POKéMON™

POCKET COMICS
Legendary Pokémon

STORY & ART BY SANTA HARUKAZE

FOUR-PANEL GAGS, POKÉMON TRIVIA, AND FUN PUZZLES BASED ON THE CHARACTERS FROM THE BEST-SELLING POKÉMON BLACK AND WHITE VIDEO GAMES!

THE LEGENDARY JOKE... IT'S UP TO ME TO FIND IT!
THERE MUST BE A JOKE SOMEWHERE IN THIS WORLD THAT CAN BRING BACK PIKACHU'S SMILE!

Available now!

POKéMON
POCKET COMICS
Legendary Pokémon
STORY & ART BY SANTA HARUKAZE

To the forest! To the sea! To Legendary Island!

Join our Pokémon pals on their quest through Unova—while testing your knowledge and laughing all the way!

Ask for it at your local comic book shop or bookstore!

ISBN: 978-1-4215-8128-6

RATED A ALL AGES ratings.viz.com

PERFECT SQUARE www.PerfectSquare.com

VIZ media www.viz.com

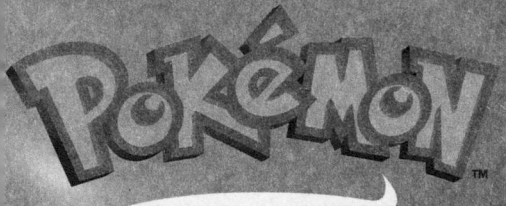

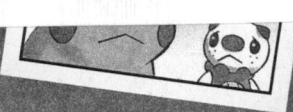

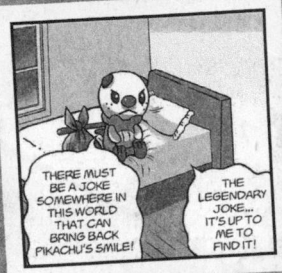

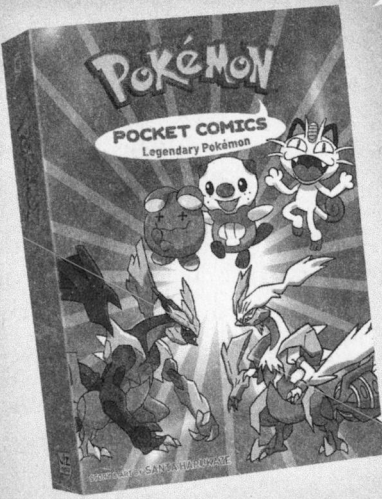

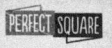

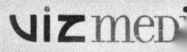

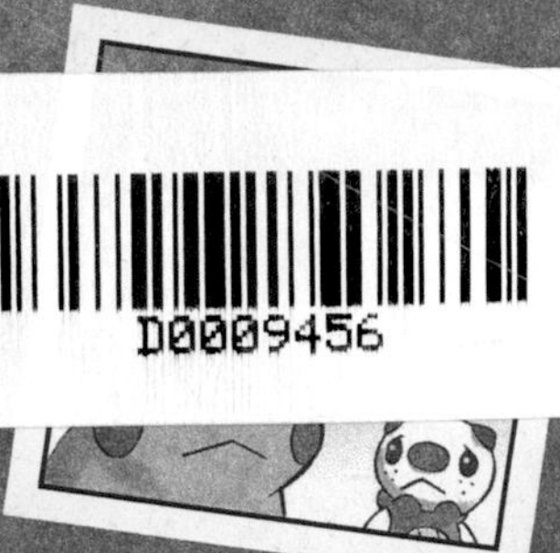

POKéMON ADVENTURES
HEARTGOLD & SOULSILVER

Story by HIDENORI KUSAKA
Art by SATOSHI YAMAMOTO

In this **two-volume** thriller, troublemaker Gold and feisty Silver must team up again to find their old enemy Lance and the Legendary Pokémon Arceus!

Available now!

www.viz.com

POKÉMON
ADVENTURES
TM

Pokémon ADVENTURES
Volume 7
Perfect Square Edition

Story by **HIDENORI KUSAKA**
Art by **MATO**

English Adaptation/Gerard Jones
Translation/Kaori Inoue
Miscellaneous Text Adaptation/Ben Costa
Touch-up & Lettering/Annaliese Christman
Design/Sam Elzway
Editor, 1st Edition/William Flanagan
Editor, Perfect Square Edition/Jann Jones

The stories, characters and incidents mentioned
in this publication are entirely fictional.

Printed in the U.S.A.

Published by VIZ Media, LLC
P.O. Box 77010
San Francisco, CA 94107

11
First printing, June 2010
Eleventh printing, December 2016

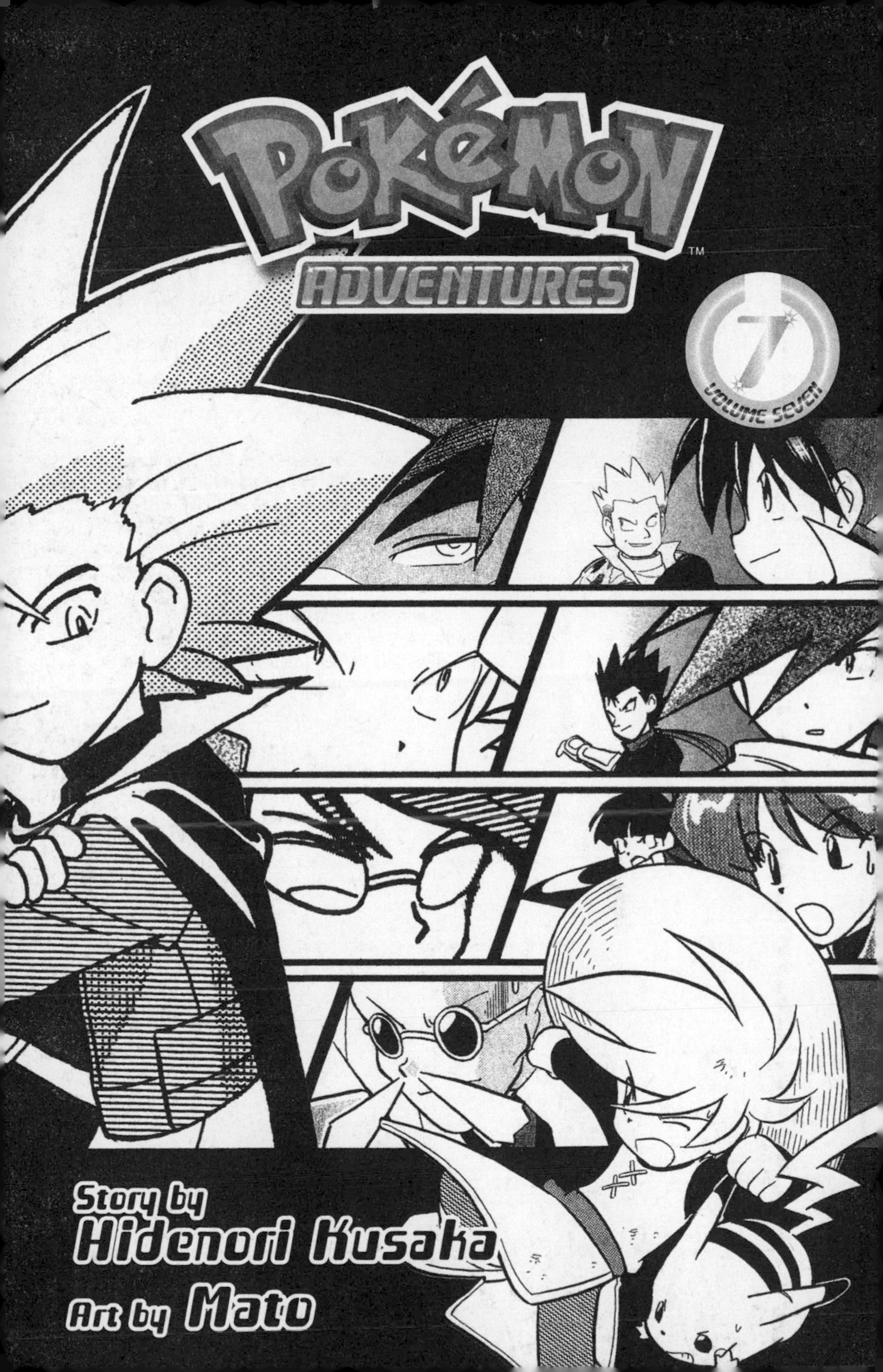
Pokémon™
Adventures
7
Volume Seven
Story by
Hidenori Kusaka
Art by Mato

CHARACTERS THUS FAR...

In an effort to defeat the Elite Four, Yellow and the eight Trainers scatter to various parts of Cerise Island! But as Bill and Lt. Surge struggle against Bruno's Fighting-type Pokémon, who would arrive to save the day?

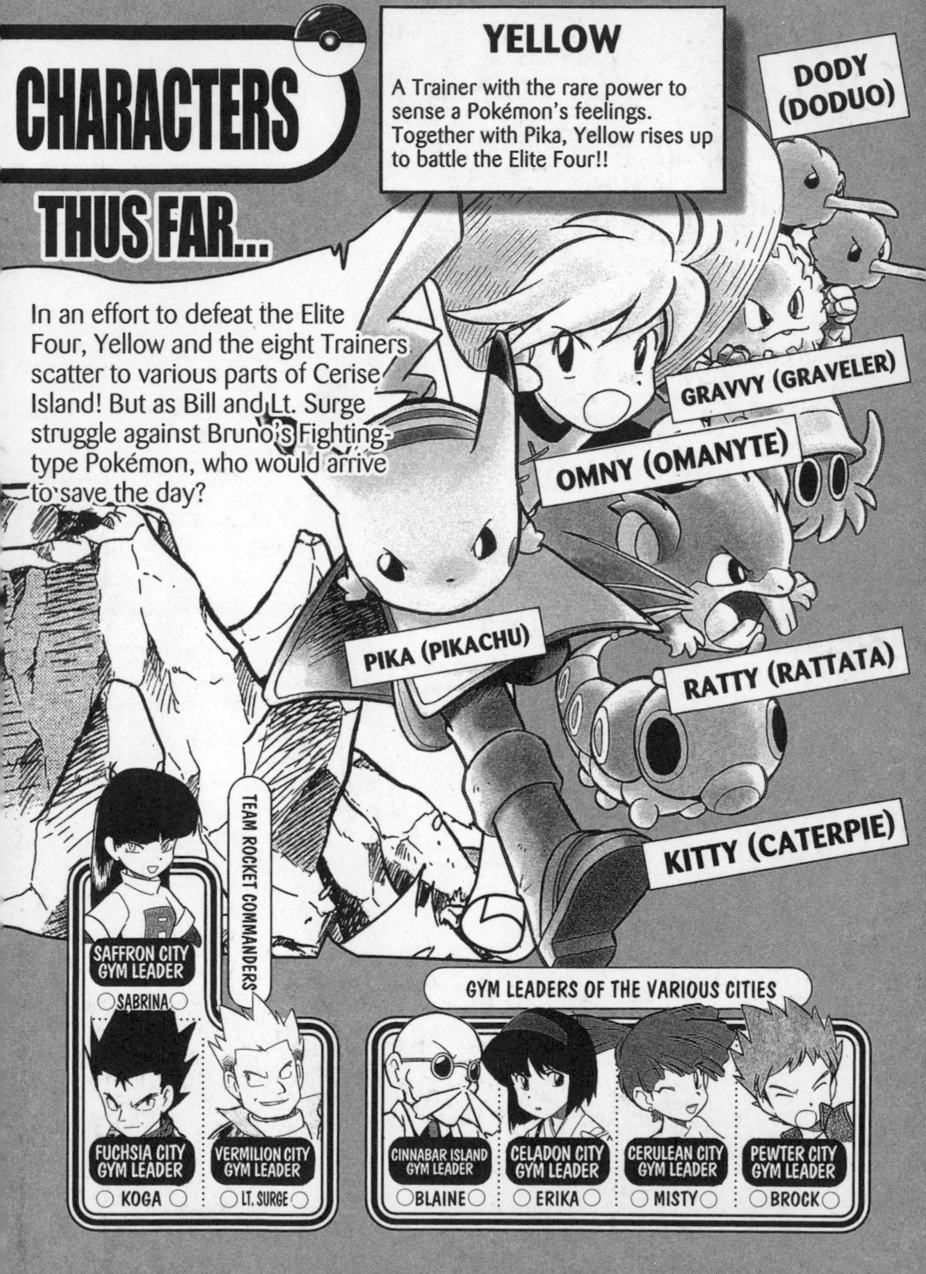
YELLOW
A Trainer with the rare power to sense a Pokémon's feelings. Together with Pika, Yellow rises up to battle the Elite Four!!
DODY (DODUO)
GRAVVY (GRAVELER)
OMNY (OMANYTE)
PIKA (PIKACHU)
RATTY (RATTATA)
KITTY (CATERPIE)
TEAM ROCKET COMMANDERS
SAFFRON CITY GYM LEADER
SABRINA
FUCHSIA CITY GYM LEADER
KOGA
VERMILION CITY GYM LEADER
LT. SURGE
GYM LEADERS OF THE VARIOUS CITIES
CINNABAR ISLAND GYM LEADER
BLAINE
CELADON CITY GYM LEADER
ERIKA
CERULEAN CITY GYM LEADER
MISTY
PEWTER CITY GYM LEADER
BROCK

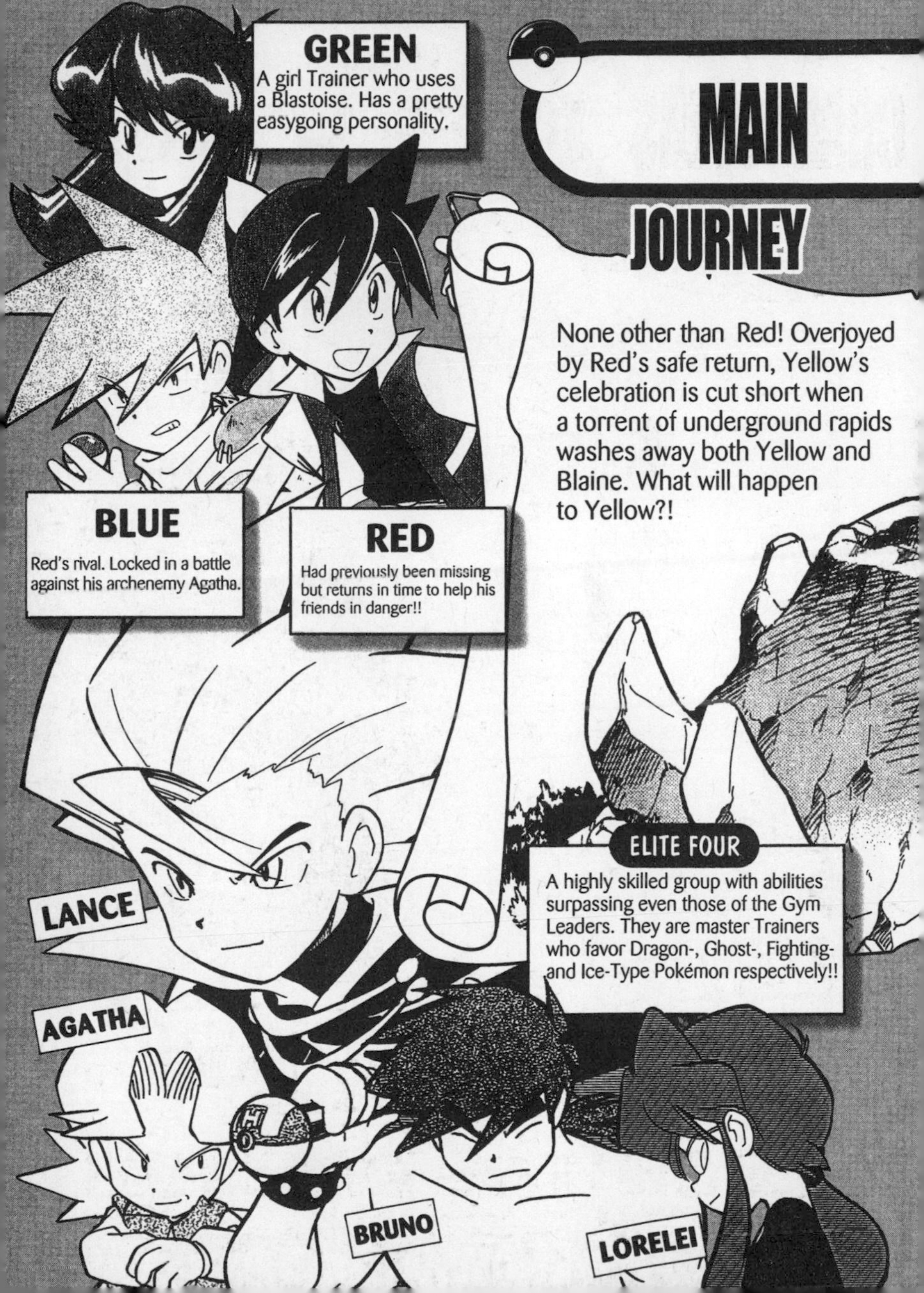
MAIN JOURNEY
None other than Red! Overjoyed by Red's safe return, Yellow's celebration is cut short when a torrent of underground rapids washes away both Yellow and Blaine. What will happen to Yellow?!
GREEN
A girl Trainer who uses a Blastoise. Has a pretty easygoing personality.
BLUE
Red's rival. Locked in a battle against his archenemy Agatha.
RED
Had previously been missing but returns in time to help his friends in danger!!
ELITE FOUR
A highly skilled group with abilities surpassing even those of the Gym Leaders. They are master Trainers who favor Dragon-, Ghost-, Fighting- and Ice-Type Pokémon respectively!!
LANCE
AGATHA
BRUNO
LORELEI

CONTENTS

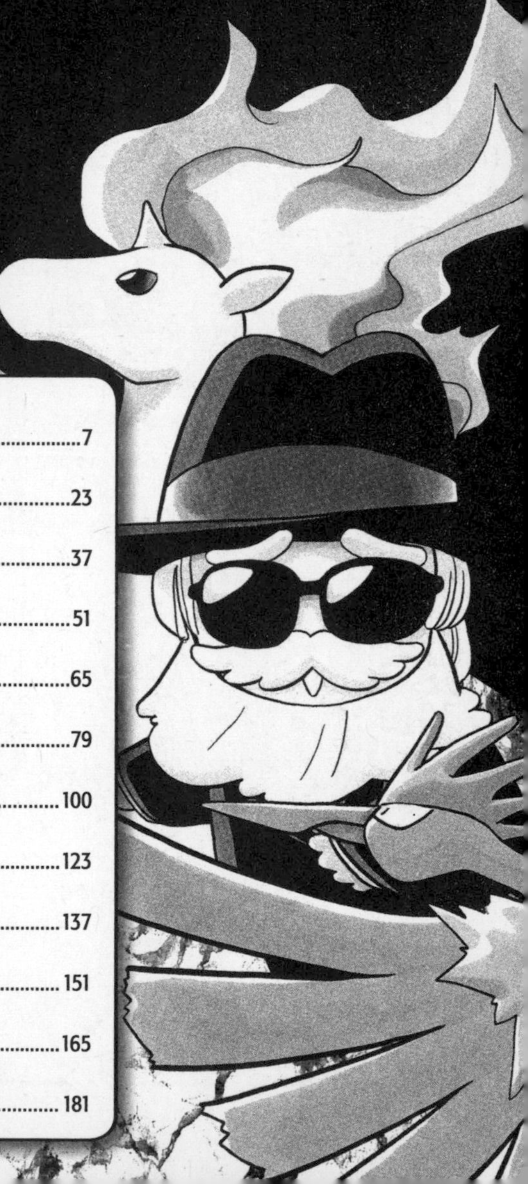

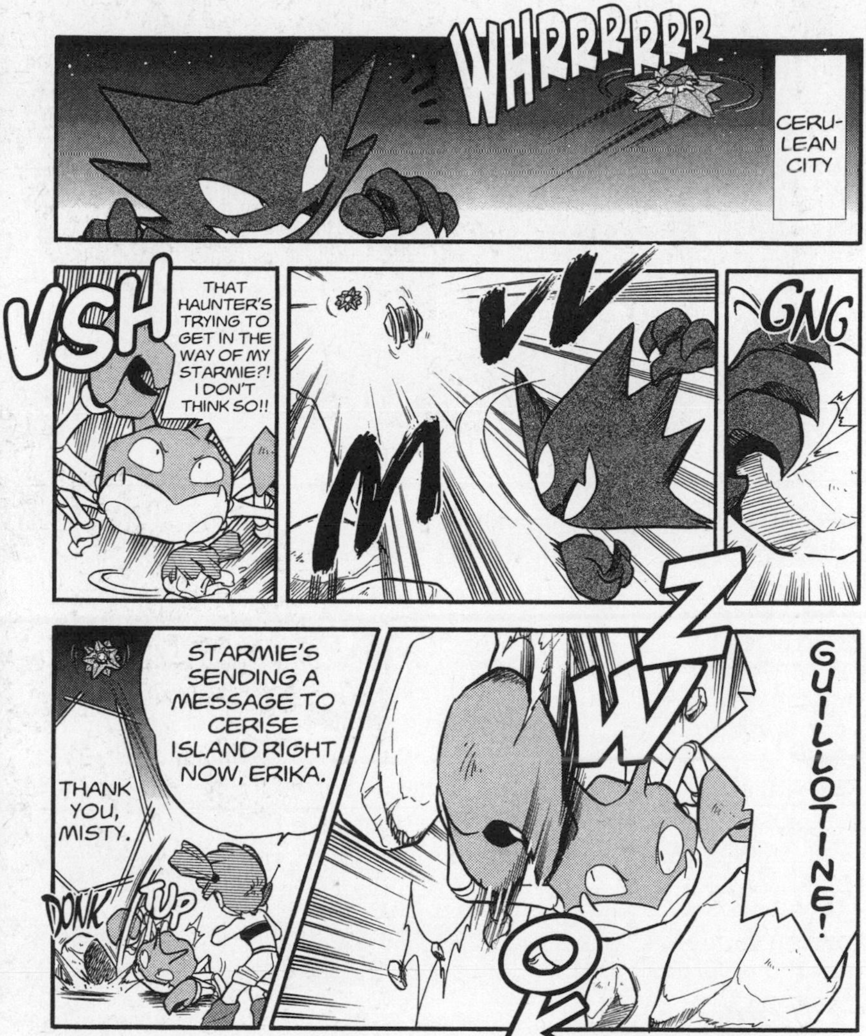
WHRRRRRR
CERULEAN CITY
GNG
VVM
VSH
THAT HAUNTER'S TRYING TO GET IN THE WAY OF MY STARMIE?! I DON'T THINK SO!!
GUILLOTINE!
ZWOK
STARMIE'S SENDING A MESSAGE TO CERISE ISLAND RIGHT NOW, ERIKA.
THANK YOU, MISTY.
TUP
DONK
BUT WAIT A MOMENT.
THERE IS MORE.
?!

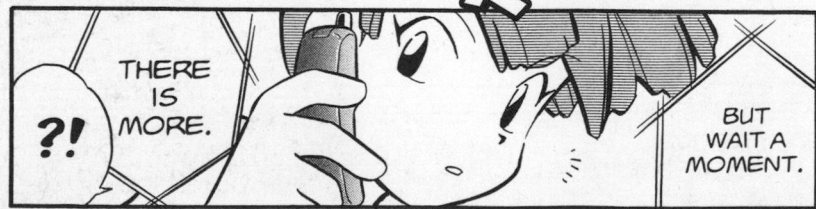

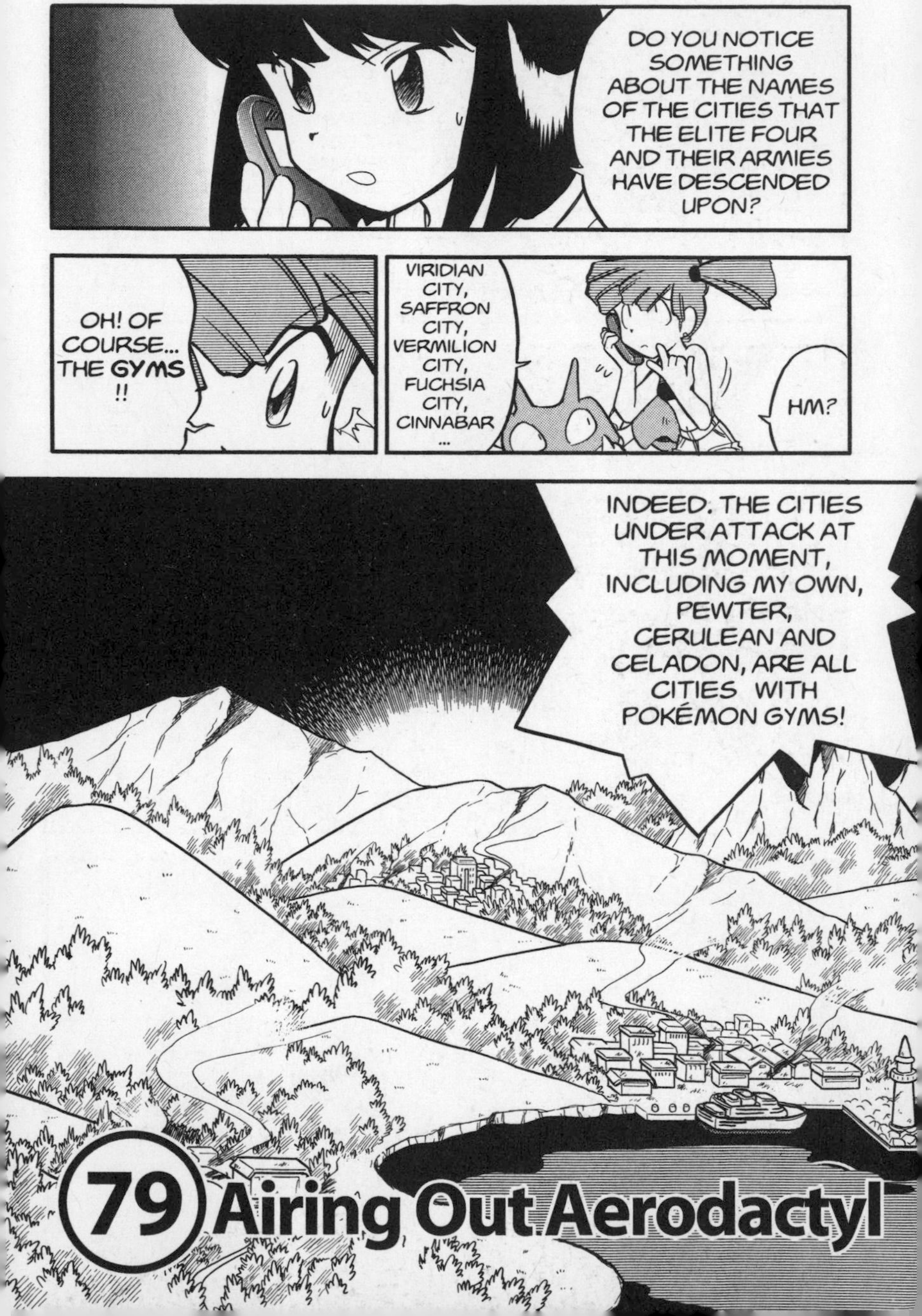
DO YOU NOTICE SOMETHING ABOUT THE NAMES OF THE CITIES THAT THE ELITE FOUR AND THEIR ARMIES HAVE DESCENDED UPON?
HM?
VIRIDIAN CITY, SAFFRON CITY, VERMILION CITY, FUCHSIA CITY, CINNABAR ...
OH! OF COURSE... THE GYMS !!
INDEED. THE CITIES UNDER ATTACK AT THIS MOMENT, INCLUDING MY OWN, PEWTER, CERULEAN AND CELADON, ARE ALL CITIES WITH POKÉMON GYMS!
79 Airing Out Aerodactyl

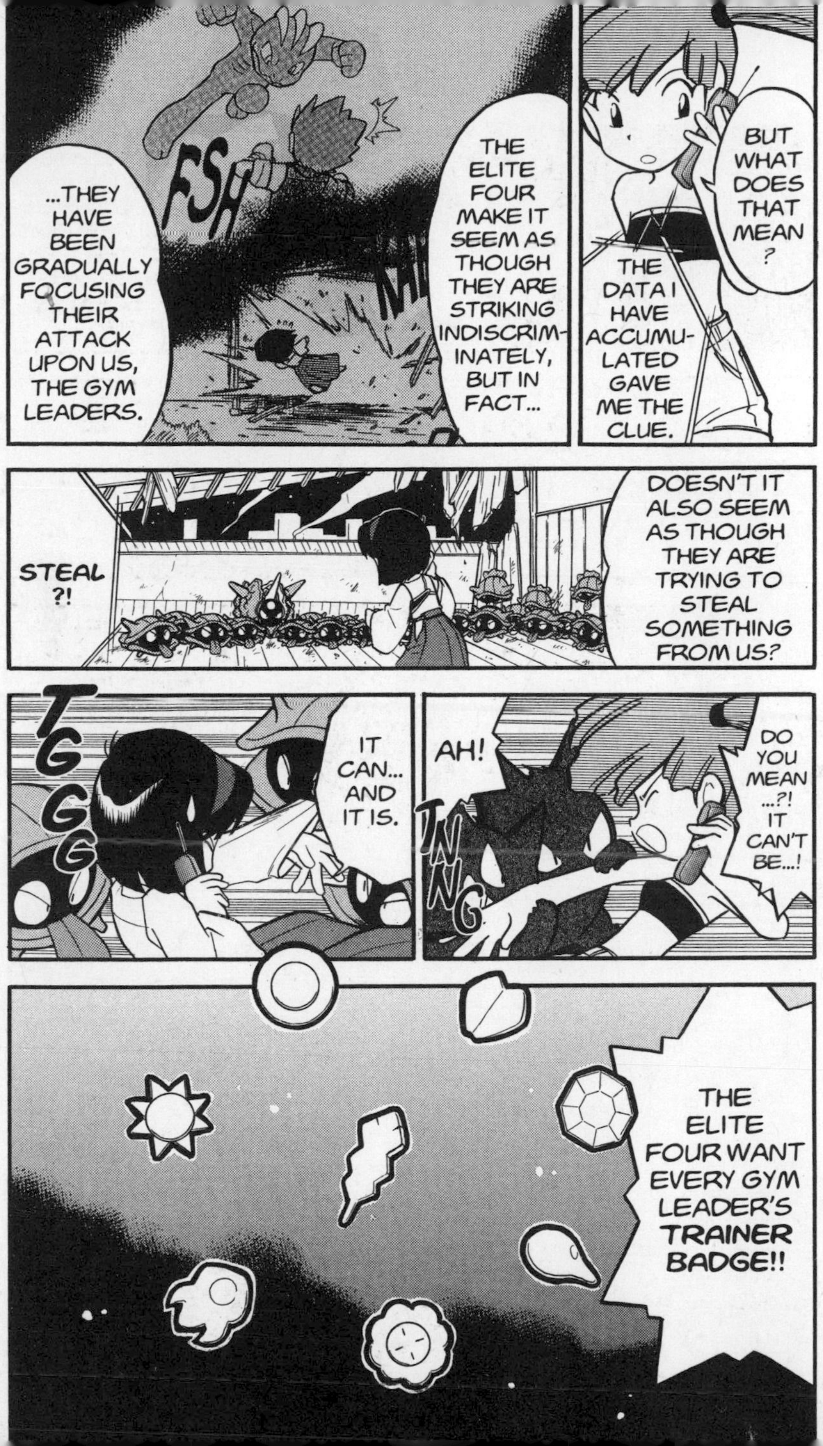
BUT WHAT DOES THAT MEAN?
THE DATA I HAVE ACCUMULATED GAVE ME THE CLUE.
THE ELITE FOUR MAKE IT SEEM AS THOUGH THEY ARE STRIKING INDISCRIMINATELY, BUT IN FACT...
FSH
...THEY HAVE BEEN GRADUALLY FOCUSING THEIR ATTACK UPON US, THE GYM LEADERS.
DOESN'T IT ALSO SEEM AS THOUGH THEY ARE TRYING TO STEAL SOMETHING FROM US?
STEAL?!
DO YOU MEAN...?! IT CAN'T BE...!
AH!
TNNG
IT CAN... AND IT IS.
TGGG
THE ELITE FOUR WANT EVERY GYM LEADER'S TRAINER BADGE!!

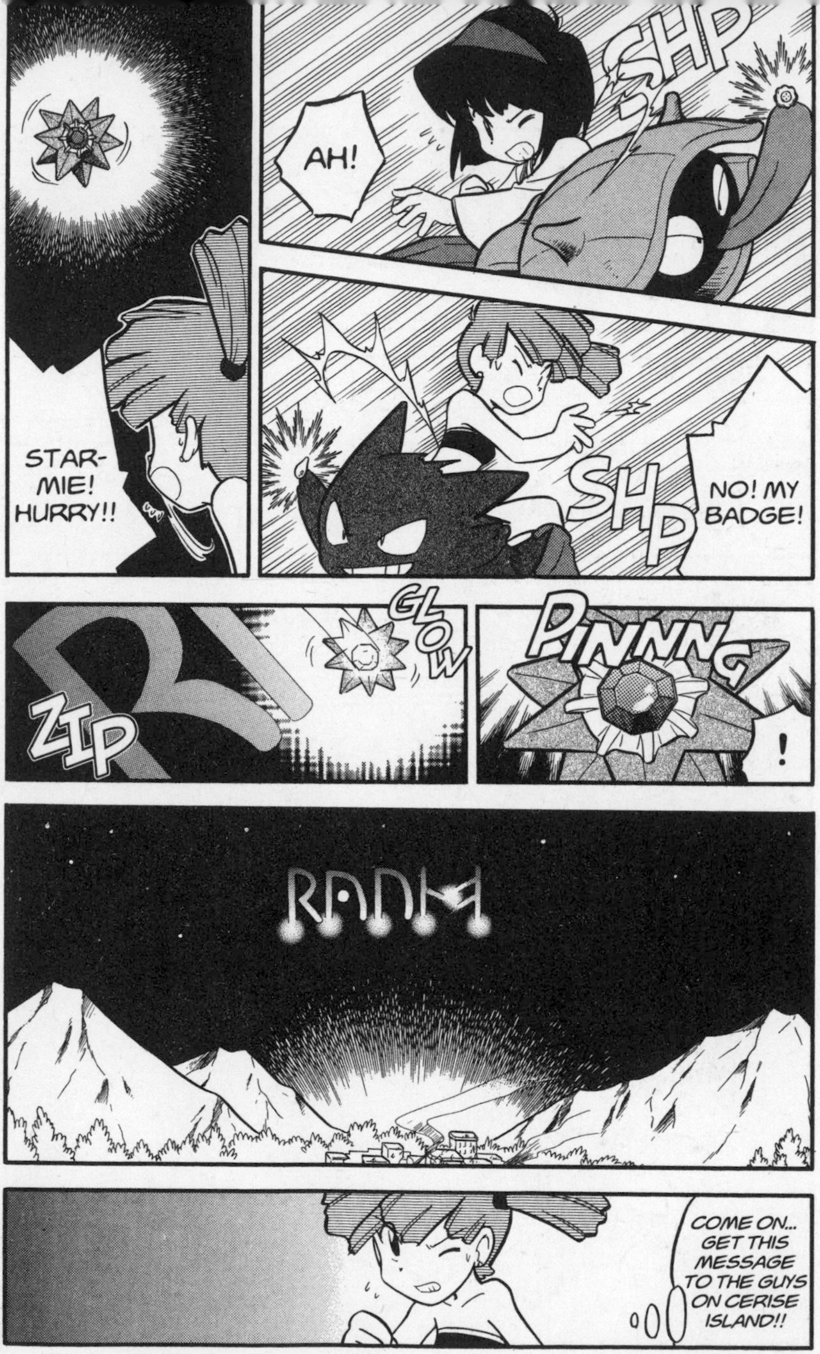
SHP
AH!
SHP
NO! MY BADGE!
STAR-MIE! HURRY!!
PINNNG
!
GLOW
ZIP
COME ON... GET THIS MESSAGE TO THE GUYS ON CERISE ISLAND!!

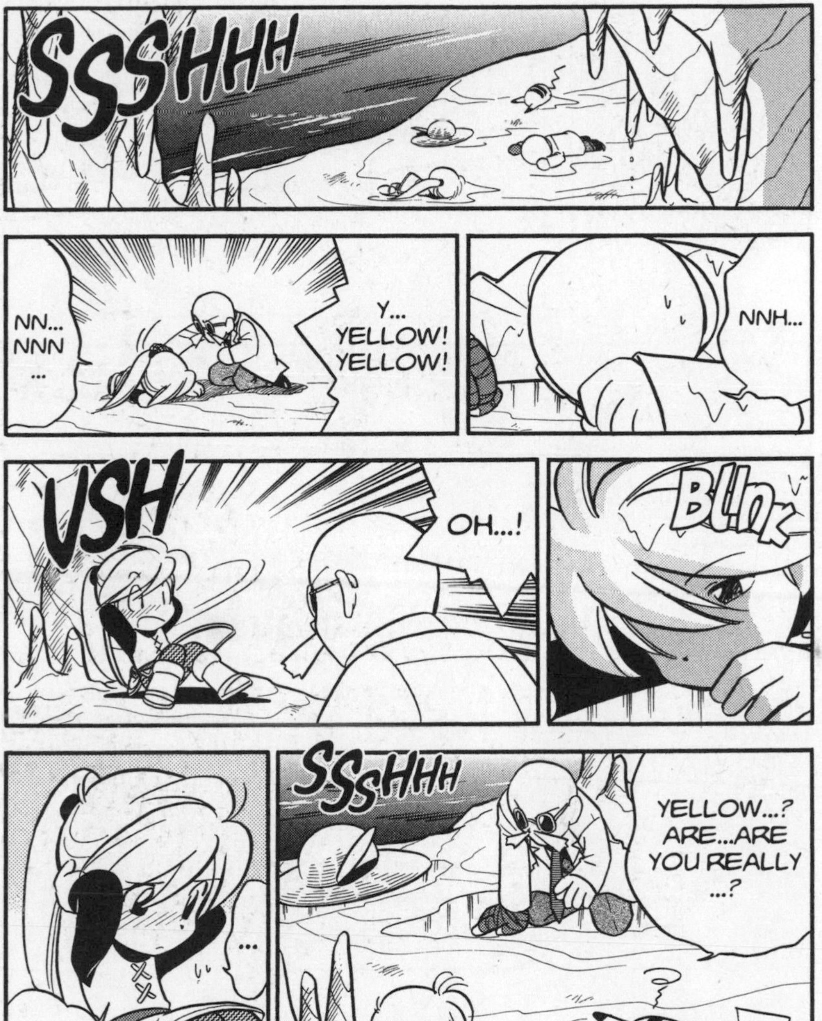
SSSHHH
NNH...
Y... YELLOW! YELLOW!
NN... NNN ...
BLINK
OH...!
USH
SSSHHH
YELLOW...? ARE...ARE YOU REALLY ...?
...
PLEASE... DON'T ASK NOW.

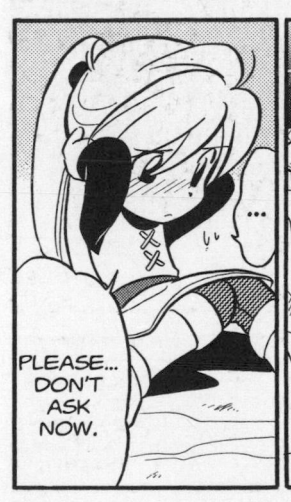

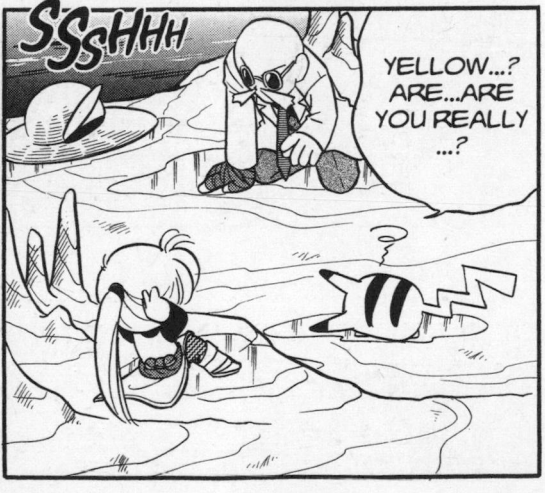

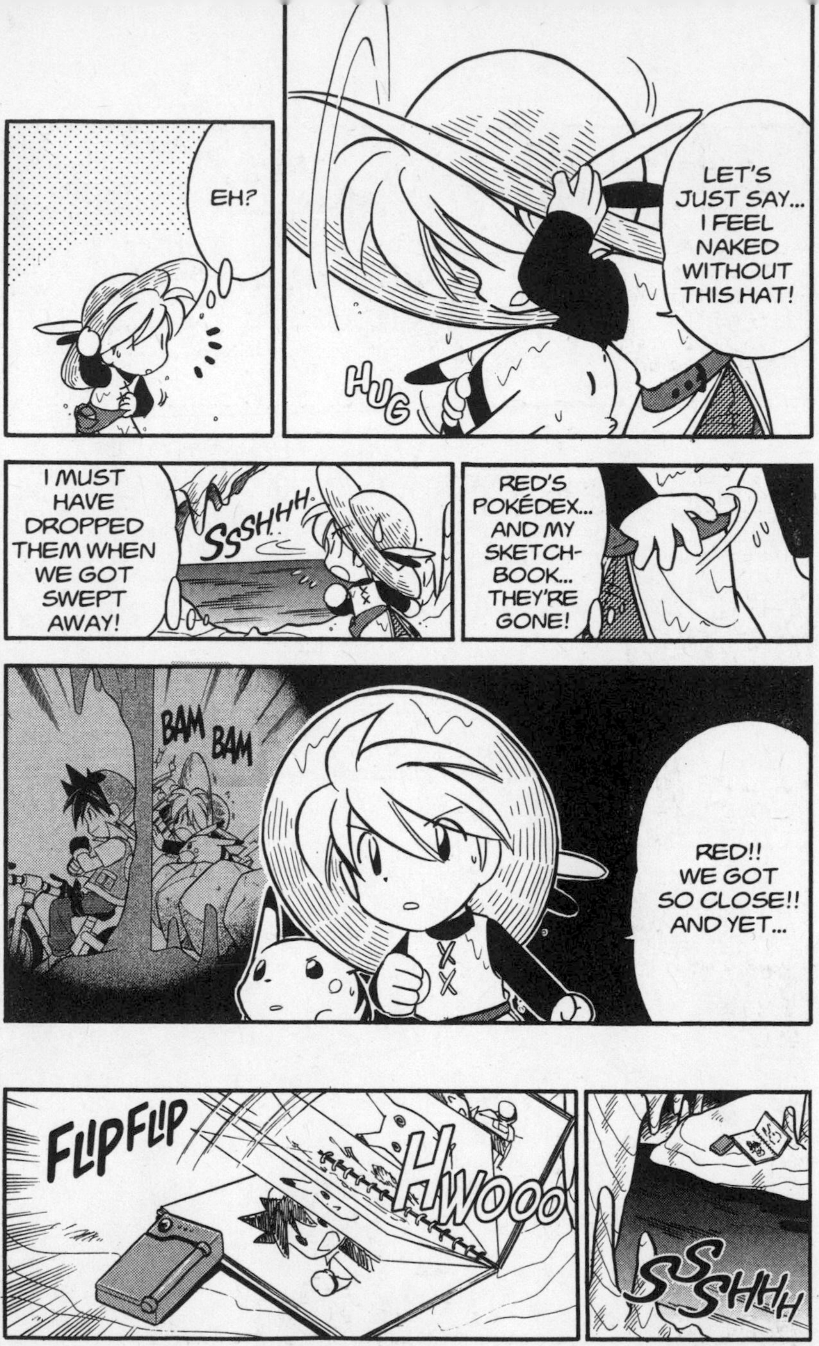
LET'S JUST SAY... I FEEL NAKED WITHOUT THIS HAT!
HUG
EH?
RED'S POKÉDEX... AND MY SKETCH-BOOK... THEY'RE GONE!
I MUST HAVE DROPPED THEM WHEN WE GOT SWEPT AWAY!
SSSHHH
RED!! WE GOT SO CLOSE!! AND YET...
BAM BAM
SSSHHH
FLIPFLIP
HWOOO

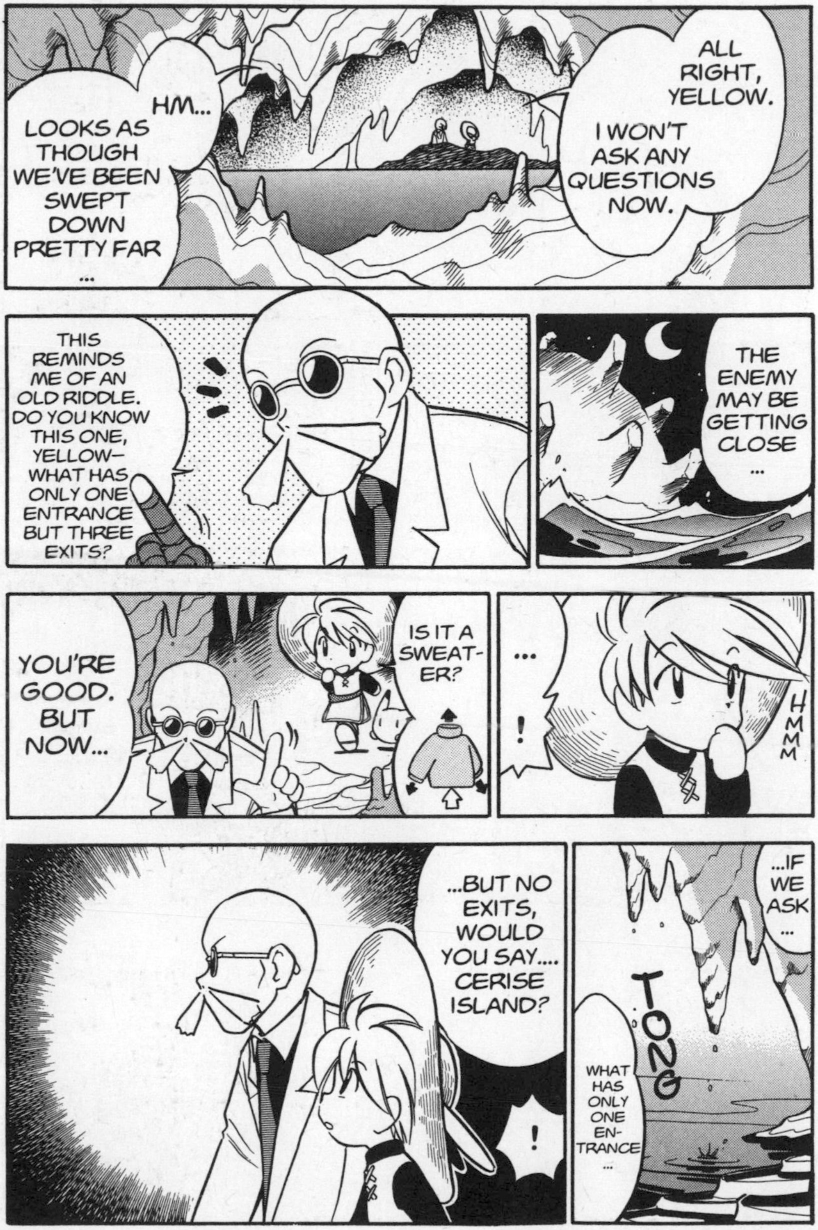
ALL RIGHT, YELLOW.
I WON'T ASK ANY QUESTIONS NOW.
HM... LOOKS AS THOUGH WE'VE BEEN SWEPT DOWN PRETTY FAR ...
THE ENEMY MAY BE GETTING CLOSE ...
THIS REMINDS ME OF AN OLD RIDDLE. DO YOU KNOW THIS ONE, YELLOW— WHAT HAS ONLY ONE ENTRANCE BUT THREE EXITS?
HMMM
...
!
IS IT A SWEAT-ER?
YOU'RE GOOD. BUT NOW...
...IF WE ASK ...
TONG
WHAT HAS ONLY ONE EN-TRANCE ...
...BUT NO EXITS, WOULD YOU SAY.... CERISE ISLAND?
!

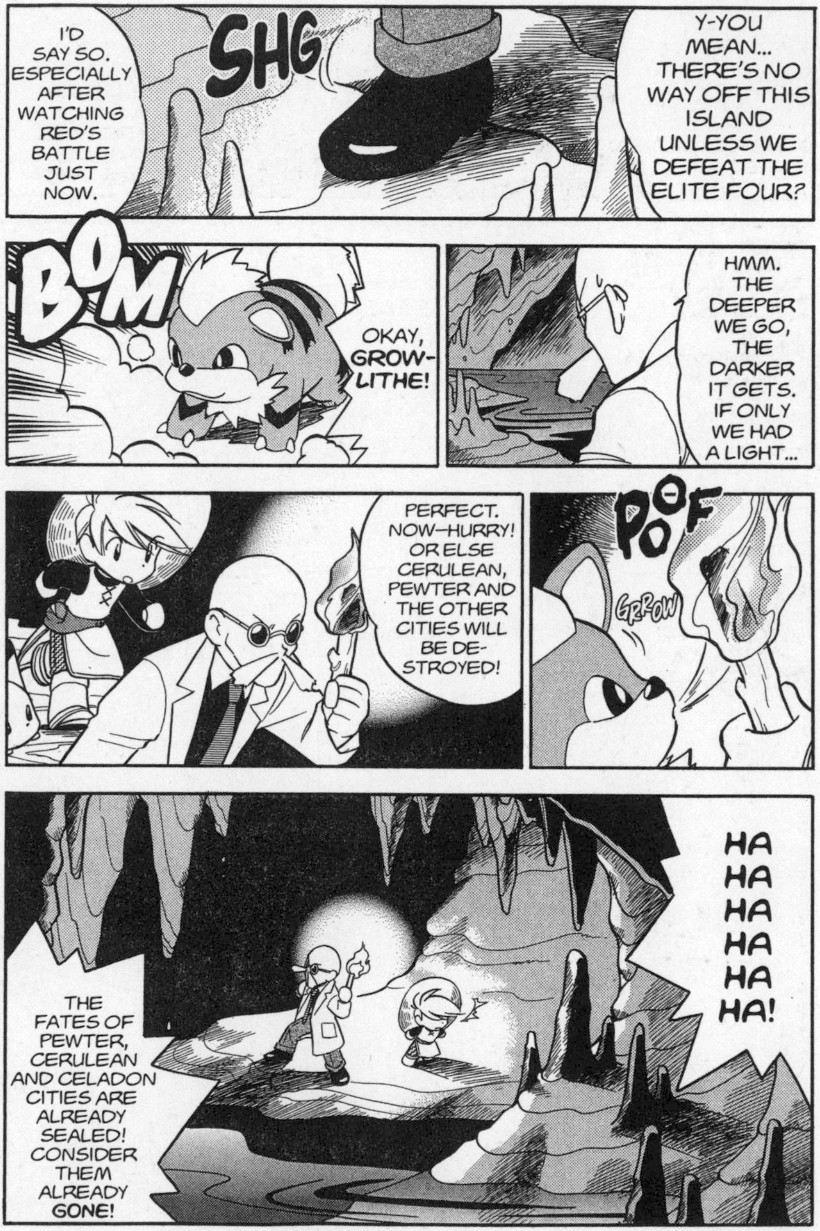

Y-YOU MEAN... THERE'S NO WAY OFF THIS ISLAND UNLESS WE DEFEAT THE ELITE FOUR?
SHG
I'D SAY SO. ESPECIALLY AFTER WATCHING RED'S BATTLE JUST NOW.
HMM. THE DEEPER WE GO, THE DARKER IT GETS. IF ONLY WE HAD A LIGHT...
BOM
OKAY, GROWLITHE!
POOF
GRROW
PERFECT. NOW—HURRY! OR ELSE CERULEAN, PEWTER AND THE OTHER CITIES WILL BE DESTROYED!
HA HA HA HA HA HA!
THE FATES OF PEWTER, CERULEAN AND CELADON CITIES ARE ALREADY SEALED! CONSIDER THEM ALREADY GONE!

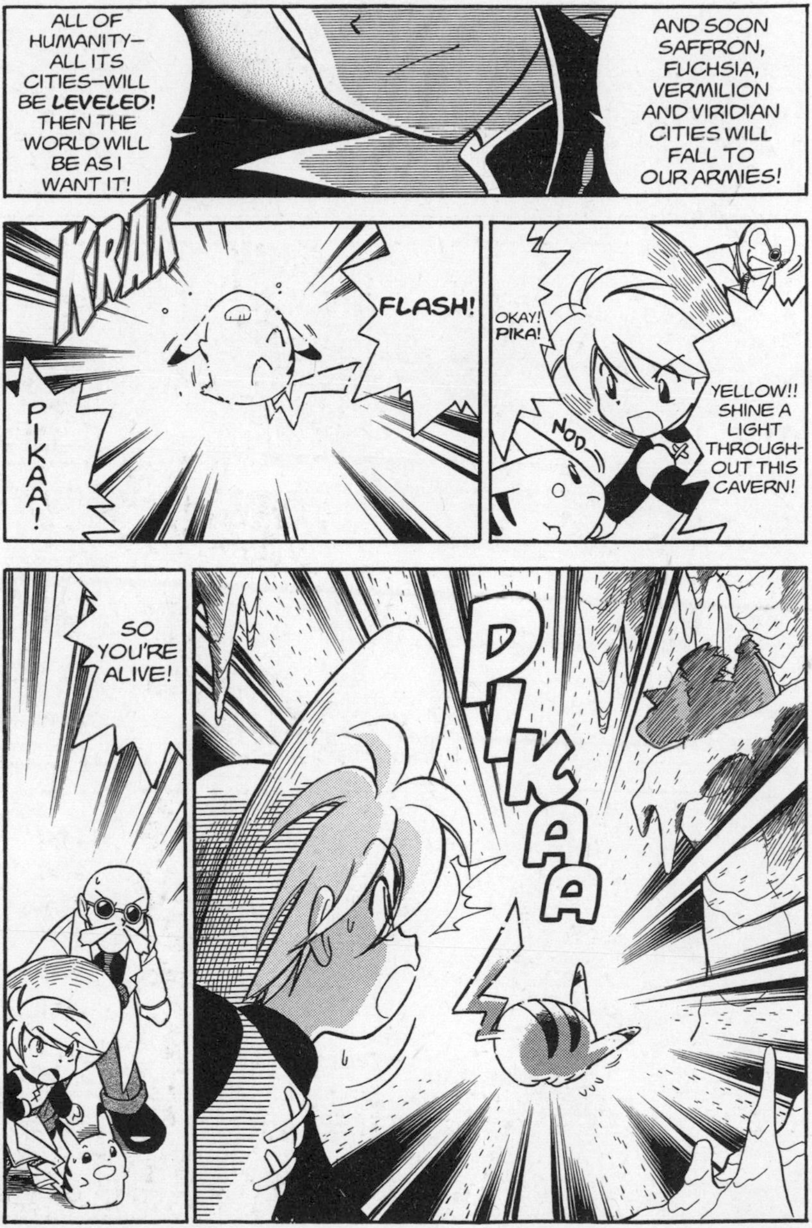
AND SOON SAFFRON, FUCHSIA, VERMILION AND VIRIDIAN CITIES WILL FALL TO OUR ARMIES!
ALL OF HUMANITY—ALL ITS CITIES—WILL BE **LEVELED**! THEN THE WORLD WILL BE AS I WANT IT!
YELLOW!! SHINE A LIGHT THROUGH-OUT THIS CAVERN!
OKAY! PIKA!
NOD
FLASH!
KRAK
PIKAA!
PIKAA
SO YOU'RE ALIVE!

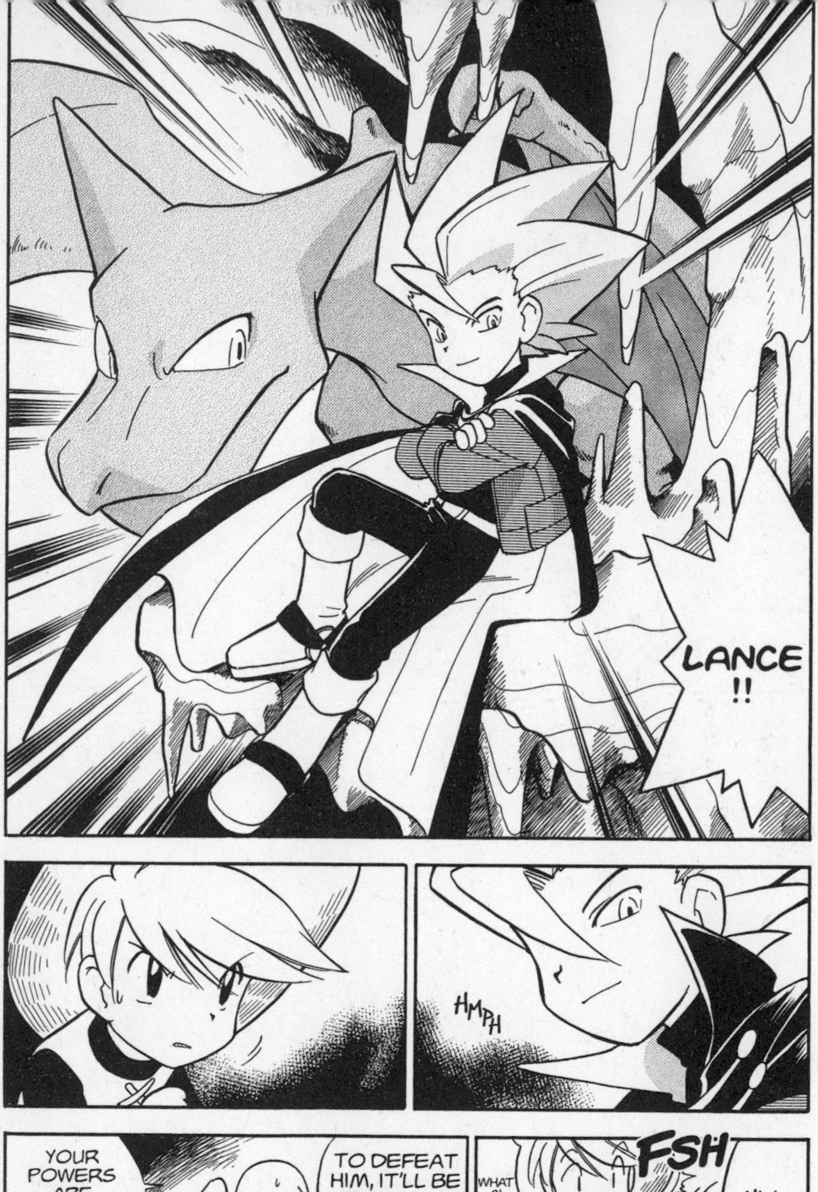
LANCE !!
HMPH
FSH
I'LL TAKE THIS.
WHAT ?!
TO DEFEAT HIM, IT'LL BE NECESSARY TO MERGE OUR POWERS.
YOUR POWERS ARE IMPRESSIVE, YELLOW... BUT... WELL...

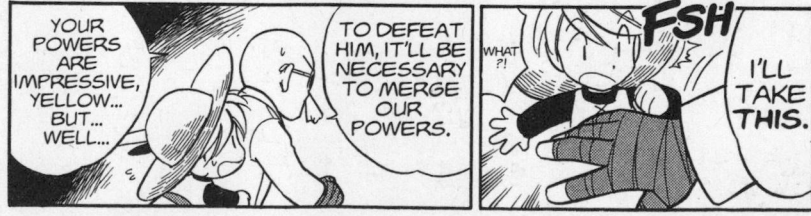

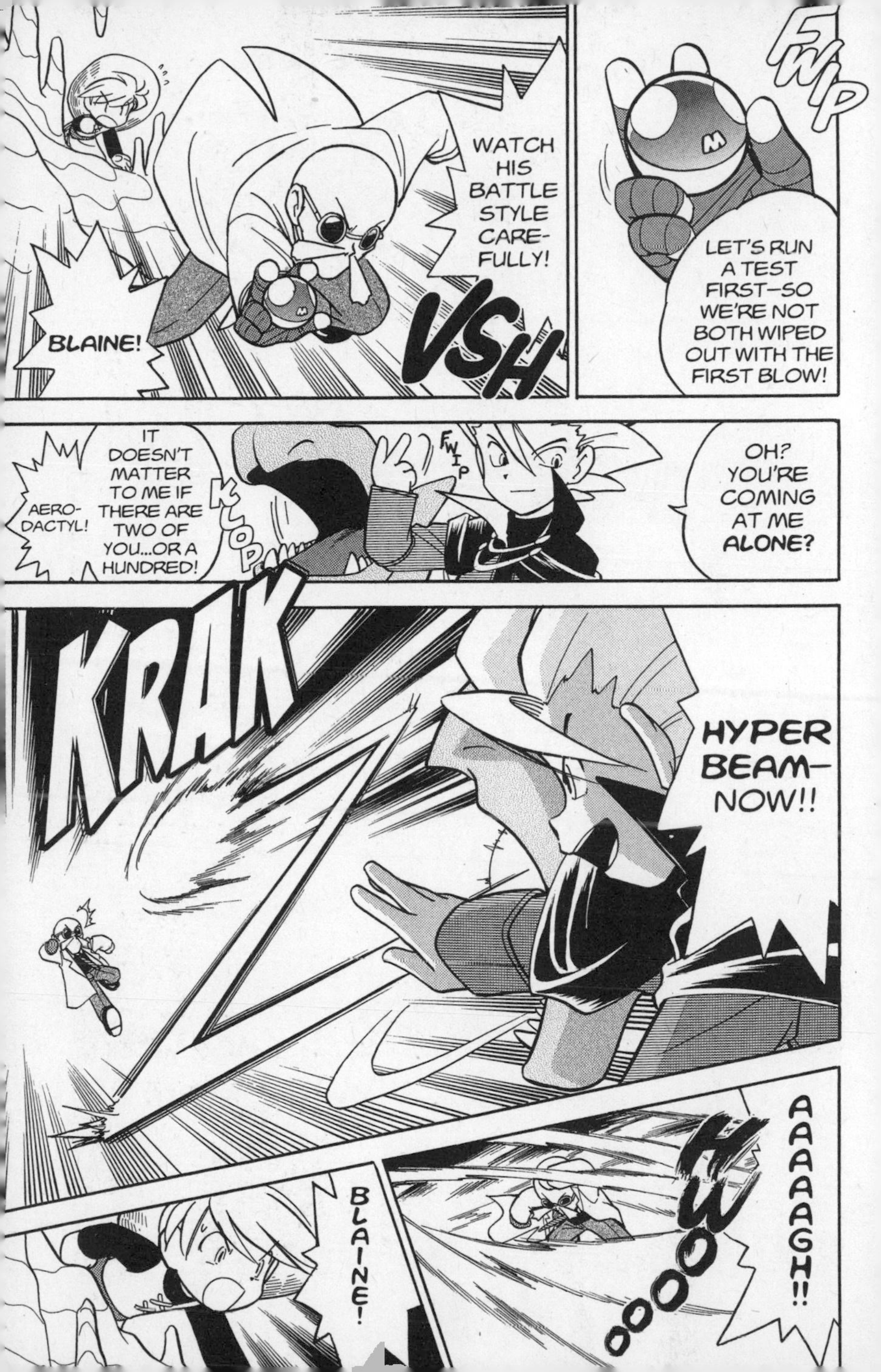
FWIP
LET'S RUN A TEST FIRST—SO WE'RE NOT BOTH WIPED OUT WITH THE FIRST BLOW!
WATCH HIS BATTLE STYLE CARE-FULLY!
VSH
BLAINE!
OH? YOU'RE COMING AT ME ALONE?
FWIP
KLOP
IT DOESN'T MATTER TO ME IF THERE ARE TWO OF YOU...OR A HUNDRED!
AERO-DACTYL!
HYPER BEAM—NOW!!
KRAK
AAAAAAGH!!
HWOOOO
BLAINE!

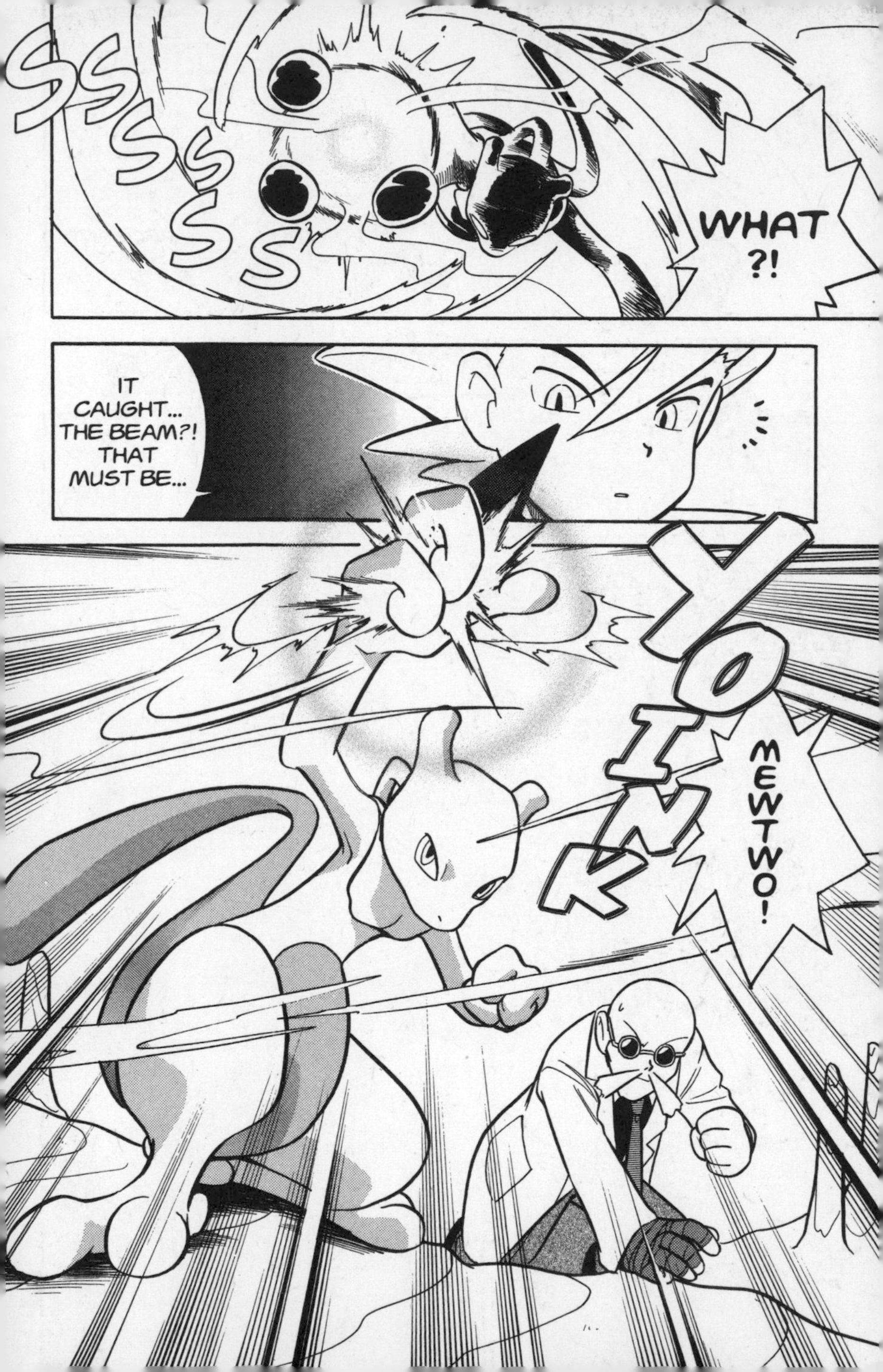
WHAT ?!
SSSSSSS
IT CAUGHT... THE BEAM?! THAT MUST BE...
YOINK
MEWTWO!

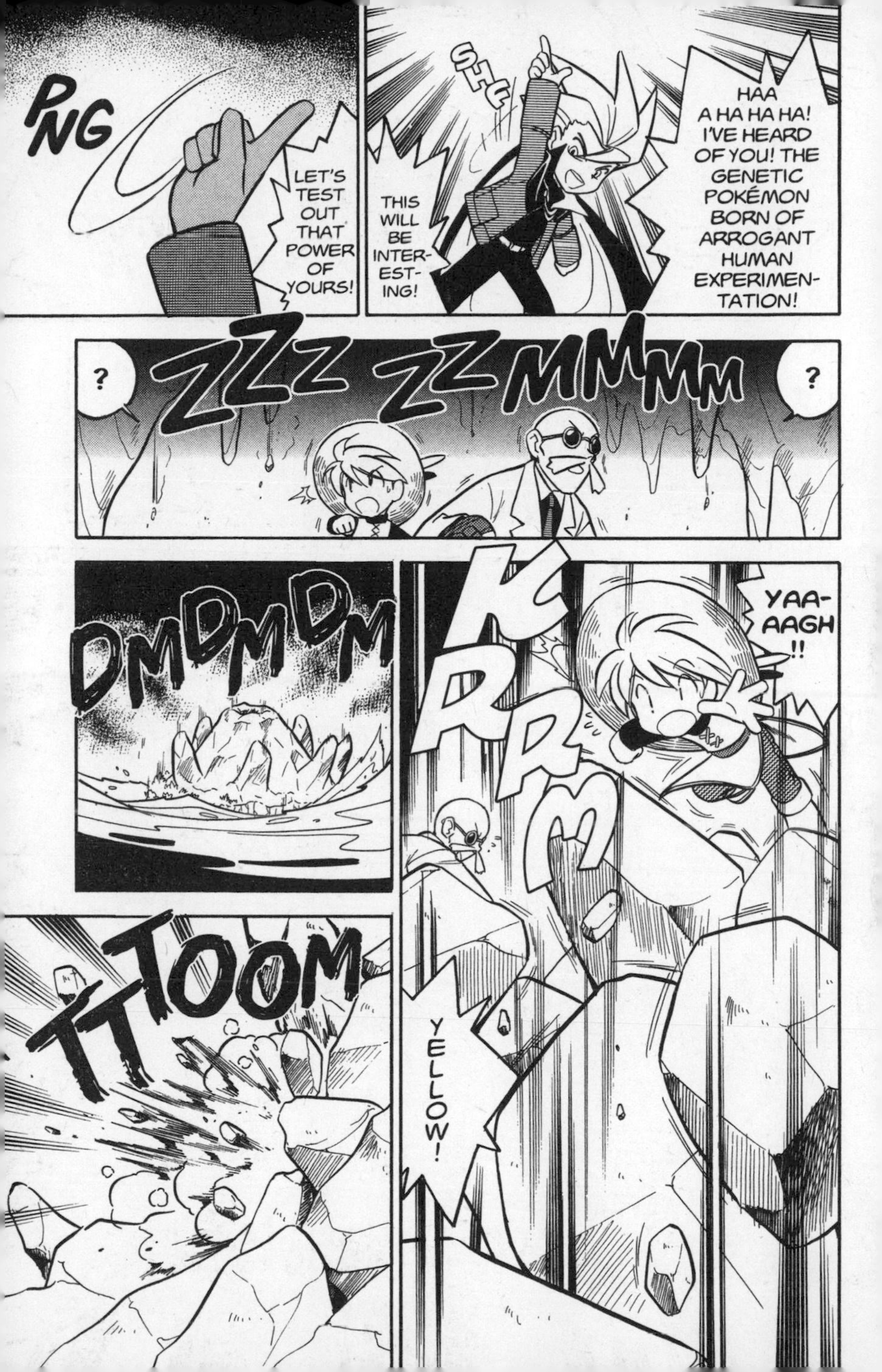
HAA A HA HA HA! I'VE HEARD OF YOU! THE GENETIC POKÉMON BORN OF ARROGANT HUMAN EXPERIMENTATION!
SHF
THIS WILL BE INTERESTING!
PNG
LET'S TEST OUT THAT POWER OF YOURS!
?
ZZZ ZZMMMMM
?
KRRAM
YAA-AAGH!!
YELLOW!
DMDMDM
TTOOM

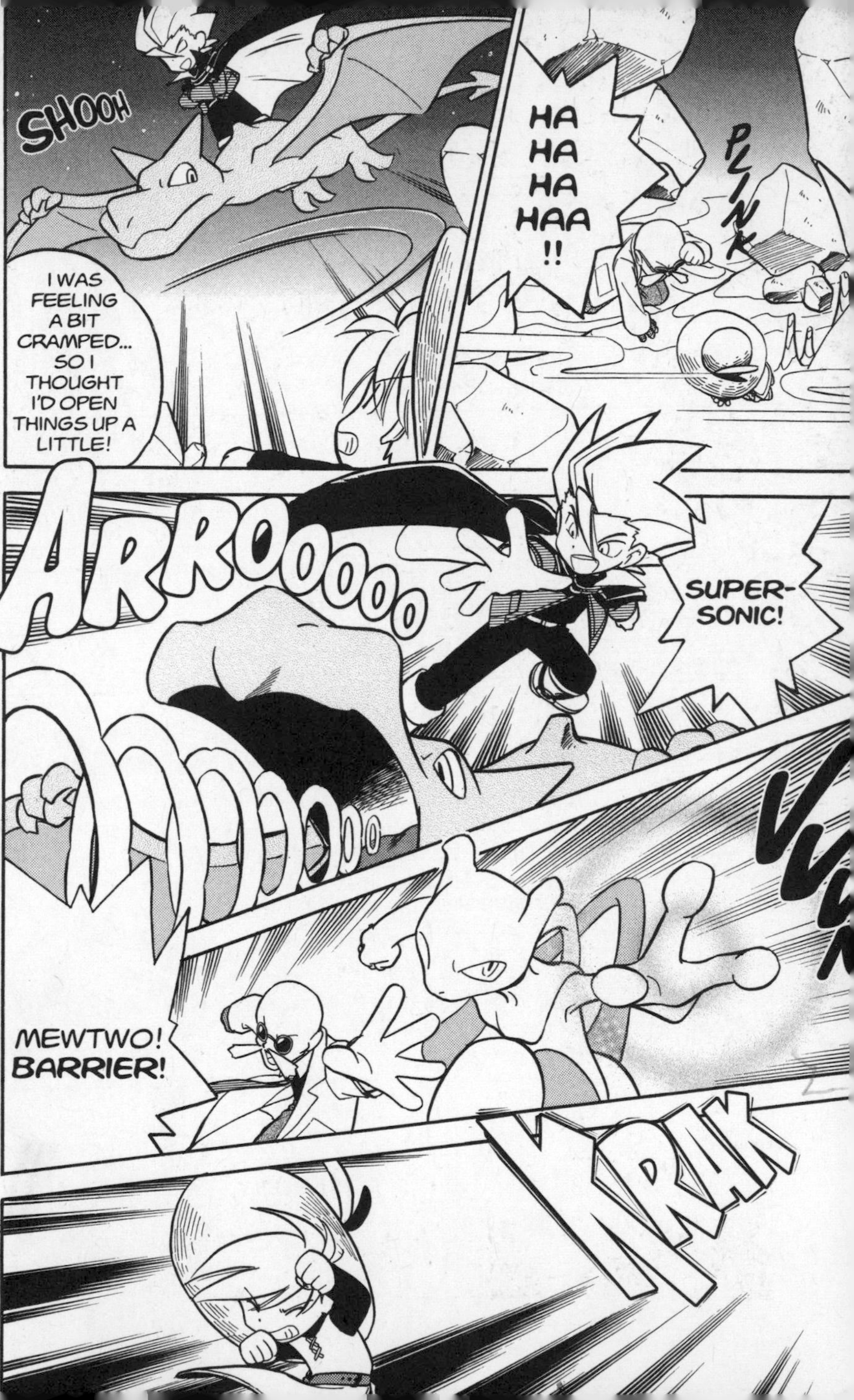
HA
HA
HA
HAA
!!
PLINK
SHOOH
I WAS FEELING A BIT CRAMPED... SO I THOUGHT I'D OPEN THINGS UP A LITTLE!
SUPER-SONIC!
ARROOOOOO
VVVN
MEWTWO! BARRIER!
KRAK

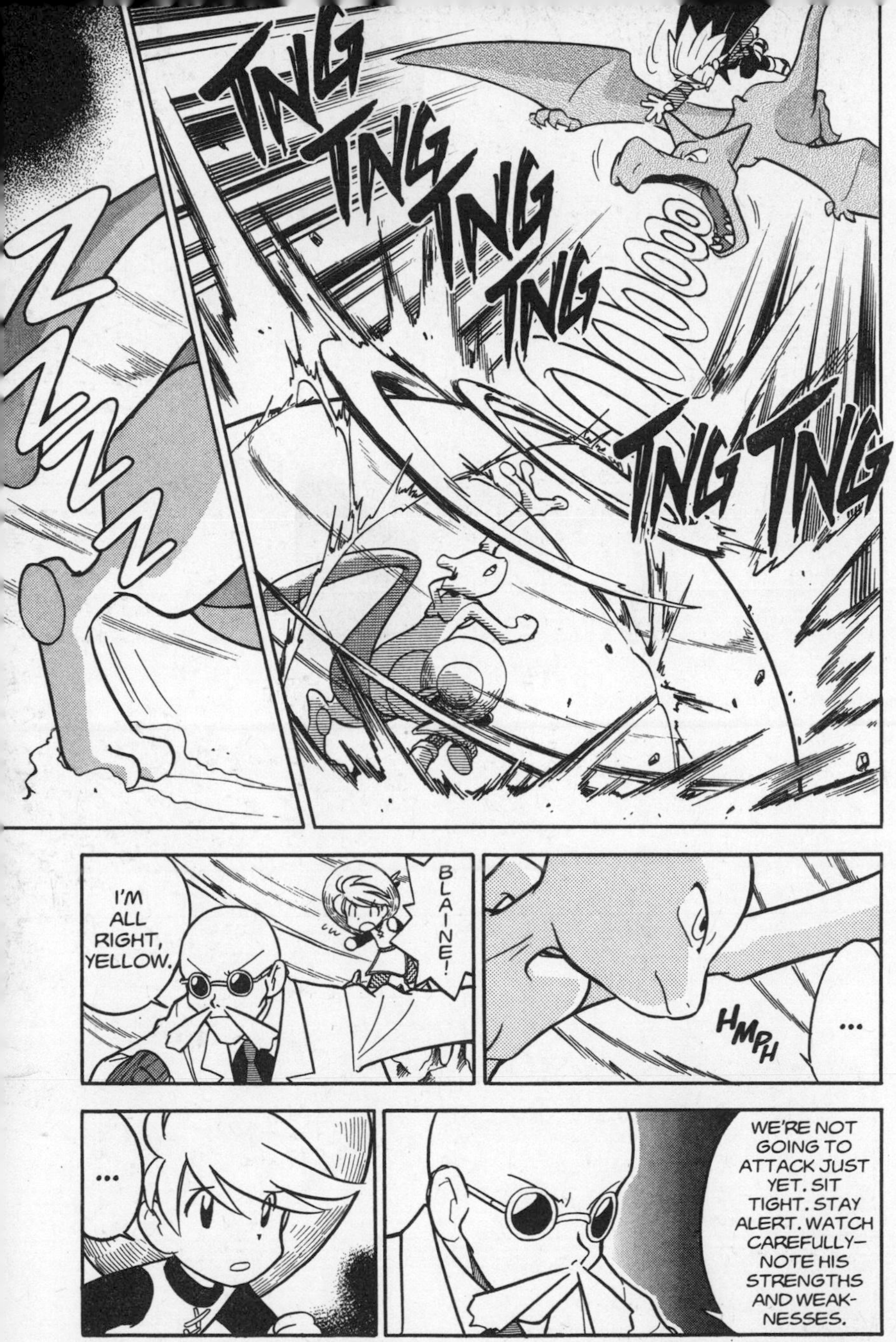
TNG
TNG
TNG
TNG
TNG TNG
ZZZZ
HMPH
...
BLAINE!
I'M ALL RIGHT, YELLOW.
WE'RE NOT GOING TO ATTACK JUST YET. SIT TIGHT. STAY ALERT. WATCH CAREFULLY—NOTE HIS STRENGTHS AND WEAKNESSES.
...

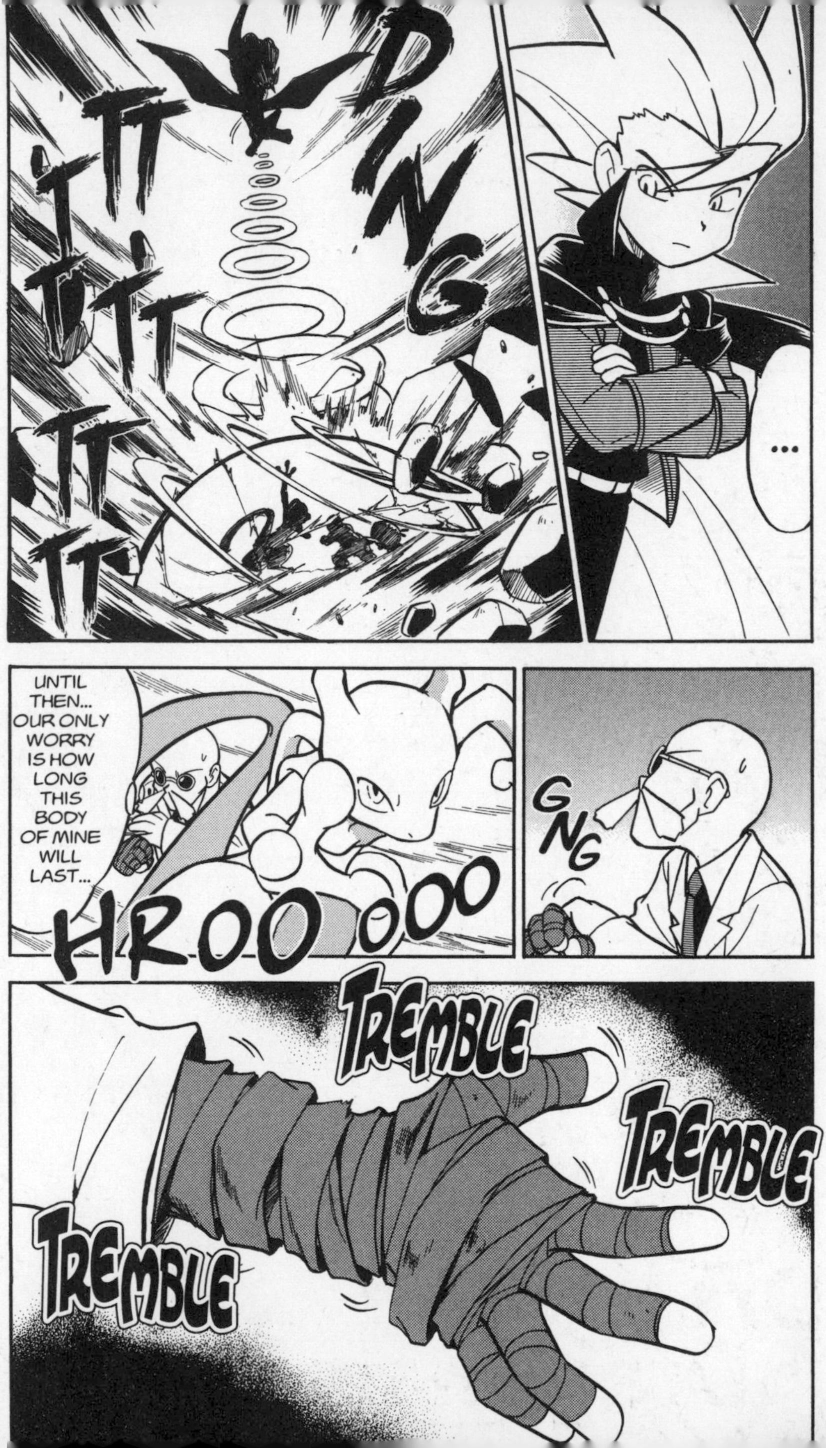
...
PING
GNG
UNTIL THEN... OUR ONLY WORRY IS HOW LONG THIS BODY OF MINE WILL LAST...
HROO OOO
TREMBLE
TREMBLE
TREMBLE

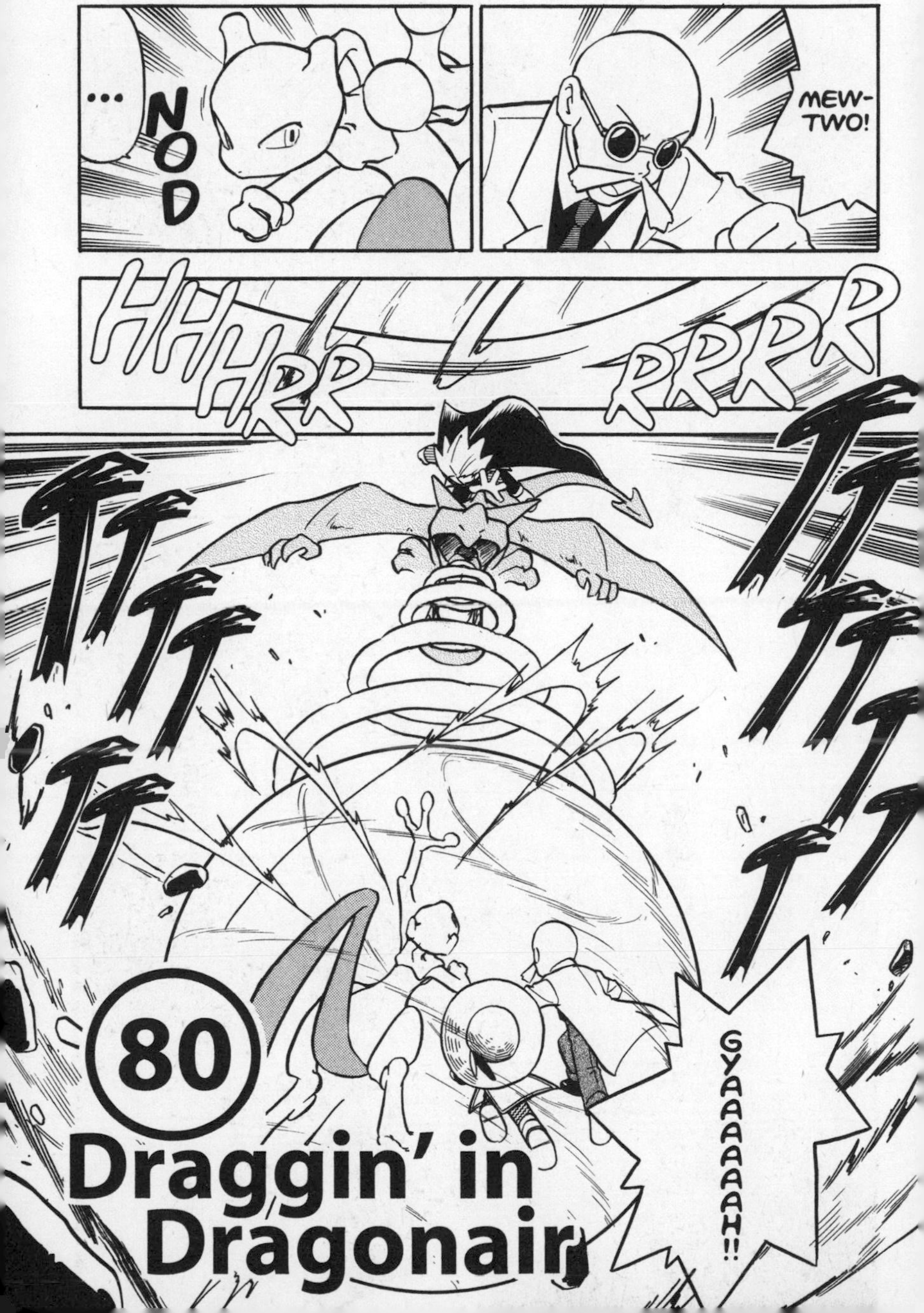
MEW-
TWO!
...
NOD
HHHRR
RRRRR
TTTTT
TTTTT
GYAAAAAAAH!!
80
Draggin' in
Dragonair

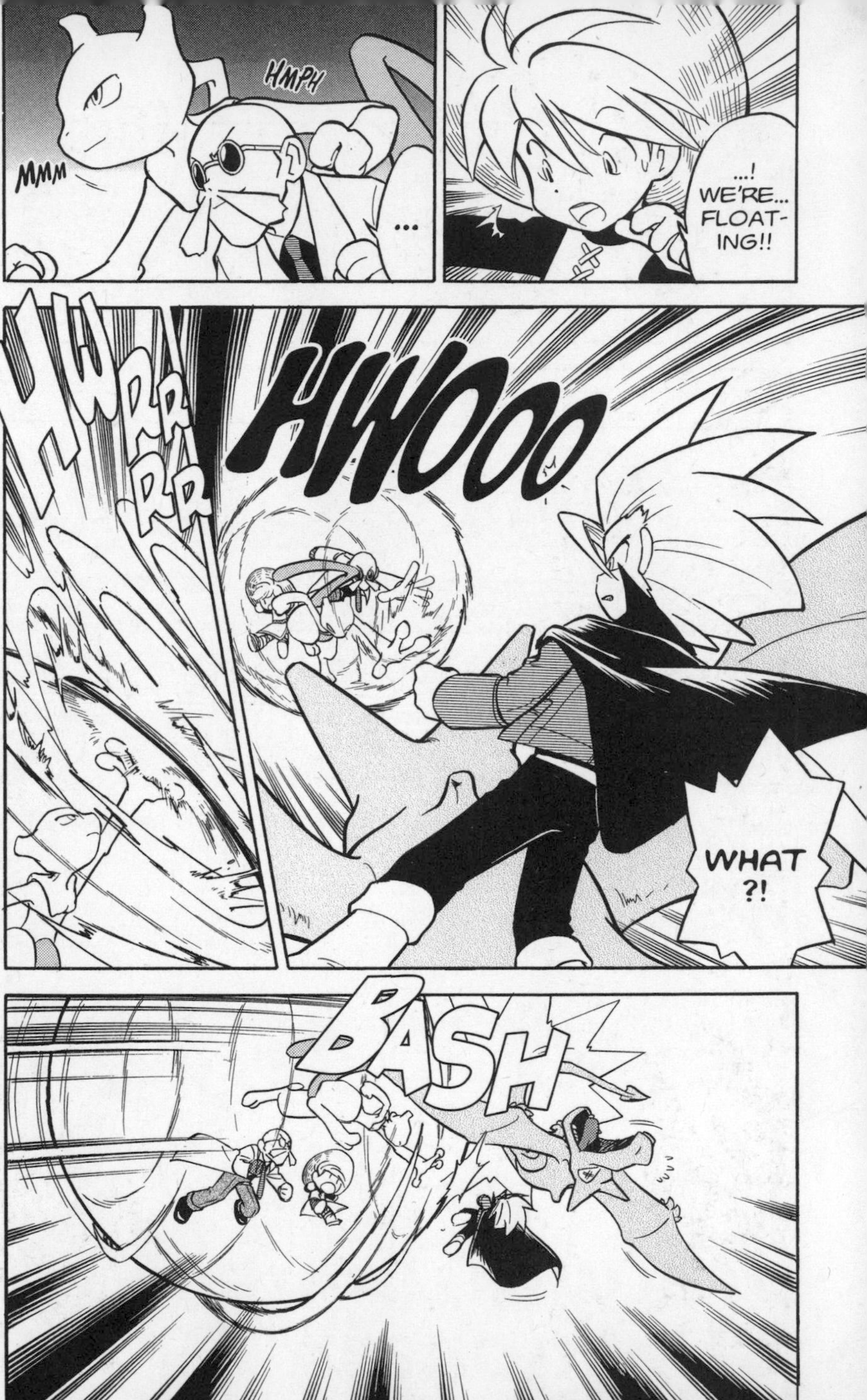
...! WE'RE... FLOAT-ING!!
HMPH
...
MMM
HWOOO
WHAT ?!
HWRRRR
BASH

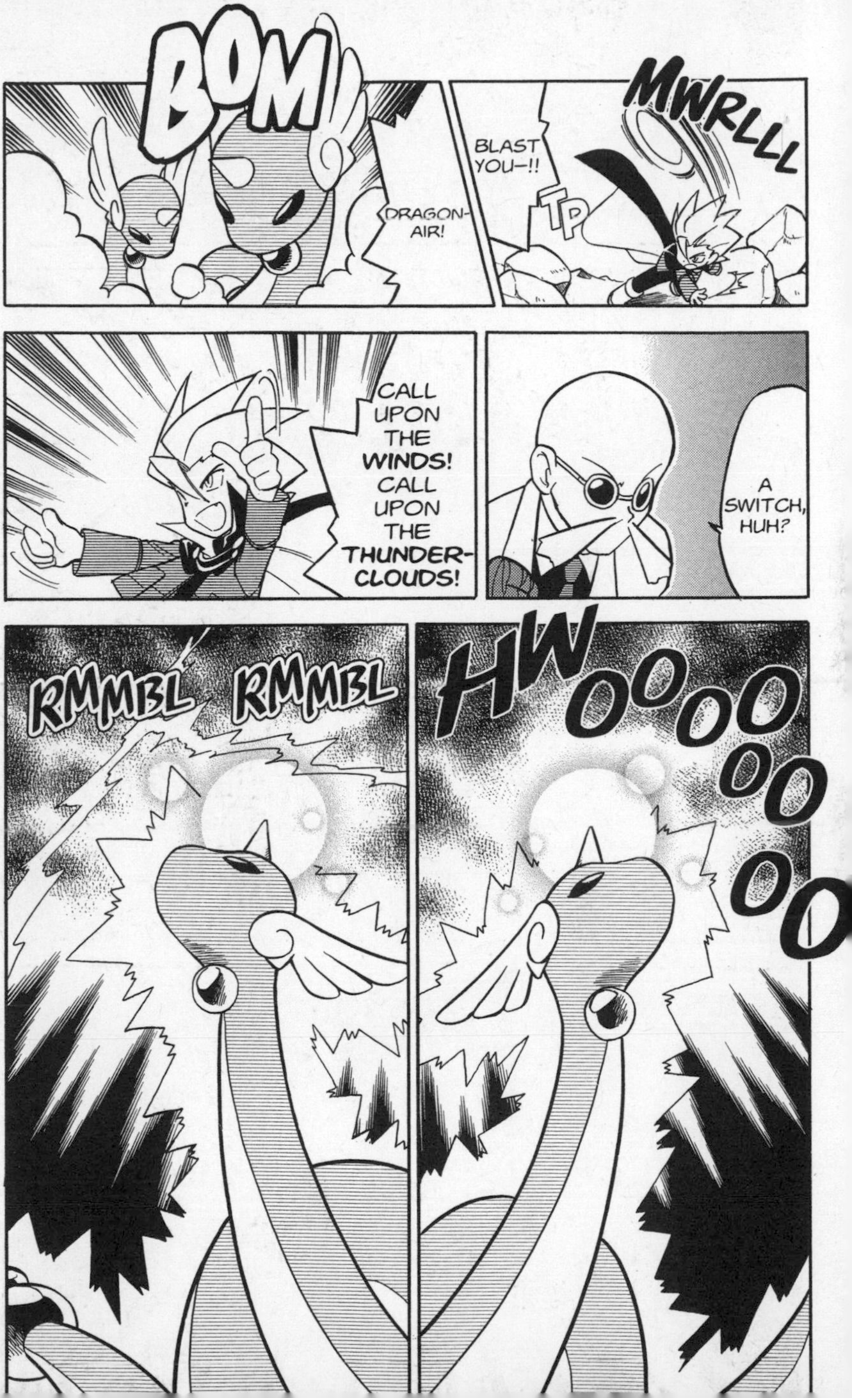
MWRLLL
BLAST YOU—!!
TP
BOM
DRAGON-AIR!
A SWITCH, HUH?
CALL UPON THE WINDS! CALL UPON THE THUNDER-CLOUDS!
HWOOOOOOOOOO
RMMBL RMMBL

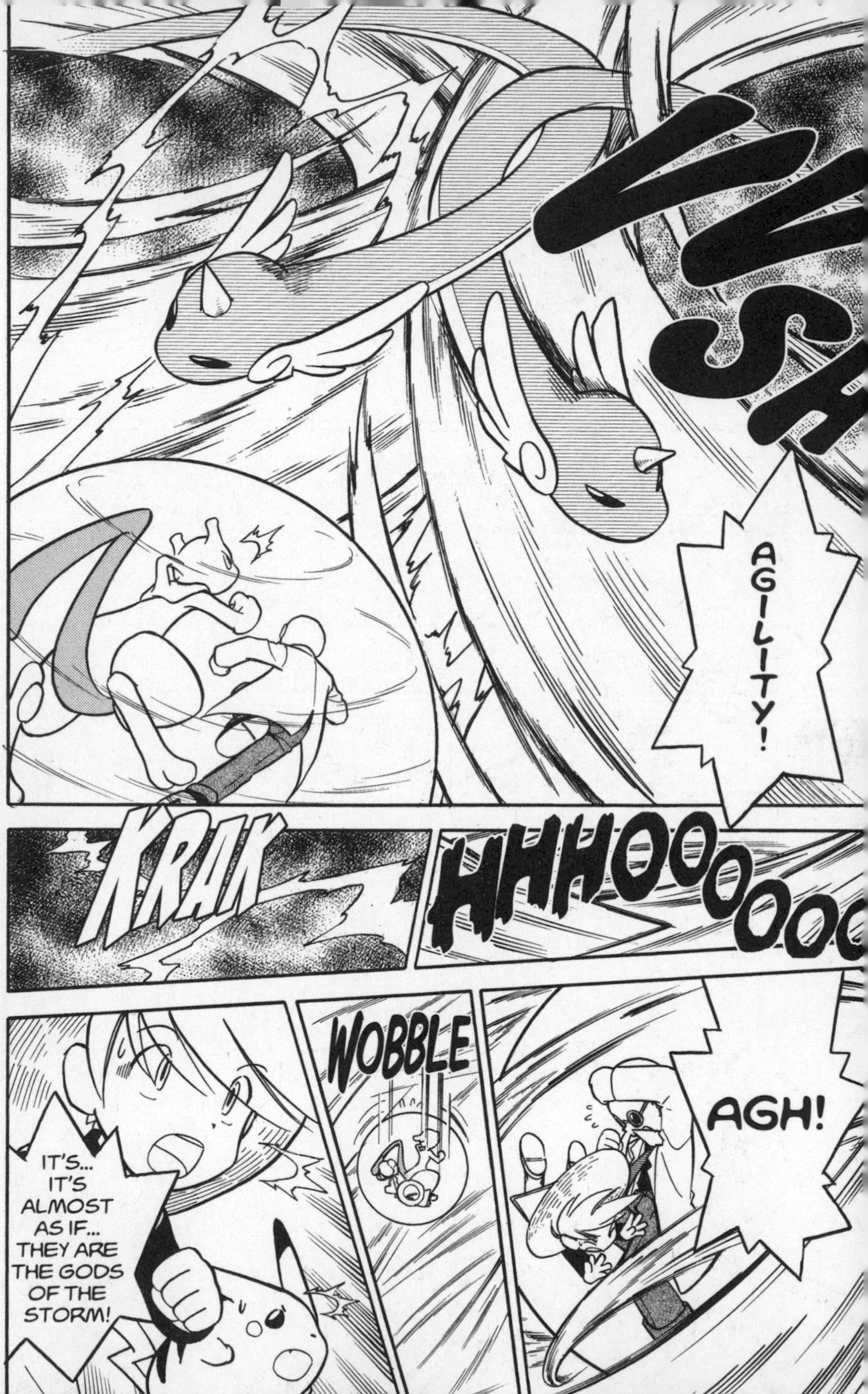
AGILITY!
HHHOOOOO
KRAK
AGH!
WOBBLE
IT'S... IT'S ALMOST AS IF... THEY ARE THE GODS OF THE STORM!

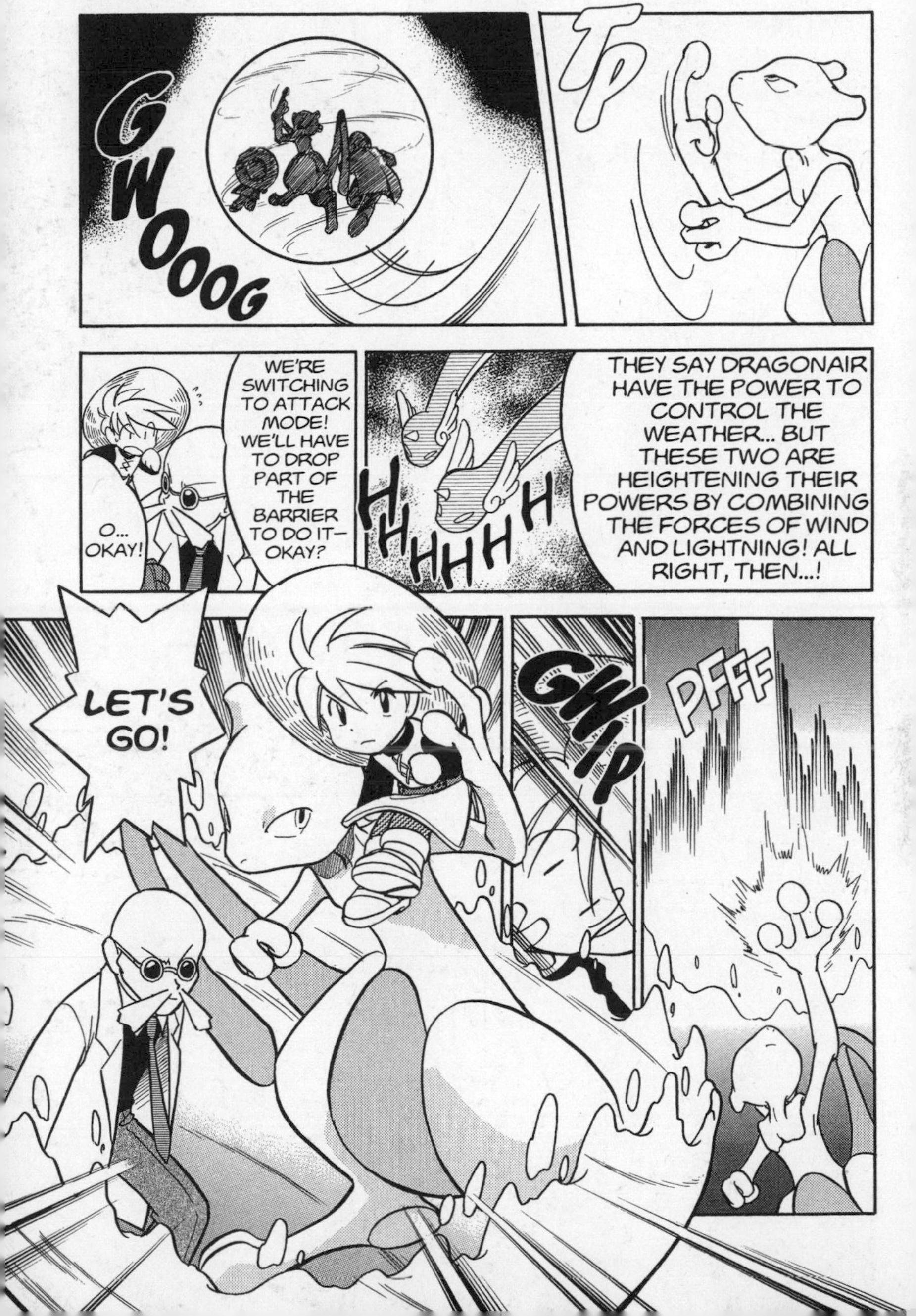
TP
GWOOOG
THEY SAY DRAGONAIR HAVE THE POWER TO CONTROL THE WEATHER... BUT THESE TWO ARE HEIGHTENING THEIR POWERS BY COMBINING THE FORCES OF WIND AND LIGHTNING! ALL RIGHT, THEN...!
HHHHHHH
WE'RE SWITCHING TO ATTACK MODE! WE'LL HAVE TO DROP PART OF THE BARRIER TO DO IT—OKAY?
O... OKAY!
PFFF
GWIP
LET'S GO!

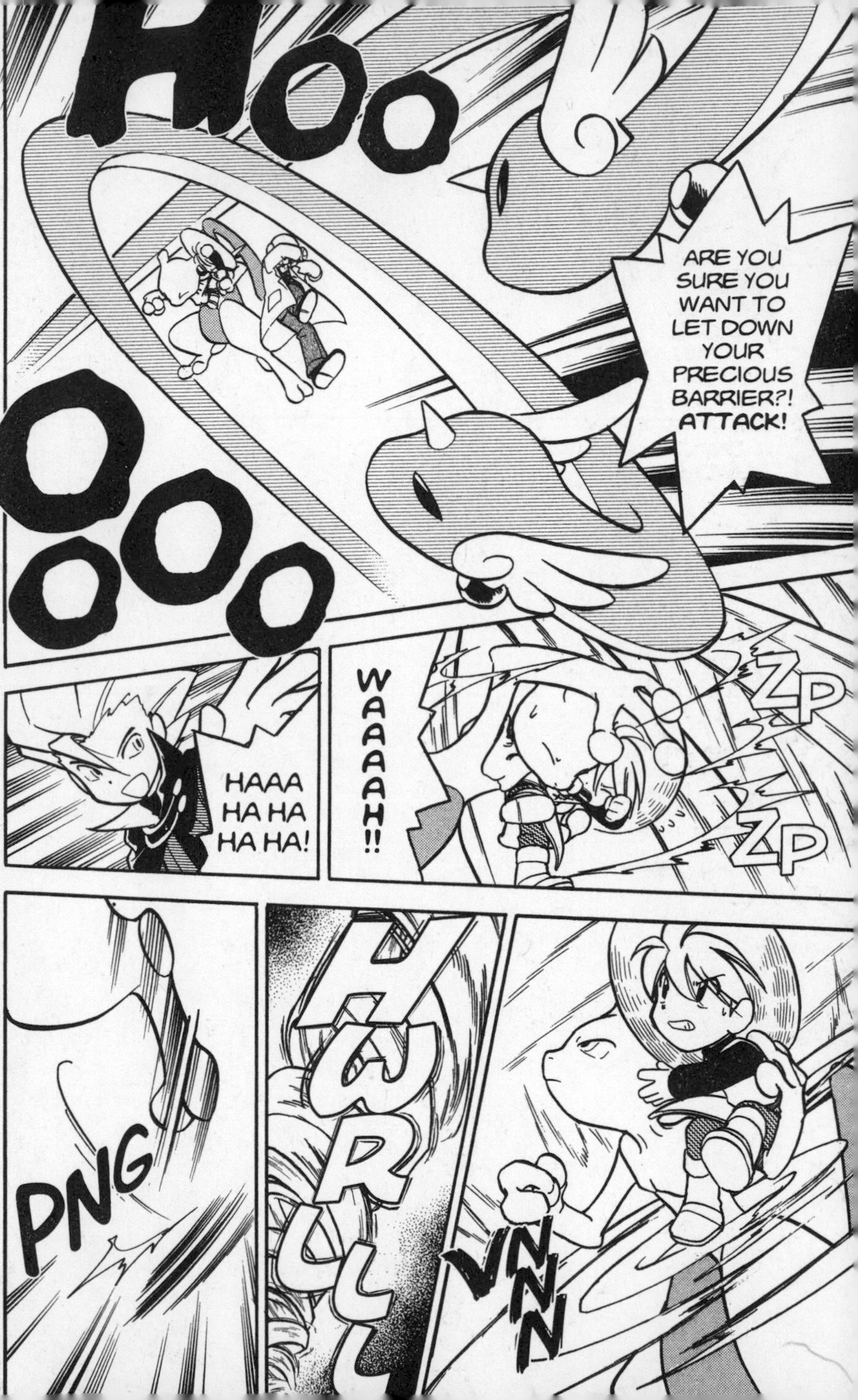
HOOOOOOO
ARE YOU SURE YOU WANT TO LET DOWN YOUR PRECIOUS BARRIER?! ATTACK!
ZP
ZP
WAAAAAH!!
HAAA HA HA HA HA!
VNNNN
HWRLL
PNG

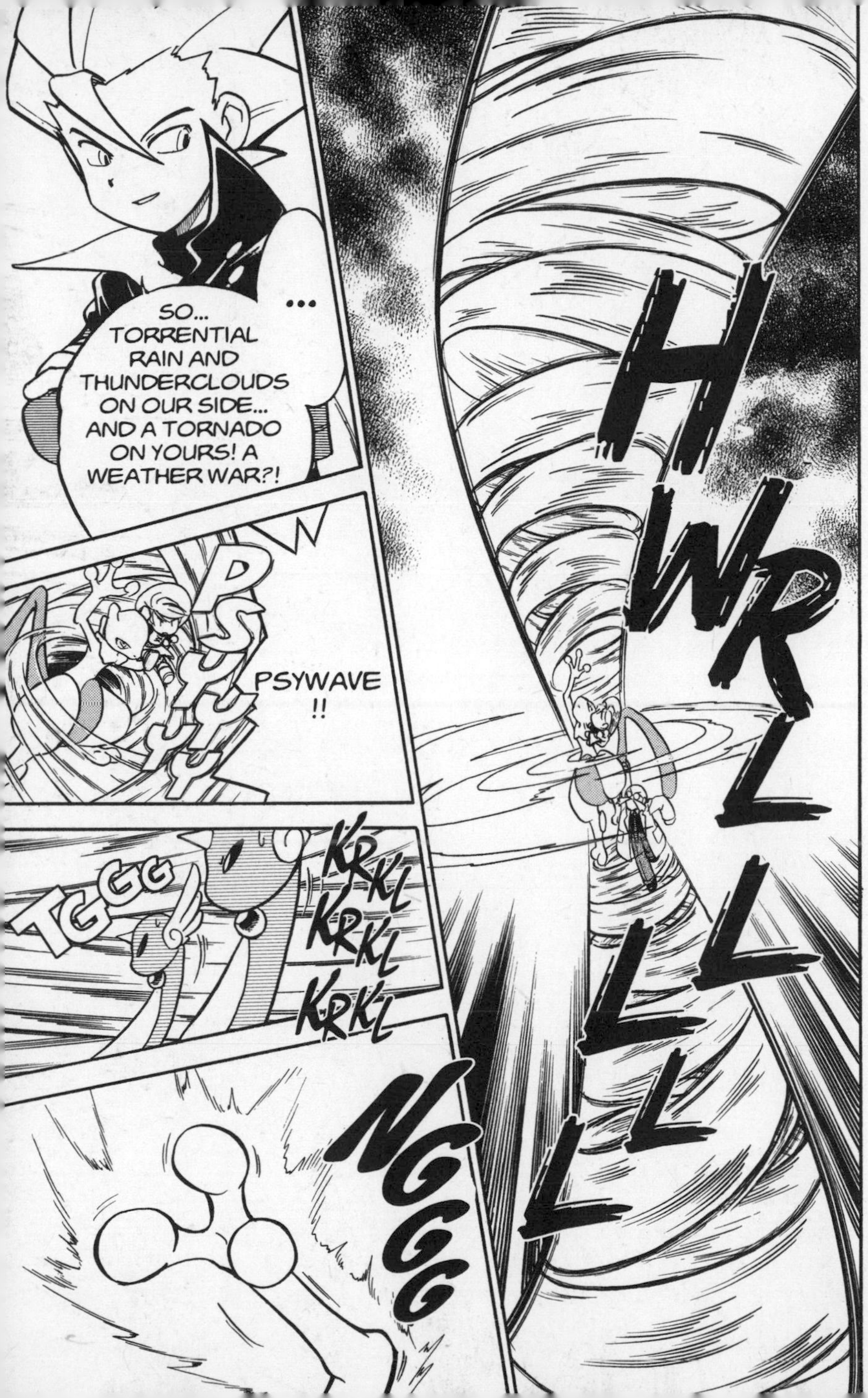
HWRLLLLL
NGGG
...
SO... TORRENTIAL RAIN AND THUNDERCLOUDS ON OUR SIDE... AND A TORNADO ON YOURS! A WEATHER WAR?!
PSYWAVE !!
KRKL KRKL KRKL
TGGG

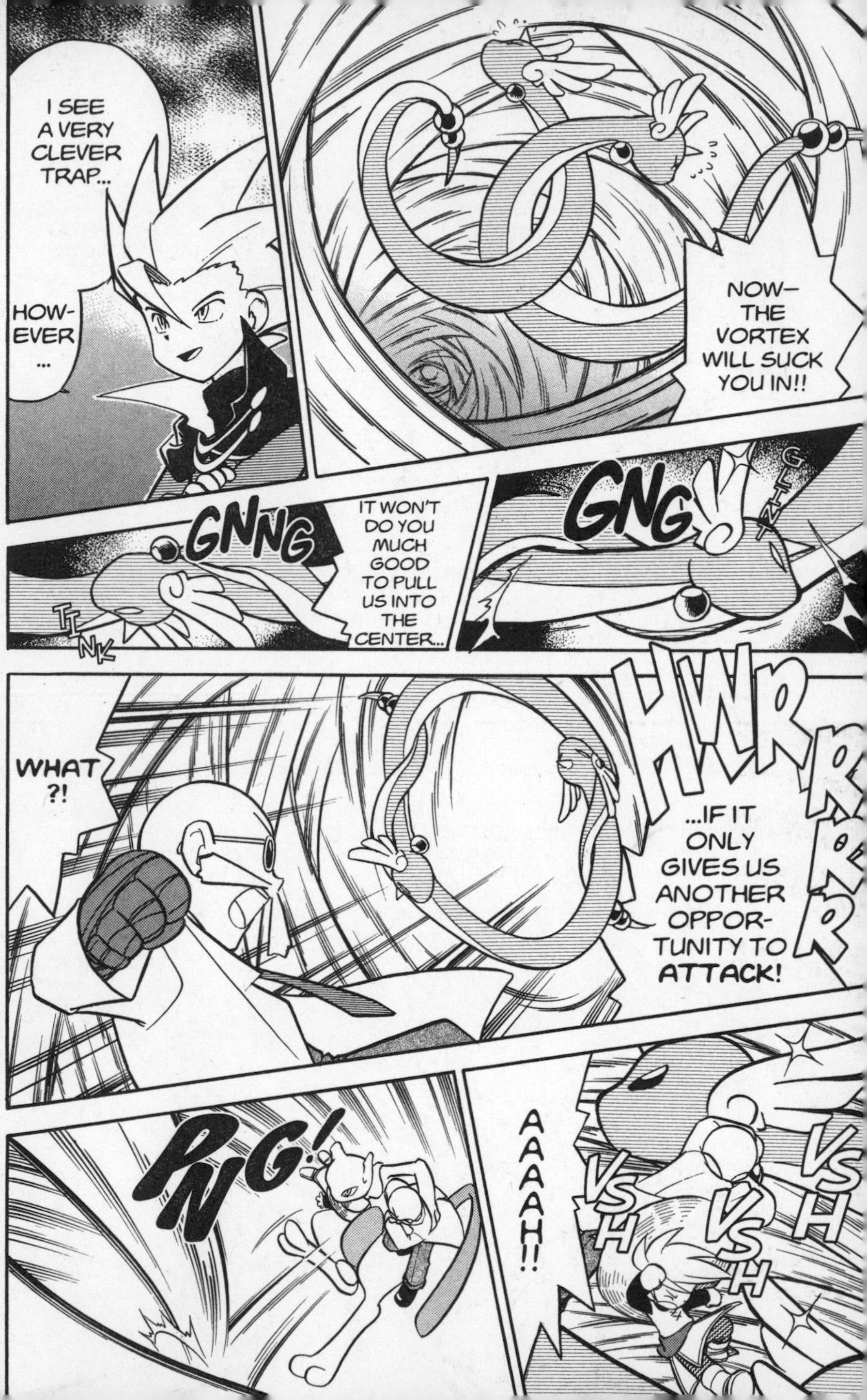
NOW— THE VORTEX WILL SUCK YOU IN!!
I SEE A VERY CLEVER TRAP...
HOW-EVER ...
GNG
GLINT
IT WON'T DO YOU MUCH GOOD TO PULL US INTO THE CENTER...
GNNG
TINK
HWR
...IF IT ONLY GIVES US ANOTHER OPPOR-TUNITY TO ATTACK!
WHAT ?!
VSH
VSH
VSH
AAAAAH!!
PNG!

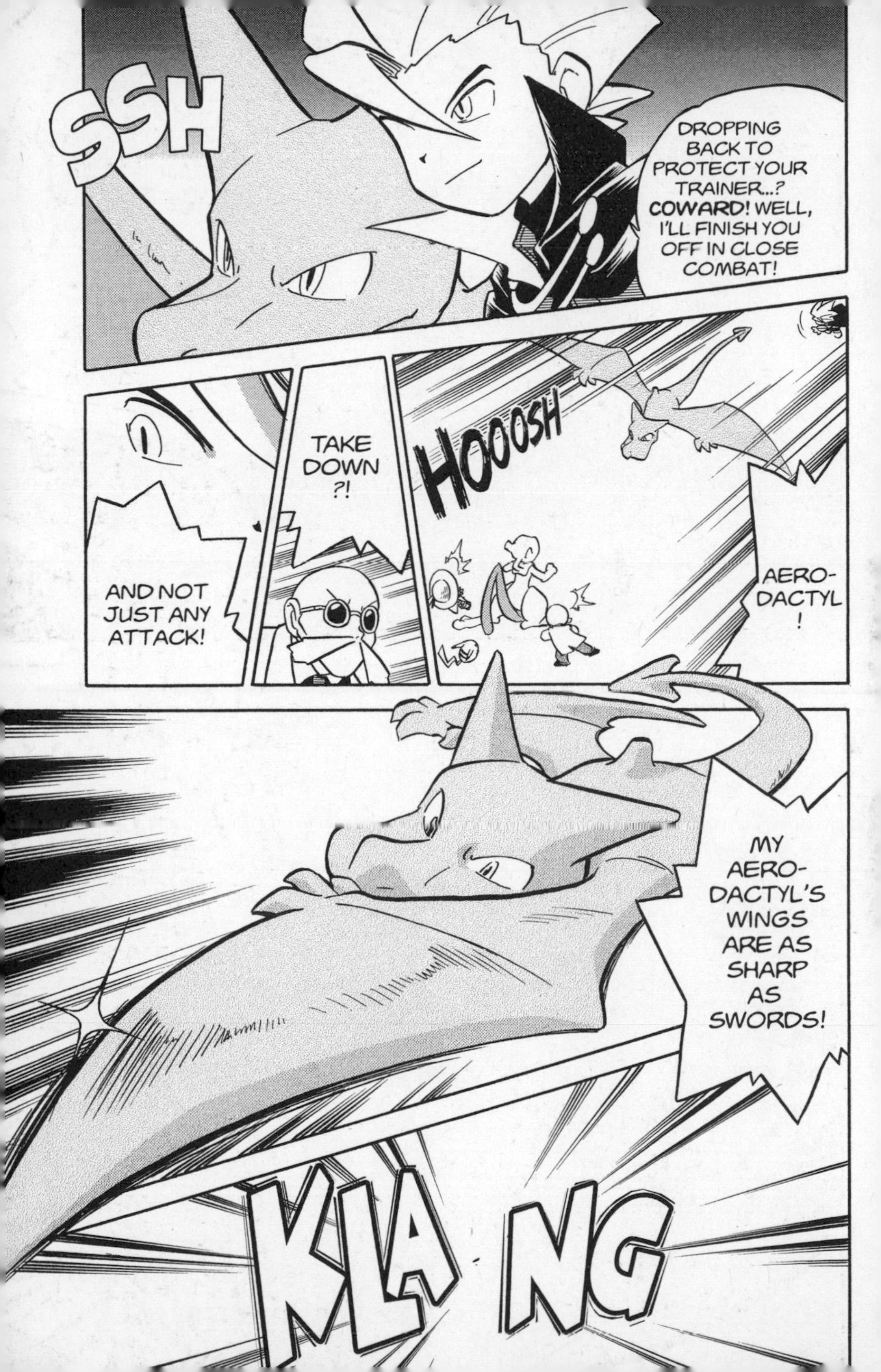
SSH
DROPPING BACK TO PROTECT YOUR TRAINER...? COWARD! WELL, I'LL FINISH YOU OFF IN CLOSE COMBAT!
HOOOSH
AERO-DACTYL!
TAKE DOWN ?!
AND NOT JUST ANY ATTACK!
MY AERO-DACTYL'S WINGS ARE AS SHARP AS SWORDS!
KLANG

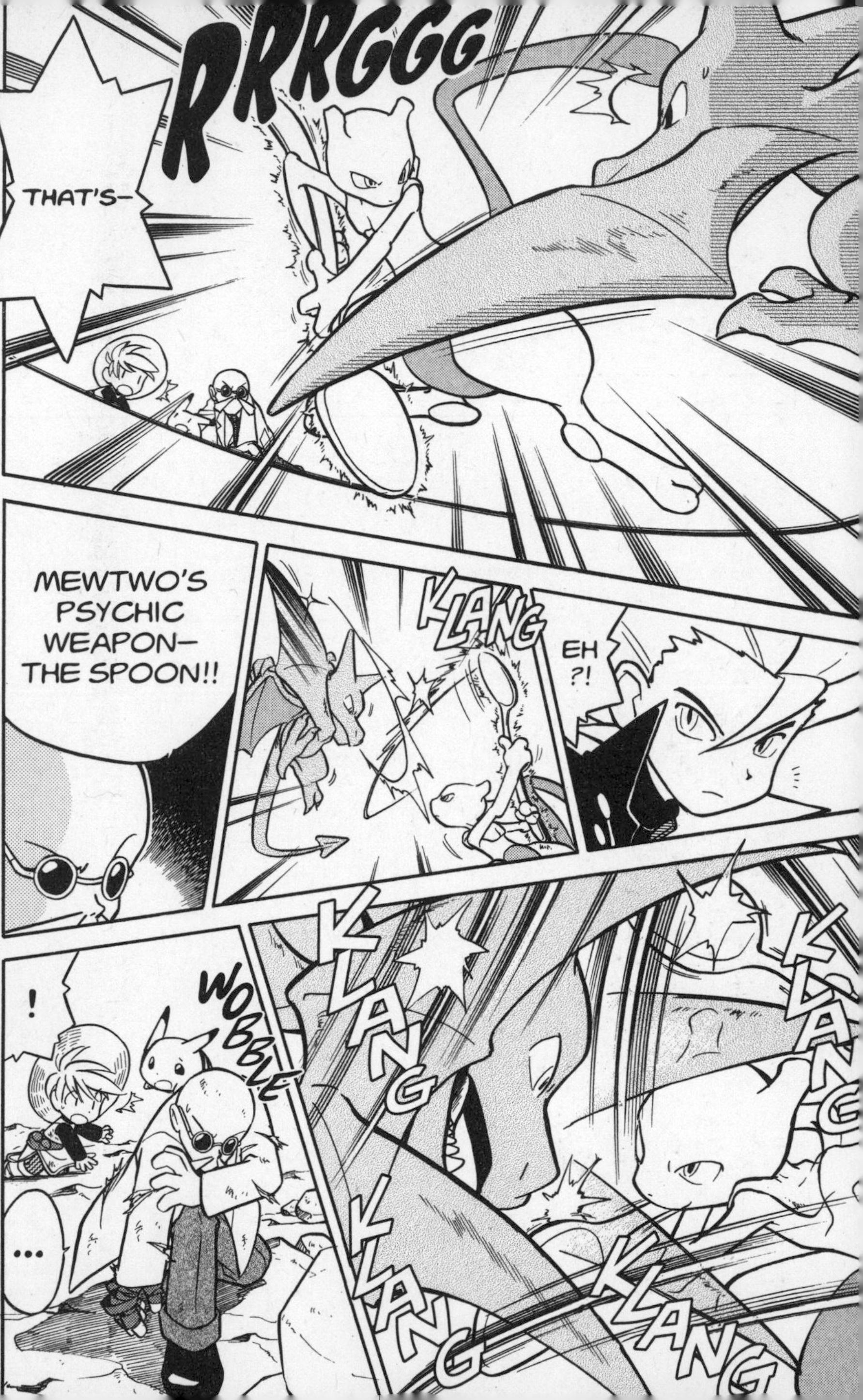
RRRGGG
THAT'S—
EH ?!
KLANG
MEWTWO'S PSYCHIC WEAPON— THE SPOON!!
KLANG
KLANG
KLANG
KLANG
KLANG
!
WOBBLE
...

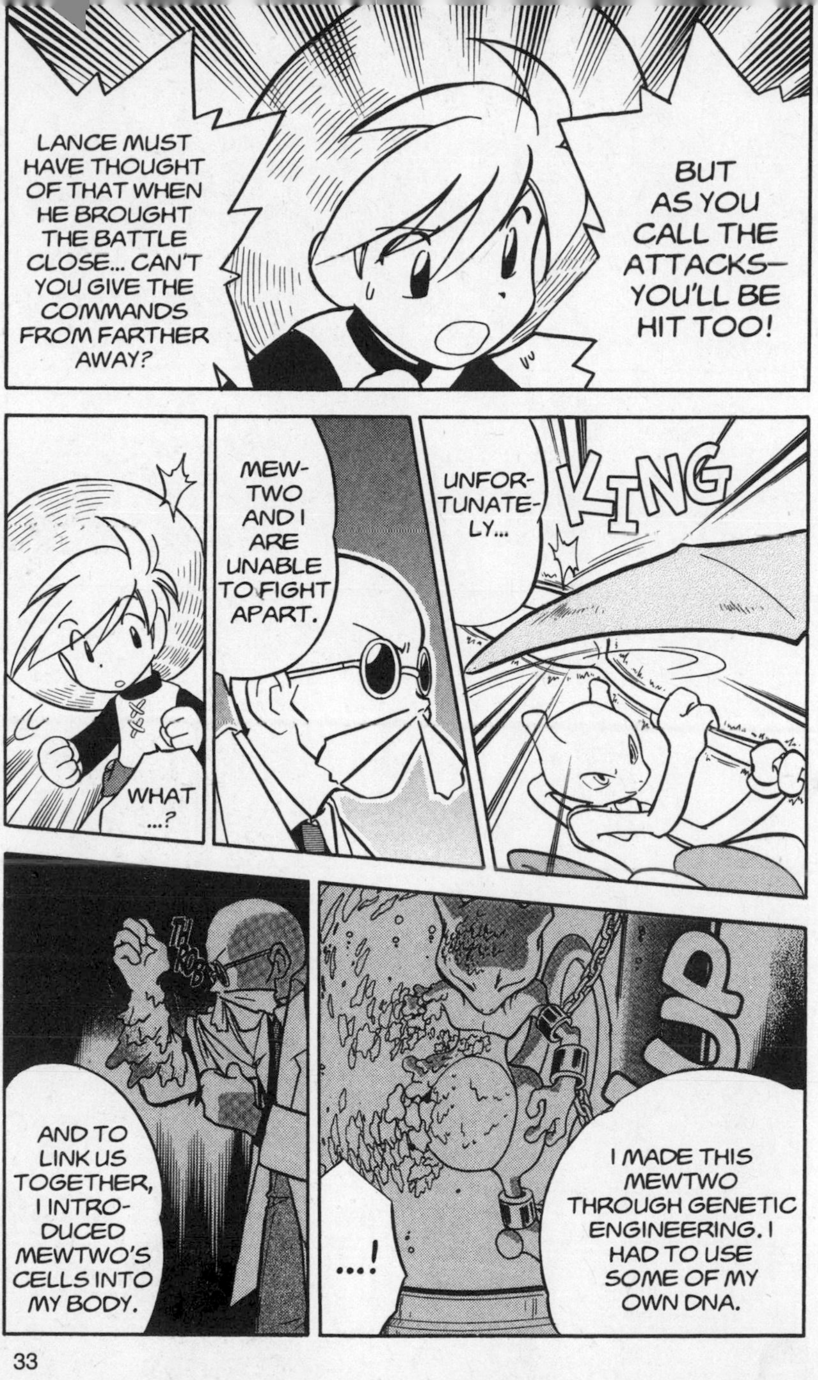
BUT AS YOU CALL THE ATTACKS—YOU'LL BE HIT TOO!
LANCE MUST HAVE THOUGHT OF THAT WHEN HE BROUGHT THE BATTLE CLOSE... CAN'T YOU GIVE THE COMMANDS FROM FARTHER AWAY?
KING
UNFOR-TUNATE-LY...
MEW-TWO AND I ARE UNABLE TO FIGHT APART.
WHAT ...?
I MADE THIS MEWTWO THROUGH GENETIC ENGINEERING. I HAD TO USE SOME OF MY OWN DNA.
...!
THROB
AND TO LINK US TOGETHER, I INTRO-DUCED MEWTWO'S CELLS INTO MY BODY.

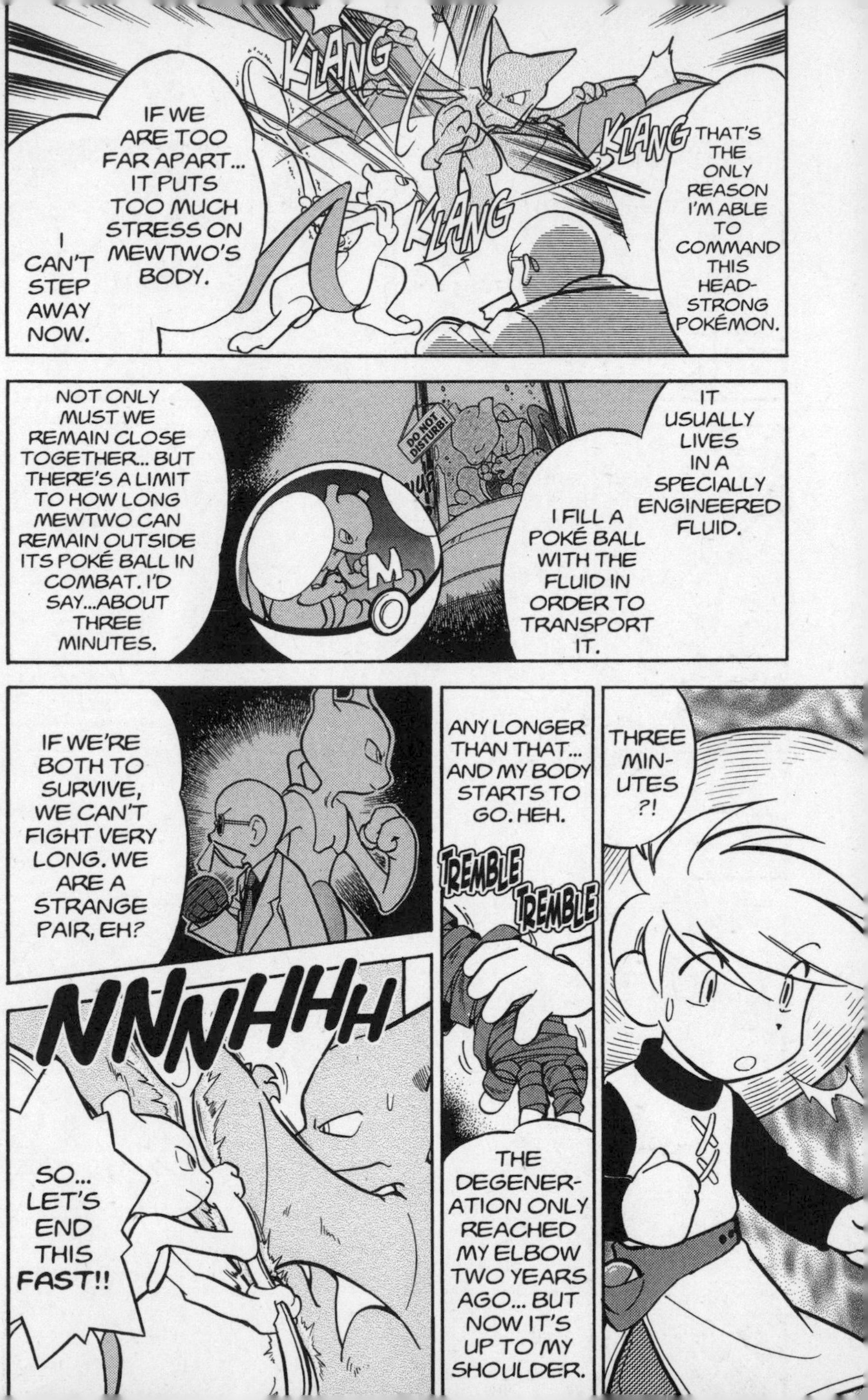
THAT'S THE ONLY REASON I'M ABLE TO COMMAND THIS HEAD-STRONG POKÉMON.
KLANG
KLANG
KLANG
IF WE ARE TOO FAR APART... IT PUTS TOO MUCH STRESS ON MEWTWO'S BODY.
I CAN'T STEP AWAY NOW.
IT USUALLY LIVES IN A SPECIALLY ENGINEERED FLUID.
I FILL A POKÉ BALL WITH THE FLUID IN ORDER TO TRANSPORT IT.
DO NOT DISTURB!
NOT ONLY MUST WE REMAIN CLOSE TOGETHER... BUT THERE'S A LIMIT TO HOW LONG MEWTWO CAN REMAIN OUTSIDE ITS POKÉ BALL IN COMBAT. I'D SAY...ABOUT THREE MINUTES.
THREE MIN-UTES?!
ANY LONGER THAN THAT... AND MY BODY STARTS TO GO. HEH.
TREMBLE
TREMBLE
THE DEGENER-ATION ONLY REACHED MY ELBOW TWO YEARS AGO... BUT NOW IT'S UP TO MY SHOULDER.
IF WE'RE BOTH TO SURVIVE, WE CAN'T FIGHT VERY LONG. WE ARE A STRANGE PAIR, EH?
NNNHHH
SO... LET'S END THIS FAST!!

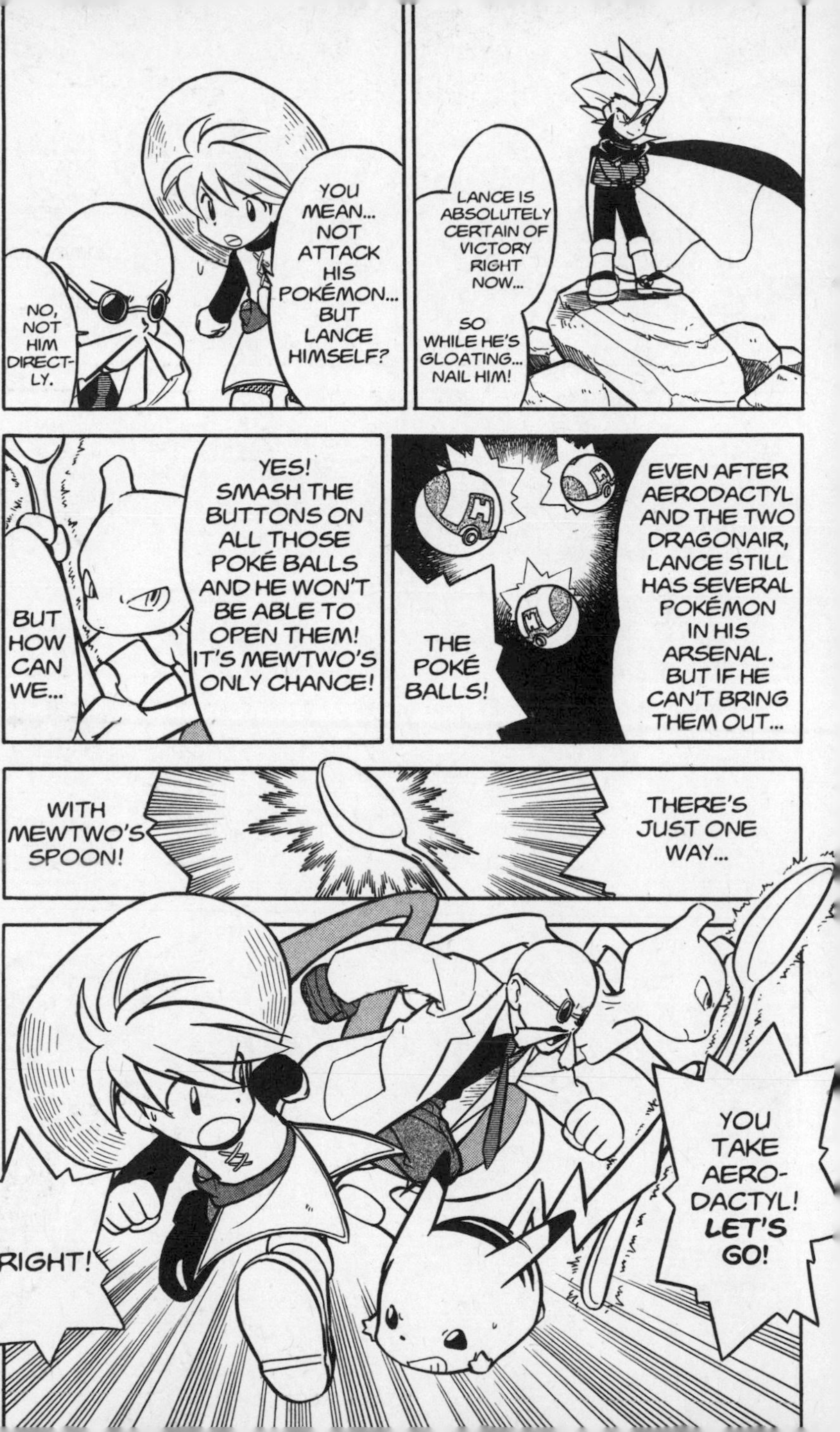
LANCE IS ABSOLUTELY CERTAIN OF VICTORY RIGHT NOW...
SO WHILE HE'S GLOATING... NAIL HIM!
YOU MEAN... NOT ATTACK HIS POKÉMON... BUT LANCE HIMSELF?
NO, NOT HIM DIRECTLY.
EVEN AFTER AERODACTYL AND THE TWO DRAGONAIR, LANCE STILL HAS SEVERAL POKÉMON IN HIS ARSENAL. BUT IF HE CAN'T BRING THEM OUT...
THE POKÉ BALLS!
YES! SMASH THE BUTTONS ON ALL THOSE POKÉ BALLS AND HE WON'T BE ABLE TO OPEN THEM! IT'S MEWTWO'S ONLY CHANCE!
BUT HOW CAN WE...
THERE'S JUST ONE WAY...
WITH MEWTWO'S SPOON!
YOU TAKE AERODACTYL! LET'S GO!
RIGHT!

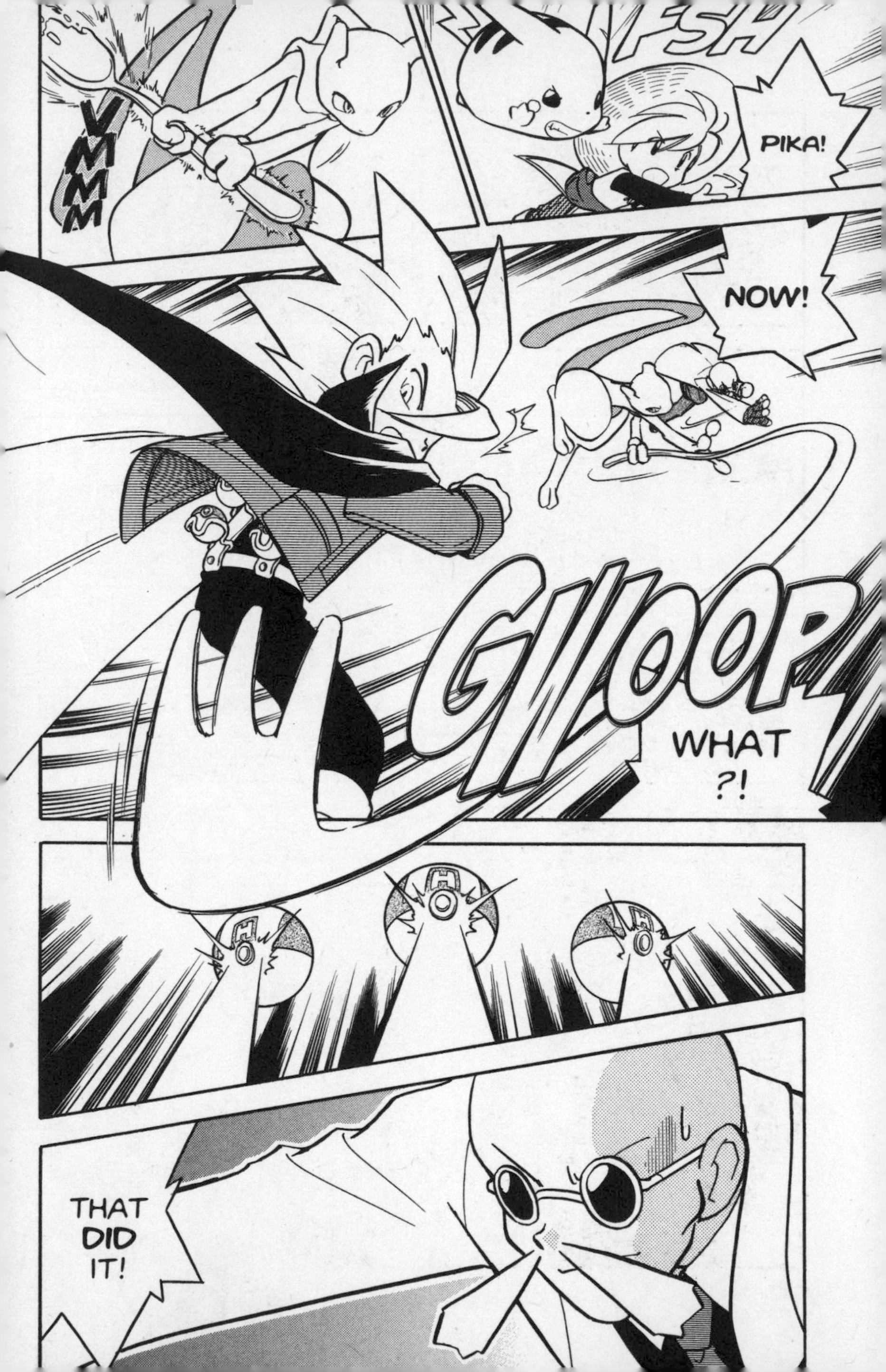
FSH
PIKA!
VMMM
NOW!
GLOOP
WHAT ?!
THAT DID IT!

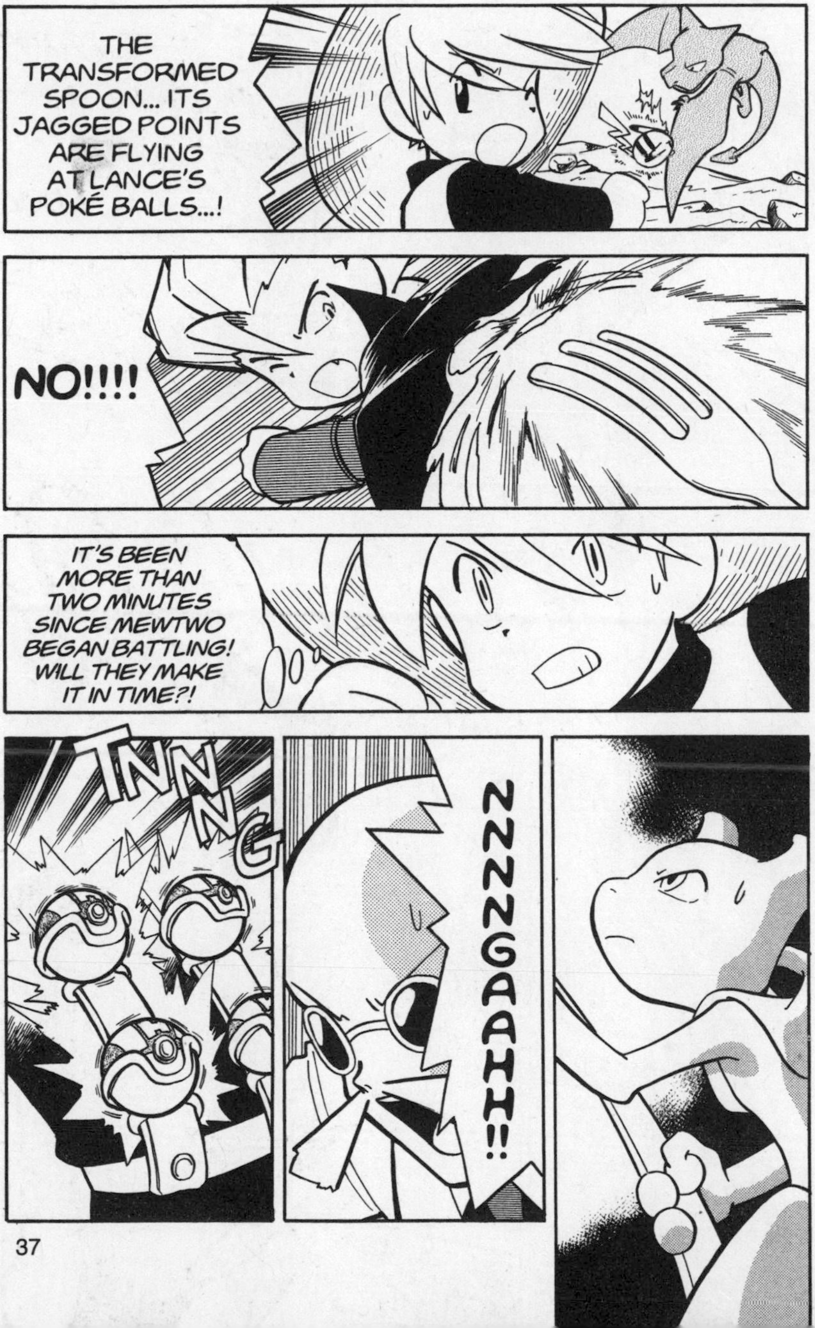
THE TRANSFORMED SPOON... ITS JAGGED POINTS ARE FLYING AT LANCE'S POKÉ BALLS...!
NO!!!!
IT'S BEEN MORE THAN TWO MINUTES SINCE MEWTWO BEGAN BATTLING! WILL THEY MAKE IT IN TIME?!
NNNNGAAHH!!
TNNNG

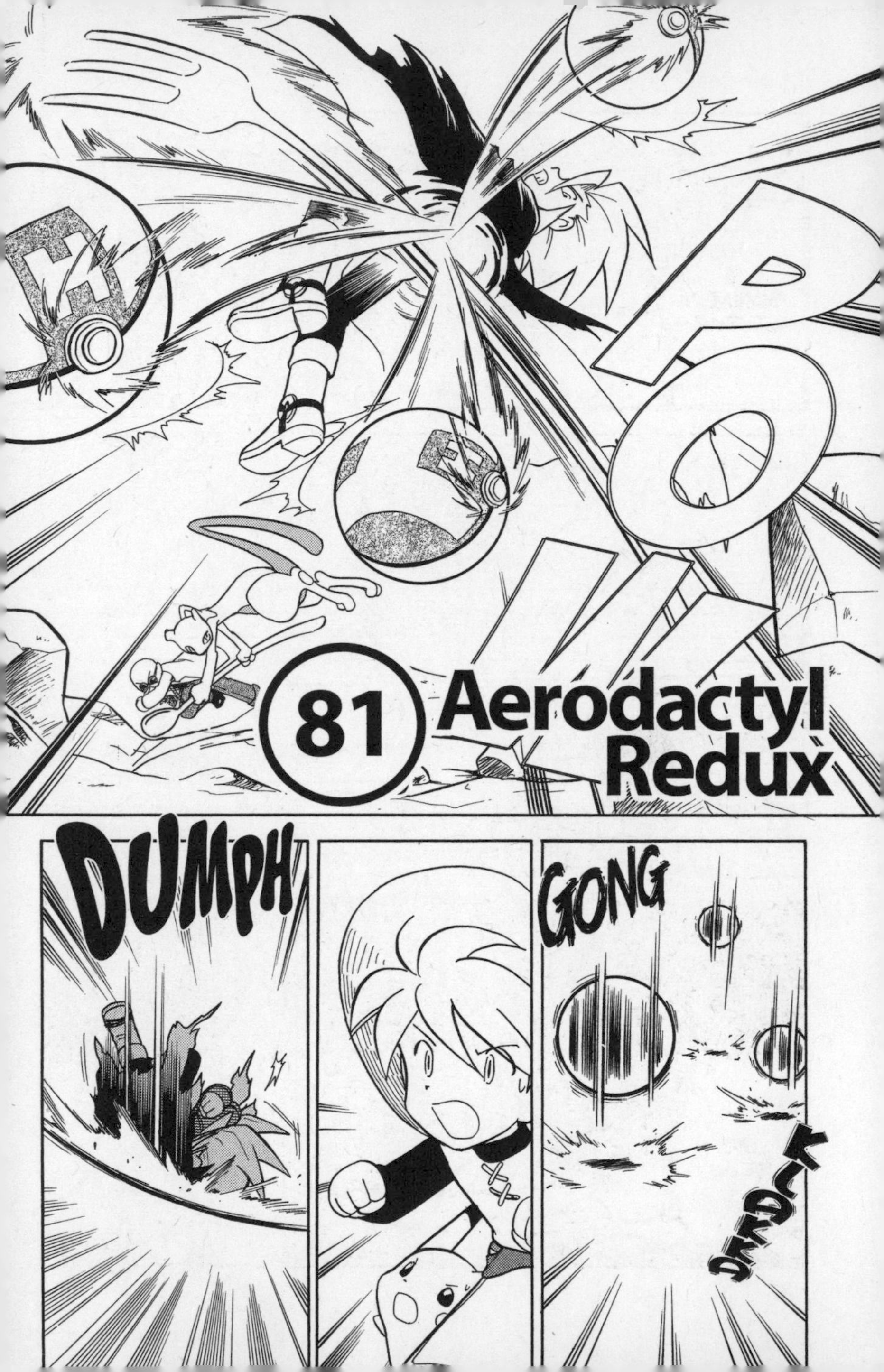
81 Aerodactyl Redux
GONG
DUMPH

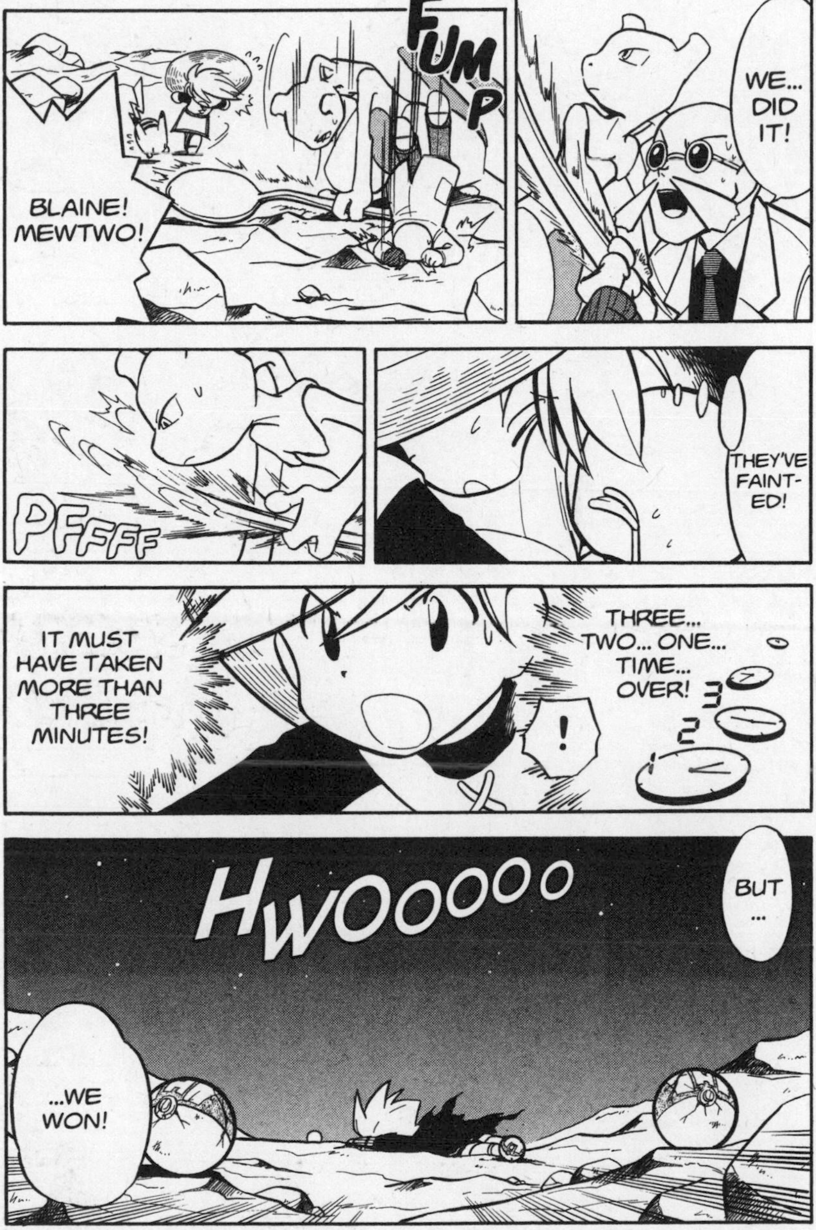
WE... DID IT!
FUMP
BLAINE! MEWTWO!
THEY'VE FAINT-ED!
PFFFF
THREE... TWO... ONE... TIME... OVER!
3
2
1
!
IT MUST HAVE TAKEN MORE THAN THREE MINUTES!
BUT ...
HWOOOOO
...WE WON!

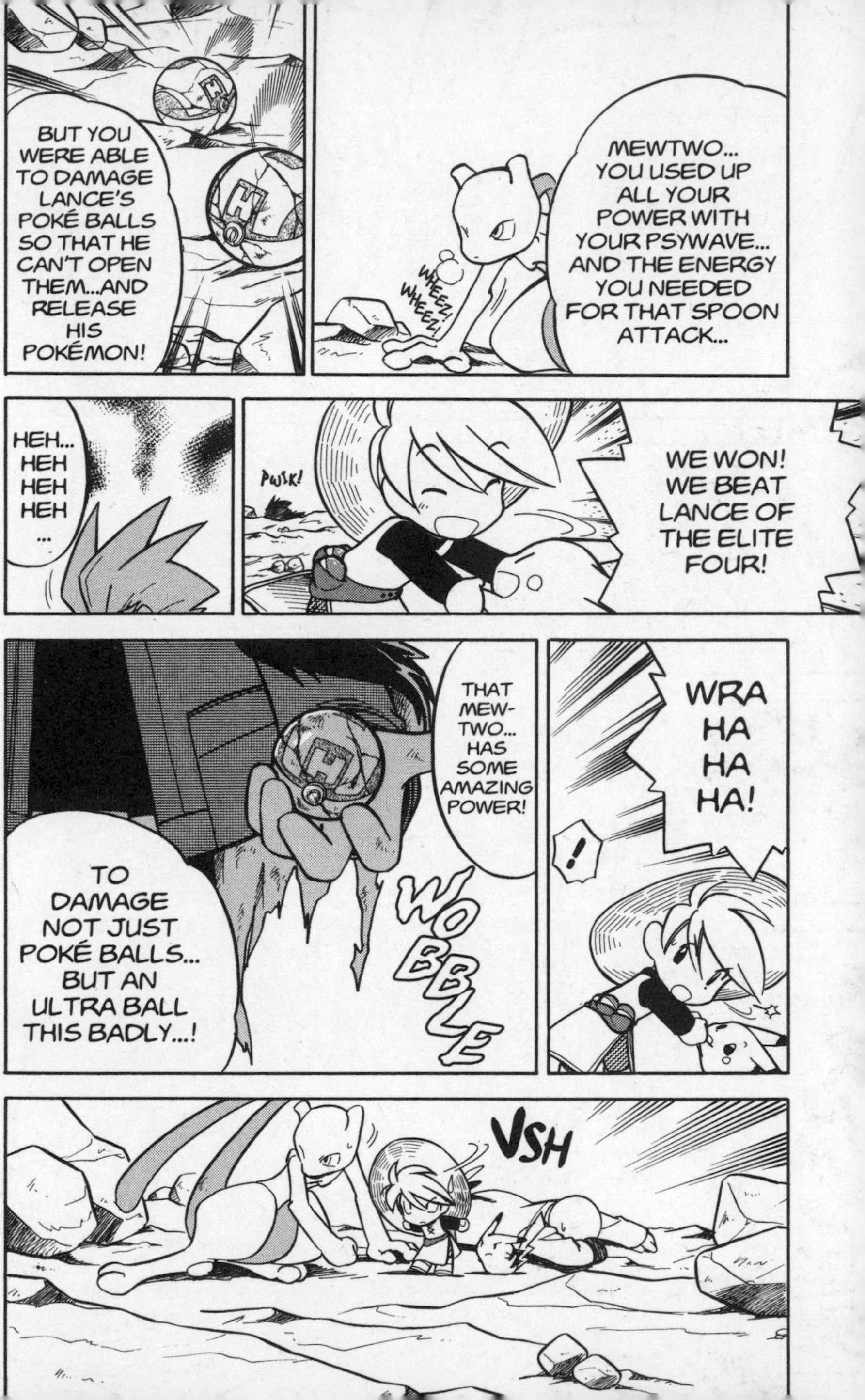
MEWTWO... YOU USED UP ALL YOUR POWER WITH YOUR PSYWAVE... AND THE ENERGY YOU NEEDED FOR THAT SPOON ATTACK...
WHEEZ! WHEEZ!
BUT YOU WERE ABLE TO DAMAGE LANCE'S POKÉ BALLS SO THAT HE CAN'T OPEN THEM...AND RELEASE HIS POKÉMON!
PWIK!
WE WON! WE BEAT LANCE OF THE ELITE FOUR!
HEH... HEH HEH HEH ...
WRA HA HA HA!
!
THAT MEW-TWO... HAS SOME AMAZING POWER!
TO DAMAGE NOT JUST POKÉ BALLS... BUT AN ULTRA BALL THIS BADLY...!
WOBBLE
VSH

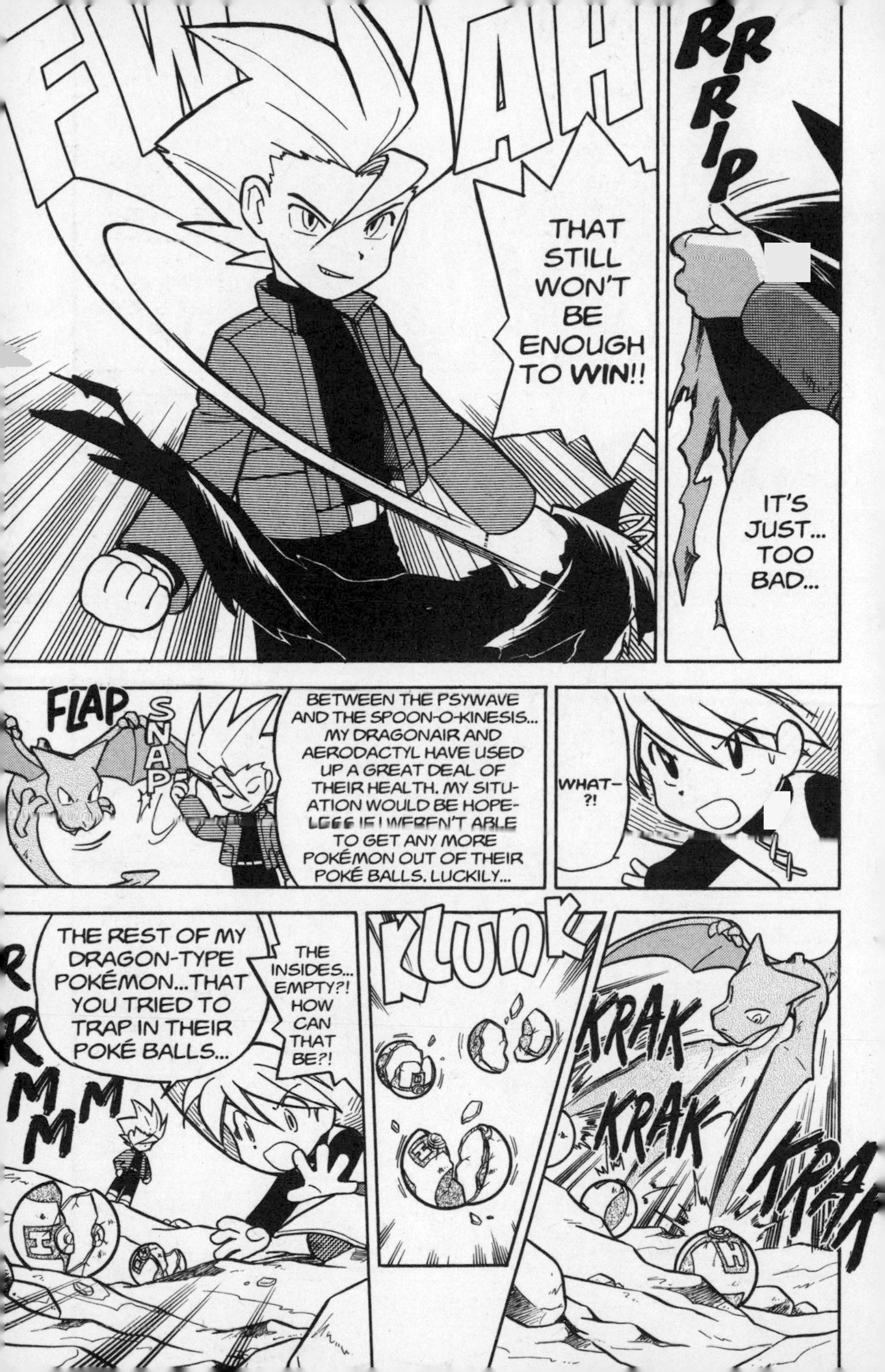
RRRIP
IT'S JUST... TOO BAD...
FWAH
THAT STILL WON'T BE ENOUGH TO WIN!!
WHAT—?!
BETWEEN THE PSYWAVE AND THE SPOON-O-KINESIS... MY DRAGONAIR AND AERODACTYL HAVE USED UP A GREAT DEAL OF THEIR HEALTH. MY SITUATION WOULD BE HOPELESS IF I WEREN'T ABLE TO GET ANY MORE POKÉMON OUT OF THEIR POKÉ BALLS. LUCKILY...
SNAP
FLAP
KRAK KRAK KRAK
KLUNK
THE INSIDES... EMPTY?! HOW CAN THAT BE?!
THE REST OF MY DRAGON-TYPE POKÉMON...THAT YOU TRIED TO TRAP IN THEIR POKÉ BALLS...
RRMMMM

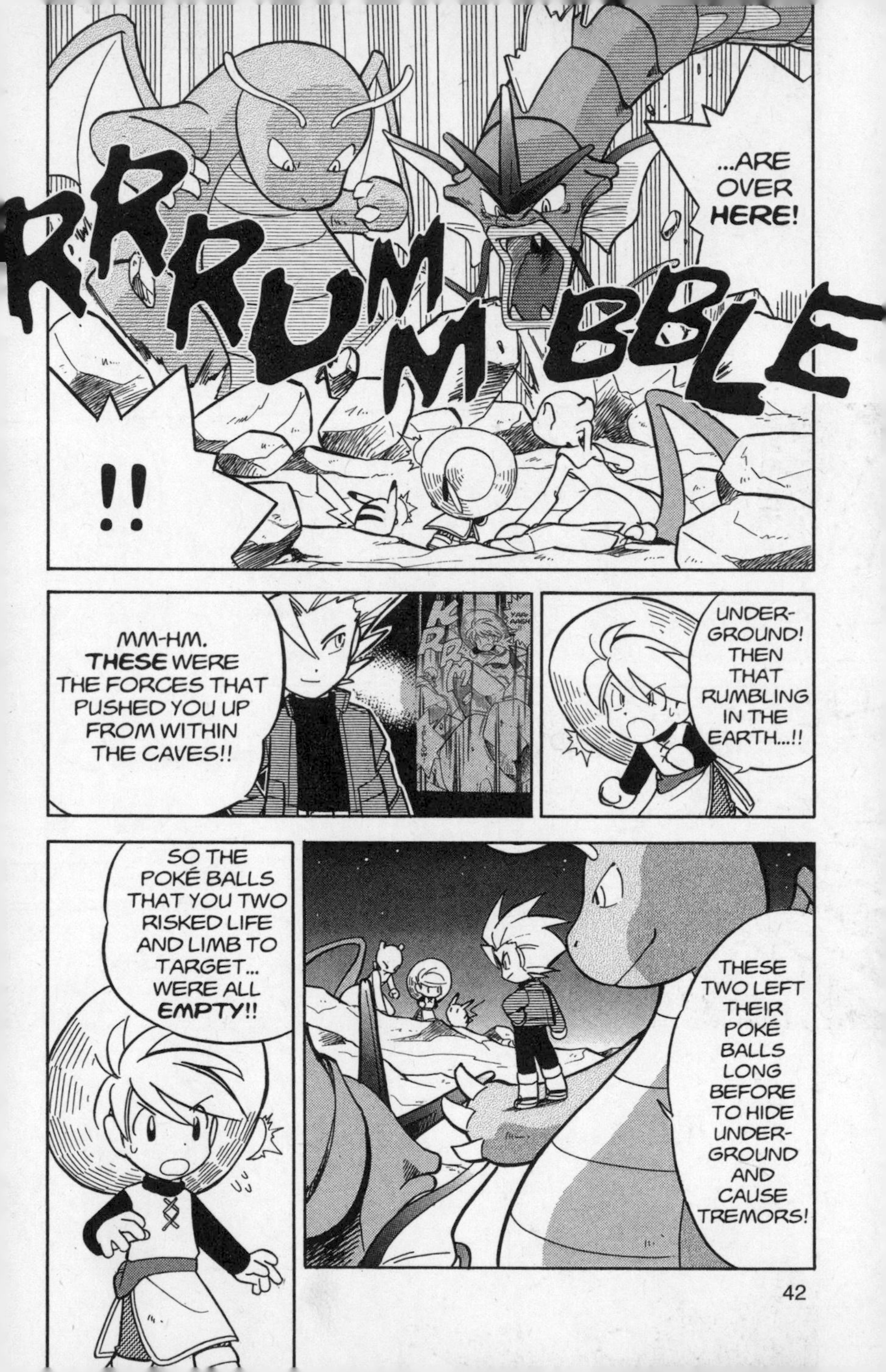
...ARE OVER HERE!
RRRUMMBBLE
!!
UNDER-GROUND! THEN THAT RUMBLING IN THE EARTH...!!
MM-HM. THESE WERE THE FORCES THAT PUSHED YOU UP FROM WITHIN THE CAVES!!
THESE TWO LEFT THEIR POKÉ BALLS LONG BEFORE TO HIDE UNDER-GROUND AND CAUSE TREMORS!
SO THE POKÉ BALLS THAT YOU TWO RISKED LIFE AND LIMB TO TARGET... WERE ALL EMPTY!!

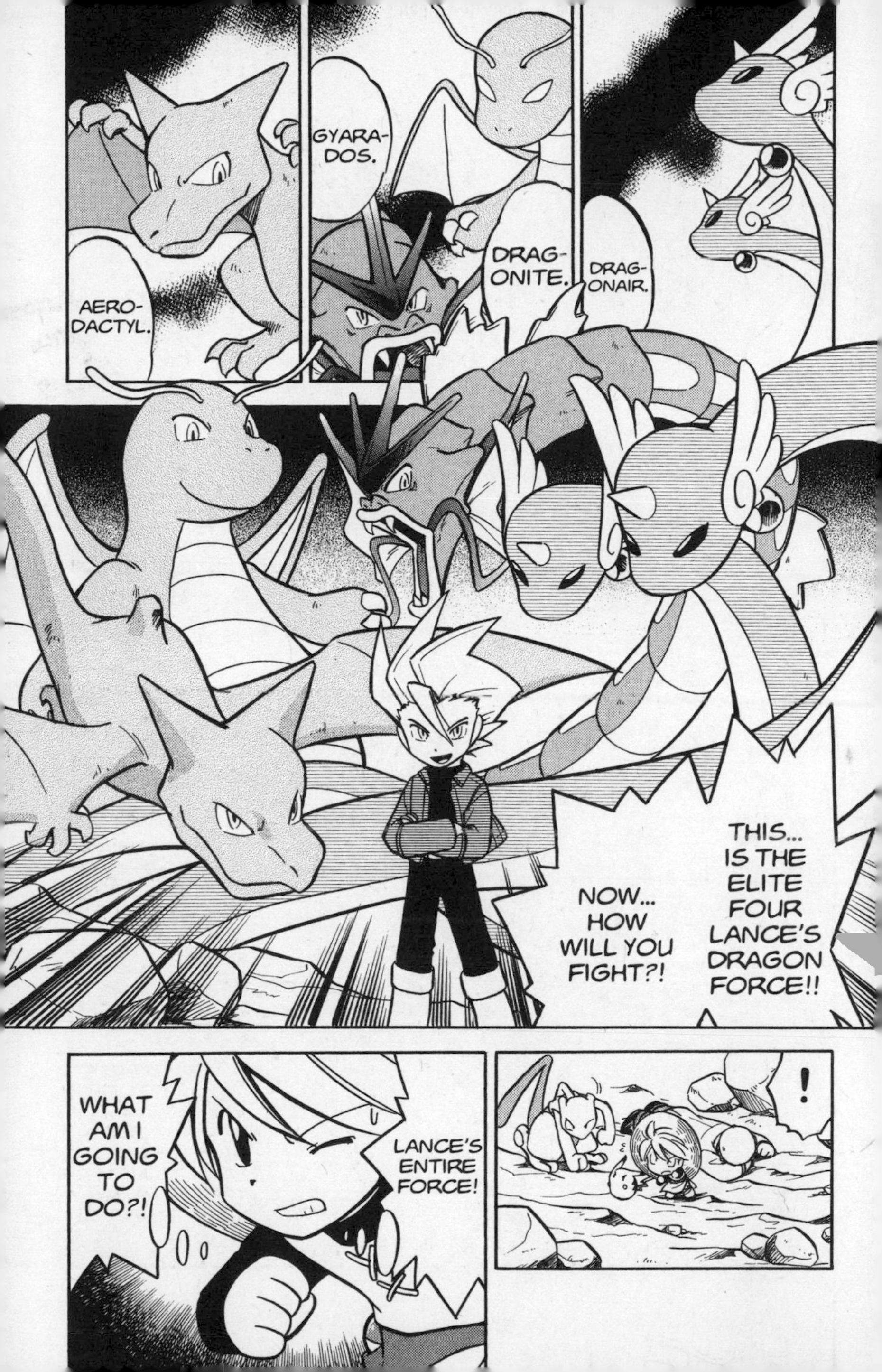
DRAG-ONAIR.
DRAG-ONITE.
GYARA-DOS.
AERO-DACTYL.
THIS... IS THE ELITE FOUR LANCE'S DRAGON FORCE!!
NOW... HOW WILL YOU FIGHT?!
!
LANCE'S ENTIRE FORCE!
WHAT AM I GOING TO DO?!

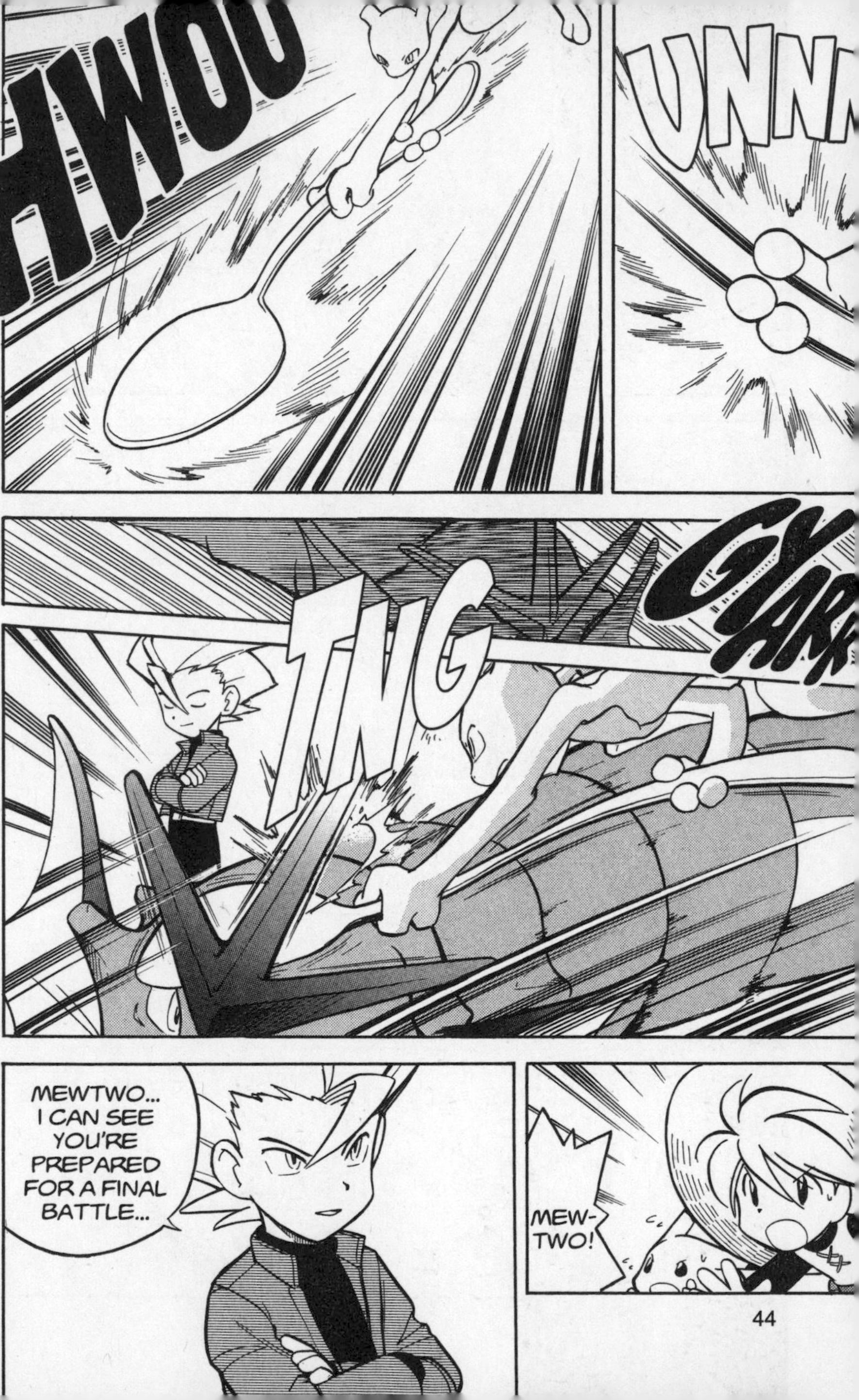
UNNN
HWOU
GYARR
TNG
MEW-TWO!
MEWTWO... I CAN SEE YOU'RE PREPARED FOR A FINAL BATTLE...

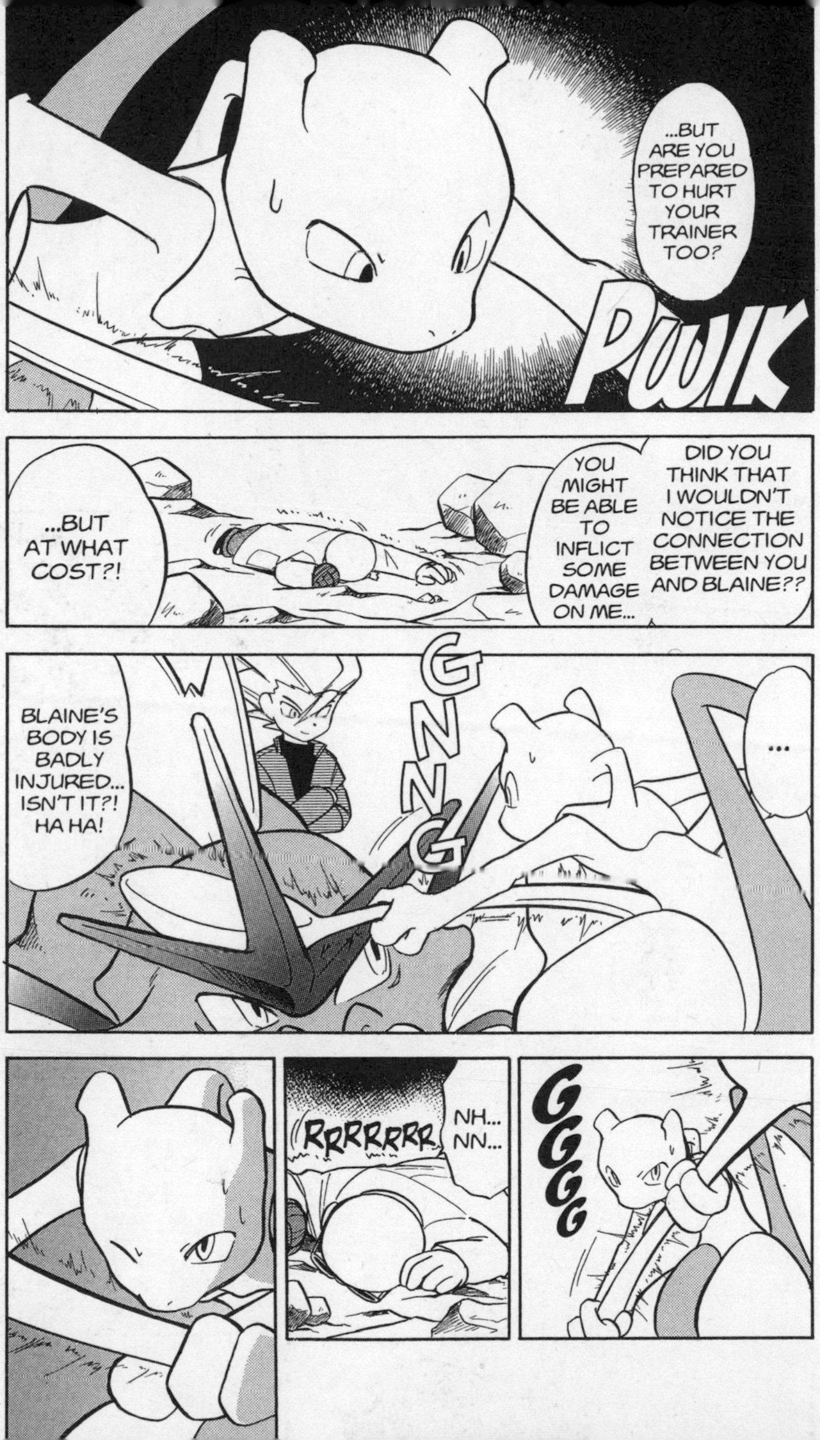
...BUT ARE YOU PREPARED TO HURT YOUR TRAINER TOO?
PWIK
DID YOU THINK THAT I WOULDN'T NOTICE THE CONNECTION BETWEEN YOU AND BLAINE??
YOU MIGHT BE ABLE TO INFLICT SOME DAMAGE ON ME...
...BUT AT WHAT COST?!
...
GNNG
BLAINE'S BODY IS BADLY INJURED... ISN'T IT?! HA HA!
GGGG
NH... NN...
RRRRRRR

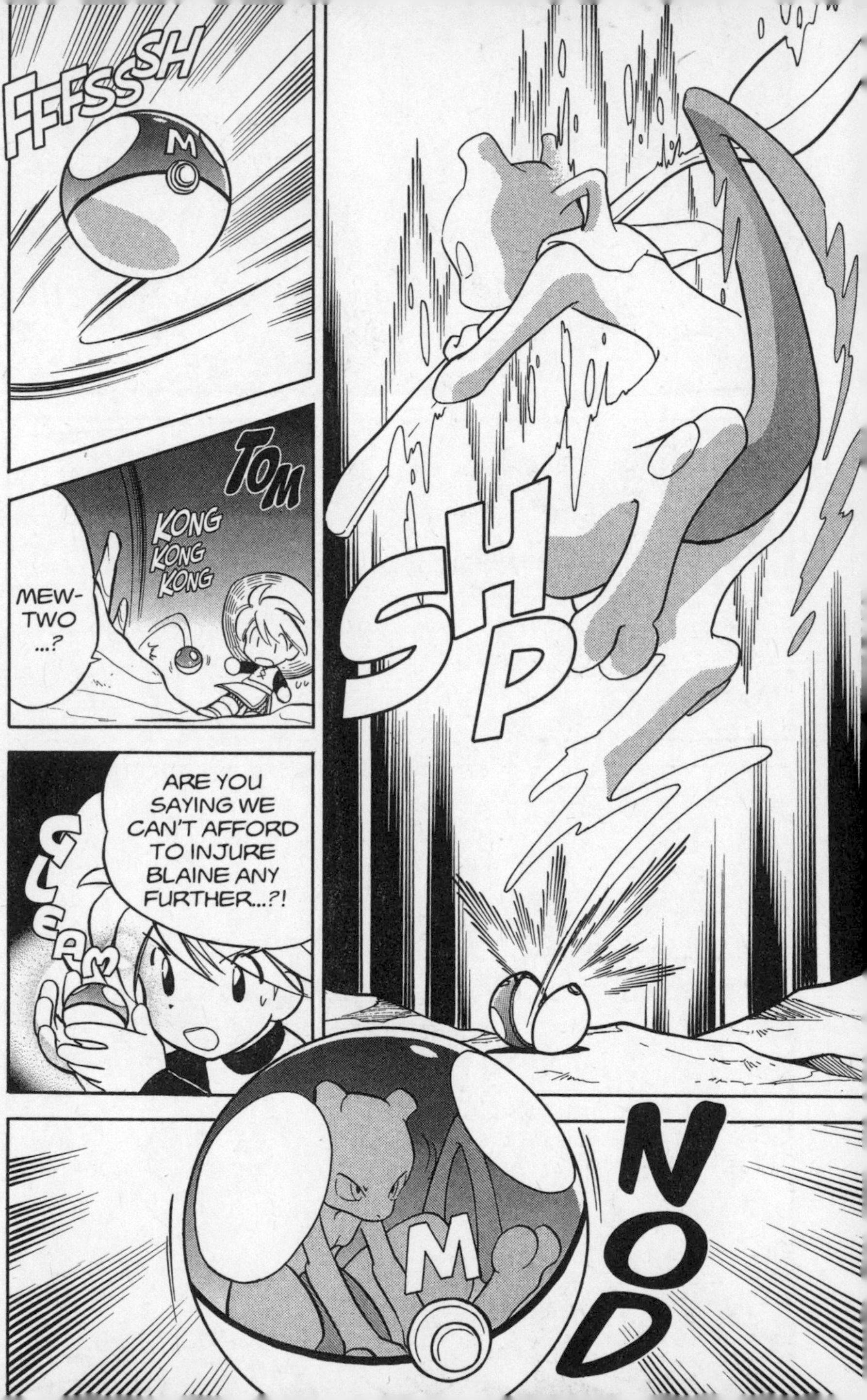
SHP
FFFSSSH
TOM
KONG KONG KONG
MEW-TWO ...?
ARE YOU SAYING WE CAN'T AFFORD TO INJURE BLAINE ANY FURTHER...?!
GLEAM
NOD

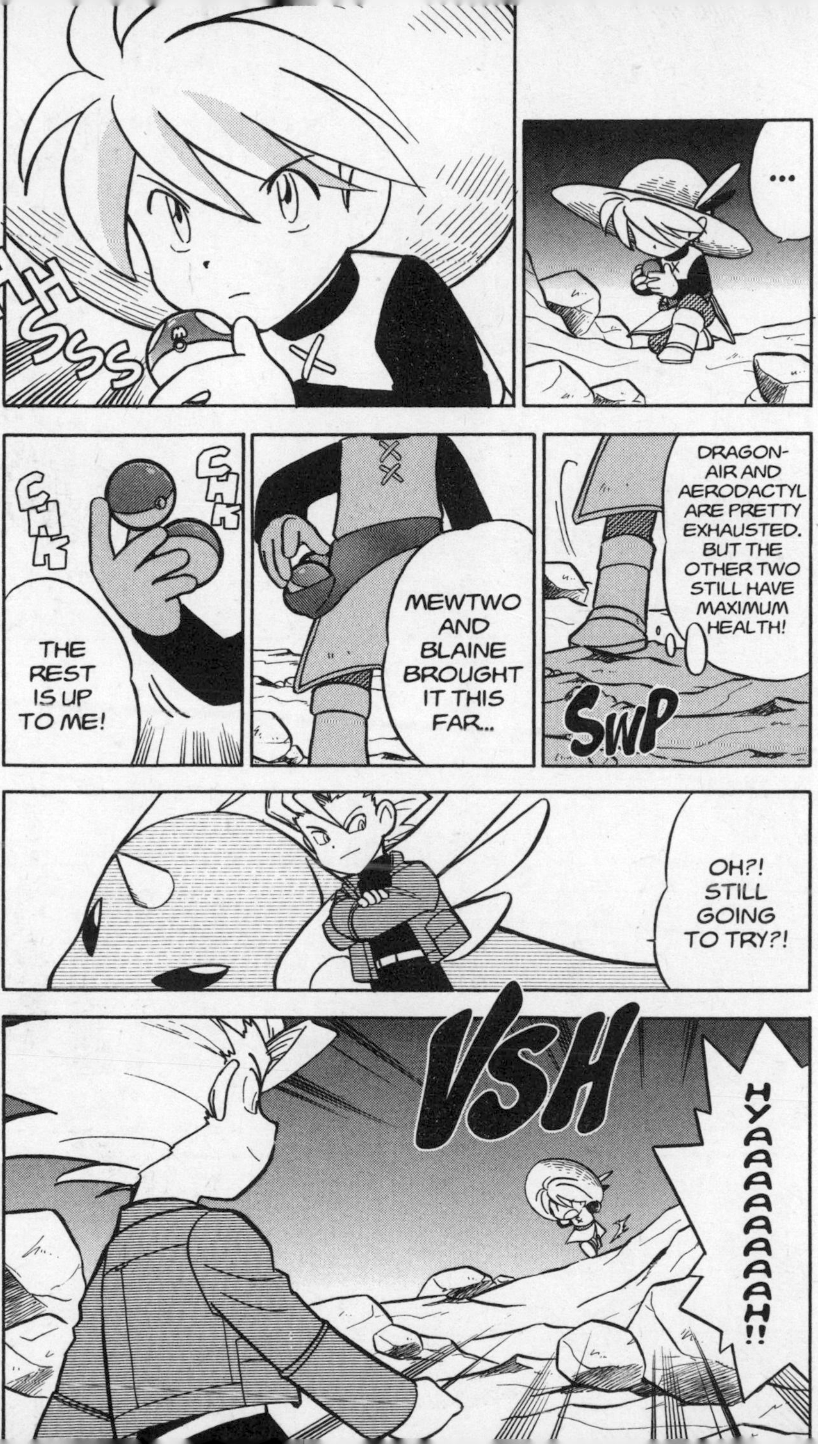
...
HHSSS
DRAGON-AIR AND AERODACTYL ARE PRETTY EXHAUSTED. BUT THE OTHER TWO STILL HAVE MAXIMUM HEALTH!
SWP
MEWTWO AND BLAINE BROUGHT IT THIS FAR...
CHK
CHK
THE REST IS UP TO ME!
OH?! STILL GOING TO TRY?!
HYAAAAAAAAH!!
VSH

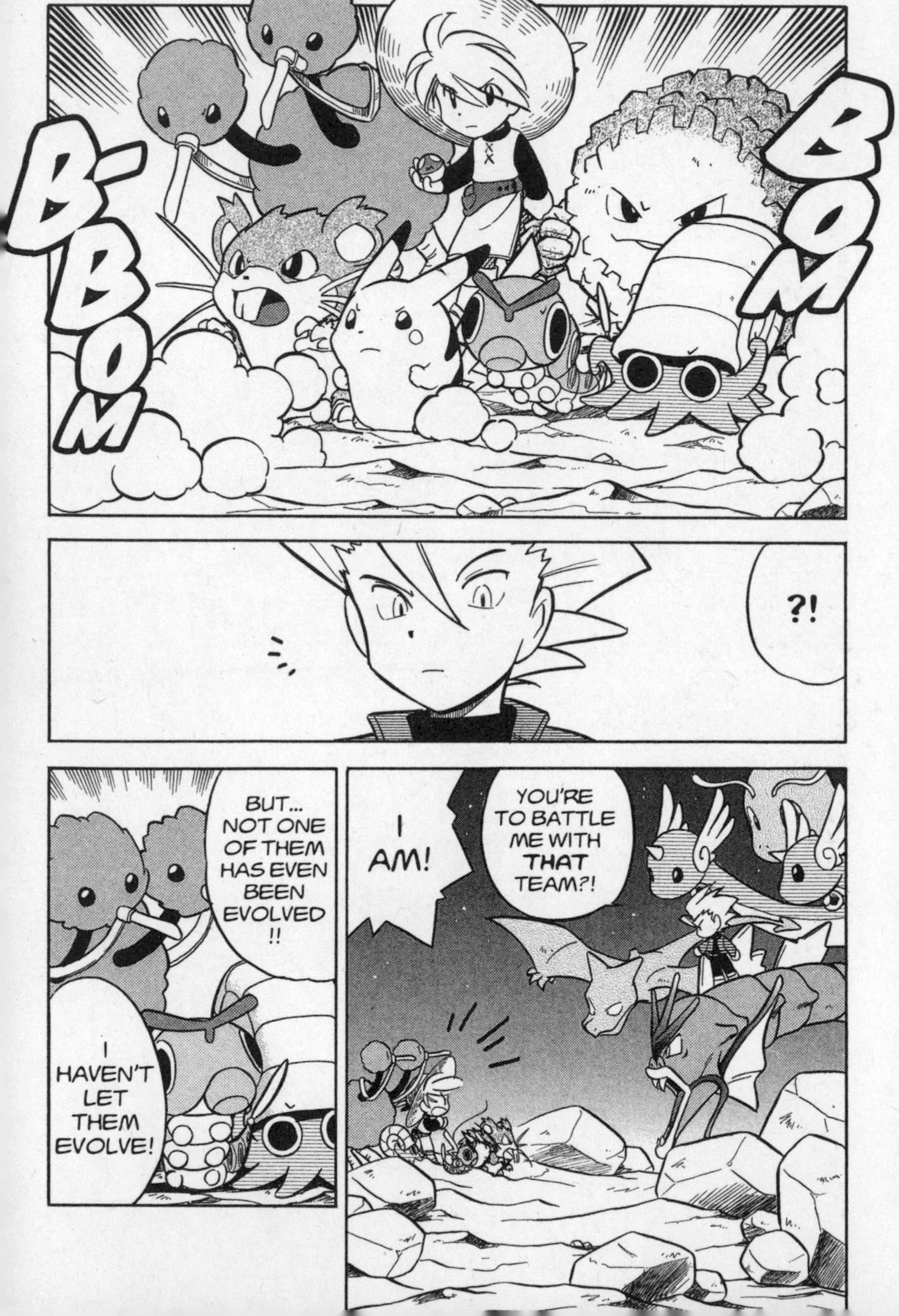
BOM
B-BOM
?!
YOU'RE TO BATTLE ME WITH THAT TEAM?!
I AM!
BUT... NOT ONE OF THEM HAS EVEN BEEN EVOLVED!!
I HAVEN'T LET THEM EVOLVE!

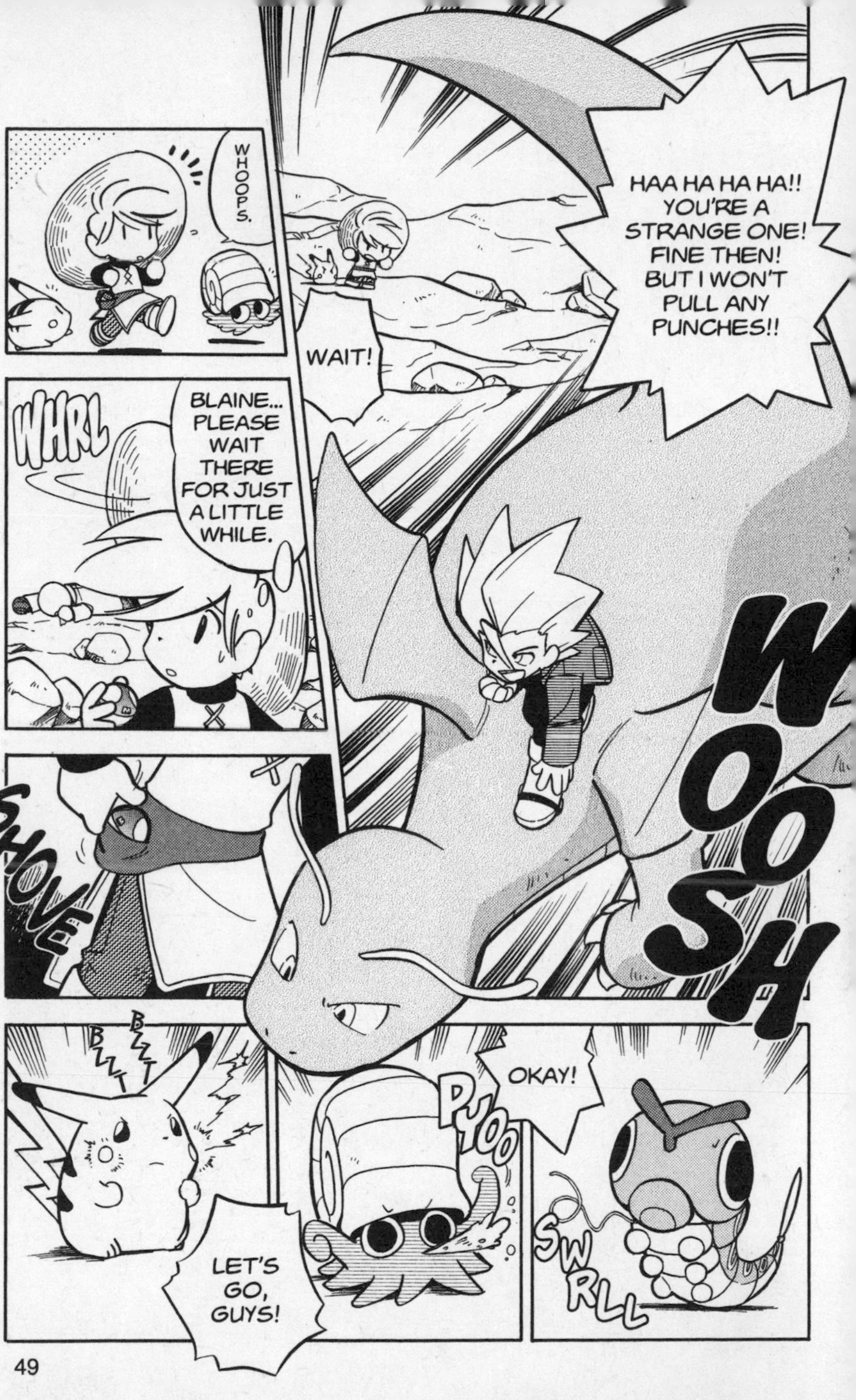
HAA HA HA HA!! YOU'RE A STRANGE ONE! FINE THEN! BUT I WON'T PULL ANY PUNCHES!!
WAIT!
WHOOSH
WHOOPS.
WHRL
BLAINE... PLEASE WAIT THERE FOR JUST A LITTLE WHILE.
SHOVE
OKAY!
PYOO
SWRLL
BZZT
BZZT
LET'S GO, GUYS!

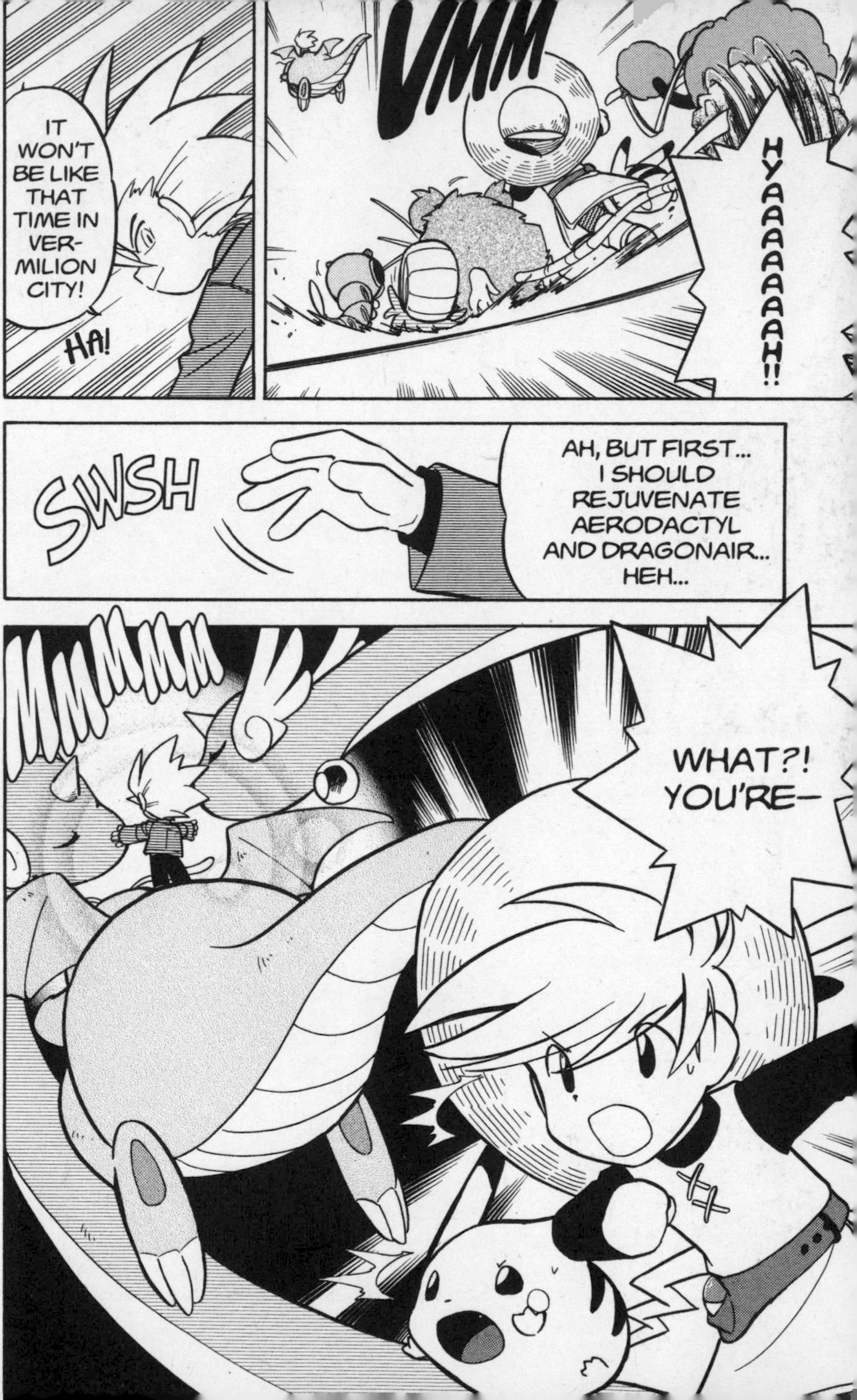
VMM
HYAAAAAAAH!!
IT WON'T BE LIKE THAT TIME IN VER-MILION CITY!
HA!
AH, BUT FIRST... I SHOULD REJUVENATE AERODACTYL AND DRAGONAIR... HEH...
SWSH
MMMMM
WHAT?! YOU'RE–

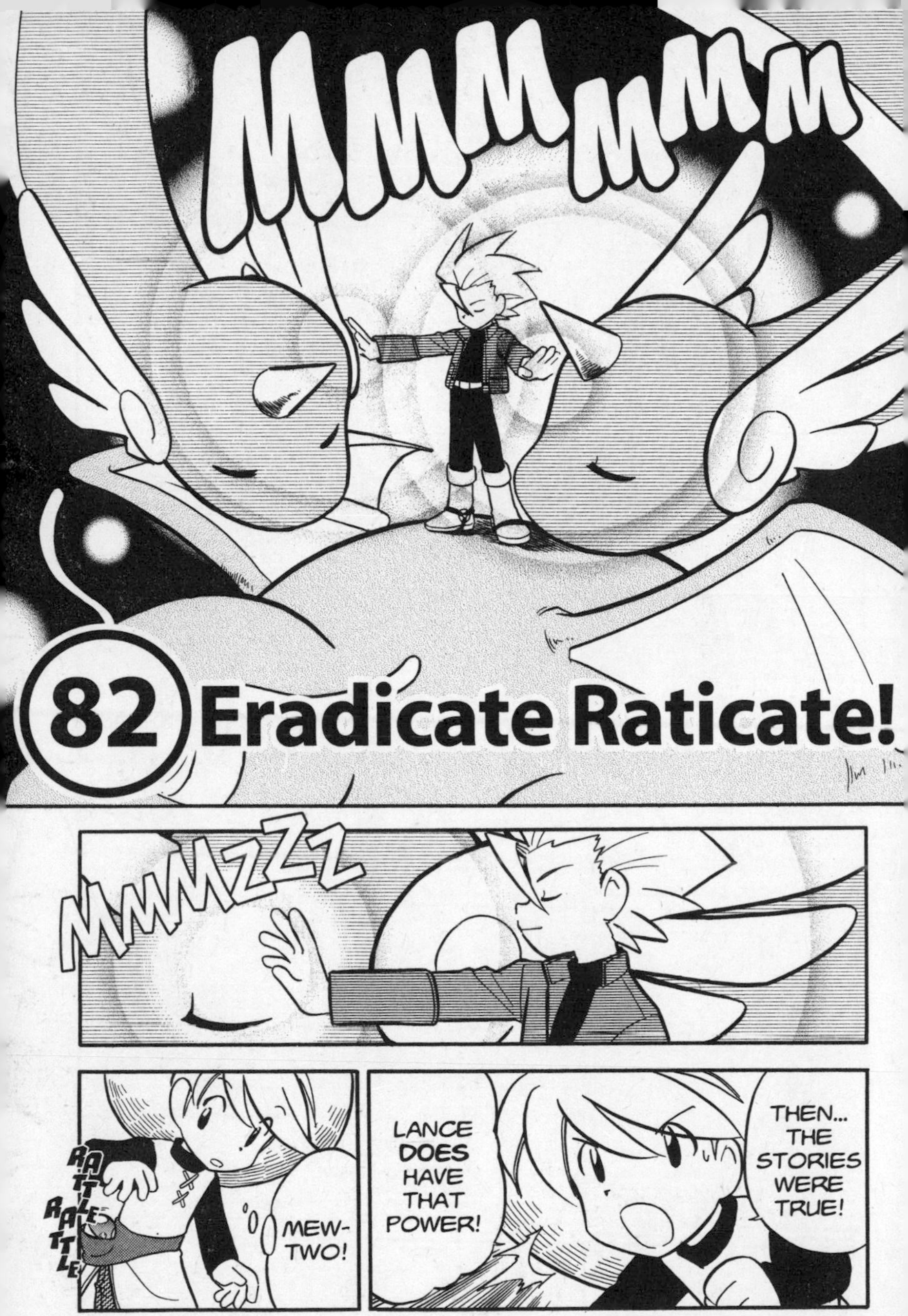
MMMMMM
82 Eradicate Raticate!
MMMMZZZ
THEN... THE STORIES WERE TRUE!
LANCE DOES HAVE THAT POWER!
MEW-TWO!
RATTLE RATTLE

DID YOU SEE THAT, MEWTWO ?!

JUST LIKE ME... LANCE IS A TRAINER...

...WHO CAN READ POKÉMON'S MINDS AND HEAL THEIR WOUNDS!!

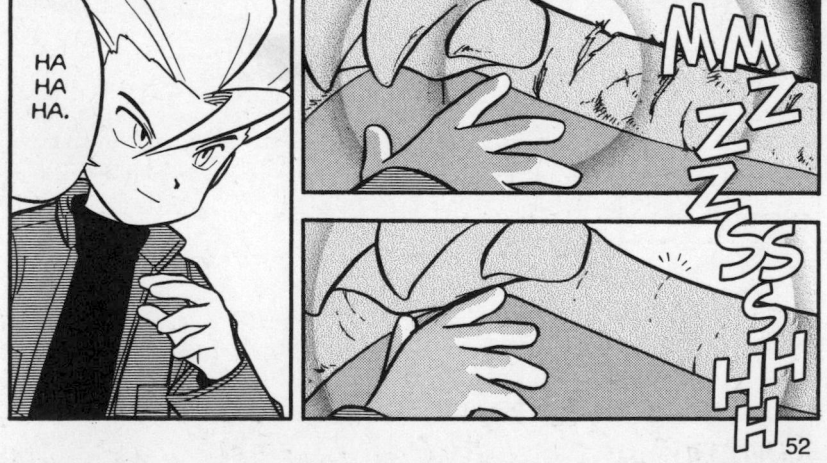

HA HA HA.

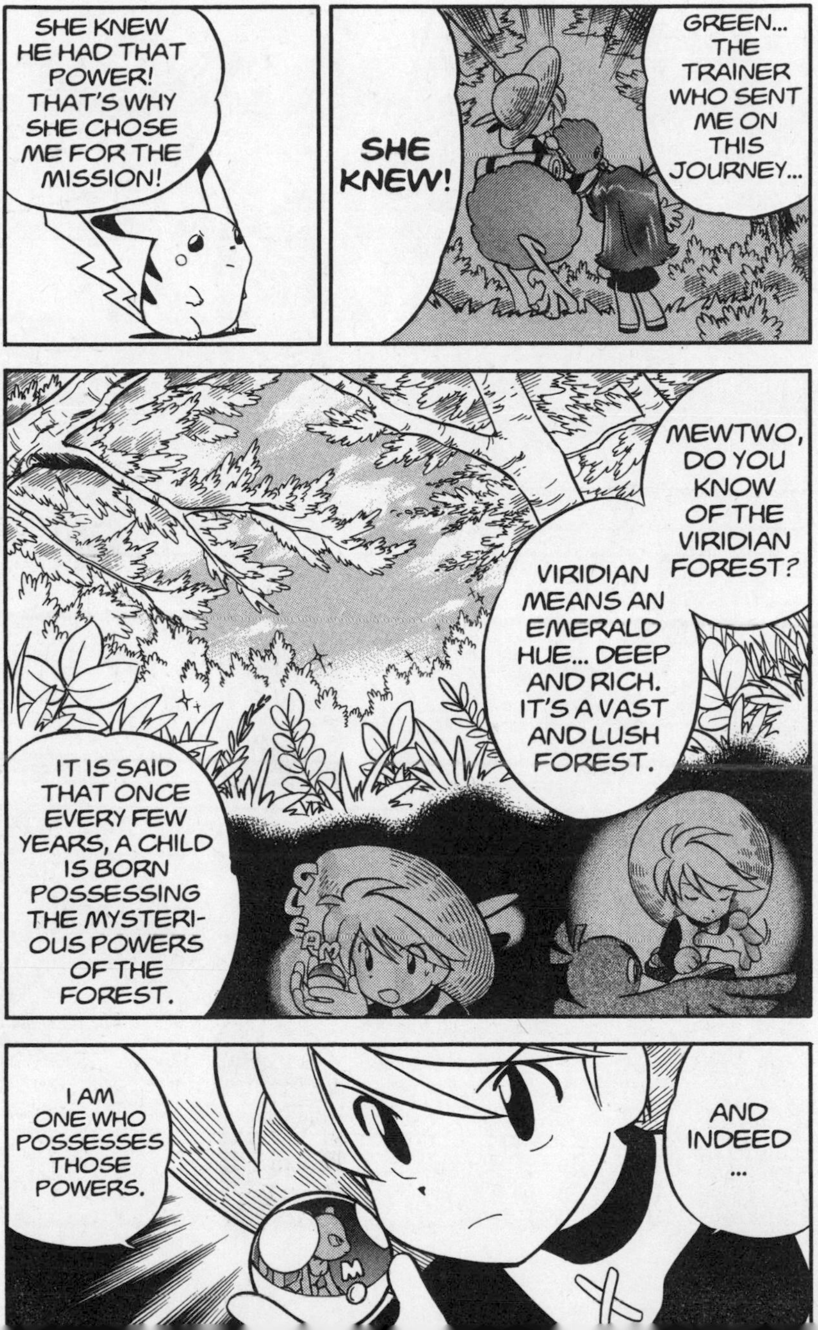
GREEN... THE TRAINER WHO SENT ME ON THIS JOURNEY...
SHE KNEW!
SHE KNEW HE HAD THAT POWER! THAT'S WHY SHE CHOSE ME FOR THE MISSION!
MEWTWO, DO YOU KNOW OF THE VIRIDIAN FOREST?
VIRIDIAN MEANS AN EMERALD HUE... DEEP AND RICH. IT'S A VAST AND LUSH FOREST.
IT IS SAID THAT ONCE EVERY FEW YEARS, A CHILD IS BORN POSSESSING THE MYSTERIOUS POWERS OF THE FOREST.
AND INDEED ...
I AM ONE WHO POSSESSES THOSE POWERS.

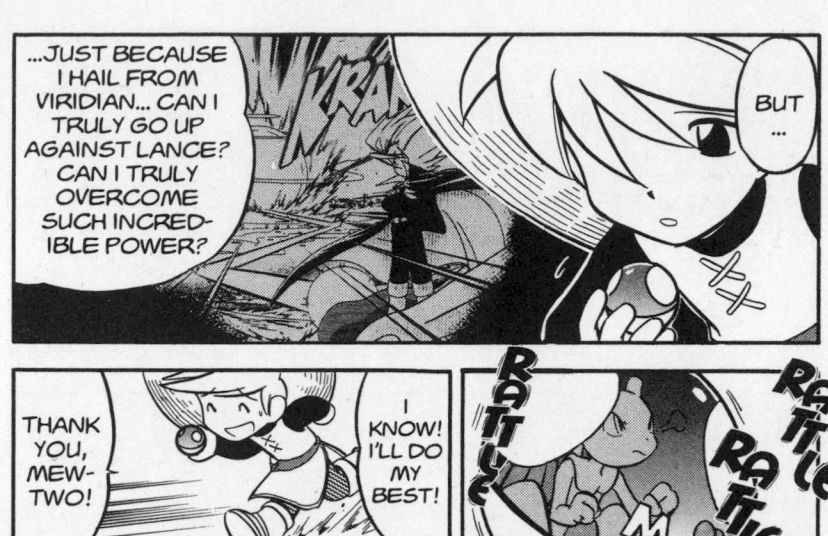

BUT ...
...JUST BECAUSE I HAIL FROM VIRIDIAN... CAN I TRULY GO UP AGAINST LANCE? CAN I TRULY OVERCOME SUCH INCREDIBLE POWER?
RATTLE
RATTLE
RATTLE
I KNOW! I'LL DO MY BEST!
THANK YOU, MEW-TWO!
EVERY-ONE...
HEH
LET'S GO!

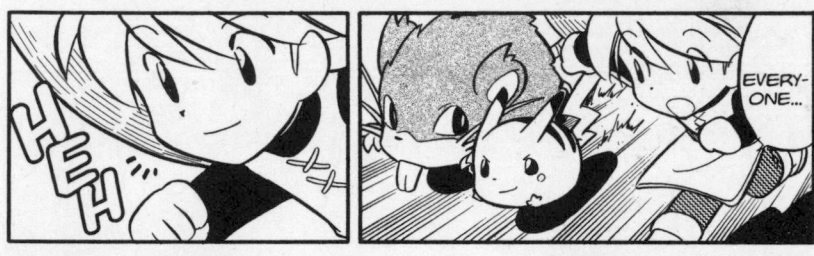

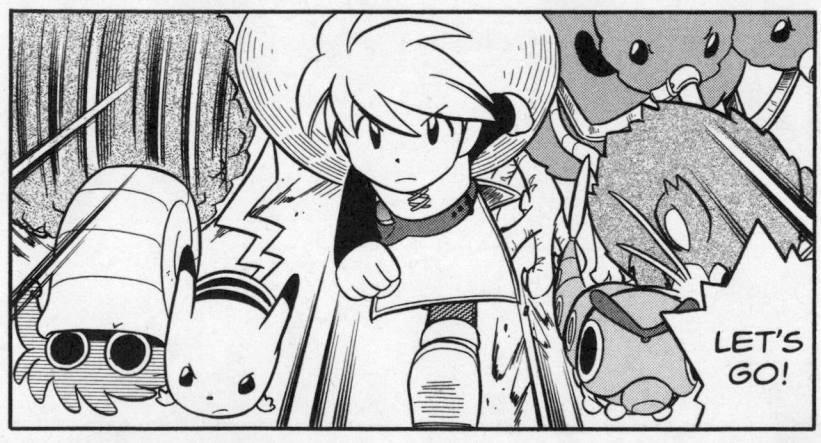

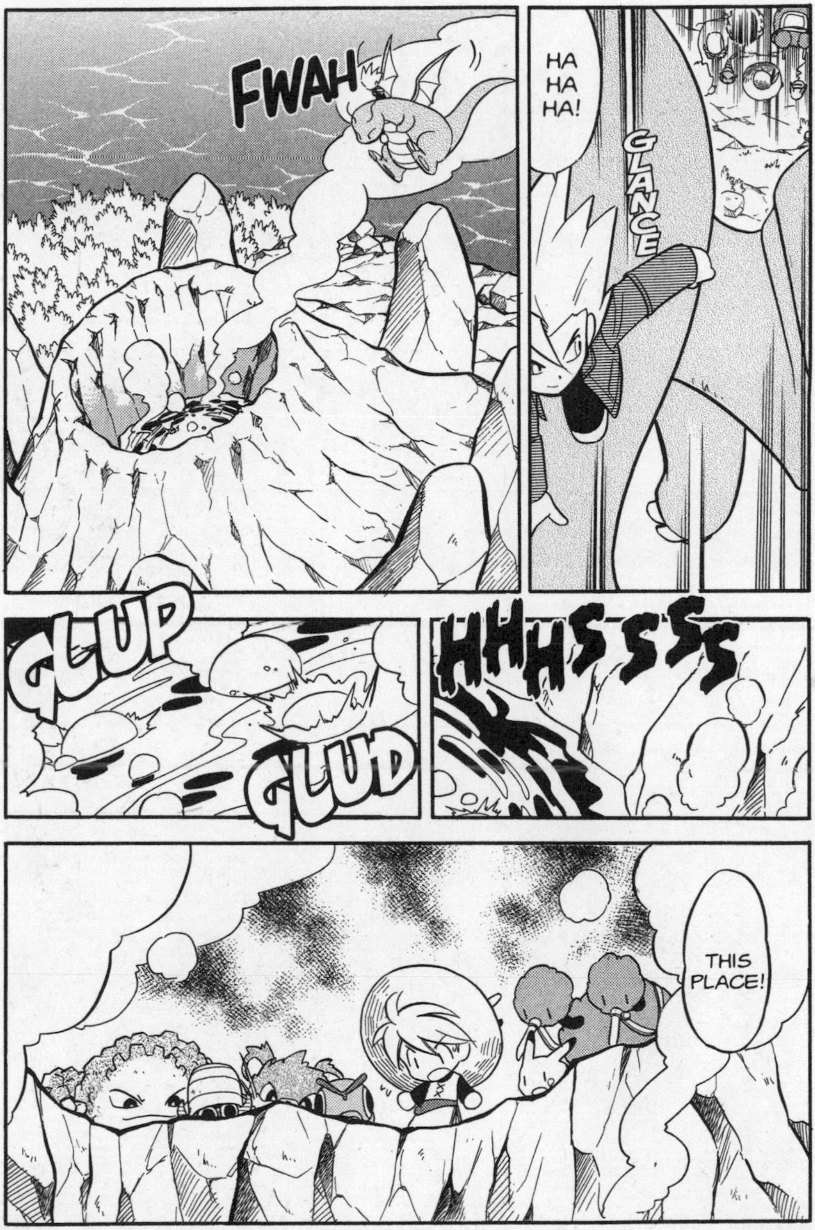
HA HA HA!
GLANCE
FWAH
HHHSSSS
GLUP
GLUD
THIS PLACE!

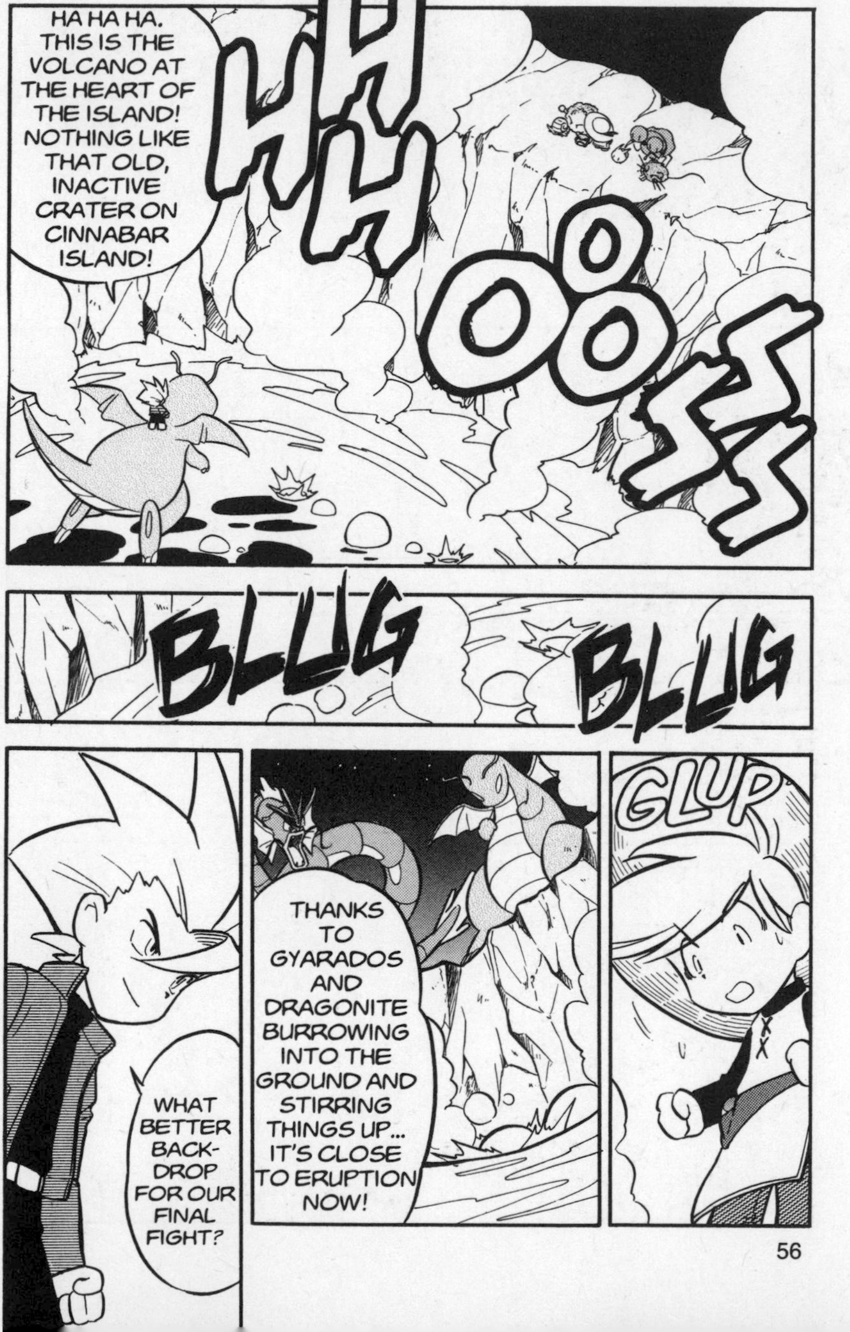
HA HA HA. THIS IS THE VOLCANO AT THE HEART OF THE ISLAND! NOTHING LIKE THAT OLD, INACTIVE CRATER ON CINNABAR ISLAND!
BLUG
BLUG
GLUP
THANKS TO GYARADOS AND DRAGONITE BURROWING INTO THE GROUND AND STIRRING THINGS UP... IT'S CLOSE TO ERUPTION NOW!
WHAT BETTER BACK-DROP FOR OUR FINAL FIGHT?

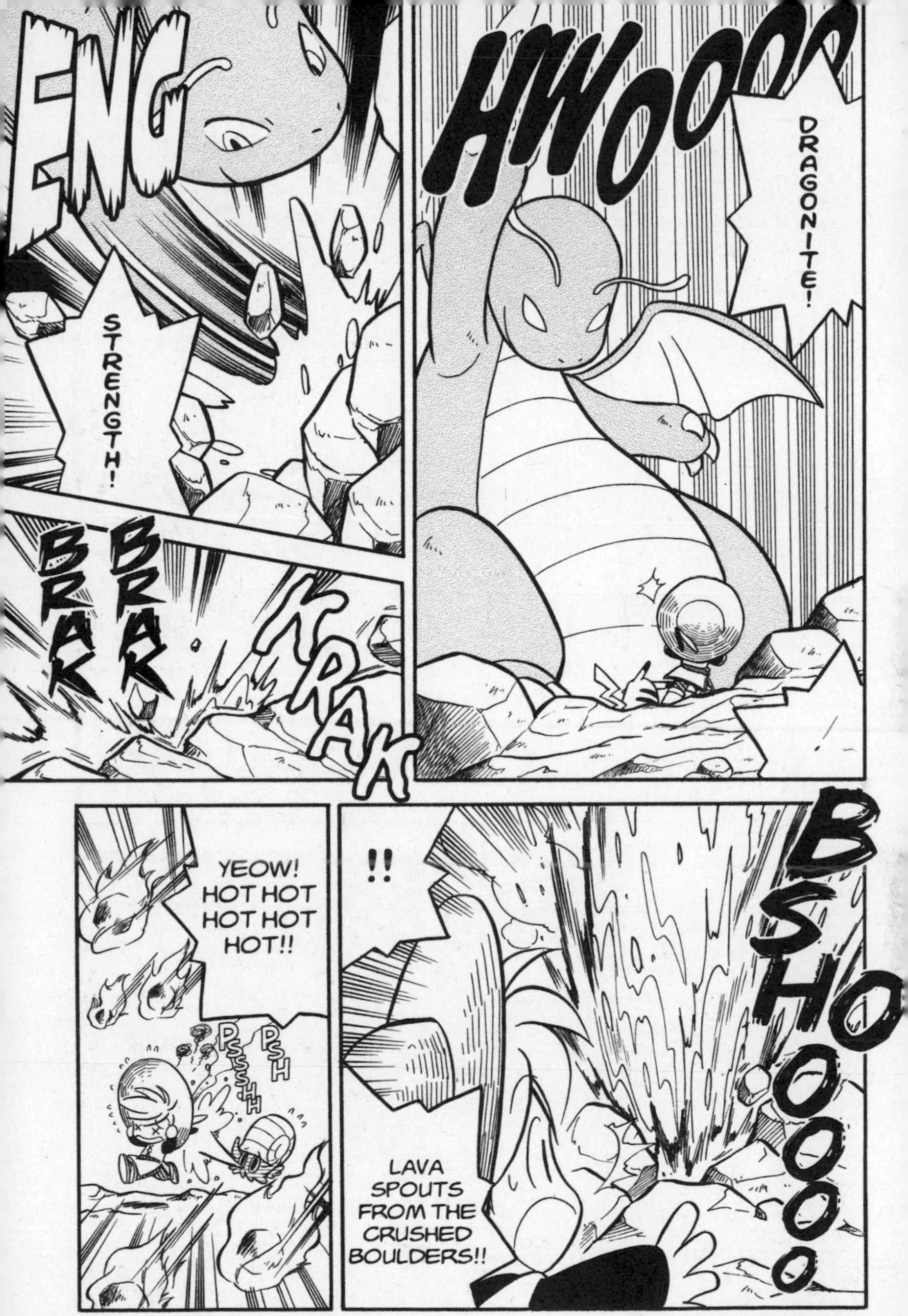
HWOOOO
DRAGONITE!
ENG
STRENGTH!
BRAK BRAK
KRAK
BSHOOOOO
!!
LAVA SPOUTS FROM THE CRUSHED BOULDERS!!
YEOW! HOT HOT HOT HOT HOT!!
PSH
PSSSHH

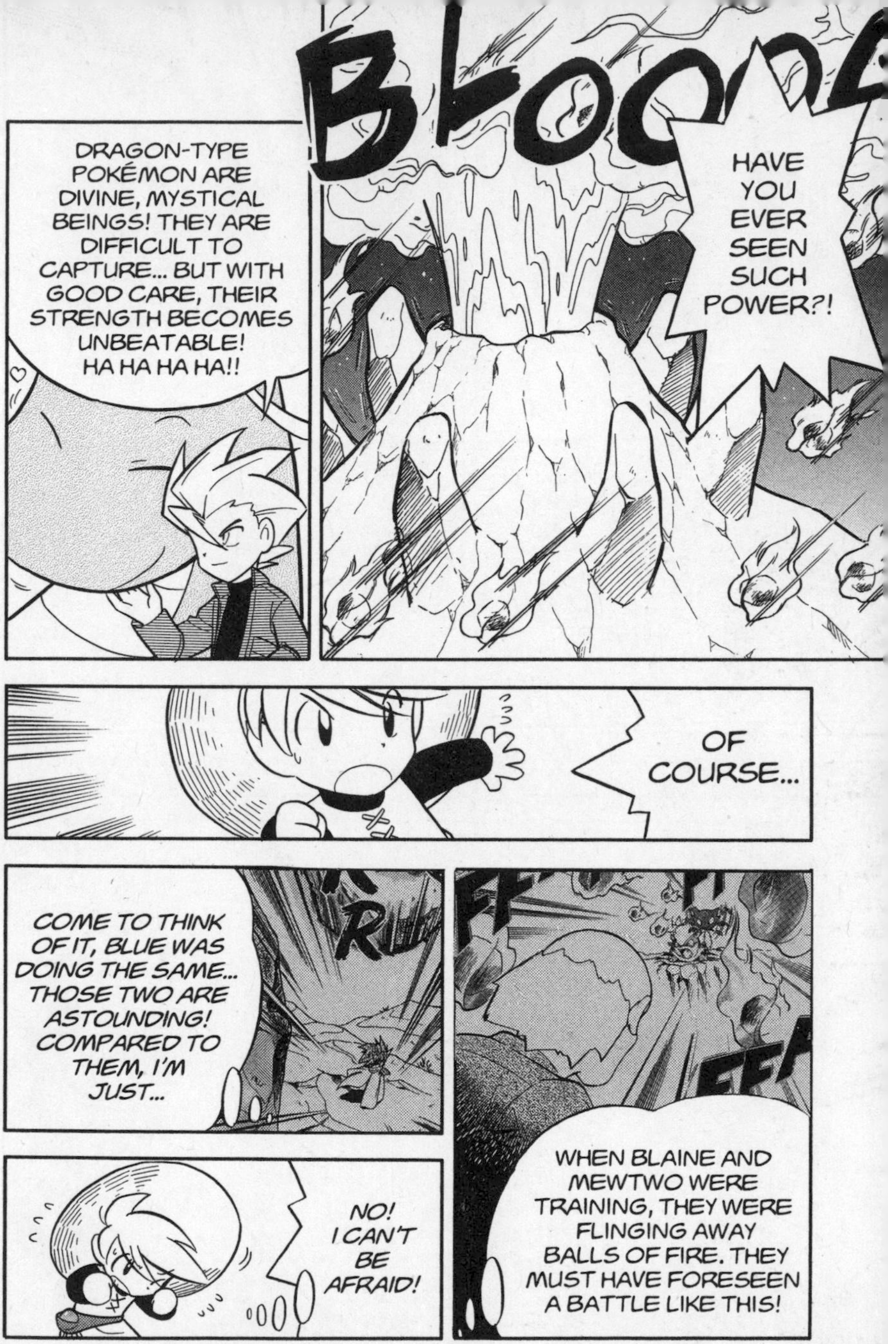
HAVE YOU EVER SEEN SUCH POWER?!
DRAGON-TYPE POKÉMON ARE DIVINE, MYSTICAL BEINGS! THEY ARE DIFFICULT TO CAPTURE... BUT WITH GOOD CARE, THEIR STRENGTH BECOMES UNBEATABLE! HA HA HA HA!!
OF COURSE...
WHEN BLAINE AND MEWTWO WERE TRAINING, THEY WERE FLINGING AWAY BALLS OF FIRE. THEY MUST HAVE FORESEEN A BATTLE LIKE THIS!
COME TO THINK OF IT, BLUE WAS DOING THE SAME... THOSE TWO ARE ASTOUNDING! COMPARED TO THEM, I'M JUST...
NO! I CAN'T BE AFRAID!

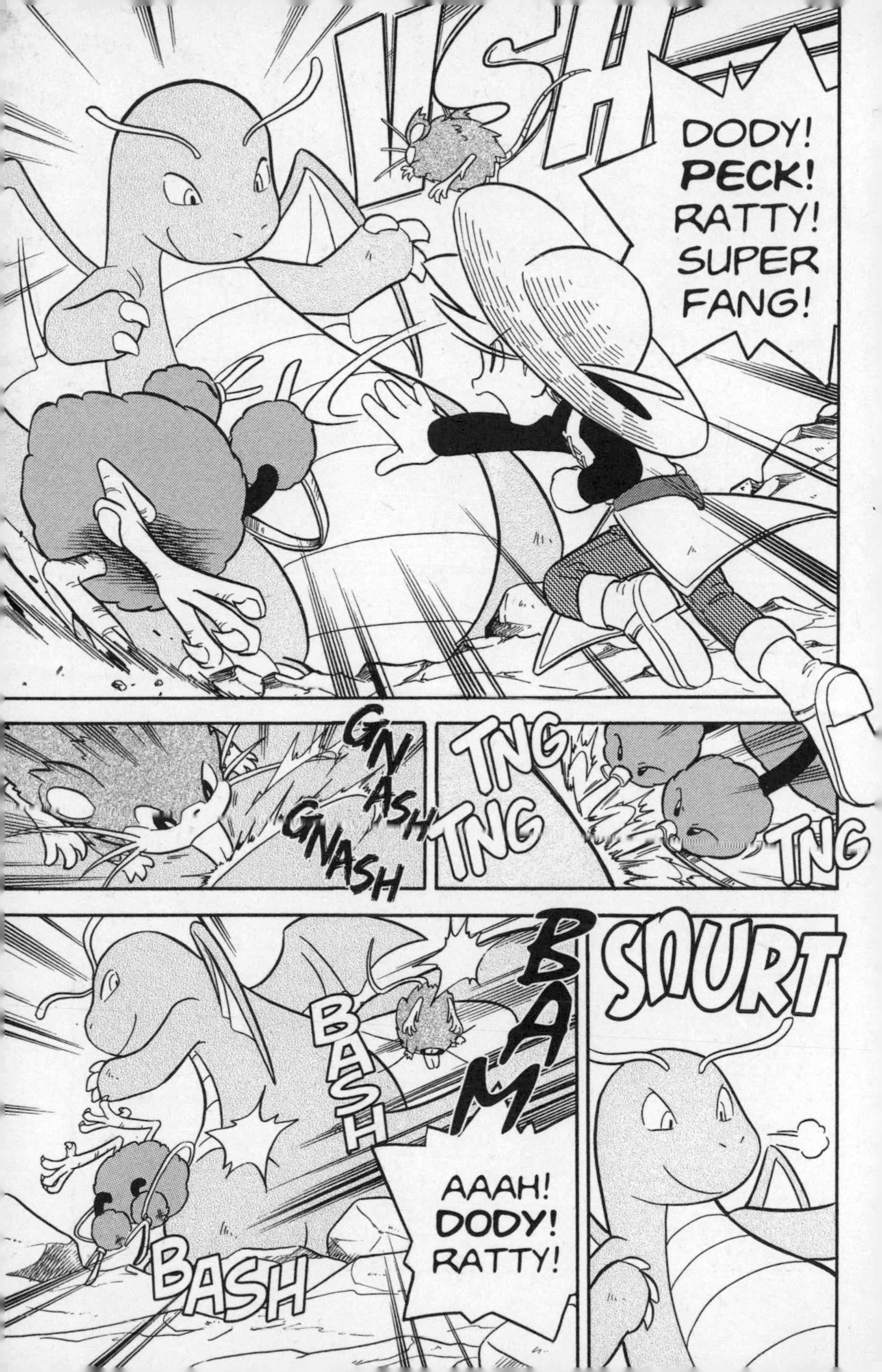
DODY! PECK! RATTY! SUPER FANG!
TNG
TNG
TNG
GNASH
GNASH
SNURT
BAM
BASH
AAAH! DODY! RATTY!
BASH

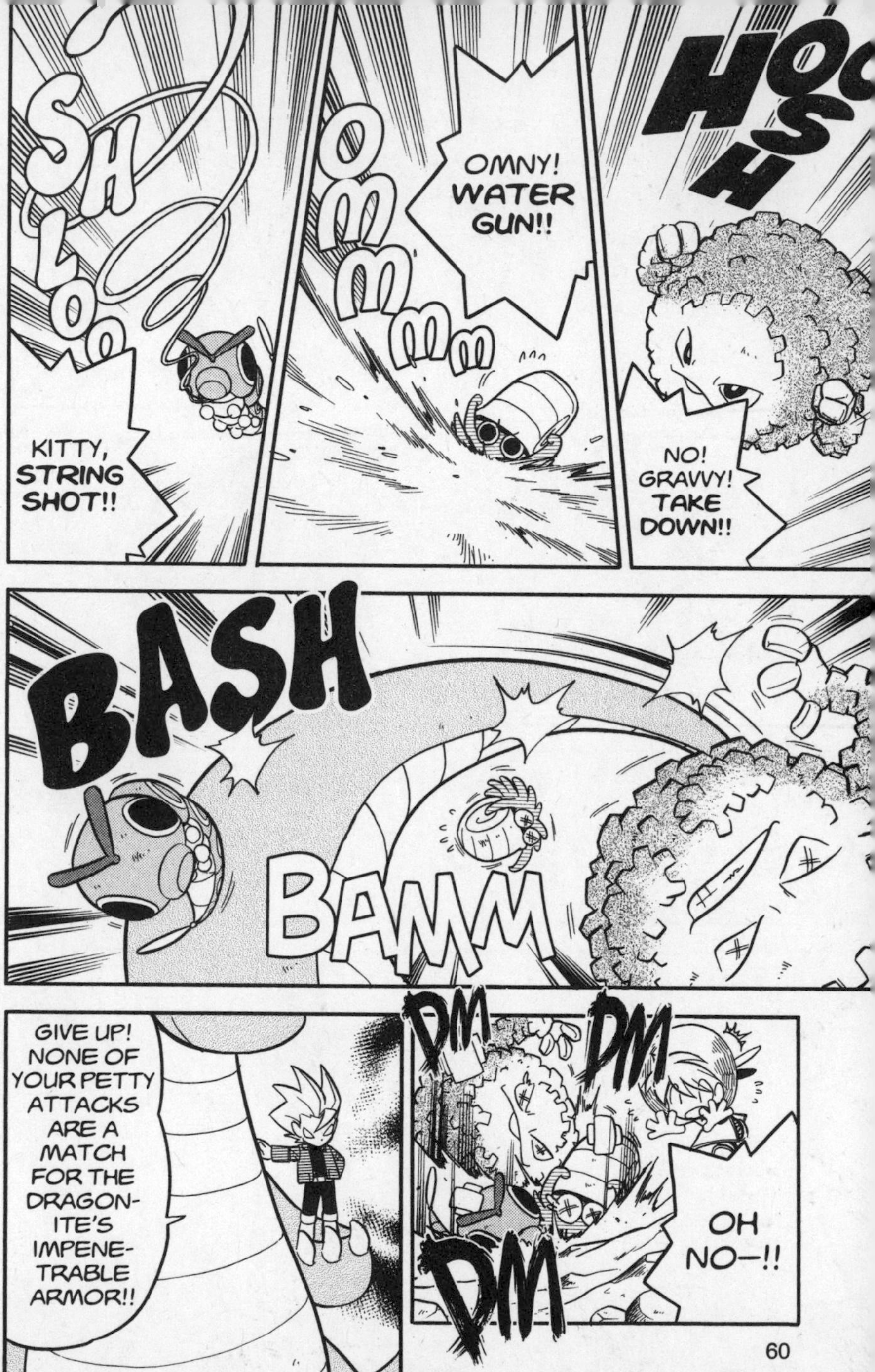
HOOSH
NO! GRAVVY! TAKE DOWN!!
OMNY! WATER GUN!!
OMMMMMM
SHLOOO
KITTY, STRING SHOT!!
BASH
BAMM
DM DM DM
OH NO—!!
GIVE UP! NONE OF YOUR PETTY ATTACKS ARE A MATCH FOR THE DRAGON-ITE'S IMPENE-TRABLE ARMOR!!

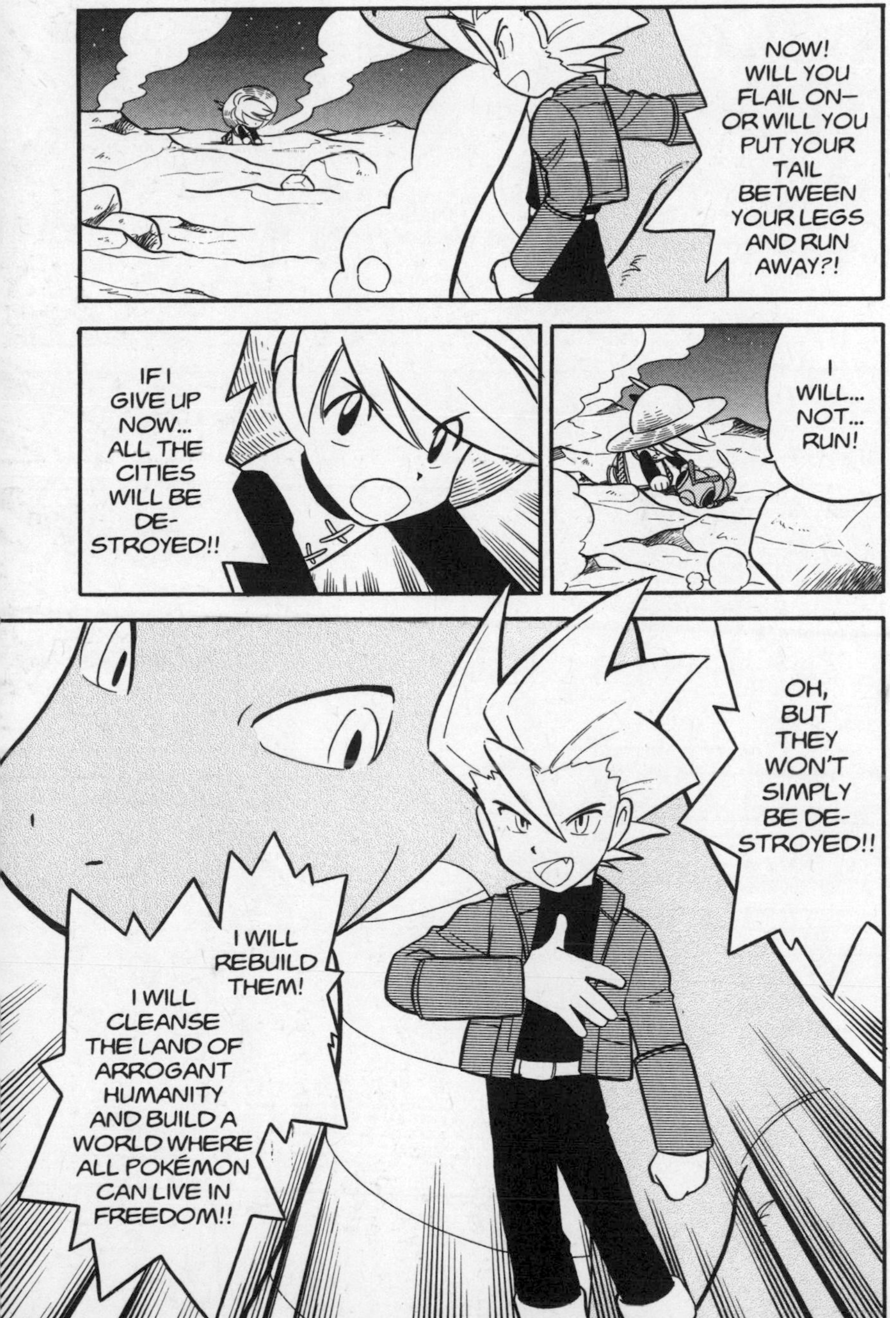
NOW! WILL YOU FLAIL ON—OR WILL YOU PUT YOUR TAIL BETWEEN YOUR LEGS AND RUN AWAY?!
IF I GIVE UP NOW... ALL THE CITIES WILL BE DE-STROYED!!
I WILL... NOT... RUN!
OH, BUT THEY WON'T SIMPLY BE DE-STROYED!!
I WILL REBUILD THEM!
I WILL CLEANSE THE LAND OF ARROGANT HUMANITY AND BUILD A WORLD WHERE ALL POKÉMON CAN LIVE IN FREEDOM!!

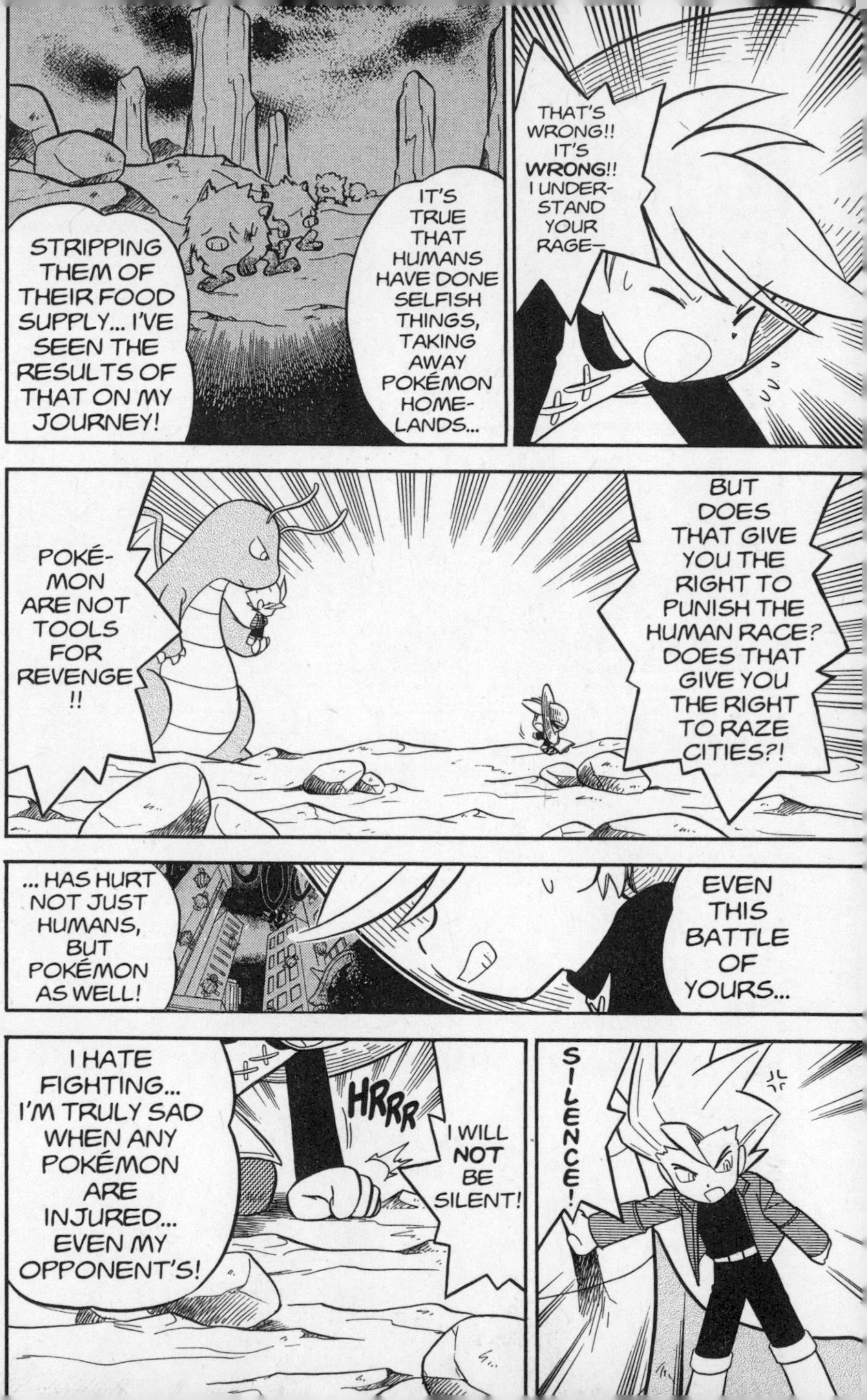
THAT'S WRONG!! IT'S **WRONG**!! I UNDER-STAND YOUR RAGE—
IT'S TRUE THAT HUMANS HAVE DONE SELFISH THINGS, TAKING AWAY POKÉMON HOME-LANDS...
STRIPPING THEM OF THEIR FOOD SUPPLY... I'VE SEEN THE RESULTS OF THAT ON MY JOURNEY!
BUT DOES THAT GIVE YOU THE RIGHT TO PUNISH THE HUMAN RACE? DOES THAT GIVE YOU THE RIGHT TO RAZE CITIES?!
POKÉ-MON ARE NOT TOOLS FOR REVENGE !!
EVEN THIS BATTLE OF YOURS...
... HAS HURT NOT JUST HUMANS, BUT POKÉMON AS WELL!
SILENCE!
I WILL **NOT** BE SILENT!
HRRR
I HATE FIGHTING... I'M TRULY SAD WHEN ANY POKÉMON ARE INJURED... EVEN MY OPPONENT'S!

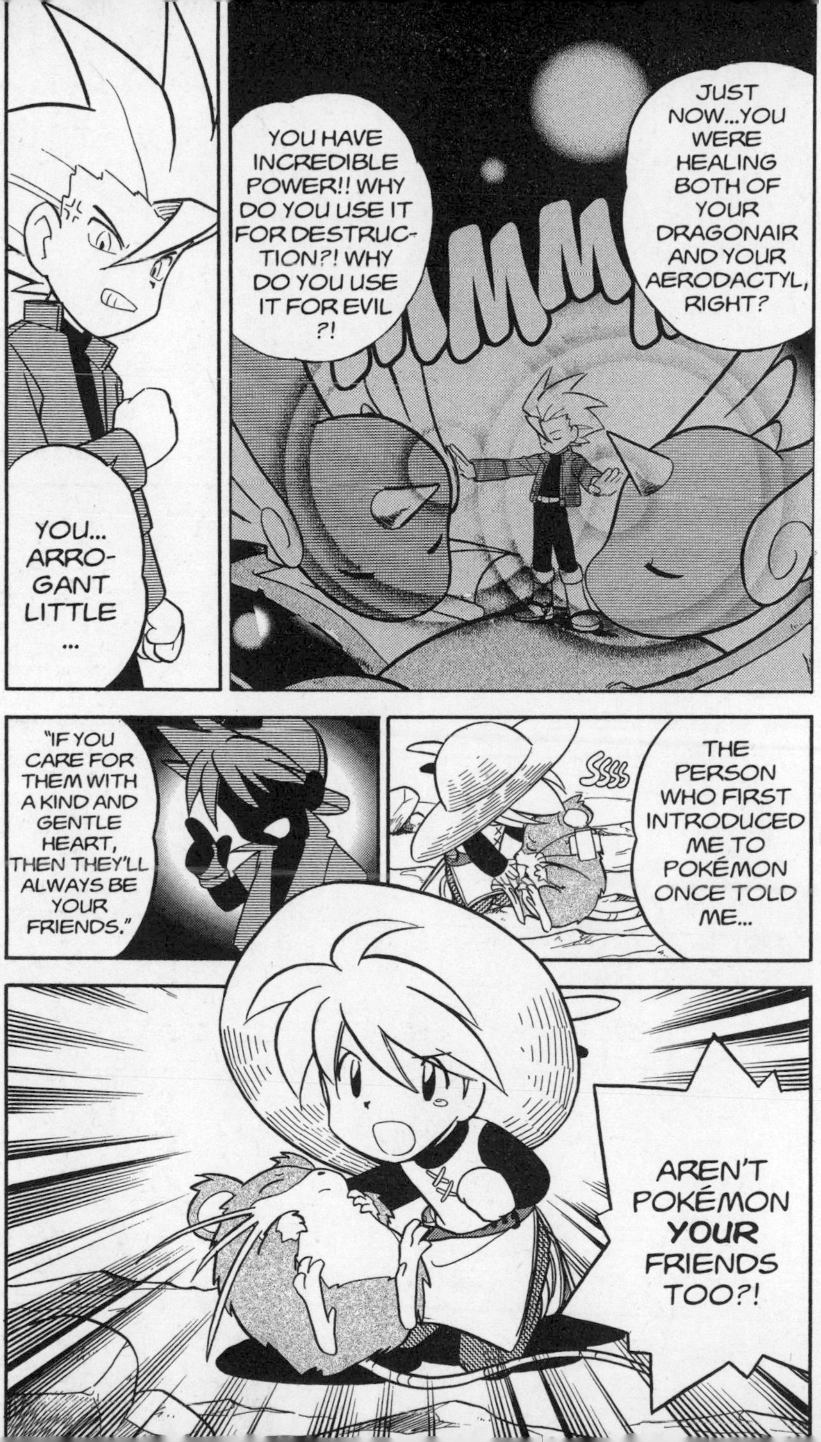
JUST NOW...YOU WERE HEALING BOTH OF YOUR DRAGONAIR AND YOUR AERODACTYL, RIGHT?
YOU HAVE INCREDIBLE POWER!! WHY DO YOU USE IT FOR DESTRUCTION?! WHY DO YOU USE IT FOR EVIL?!
YOU... ARROGANT LITTLE ...
SSSS
THE PERSON WHO FIRST INTRODUCED ME TO POKÉMON ONCE TOLD ME...
"IF YOU CARE FOR THEM WITH A KIND AND GENTLE HEART, THEN THEY'LL ALWAYS BE YOUR FRIENDS."
AREN'T POKÉMON **YOUR** FRIENDS TOO?!

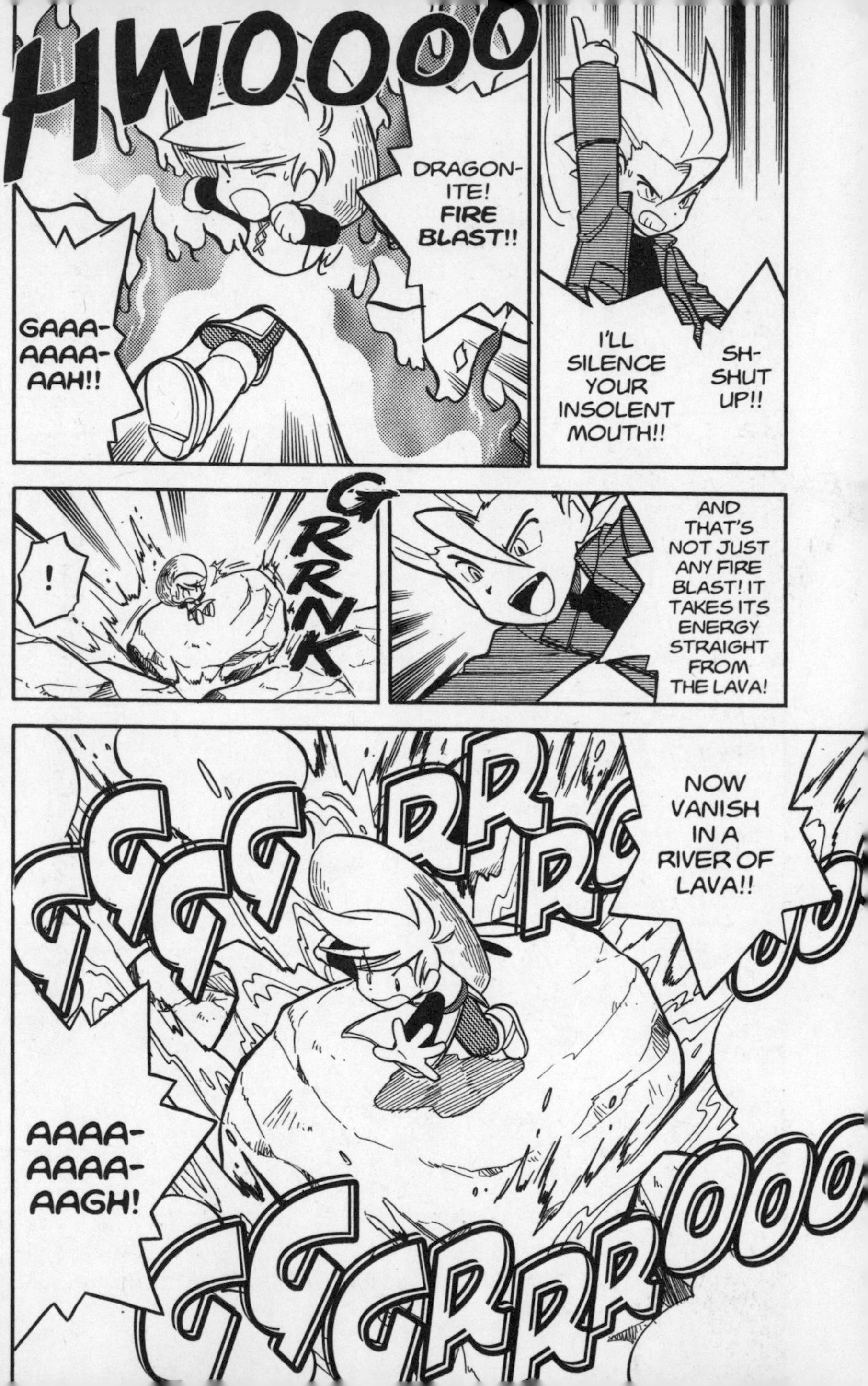
SH-SHUT UP!!
I'LL SILENCE YOUR INSOLENT MOUTH!!
HWOOOOO
DRAGON-ITE! FIRE BLAST!!
GAAA-AAAA-AAH!!
AND THAT'S NOT JUST ANY FIRE BLAST! IT TAKES ITS ENERGY STRAIGHT FROM THE LAVA!
GRRNK
!
NOW VANISH IN A RIVER OF LAVA!!
GGGGRRROO
AAAA-AAAA-AAGH!
GGGRRROOOO

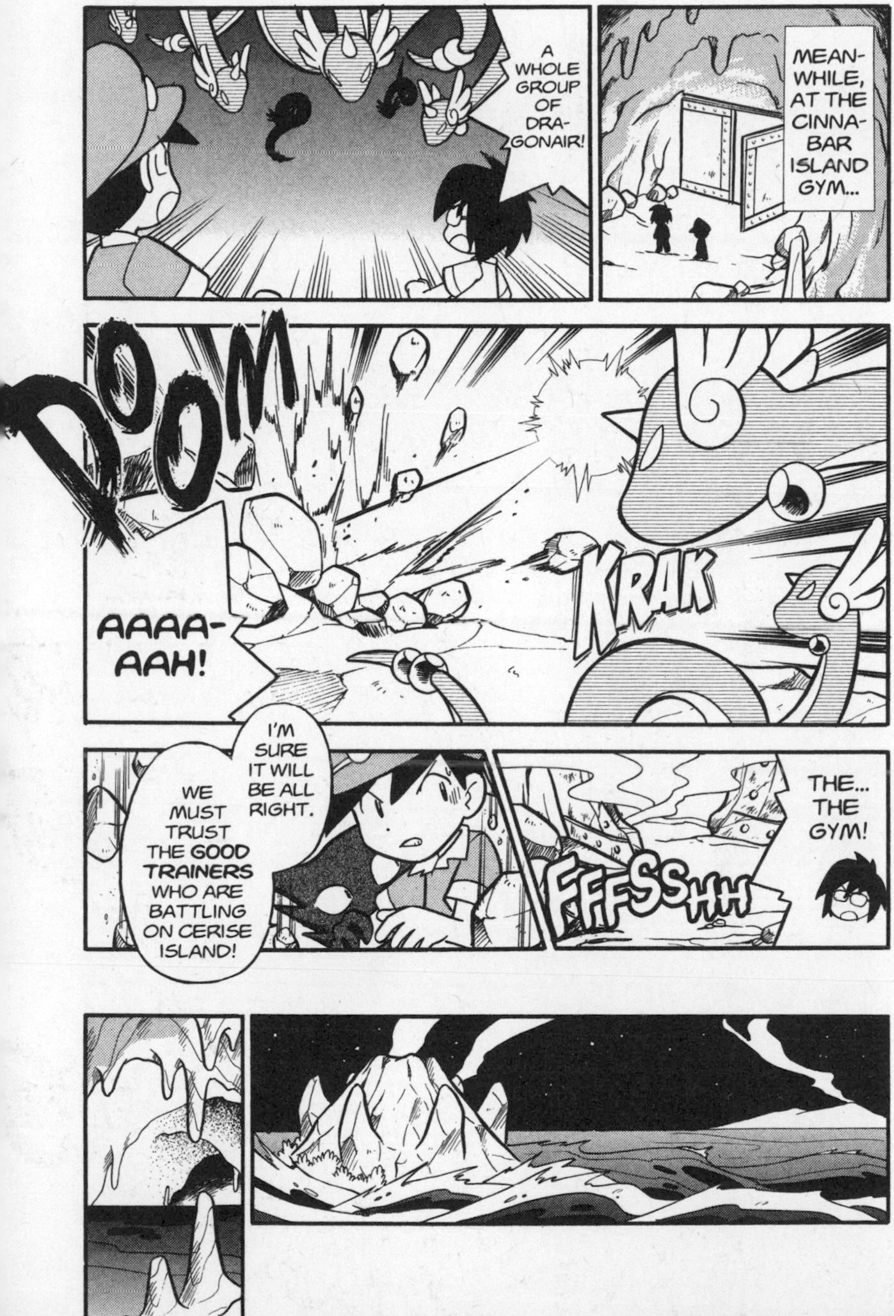
MEAN-WHILE, AT THE CINNA-BAR ISLAND GYM...
A WHOLE GROUP OF DRA-GONAIR!
DOOM
KRAK
AAAA-AAH!
THE... THE GYM!
FFFSSHH
I'M SURE IT WILL BE ALL RIGHT.
WE MUST TRUST THE GOOD TRAINERS WHO ARE BATTLING ON CERISE ISLAND!

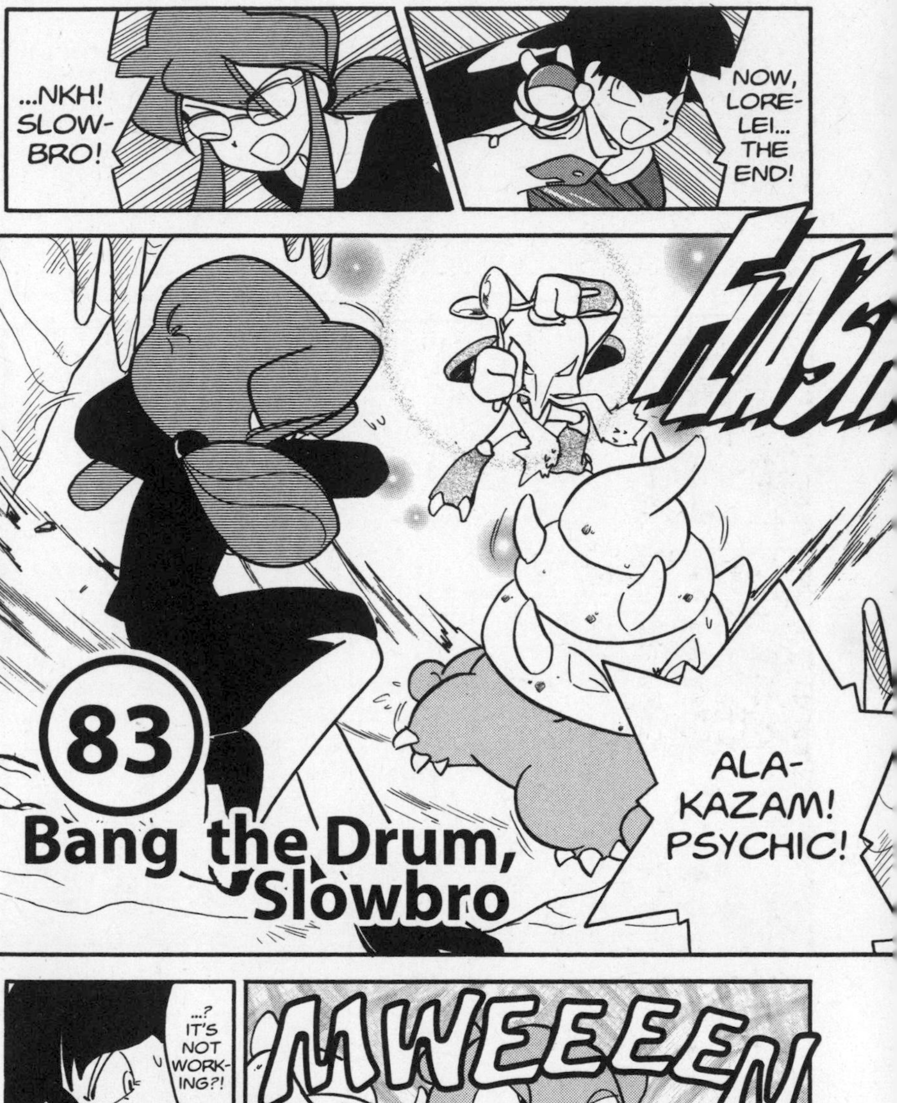
NOW, LORELEI... THE END!
...NKH! SLOWBRO!
ALAKAZAM! PSYCHIC!
83
Bang the Drum, Slowbro
MWEEEEN
SNORT
...? IT'S NOT WORKING?!

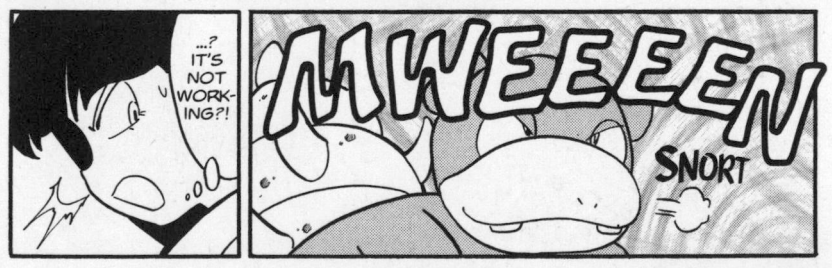

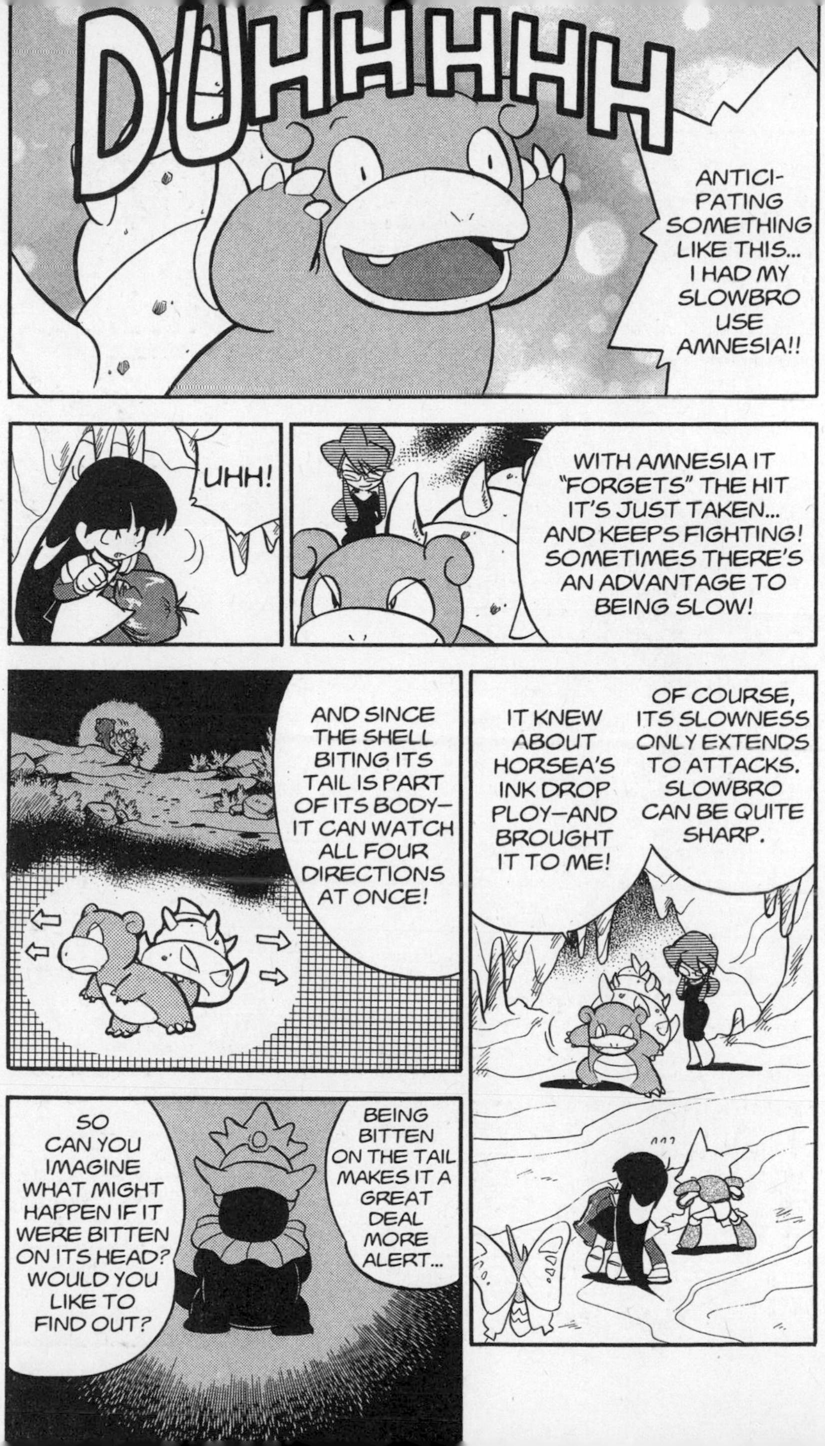
DUHHHHHH
ANTICI-PATING SOMETHING LIKE THIS... I HAD MY SLOWBRO USE AMNESIA!!
WITH AMNESIA IT "FORGETS" THE HIT IT'S JUST TAKEN... AND KEEPS FIGHTING! SOMETIMES THERE'S AN ADVANTAGE TO BEING SLOW!
UHH!
OF COURSE, ITS SLOWNESS ONLY EXTENDS TO ATTACKS. SLOWBRO CAN BE QUITE SHARP.
IT KNEW ABOUT HORSEA'S INK DROP PLOY—AND BROUGHT IT TO ME!
AND SINCE THE SHELL BITING ITS TAIL IS PART OF ITS BODY—IT CAN WATCH ALL FOUR DIRECTIONS AT ONCE!
BEING BITTEN ON THE TAIL MAKES IT A GREAT DEAL MORE ALERT...
SO CAN YOU IMAGINE WHAT MIGHT HAPPEN IF IT WERE BITTEN ON ITS HEAD? WOULD YOU LIKE TO FIND OUT?

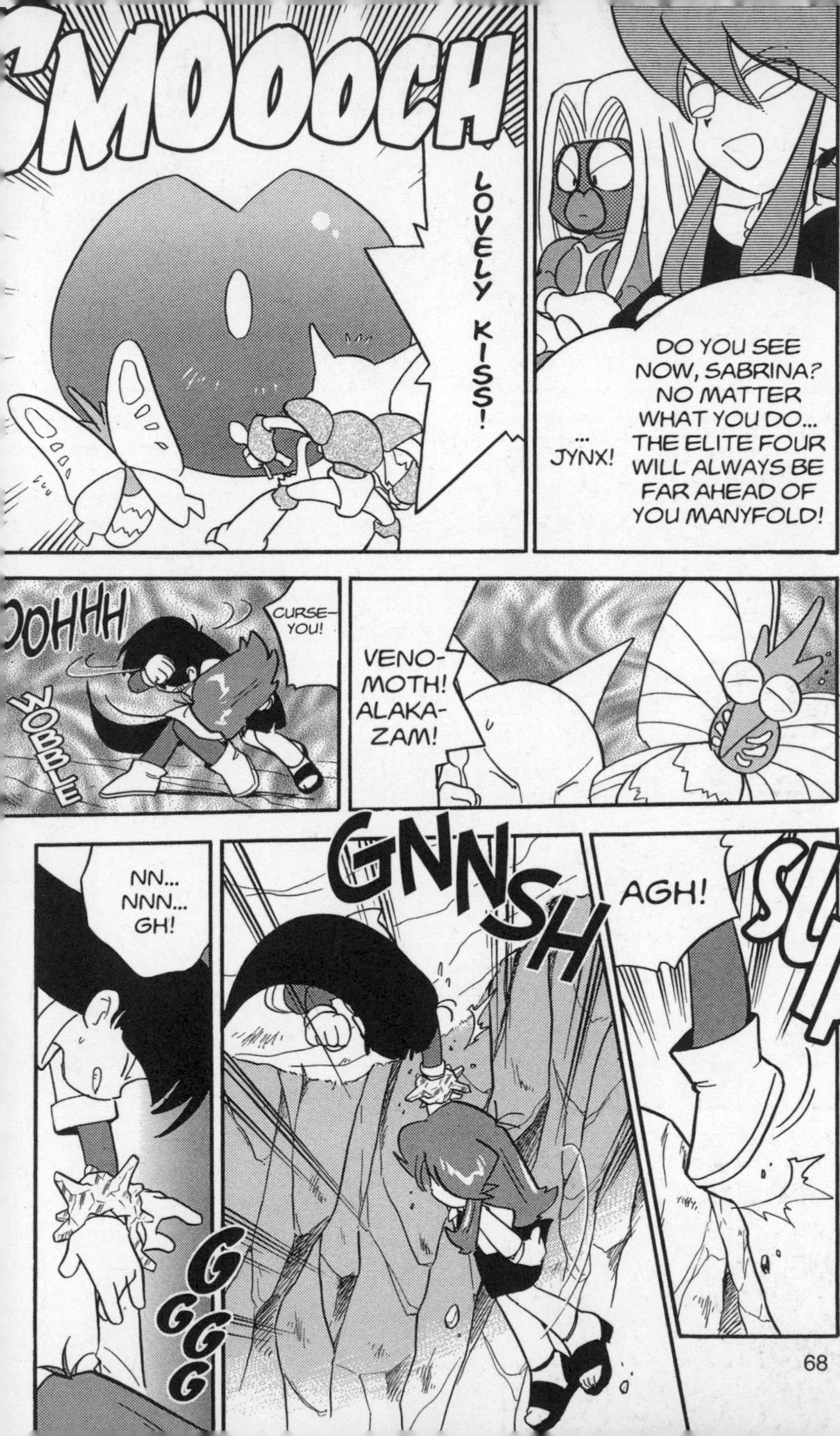
DO YOU SEE NOW, SABRINA? NO MATTER WHAT YOU DO... THE ELITE FOUR WILL ALWAYS BE FAR AHEAD OF YOU MANYFOLD!
... JYNX!
SMOOOCH
LOVELY KISS!
VENO-MOTH! ALAKA-ZAM!
CURSE-YOU!
OOHHH
WOBBLE
SLIP
AGH!
GNNSH
NN... NNN... GH!
GGGG

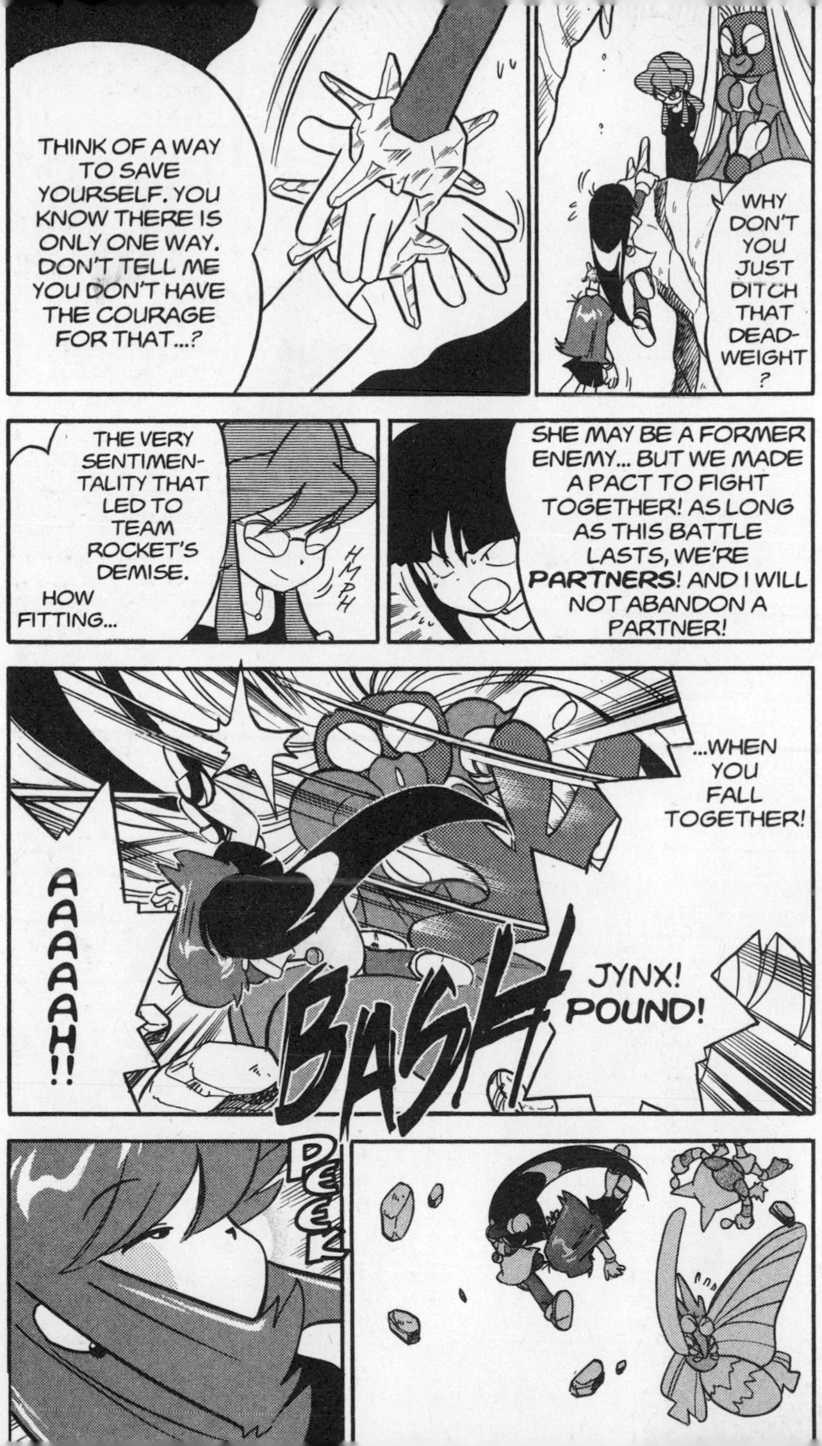
WHY DON'T YOU JUST DITCH THAT DEAD-WEIGHT?
THINK OF A WAY TO SAVE YOURSELF. YOU KNOW THERE IS ONLY ONE WAY. DON'T TELL ME YOU DON'T HAVE THE COURAGE FOR THAT...?
SHE MAY BE A FORMER ENEMY... BUT WE MADE A PACT TO FIGHT TOGETHER! AS LONG AS THIS BATTLE LASTS, WE'RE **PARTNERS**! AND I WILL NOT ABANDON A PARTNER!
THE VERY SENTIMENTALITY THAT LED TO TEAM ROCKET'S DEMISE.
HMPH
HOW FITTING...
...WHEN YOU FALL TOGETHER!
JYNX! POUND!
BASH
AAAAAAH!!
PECK

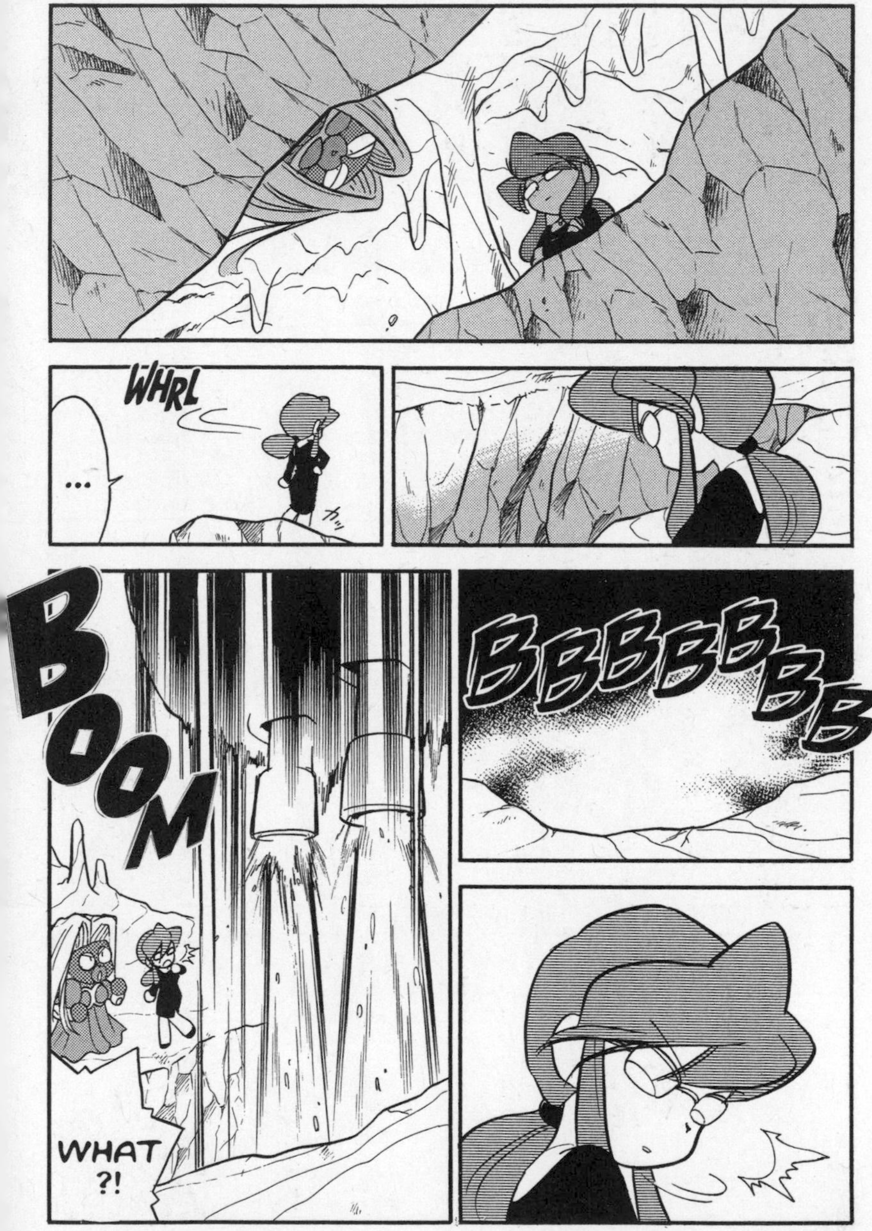
WHRL
...
BBBBBBB
BOOM
WHAT ?!

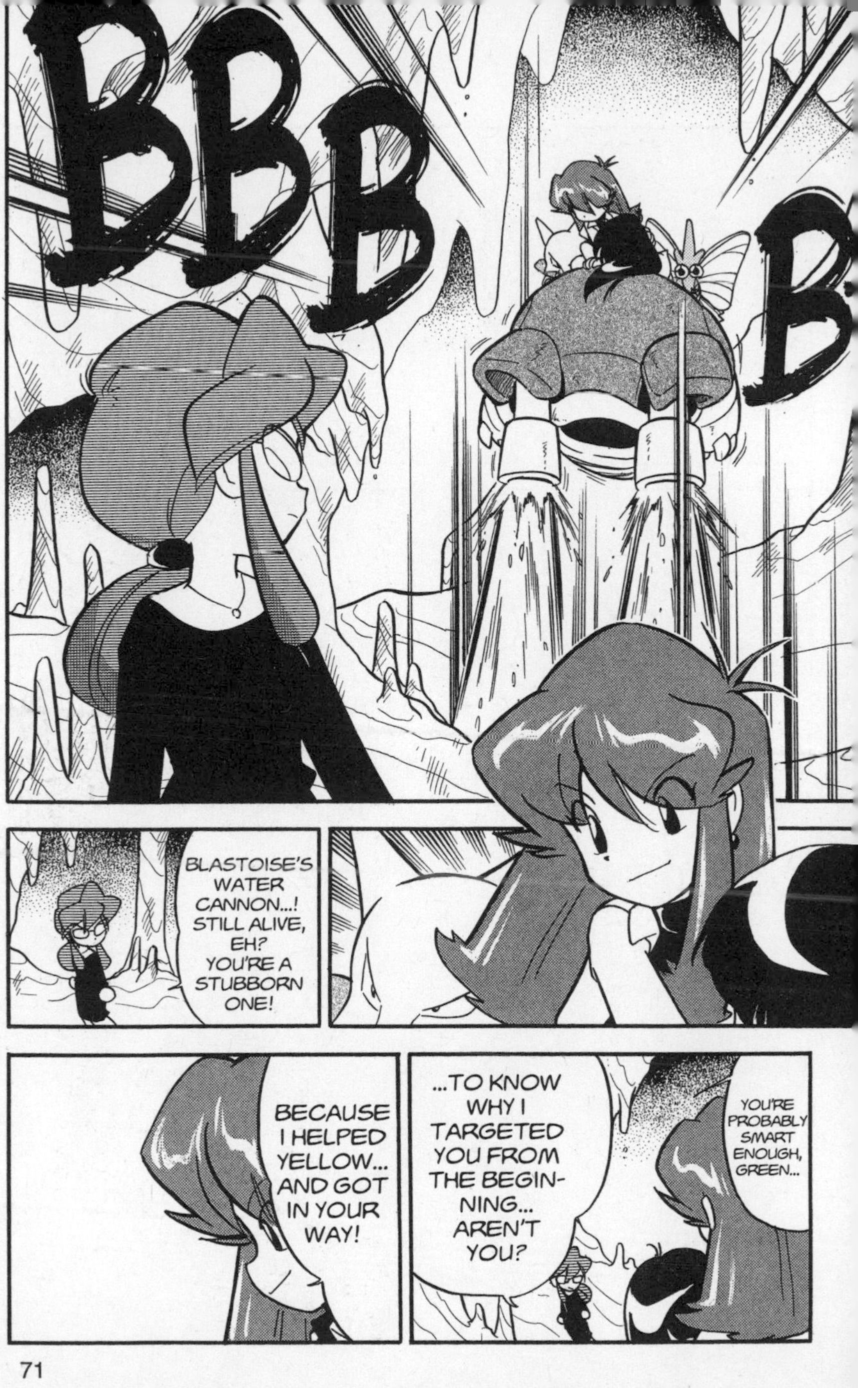
BBB
BLASTOISE'S WATER CANNON...! STILL ALIVE, EH? YOU'RE A STUBBORN ONE!
YOU'RE PROBABLY SMART ENOUGH, GREEN...
...TO KNOW WHY I TARGETED YOU FROM THE BEGIN-NING... AREN'T YOU?
BECAUSE I HELPED YELLOW... AND GOT IN YOUR WAY!

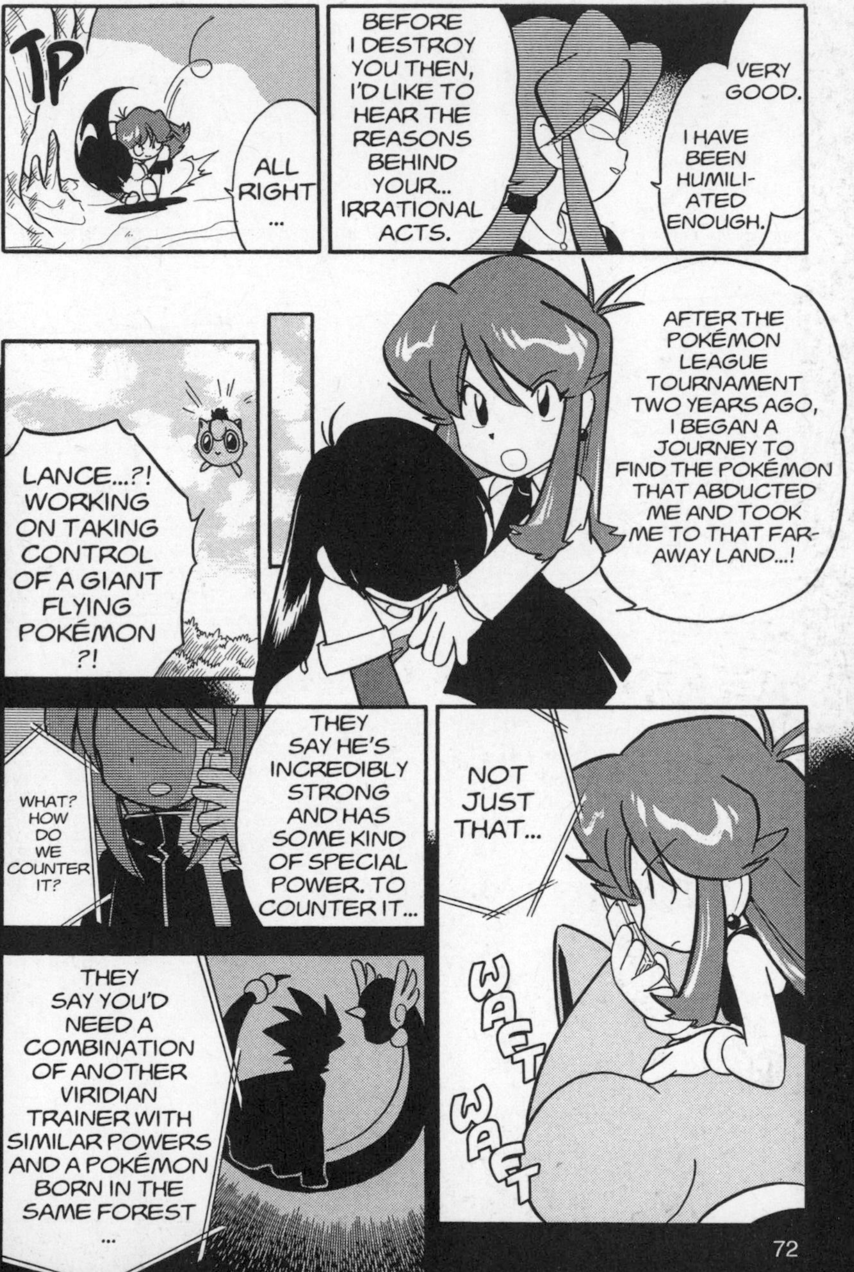
VERY GOOD.
I HAVE BEEN HUMILIATED ENOUGH.
BEFORE I DESTROY YOU THEN, I'D LIKE TO HEAR THE REASONS BEHIND YOUR... IRRATIONAL ACTS.
ALL RIGHT ...
TP
AFTER THE POKÉMON LEAGUE TOURNAMENT TWO YEARS AGO, I BEGAN A JOURNEY TO FIND THE POKÉMON THAT ABDUCTED ME AND TOOK ME TO THAT FAR-AWAY LAND...!
LANCE...?! WORKING ON TAKING CONTROL OF A GIANT FLYING POKÉMON ?!
NOT JUST THAT...
WACT
WACT
THEY SAY HE'S INCREDIBLY STRONG AND HAS SOME KIND OF SPECIAL POWER. TO COUNTER IT...
WHAT? HOW DO WE COUNTER IT?
THEY SAY YOU'D NEED A COMBINATION OF ANOTHER VIRIDIAN TRAINER WITH SIMILAR POWERS AND A POKÉMON BORN IN THE SAME FOREST ...

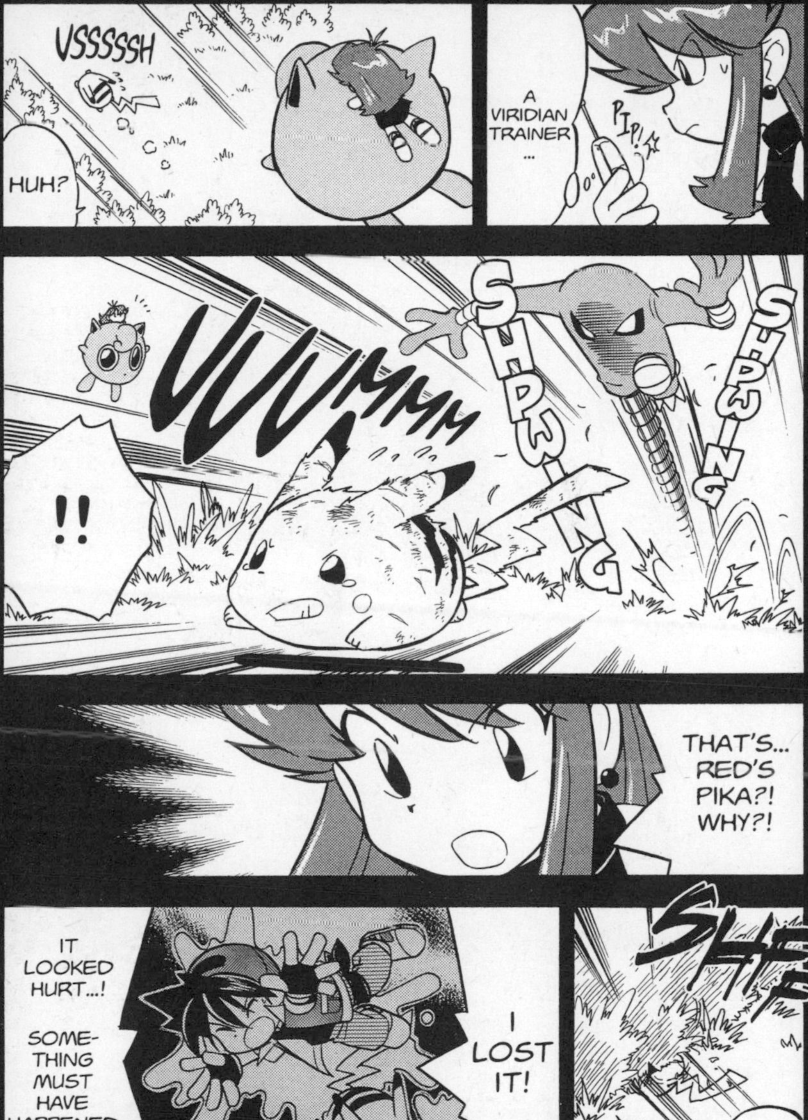
A VIRIDIAN TRAINER ...
PIP!
VSSSSSH
HUH?
SHPWING
SHPWING
UUUMMMM
!!
THAT'S... RED'S PIKA?! WHY?!
SHF
OH!
I LOST IT!
IT LOOKED HURT...!
SOME-THING MUST HAVE HAPPENED TO RED!!

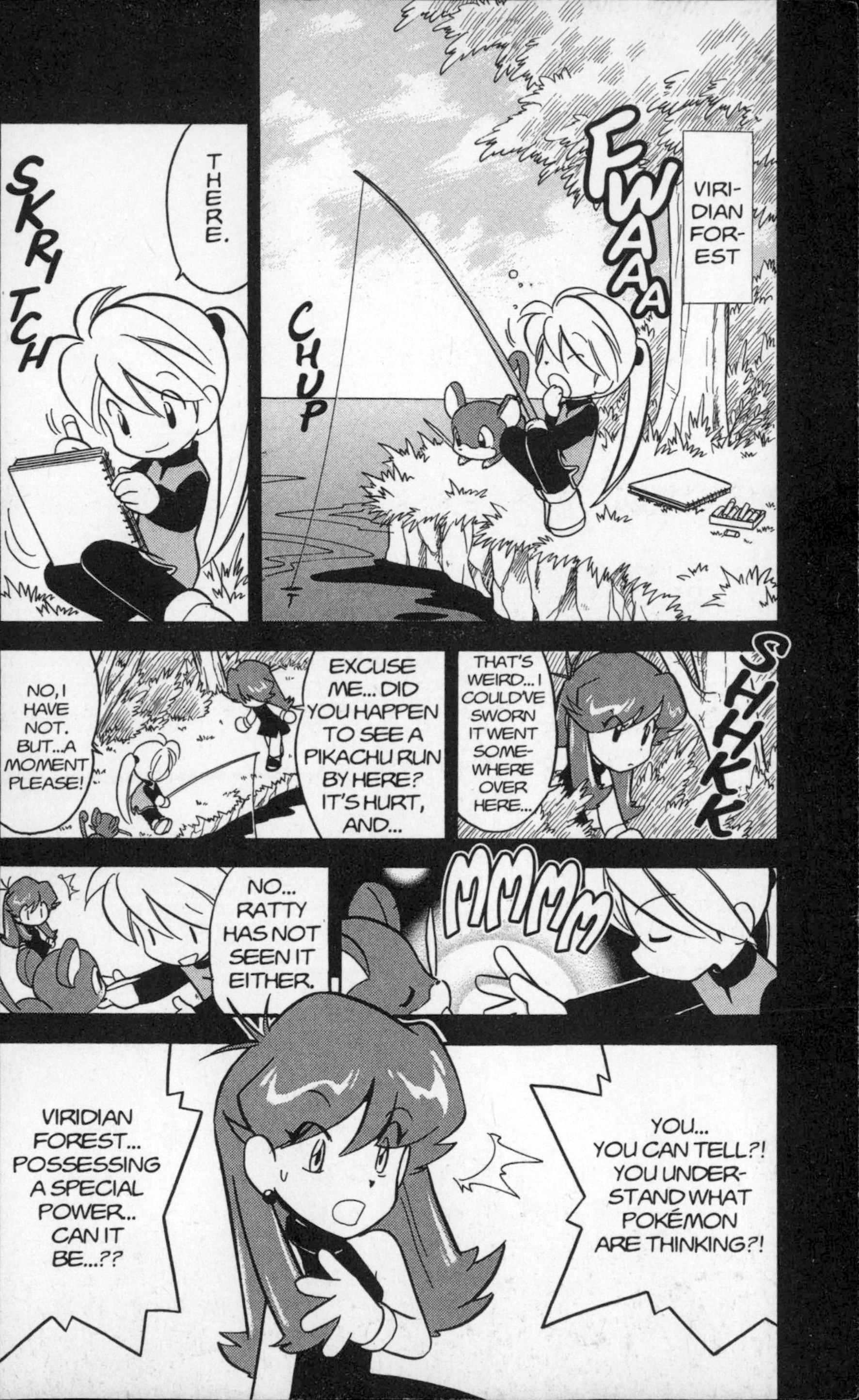
VIRIDIAN FOREST
FWAAAA
CHUP
THERE.
SKRITCH
SHHKK
THAT'S WEIRD... I COULD'VE SWORN IT WENT SOMEWHERE OVER HERE...
EXCUSE ME... DID YOU HAPPEN TO SEE A PIKACHU RUN BY HERE? IT'S HURT, AND...
NO, I HAVE NOT. BUT...A MOMENT PLEASE!
MMMM
NO... RATTY HAS NOT SEEN IT EITHER.
YOU... YOU CAN TELL?! YOU UNDERSTAND WHAT POKÉMON ARE THINKING?!
VIRIDIAN FOREST... POSSESSING A SPECIAL POWER.. CAN IT BE...??

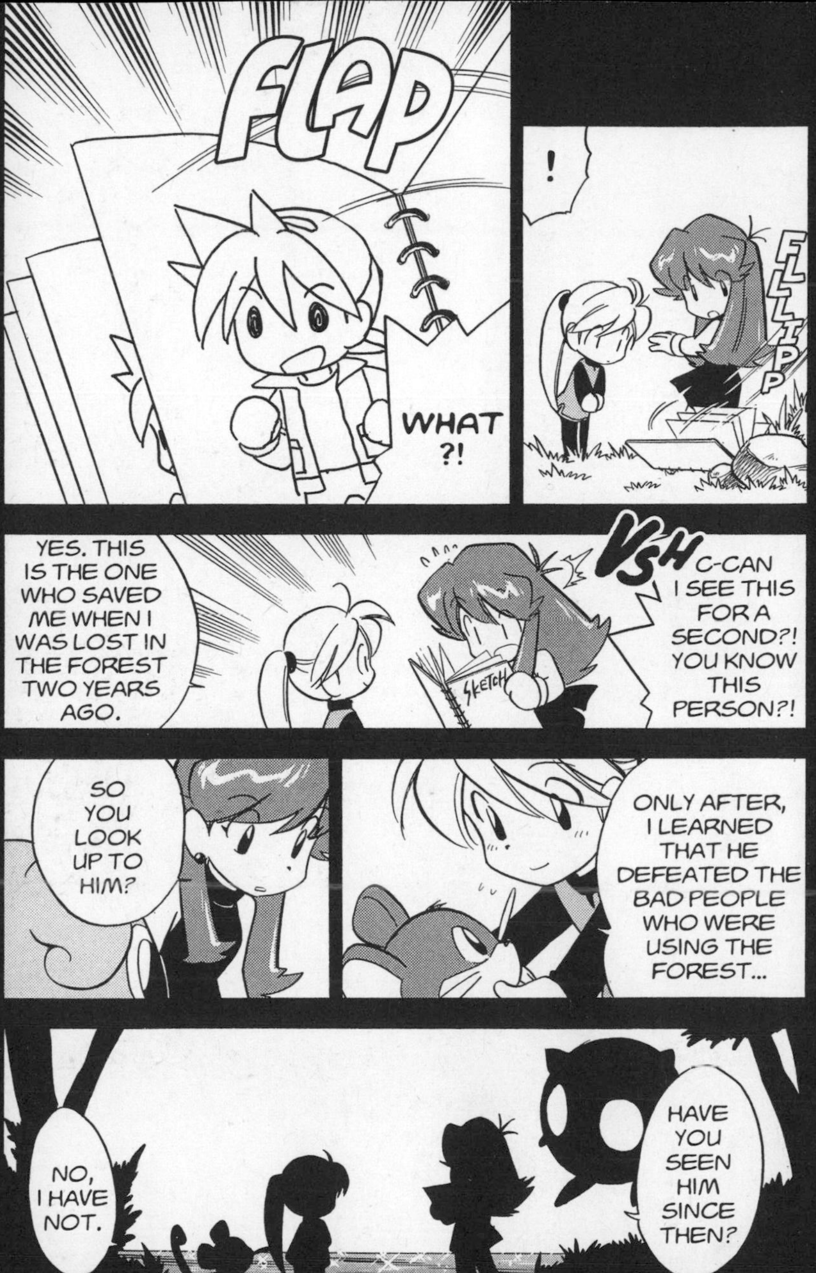
!
FLLIPP
FLAP
WHAT ?!
VSH
C-CAN I SEE THIS FOR A SECOND?! YOU KNOW THIS PERSON?!
YES. THIS IS THE ONE WHO SAVED ME WHEN I WAS LOST IN THE FOREST TWO YEARS AGO.
ONLY AFTER, I LEARNED THAT HE DEFEATED THE BAD PEOPLE WHO WERE USING THE FOREST...
SO YOU LOOK UP TO HIM?
HAVE YOU SEEN HIM SINCE THEN?
NO, I HAVE NOT.

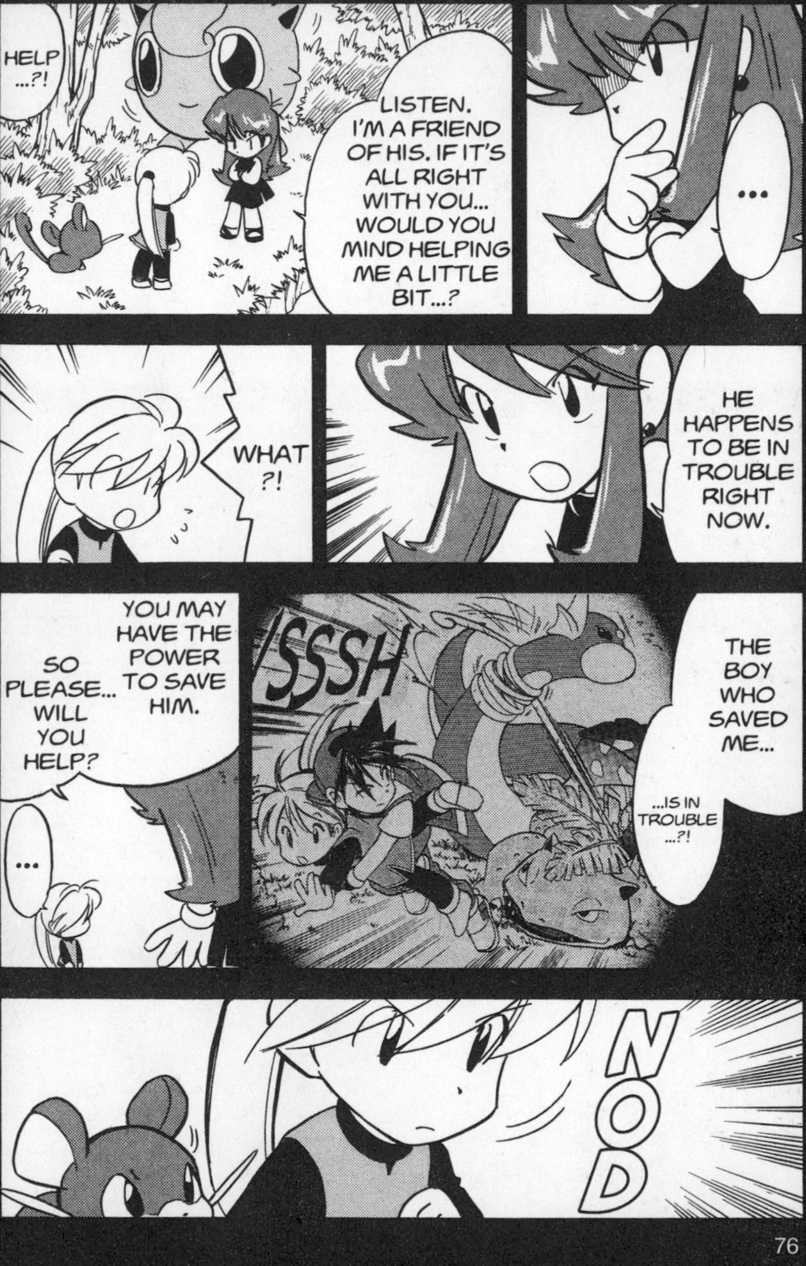
...
LISTEN. I'M A FRIEND OF HIS. IF IT'S ALL RIGHT WITH YOU... WOULD YOU MIND HELPING ME A LITTLE BIT...?
HELP ...?!
HE HAPPENS TO BE IN TROUBLE RIGHT NOW.
WHAT ?!
THE BOY WHO SAVED ME...
...IS IN TROUBLE ...?!
SSSH
YOU MAY HAVE THE POWER TO SAVE HIM.
SO PLEASE... WILL YOU HELP?
...
NOD

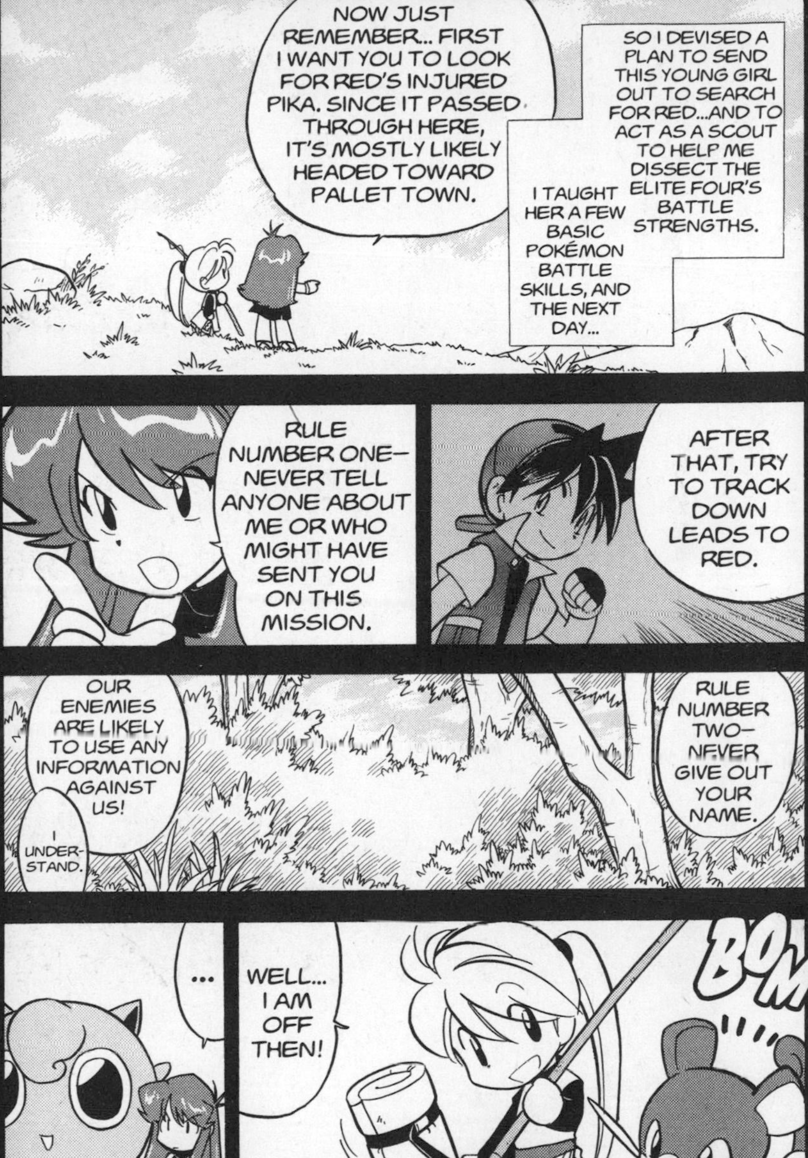
SO I DEVISED A PLAN TO SEND THIS YOUNG GIRL OUT TO SEARCH FOR RED...AND TO ACT AS A SCOUT TO HELP ME DISSECT THE ELITE FOUR'S BATTLE STRENGTHS.
I TAUGHT HER A FEW BASIC POKÉMON BATTLE SKILLS, AND THE NEXT DAY...
NOW JUST REMEMBER... FIRST I WANT YOU TO LOOK FOR RED'S INJURED PIKA. SINCE IT PASSED THROUGH HERE, IT'S MOSTLY LIKELY HEADED TOWARD PALLET TOWN.
AFTER THAT, TRY TO TRACK DOWN LEADS TO RED.
RULE NUMBER ONE— NEVER TELL ANYONE ABOUT ME OR WHO MIGHT HAVE SENT YOU ON THIS MISSION.
RULE NUMBER TWO— NEVER GIVE OUT YOUR NAME.
OUR ENEMIES ARE LIKELY TO USE ANY INFORMATION AGAINST US!
I UNDERSTAND.
BOM
WELL... I AM OFF THEN!
...

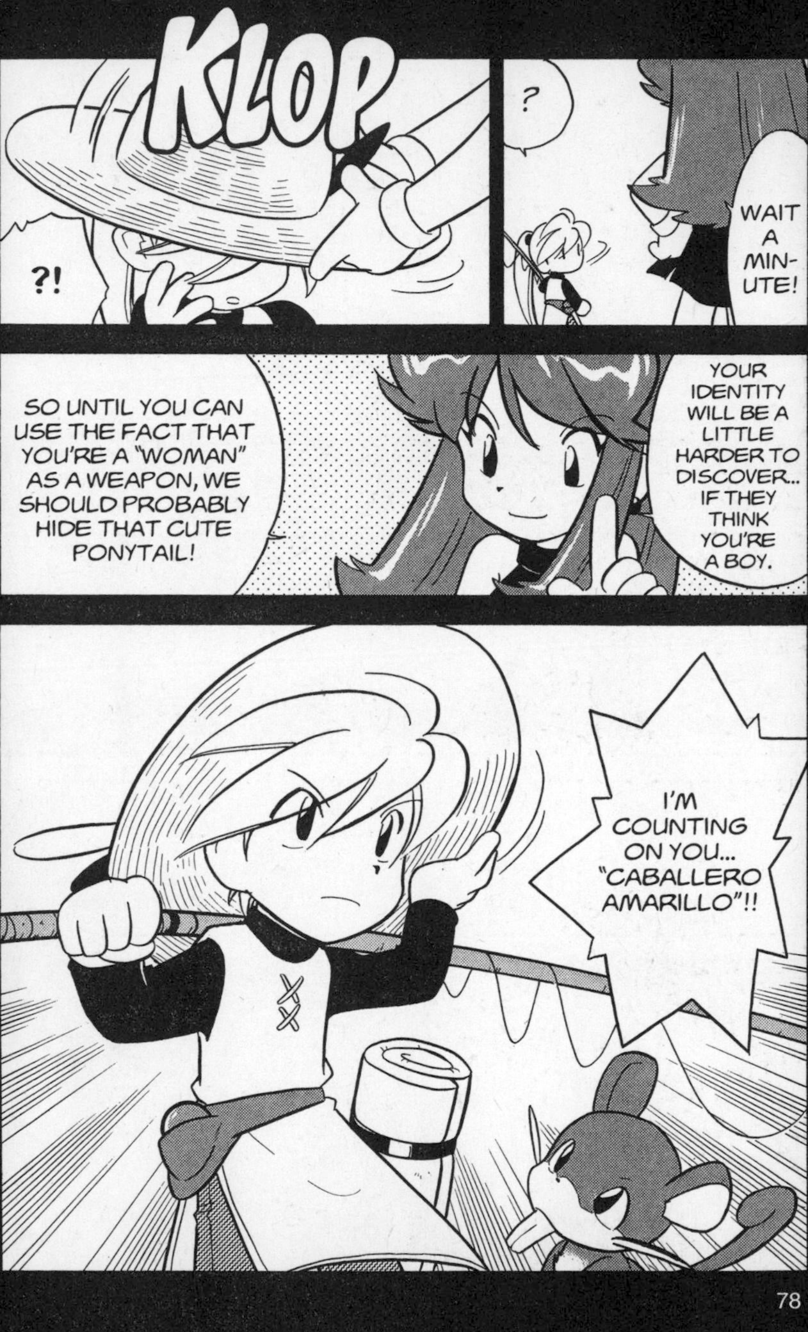
?
WAIT A MIN-UTE!
KLOP
?!
YOUR IDENTITY WILL BE A LITTLE HARDER TO DISCOVER... IF THEY THINK YOU'RE A BOY.
SO UNTIL YOU CAN USE THE FACT THAT YOU'RE A "WOMAN" AS A WEAPON, WE SHOULD PROBABLY HIDE THAT CUTE PONYTAIL!
I'M COUNTING ON YOU... "CABALLERO AMARILLO"!!

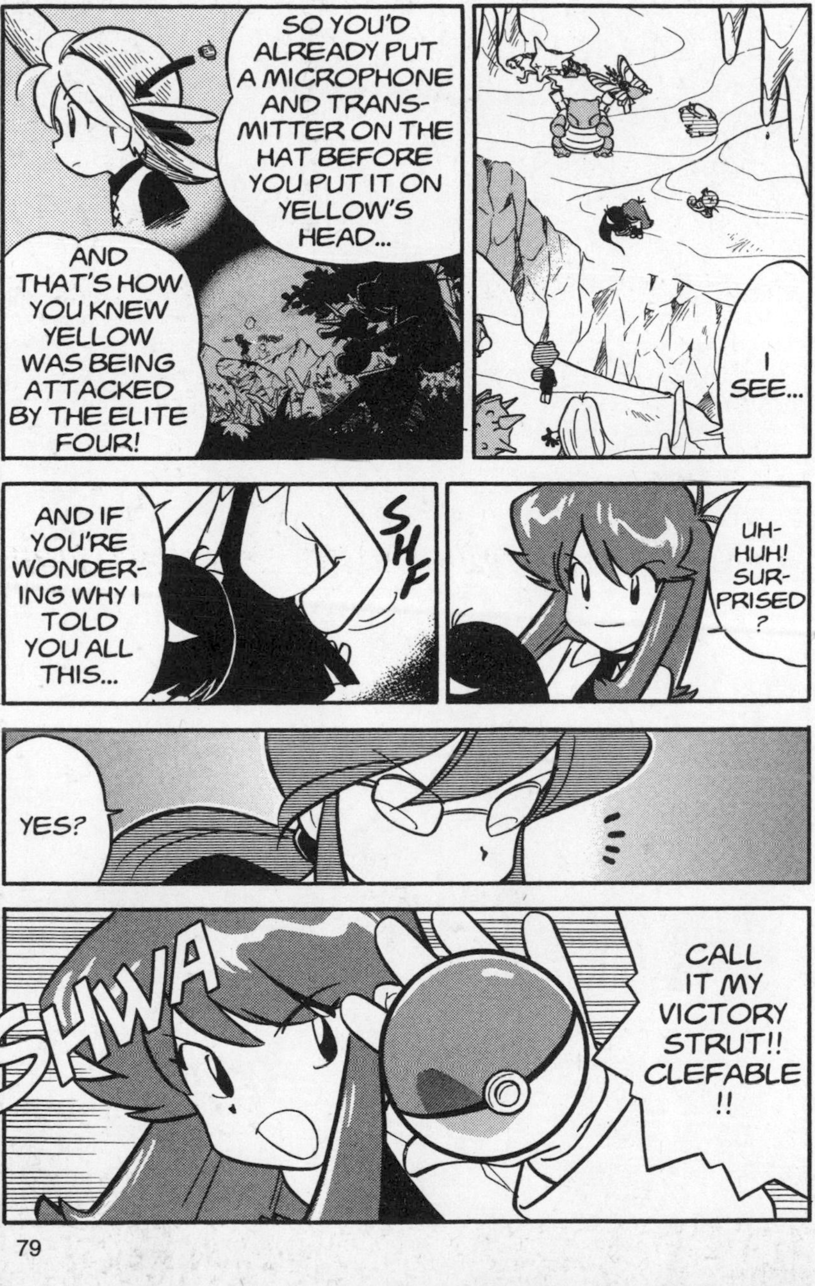
I SEE...
SO YOU'D ALREADY PUT A MICROPHONE AND TRANSMITTER ON THE HAT BEFORE YOU PUT IT ON YELLOW'S HEAD...
AND THAT'S HOW YOU KNEW YELLOW WAS BEING ATTACKED BY THE ELITE FOUR!
UH-HUH! SURPRISED?
SHF
AND IF YOU'RE WONDERING WHY I TOLD YOU ALL THIS...
YES?
CALL IT MY VICTORY STRUT!! CLEFABLE!!
SHWA

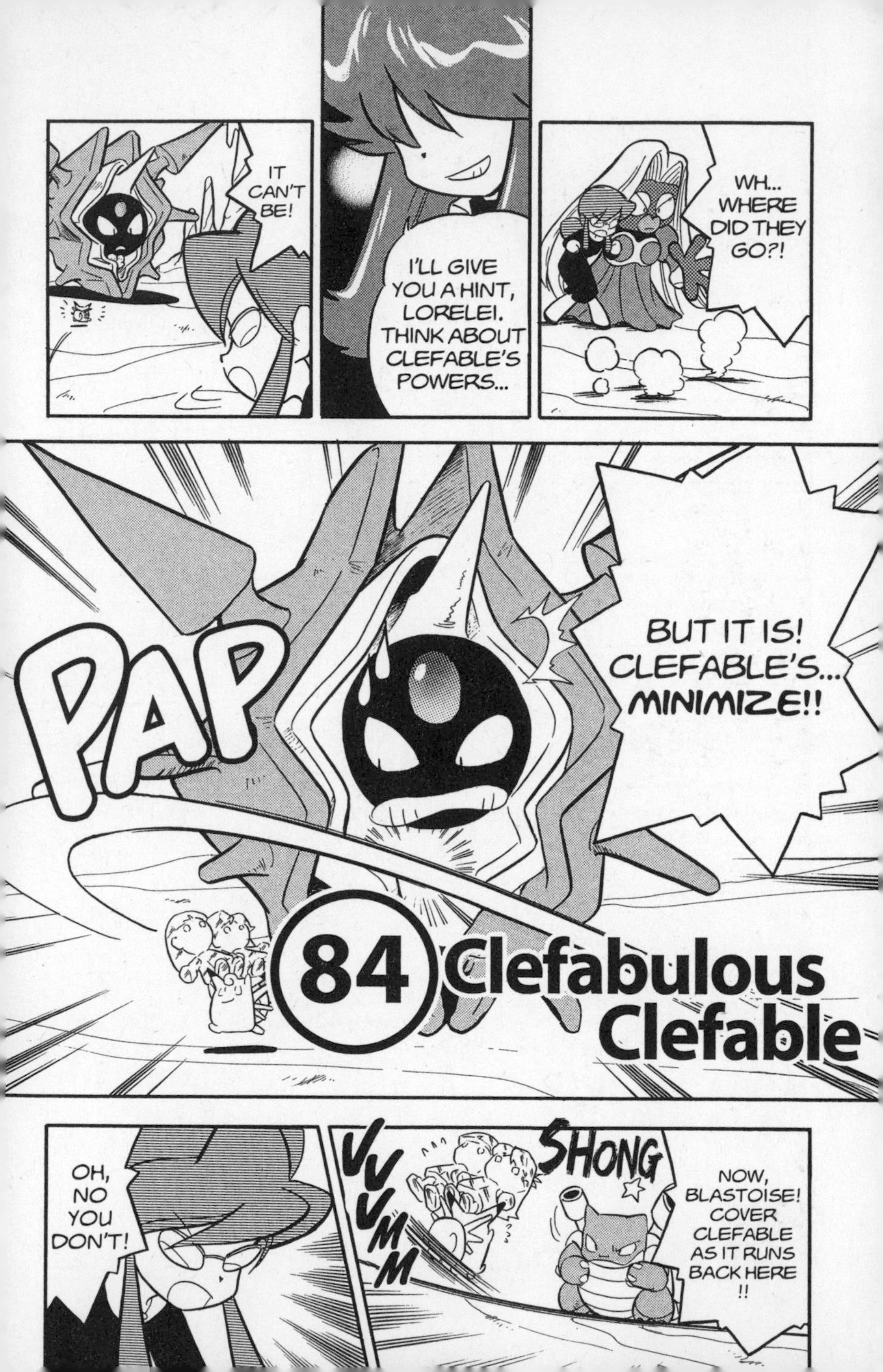
WH... WHERE DID THEY GO?!
I'LL GIVE YOU A HINT, LORELEI. THINK ABOUT CLEFABLE'S POWERS...
IT CAN'T BE!
BUT IT IS! CLEFABLE'S... MINIMIZE!!
PAP
84 Clefabulous Clefable
NOW, BLASTOISE! COVER CLEFABLE AS IT RUNS BACK HERE !!
SHONG
VVVUMM
OH, NO YOU DON'T!

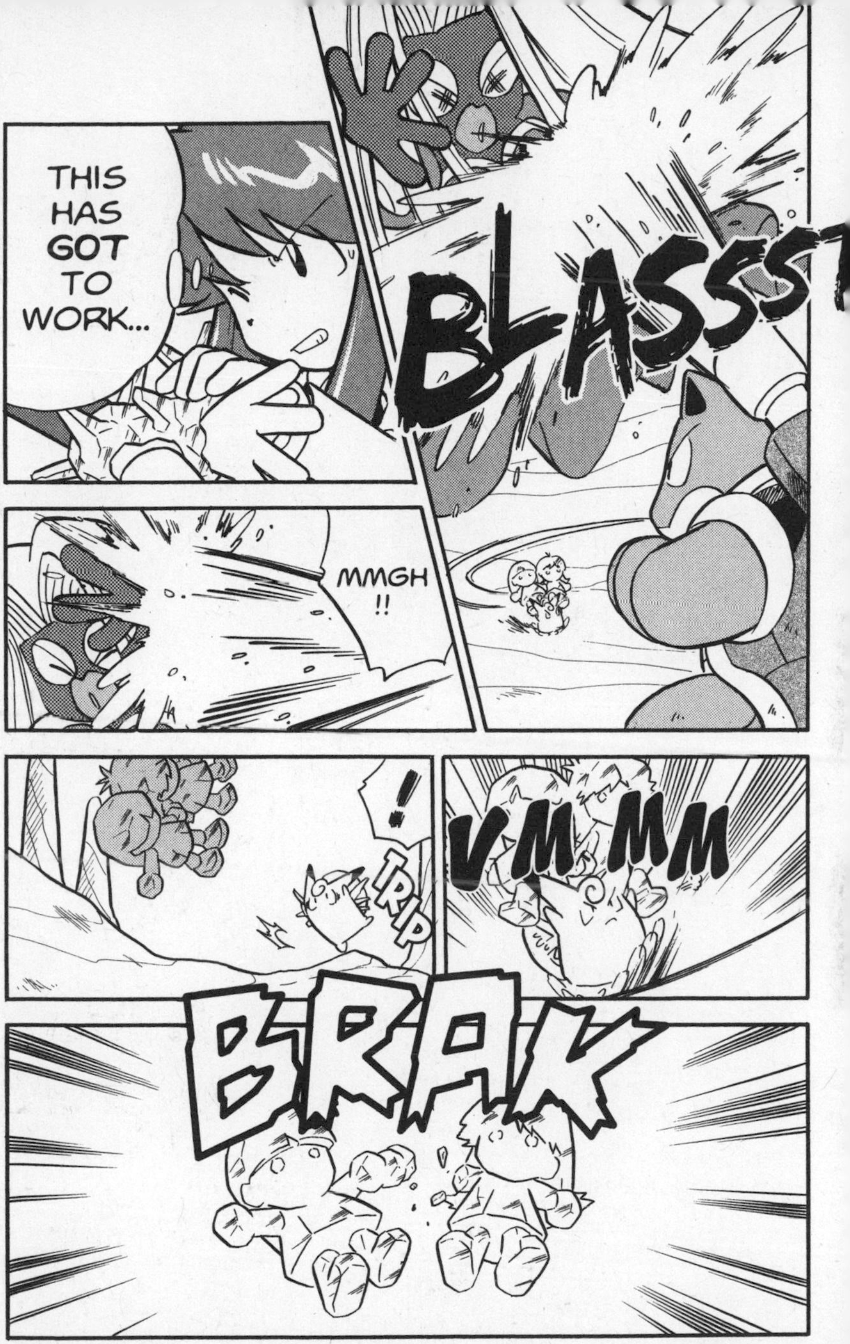
BLASSST
THIS HAS GOT TO WORK...
MMGH !!
VMMMM
!
TRIP
BRAK

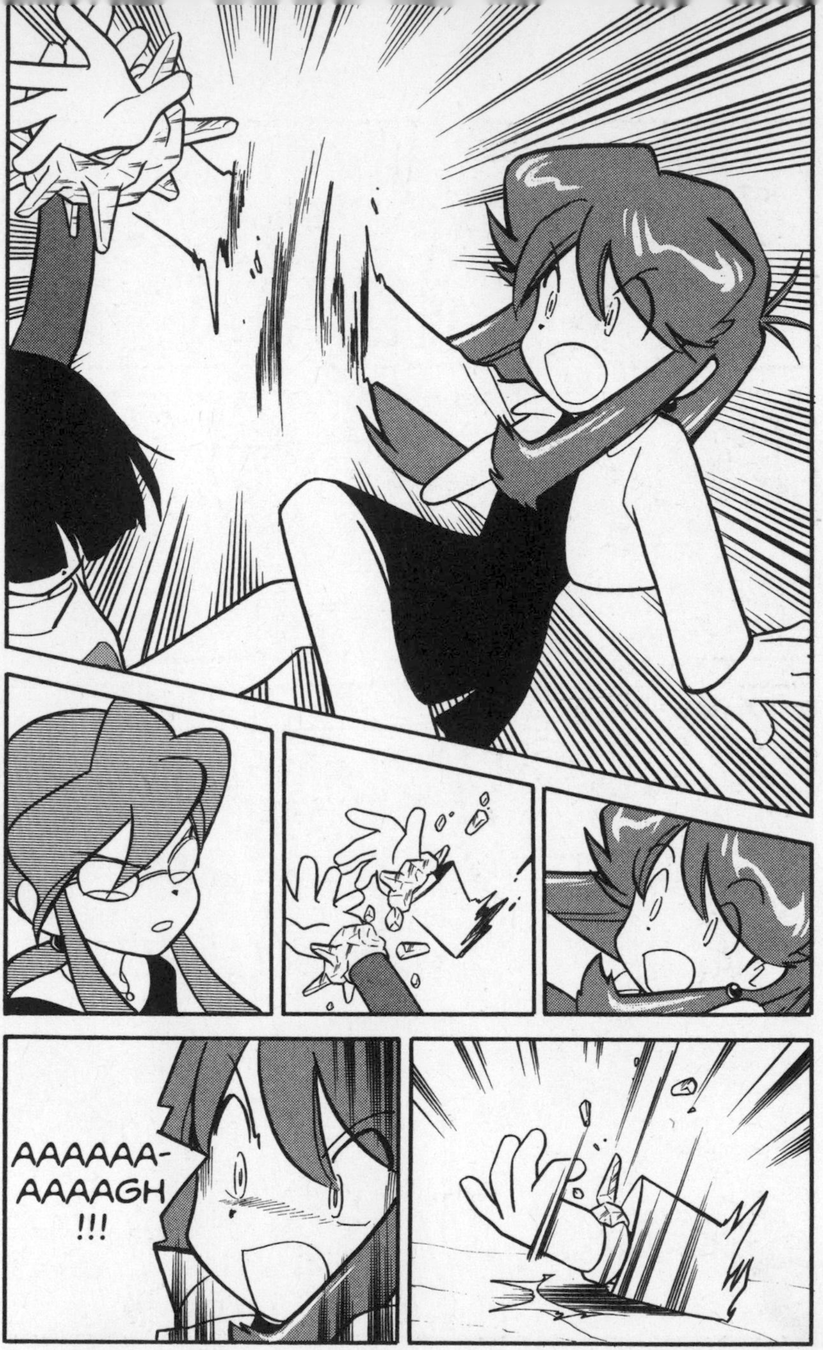
AAAAAA-
AAAAGH
!!!

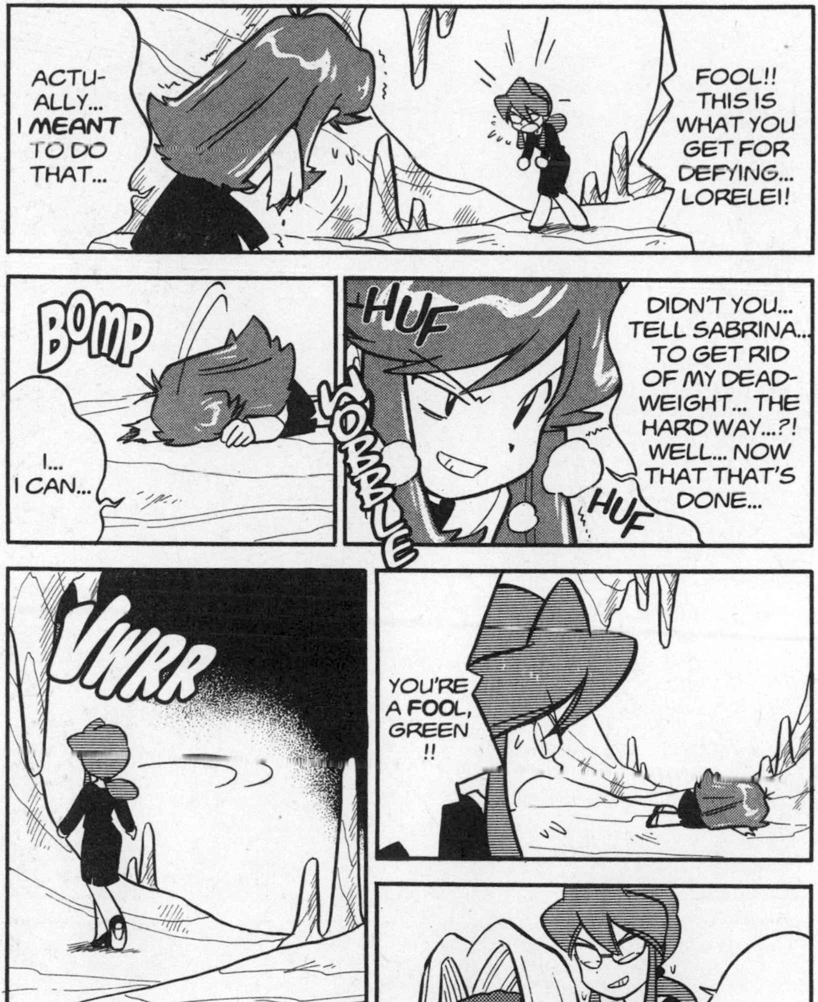
FOOL!! THIS IS WHAT YOU GET FOR DEFYING... LORELEI!
ACTU-ALLY... I MEANT TO DO THAT...
HUF
DIDN'T YOU... TELL SABRINA... TO GET RID OF MY DEAD-WEIGHT... THE HARD WAY...?! WELL... NOW THAT THAT'S DONE...
WOBBLE
HUF
BOMP
I... I CAN...
YOU'RE A FOOL, GREEN !!
IT'S OVER NOW! IT'S... ALL OVER.
VWRR

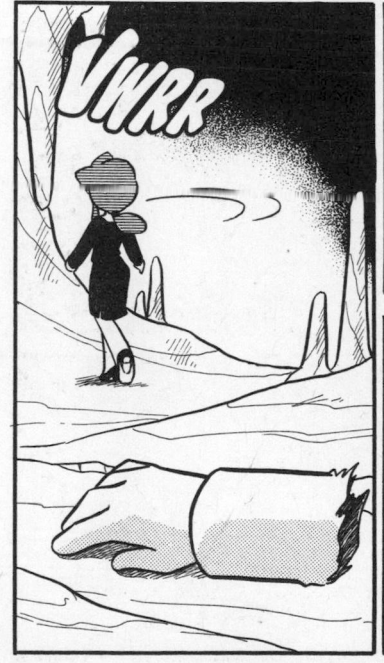

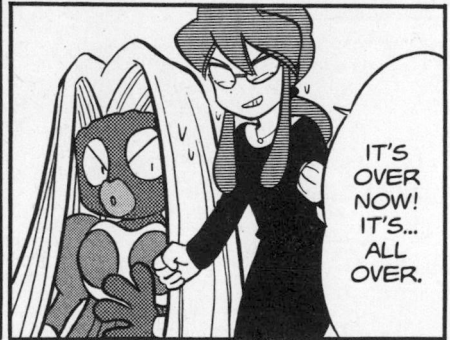

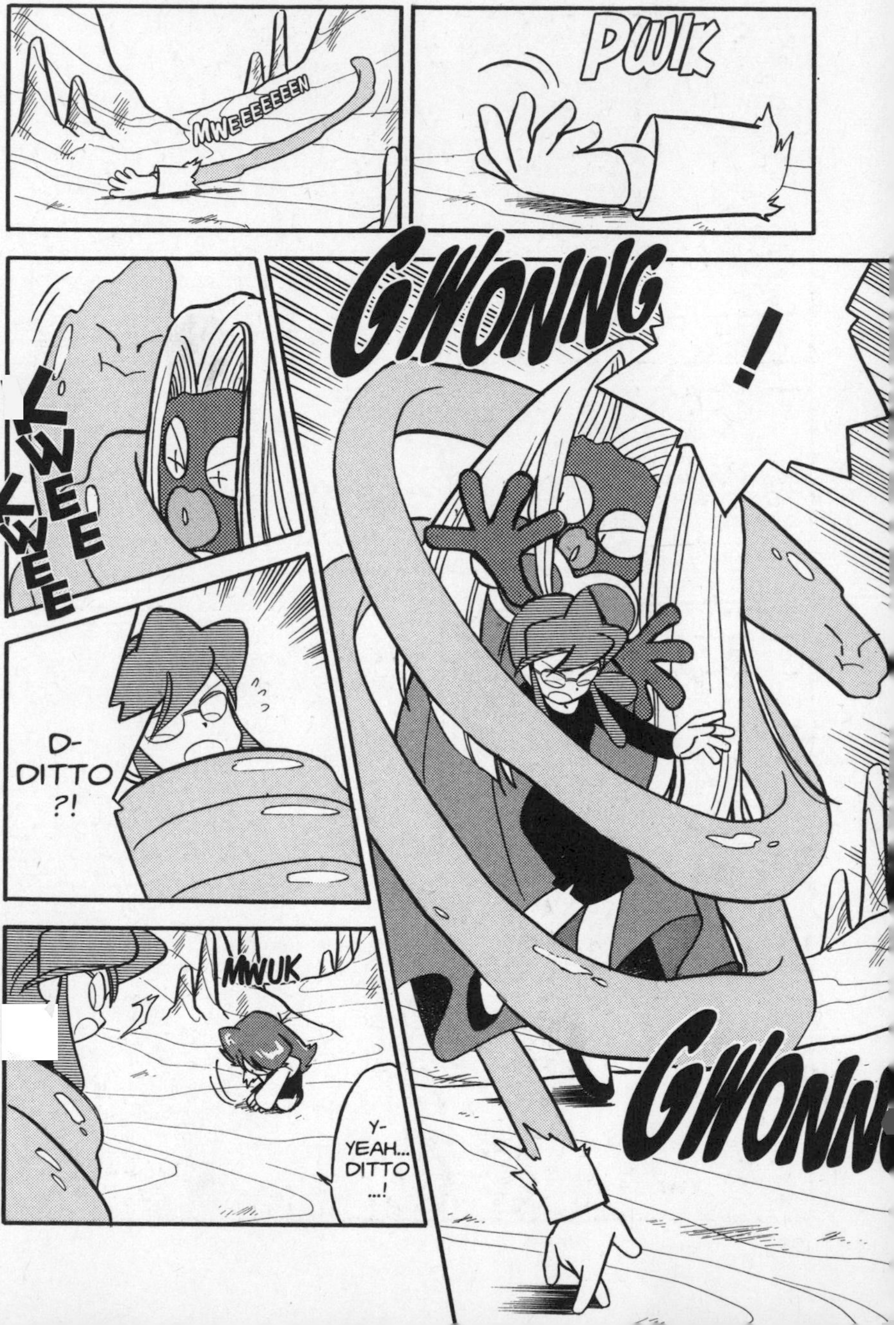
PWIK
MWEEEEEEEN
GWONNG
!
GWONNG
KWEE
KWEE
D-
DITTO
?!
MWUK
Y-
YEAH...
DITTO
...!

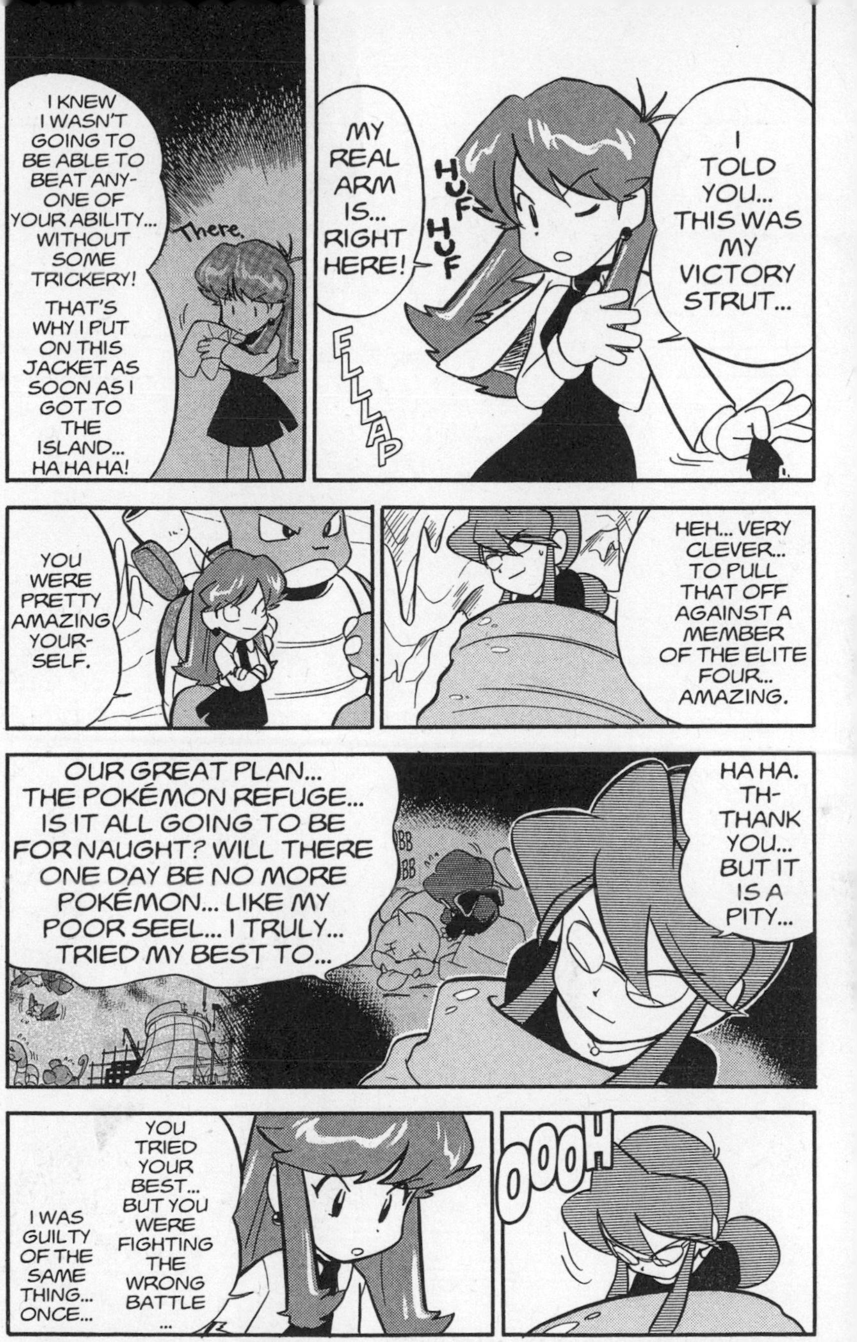
I TOLD YOU... THIS WAS MY VICTORY STRUT...
HUF HUF
MY REAL ARM IS... RIGHT HERE!
FLLLAP
There.
I KNEW I WASN'T GOING TO BE ABLE TO BEAT ANYONE OF YOUR ABILITY... WITHOUT SOME TRICKERY!
THAT'S WHY I PUT ON THIS JACKET AS SOON AS I GOT TO THE ISLAND... HA HA HA!
HEH... VERY CLEVER... TO PULL THAT OFF AGAINST A MEMBER OF THE ELITE FOUR... AMAZING.
YOU WERE PRETTY AMAZING YOURSELF.
HA HA. TH-THANK YOU... BUT IT IS A PITY...
OUR GREAT PLAN... THE POKÉMON REFUGE... IS IT ALL GOING TO BE FOR NAUGHT? WILL THERE ONE DAY BE NO MORE POKÉMON... LIKE MY POOR SEEL... I TRULY... TRIED MY BEST TO...
OOOH
YOU TRIED YOUR BEST... BUT YOU WERE FIGHTING THE WRONG BATTLE...
I WAS GUILTY OF THE SAME THING... ONCE...

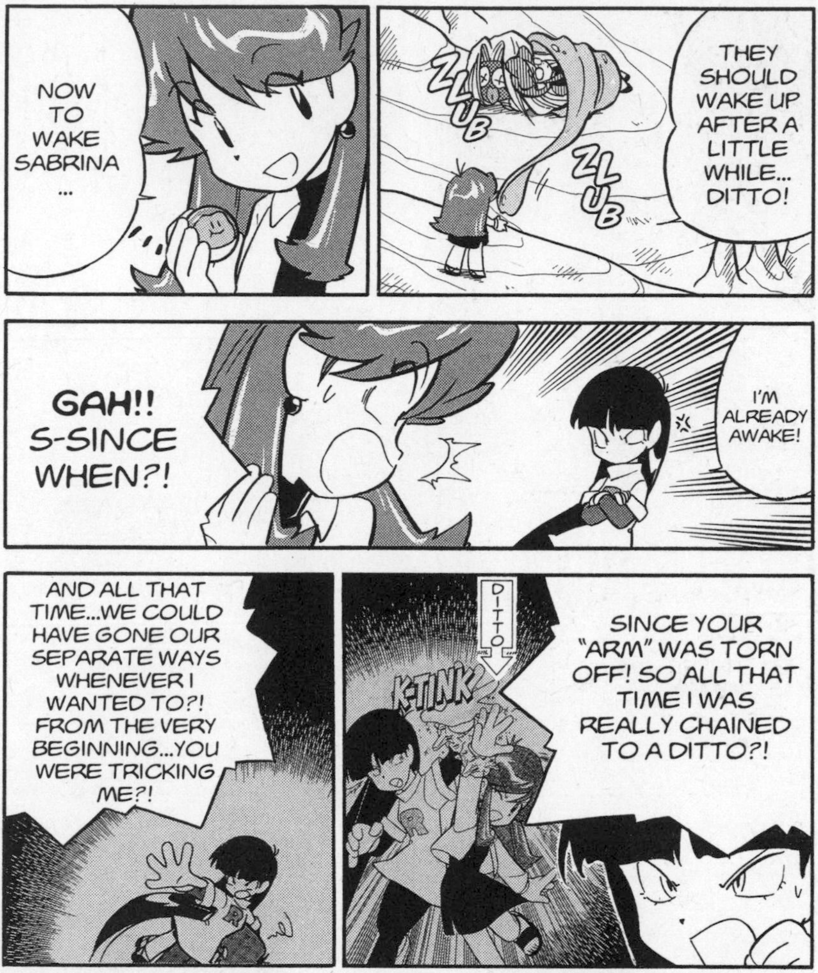
THEY SHOULD WAKE UP AFTER A LITTLE WHILE... DITTO!
ZLUB
ZLUB
NOW TO WAKE SABRINA ...
I'M ALREADY AWAKE!
GAH!! S-SINCE WHEN?!
DITTO
K-TINK
SINCE YOUR "ARM" WAS TORN OFF! SO ALL THAT TIME I WAS REALLY CHAINED TO A DITTO?!
AND ALL THAT TIME...WE COULD HAVE GONE OUR SEPARATE WAYS WHENEVER I WANTED TO?! FROM THE VERY BEGINNING...YOU WERE TRICKING ME?!
HEH HEH HEH... *AHEM.* YOU KNOW WHAT THEY SAY... TO FOOL YOUR ENEMIES, FIRST FOOL YOUR FRIENDS!
UM... SO YOU DO FORGIVE ME... RIGHT?
DON'T HOLD YOUR BREATH !!

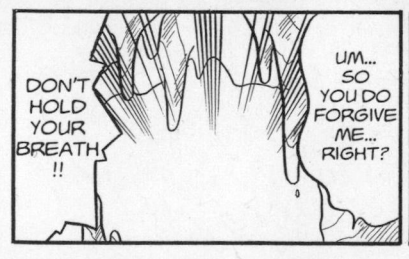

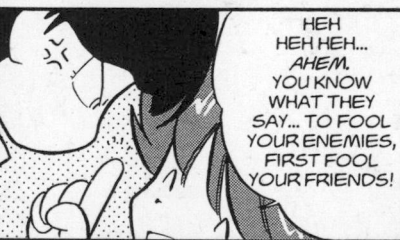

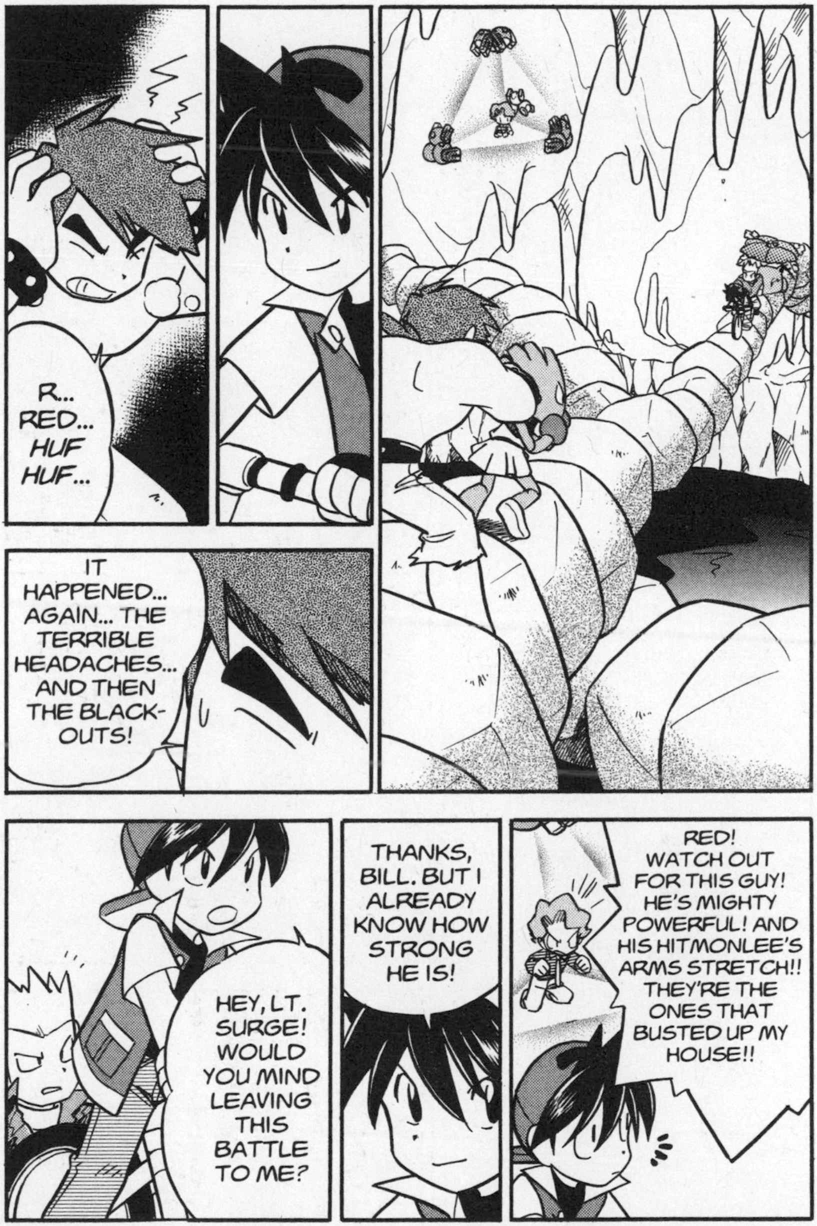
R... RED... HUF HUF...
IT HAPPENED... AGAIN... THE TERRIBLE HEADACHES... AND THEN THE BLACK-OUTS!
RED! WATCH OUT FOR THIS GUY! HE'S MIGHTY POWERFUL! AND HIS HITMONLEE'S ARMS STRETCH!! THEY'RE THE ONES THAT BUSTED UP MY HOUSE!!
THANKS, BILL. BUT I ALREADY KNOW HOW STRONG HE IS!
HEY, LT. SURGE! WOULD YOU MIND LEAVING THIS BATTLE TO ME?

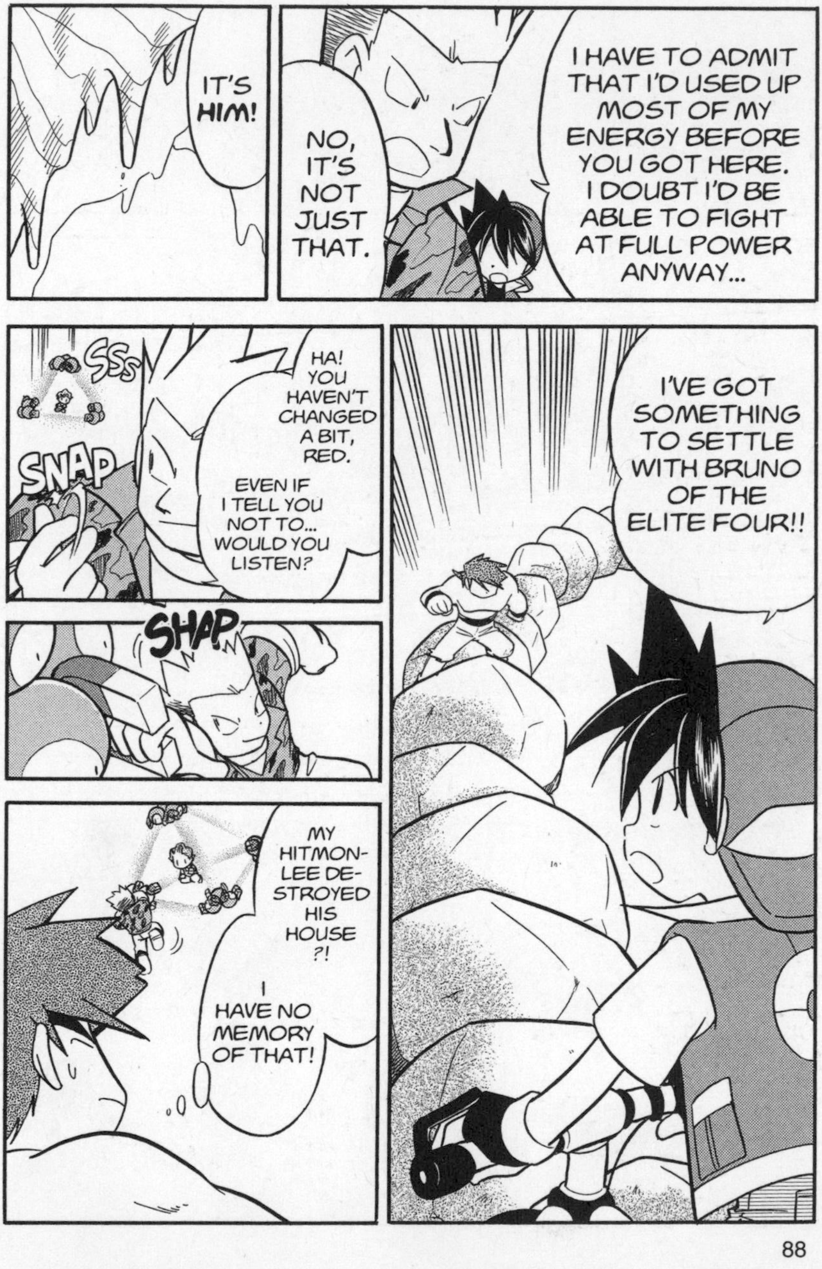
IT'S HIM!
NO, IT'S NOT JUST THAT.
I HAVE TO ADMIT THAT I'D USED UP MOST OF MY ENERGY BEFORE YOU GOT HERE. I DOUBT I'D BE ABLE TO FIGHT AT FULL POWER ANYWAY...
SSS
SNAP
HA! YOU HAVEN'T CHANGED A BIT, RED.
EVEN IF I TELL YOU NOT TO... WOULD YOU LISTEN?
SHAP
I'VE GOT SOMETHING TO SETTLE WITH BRUNO OF THE ELITE FOUR!!
MY HITMON-LEE DE-STROYED HIS HOUSE?!
I HAVE NO MEMORY OF THAT!

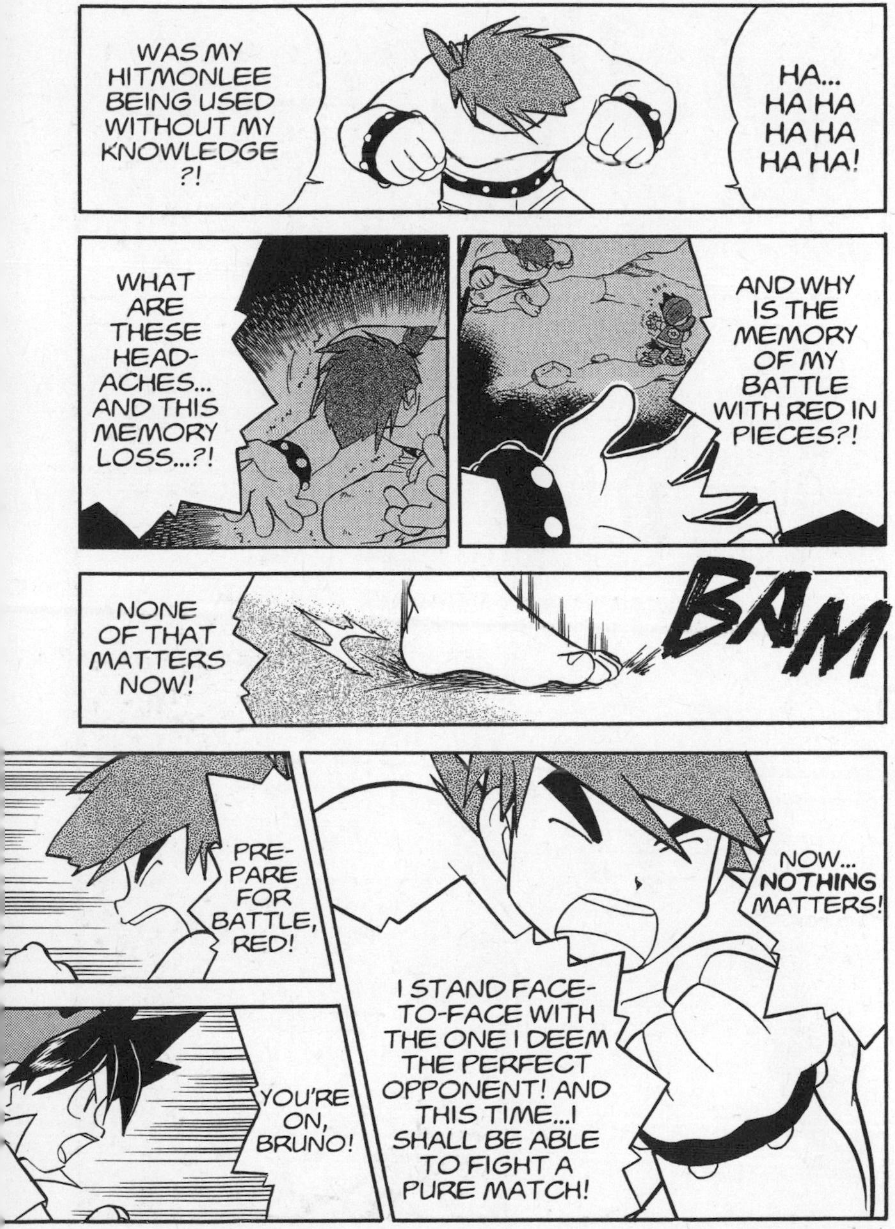
WAS MY HITMONLEE BEING USED WITHOUT MY KNOWLEDGE ?!
HA... HA HA HA HA HA HA!
WHAT ARE THESE HEAD-ACHES... AND THIS MEMORY LOSS...?!
AND WHY IS THE MEMORY OF MY BATTLE WITH RED IN PIECES?!
NONE OF THAT MATTERS NOW!
BAM
PRE-PARE FOR BATTLE, RED!
YOU'RE ON, BRUNO!
NOW... **NOTHING** MATTERS!
I STAND FACE-TO-FACE WITH THE ONE I DEEM THE PERFECT OPPONENT! AND THIS TIME...I SHALL BE ABLE TO FIGHT A PURE MATCH!

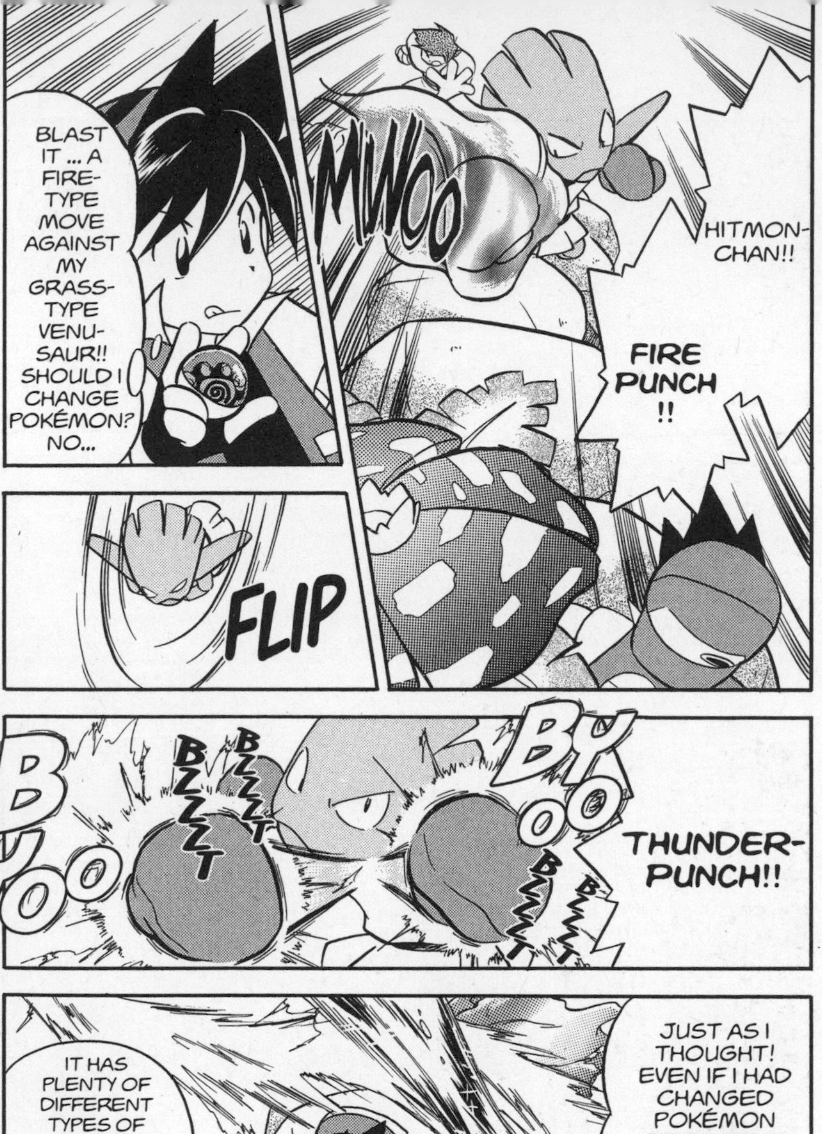
HITMON-CHAN!!
MWOO
FIRE PUNCH !!
BLAST IT ... A FIRE-TYPE MOVE AGAINST MY GRASS-TYPE VENUSAUR!! SHOULD I CHANGE POKÉMON? NO...
FLIP
THUNDER-PUNCH!!
BYOO
BZZZT
BZZZT
BZZZT
BZZZT
BYOO
JUST AS I THOUGHT! EVEN IF I HAD CHANGED POKÉMON BECAUSE IT WAS A FIRE-TYPE MOVE...
IT HAS PLENTY OF DIFFERENT TYPES OF ATTACKS! IT WOULDN'T HAVE DONE ANY GOOD TO CHANGE!! GOOD THING I DIDN'T BRING OUT POLI-WRATH...

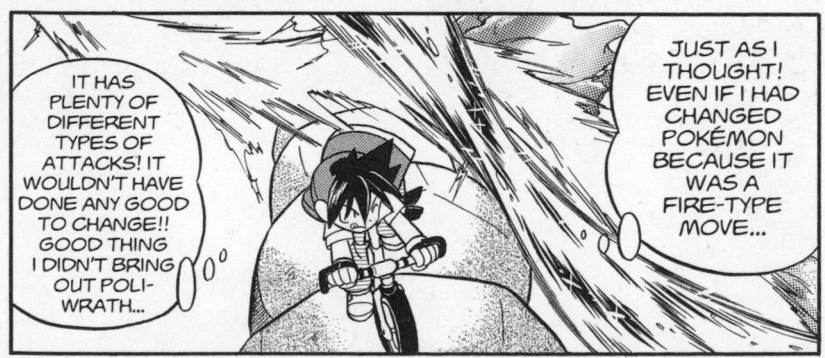

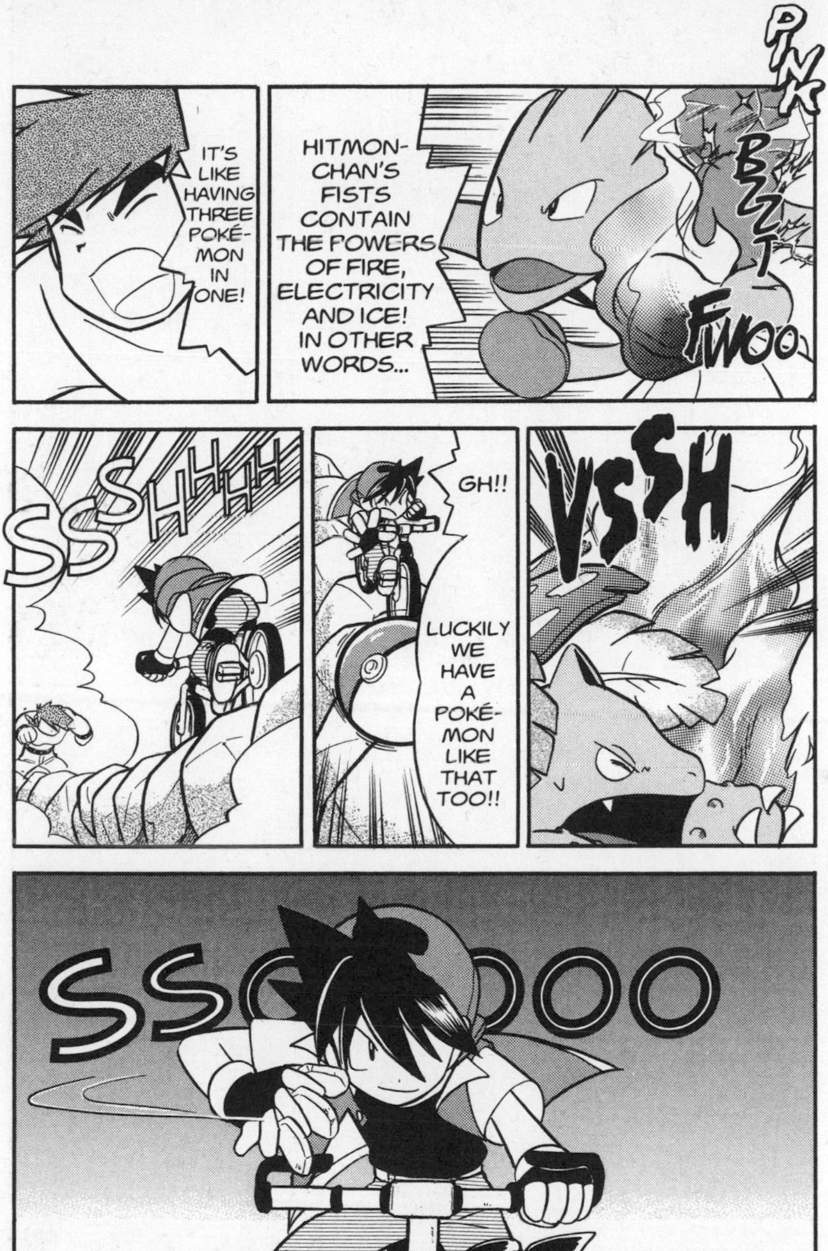

PINK
BZZT
FWOO
HITMON-CHAN'S FISTS CONTAIN THE POWERS OF FIRE, ELECTRICITY AND ICE! IN OTHER WORDS...
IT'S LIKE HAVING THREE POKÉ-MON IN ONE!
VSSH
GH!!
LUCKILY WE HAVE A POKÉ-MON LIKE THAT TOO!!
SSHHHH
SSOOOO

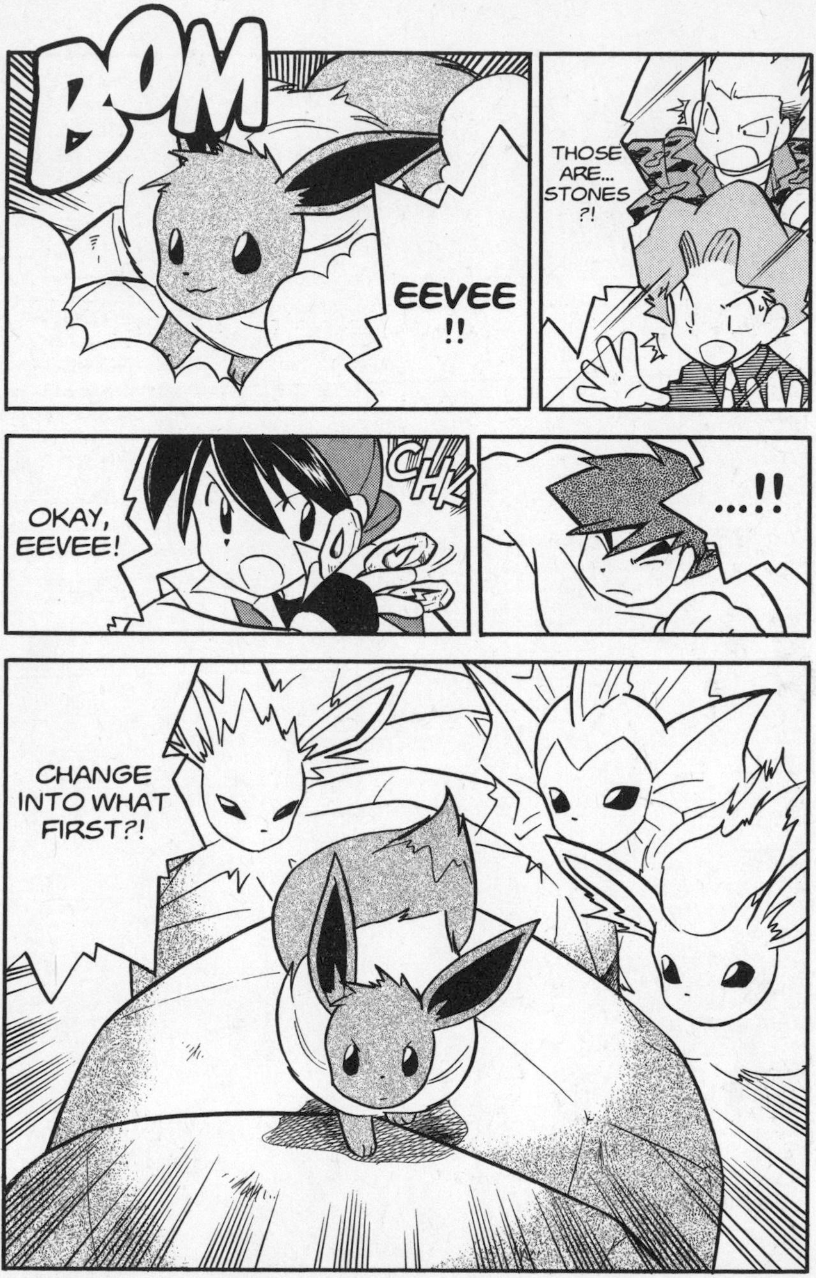
THOSE ARE... STONES ?!
BOM
EEVEE !!
...!!
CHK
OKAY, EEVEE!
CHANGE INTO WHAT FIRST?!

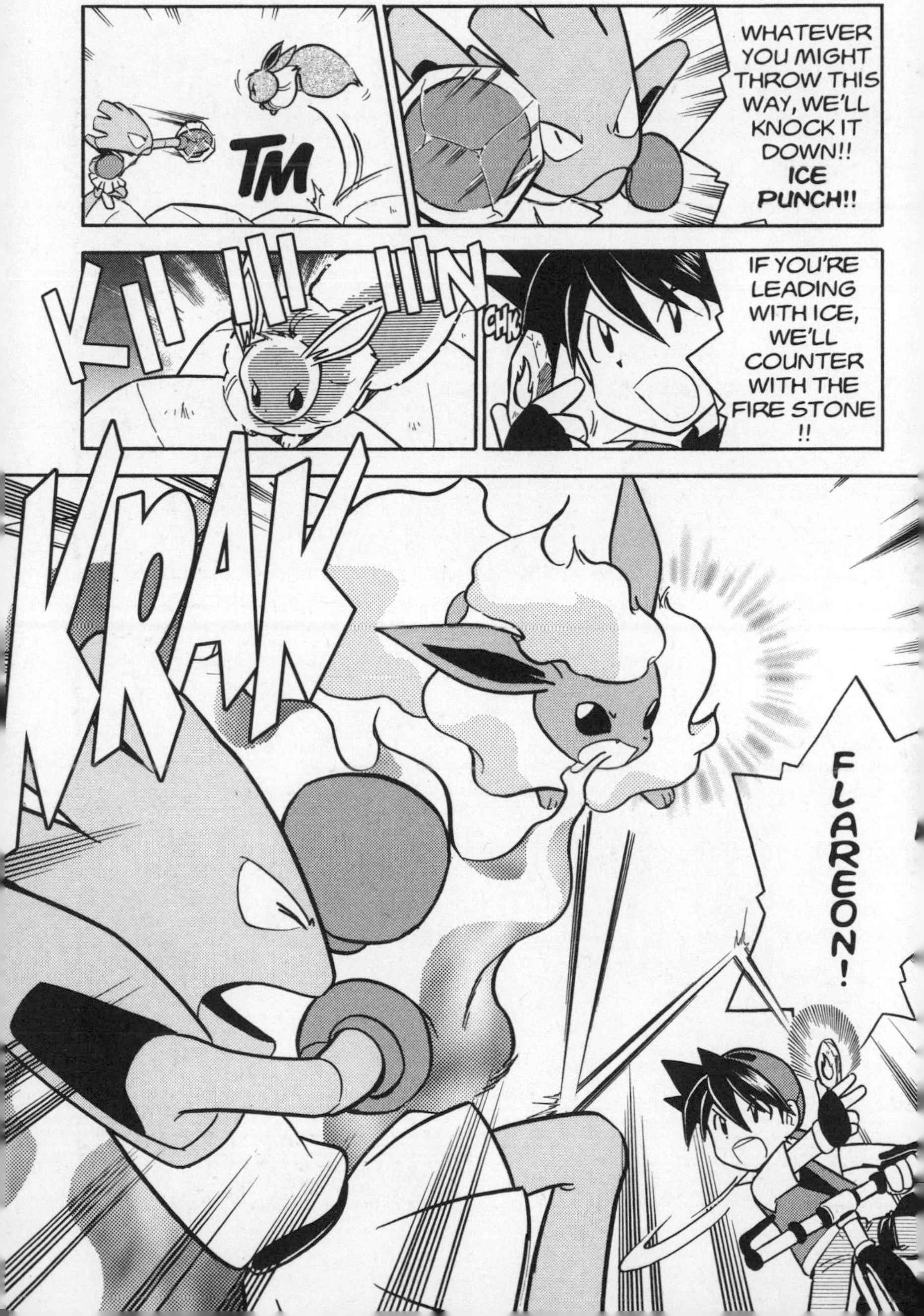
WHATEVER YOU MIGHT THROW THIS WAY, WE'LL KNOCK IT DOWN!!
ICE PUNCH!!
TM
IF YOU'RE LEADING WITH ICE, WE'LL COUNTER WITH THE FIRE STONE !!
KIIIIIIIIN
FLAREON!
KRAK

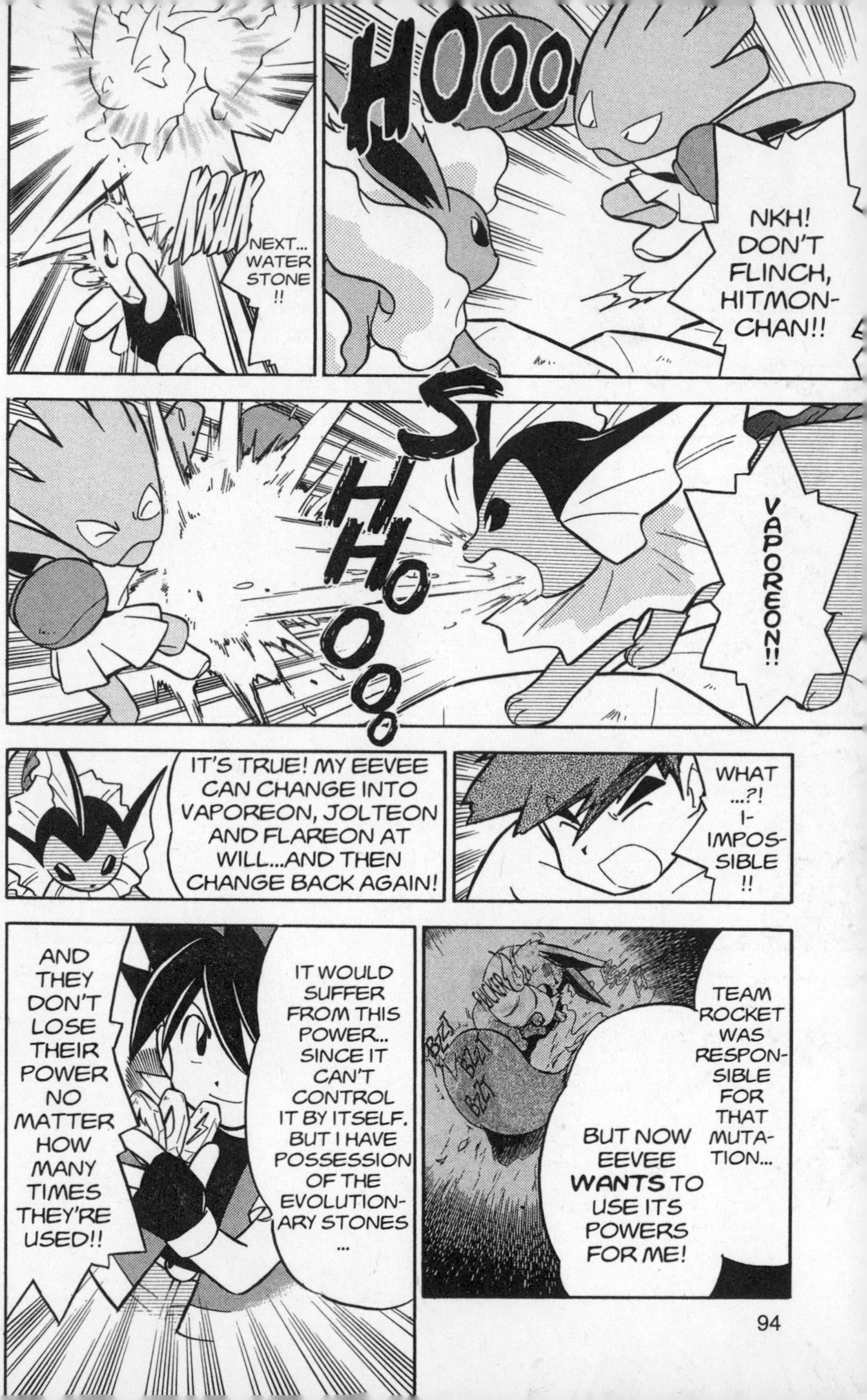
HOOO
NKH! DON'T FLINCH, HITMONCHAN!!
KRAK
NEXT... WATER STONE!!
SHHOOOO
VAPOREON!!
WHAT...?! I-IMPOSSIBLE!!
IT'S TRUE! MY EEVEE CAN CHANGE INTO VAPOREON, JOLTEON AND FLAREON AT WILL...AND THEN CHANGE BACK AGAIN!
TEAM ROCKET WAS RESPONSIBLE FOR THAT MUTATION...
BUT NOW EEVEE **WANTS** TO USE ITS POWERS FOR ME!
IT WOULD SUFFER FROM THIS POWER... SINCE IT CAN'T CONTROL IT BY ITSELF. BUT I HAVE POSSESSION OF THE EVOLUTIONARY STONES...
AND THEY DON'T LOSE THEIR POWER NO MATTER HOW MANY TIMES THEY'RE USED!!

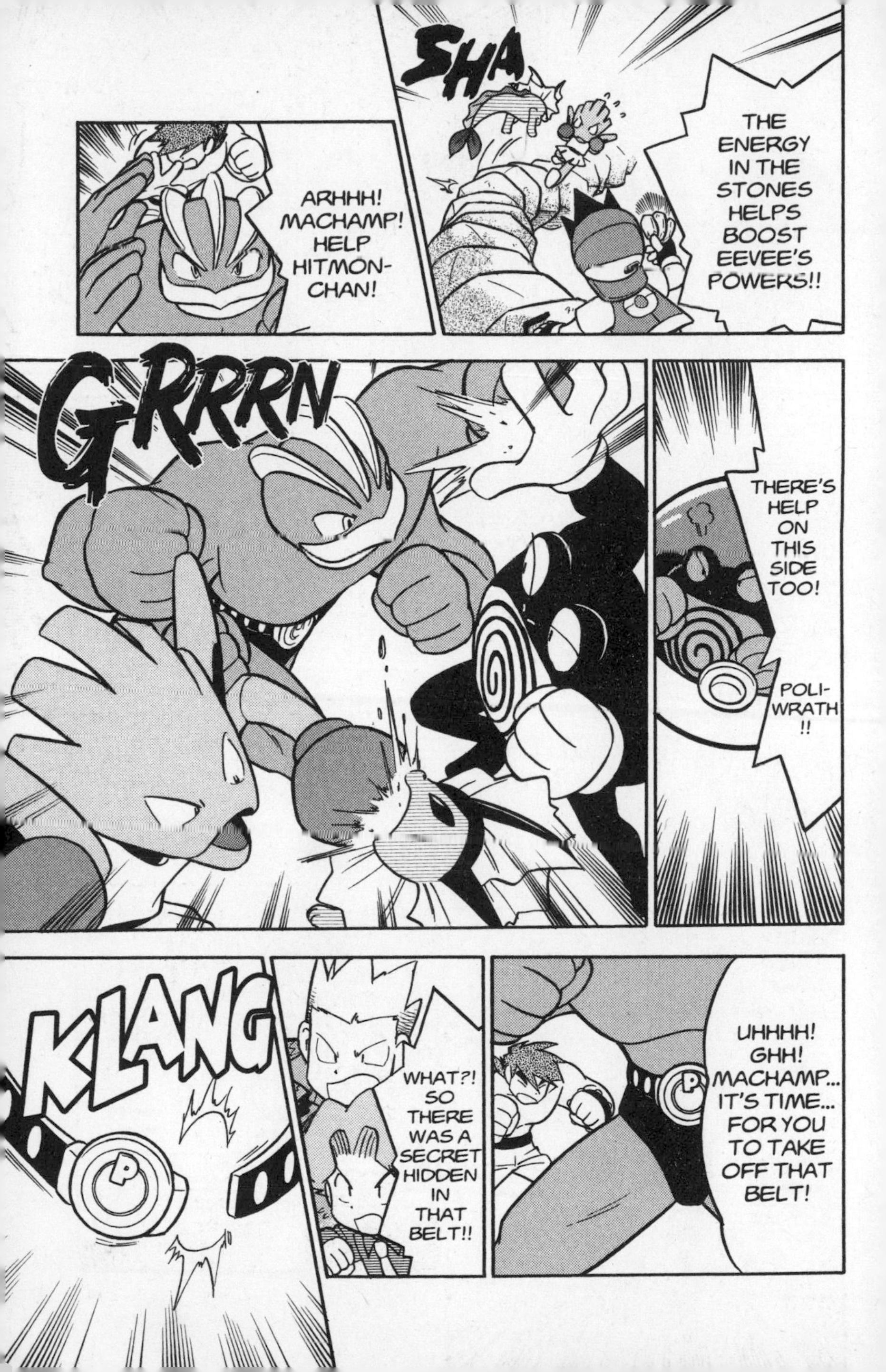
SHA
THE ENERGY IN THE STONES HELPS BOOST EEVEE'S POWERS!!
ARHHH! MACHAMP! HELP HITMON-CHAN!
THERE'S HELP ON THIS SIDE TOO!
POLI-WRATH!!
GRRRN
UHHHH! GHH! MACHAMP... IT'S TIME... FOR YOU TO TAKE OFF THAT BELT!
WHAT?! SO THERE WAS A SECRET HIDDEN IN THAT BELT!!
KLANG

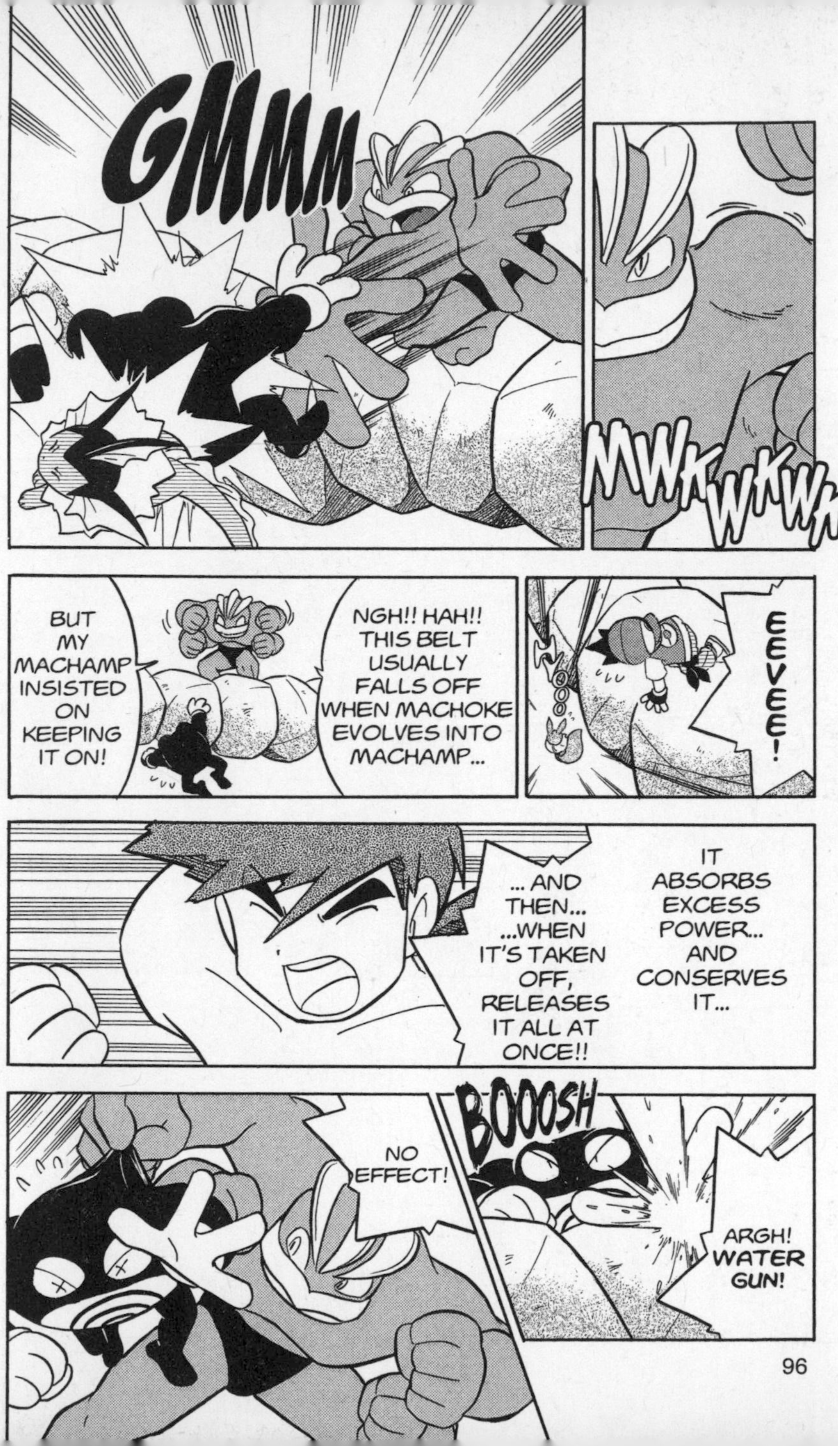
MWKWKWK
GMMM
EEVEE!
NGH!! HAH!! THIS BELT USUALLY FALLS OFF WHEN MACHOKE EVOLVES INTO MACHAMP...
BUT MY MACHAMP INSISTED ON KEEPING IT ON!
IT ABSORBS EXCESS POWER... AND CONSERVES IT...
... AND THEN... ...WHEN IT'S TAKEN OFF, RELEASES IT ALL AT ONCE!!
BOOOSH
ARGH! WATER GUN!
NO EFFECT!

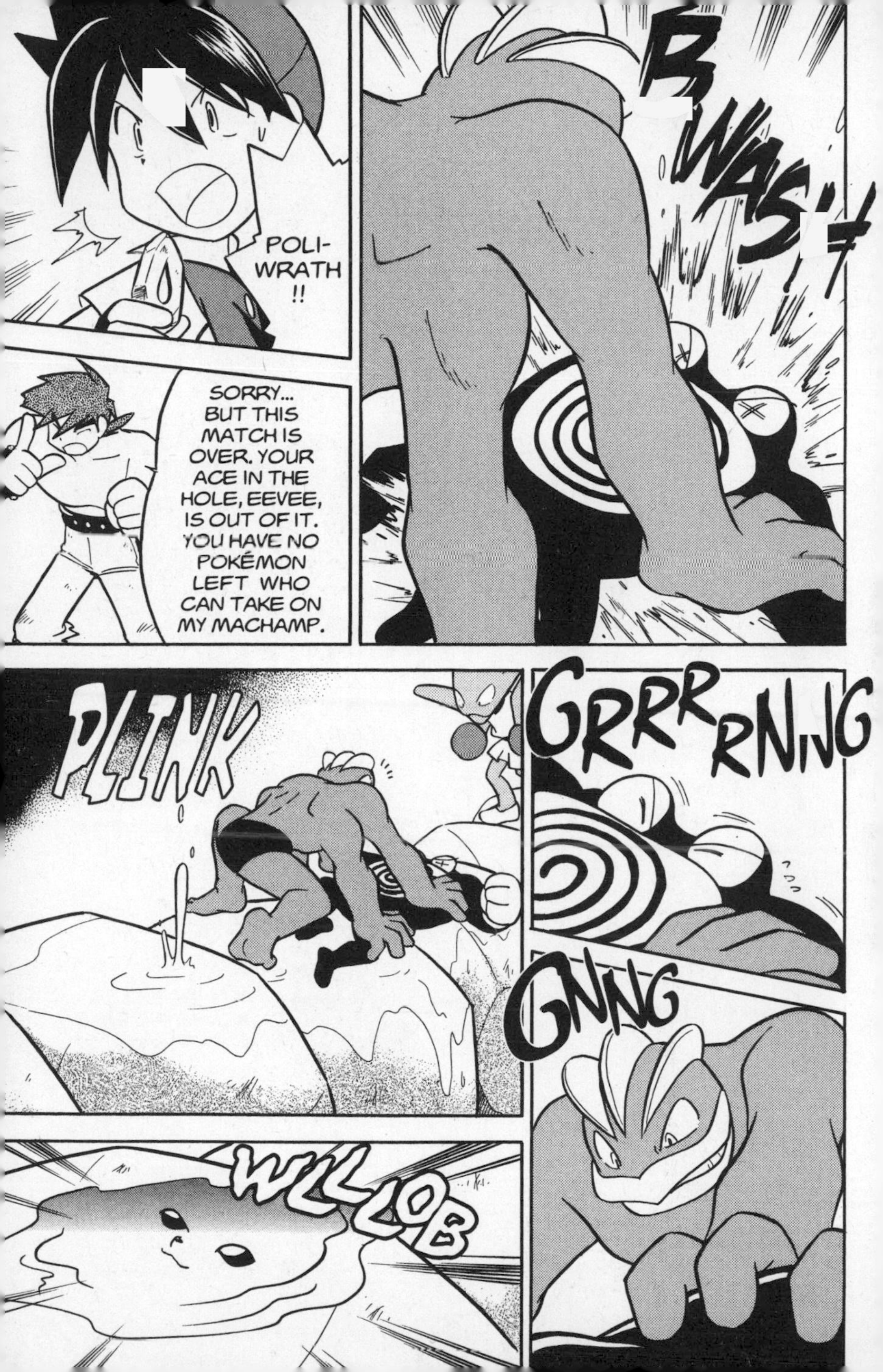
BWASH!!
POLI-WRATH!!
SORRY... BUT THIS MATCH IS OVER. YOUR ACE IN THE HOLE, EEVEE, IS OUT OF IT. YOU HAVE NO POKÉMON LEFT WHO CAN TAKE ON MY MACHAMP.
GRRRRNING
PLINK
GNNG
WLLOB

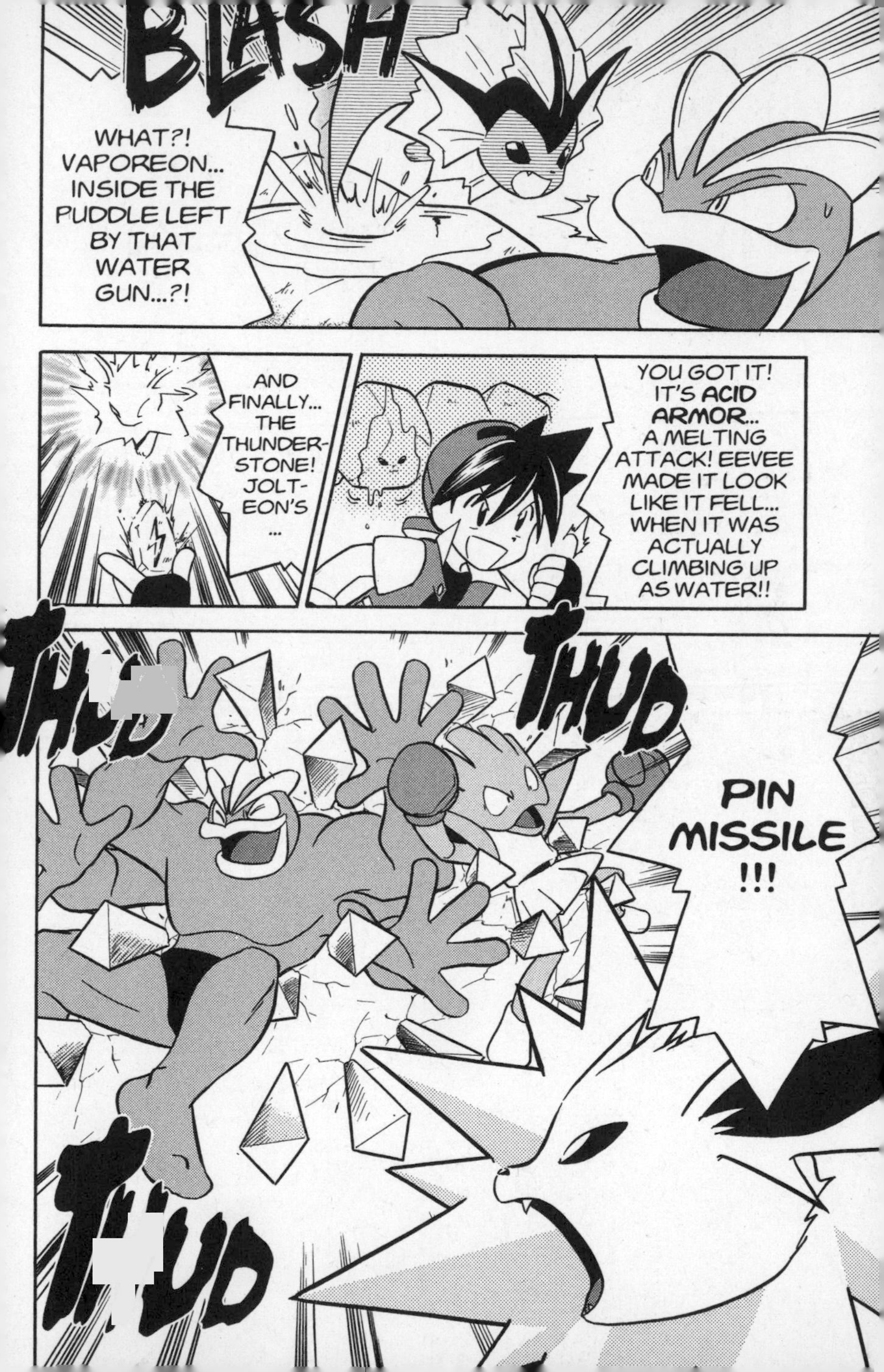
BLASH
WHAT?! VAPOREON... INSIDE THE PUDDLE LEFT BY THAT WATER GUN...?!
YOU GOT IT! IT'S **ACID ARMOR**... A MELTING ATTACK! EEVEE MADE IT LOOK LIKE IT FELL... WHEN IT WAS ACTUALLY CLIMBING UP AS WATER!!
AND FINALLY... THE THUNDER-STONE! JOLT-EON'S ...
THUD
PIN MISSILE !!!
THUD
THUD

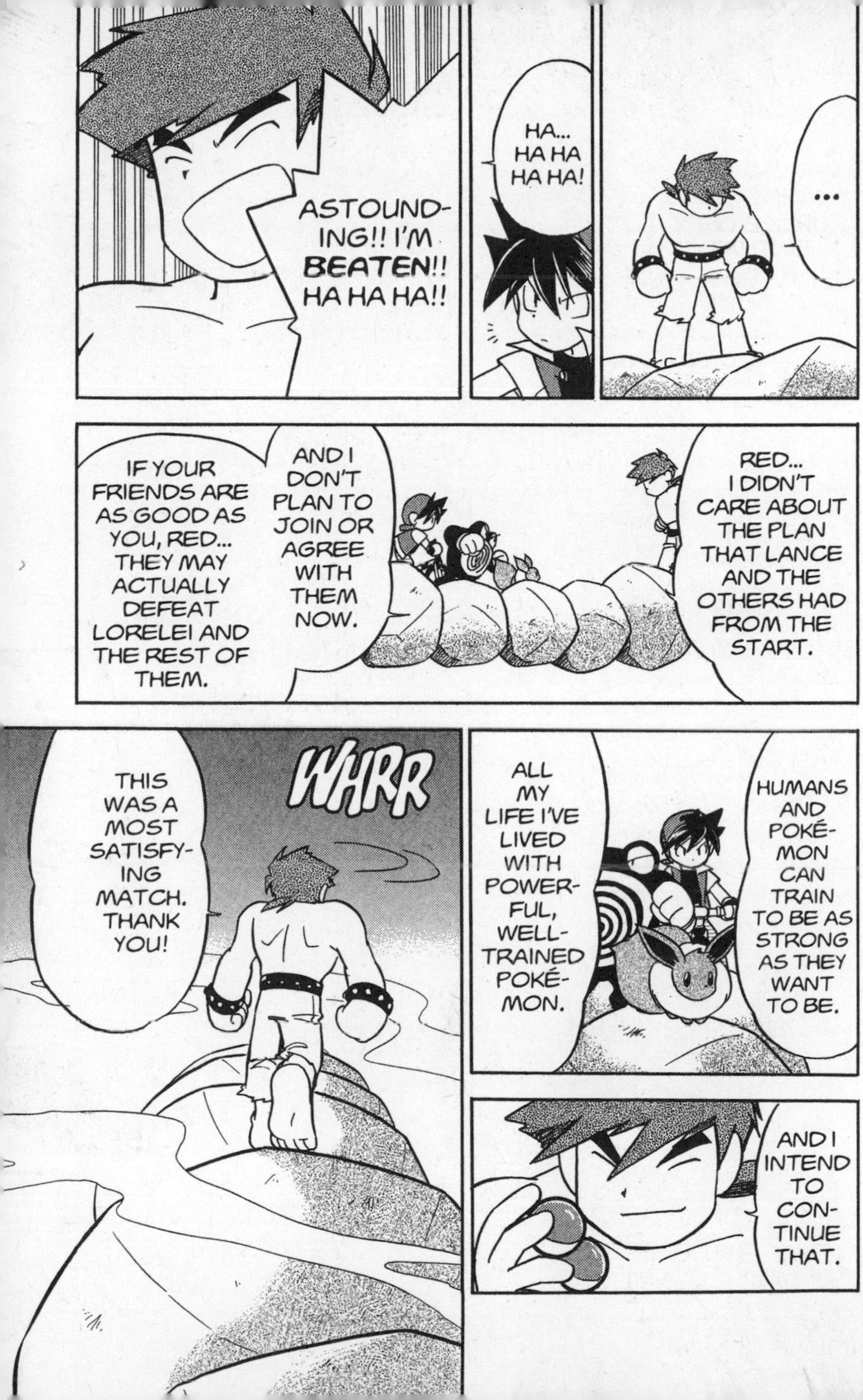
...
HA... HA HA HA HA!
ASTOUNDING!! I'M **BEATEN**!! HA HA HA!!
RED... I DIDN'T CARE ABOUT THE PLAN THAT LANCE AND THE OTHERS HAD FROM THE START.
AND I DON'T PLAN TO JOIN OR AGREE WITH THEM NOW.
IF YOUR FRIENDS ARE AS GOOD AS YOU, RED... THEY MAY ACTUALLY DEFEAT LORELEI AND THE REST OF THEM.
HUMANS AND POKÉMON CAN TRAIN TO BE AS STRONG AS THEY WANT TO BE.
ALL MY LIFE I'VE LIVED WITH POWERFUL, WELL-TRAINED POKÉMON.
AND I INTEND TO CONTINUE THAT.
WHRR
THIS WAS A MOST SATISFYING MATCH. THANK YOU!

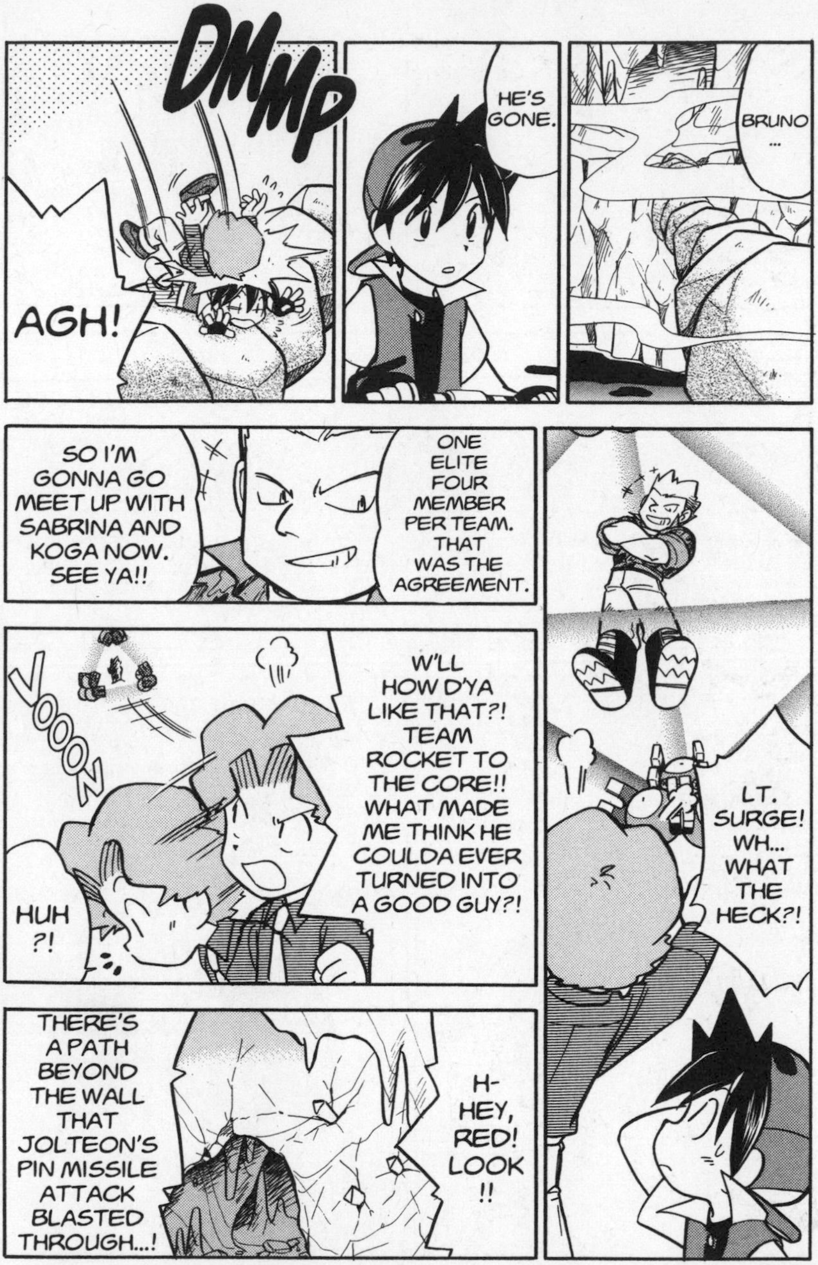
BRUNO ...
HE'S GONE.
DMMP
AGH!
LT. SURGE! WH... WHAT THE HECK?!
ONE ELITE FOUR MEMBER PER TEAM. THAT WAS THE AGREEMENT.
SO I'M GONNA GO MEET UP WITH SABRINA AND KOGA NOW. SEE YA!!
W'LL HOW D'YA LIKE THAT?! TEAM ROCKET TO THE CORE!! WHAT MADE ME THINK HE COULDA EVER TURNED INTO A GOOD GUY?!
VOOON
HUH ?!
H- HEY, RED! LOOK !!
THERE'S A PATH BEYOND THE WALL THAT JOLTEON'S PIN MISSILE ATTACK BLASTED THROUGH...!

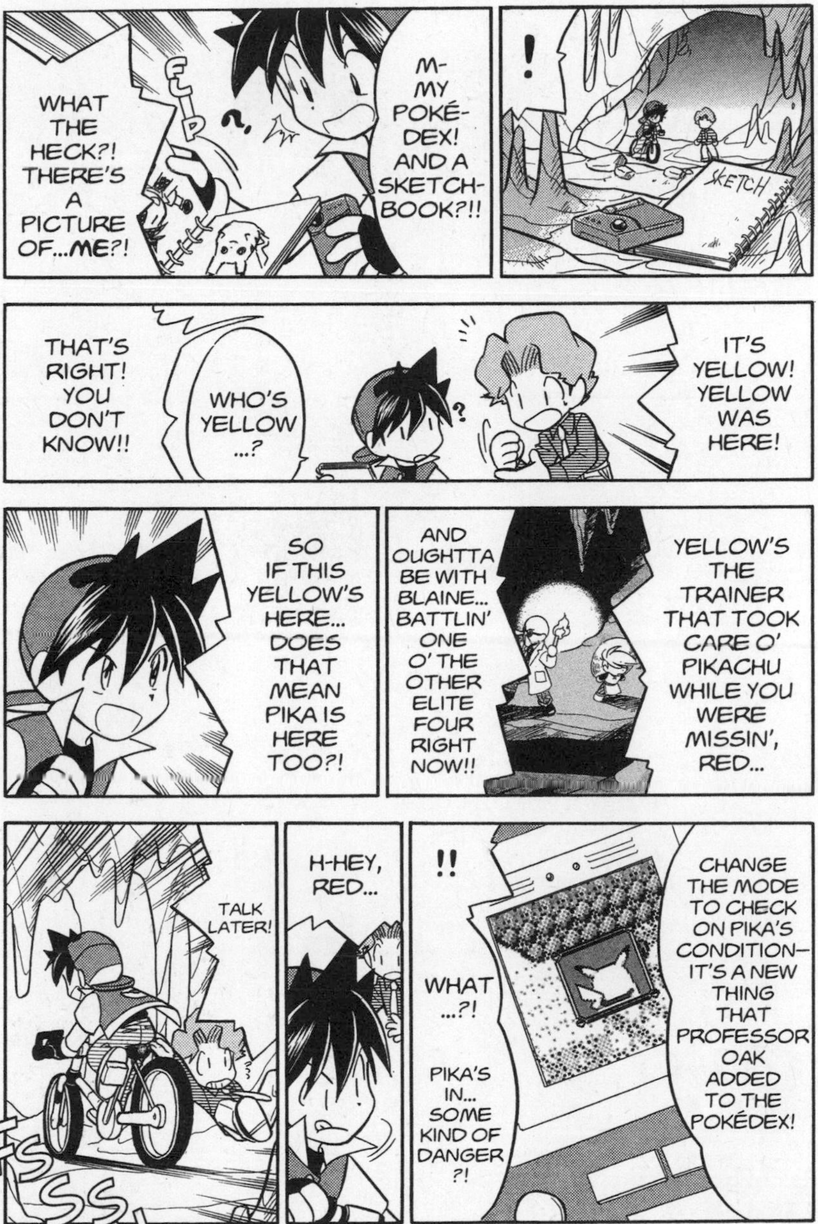
!
M-MY POKÉ-DEX! AND A SKETCH-BOOK?!!
FLIP
WHAT THE HECK?! THERE'S A PICTURE OF...ME?!
SKETCH
IT'S YELLOW! YELLOW WAS HERE!
WHO'S YELLOW...?
THAT'S RIGHT! YOU DON'T KNOW!!
YELLOW'S THE TRAINER THAT TOOK CARE O' PIKACHU WHILE YOU WERE MISSIN', RED...
AND OUGHTTA BE WITH BLAINE... BATTLIN' ONE O' THE OTHER ELITE FOUR RIGHT NOW!!
SO IF THIS YELLOW'S HERE... DOES THAT MEAN PIKA IS HERE TOO?!
CHANGE THE MODE TO CHECK ON PIKA'S CONDITION—IT'S A NEW THING THAT PROFESSOR OAK ADDED TO THE POKÉDEX!
!!
WHAT...?!
PIKA'S IN... SOME KIND OF DANGER?!
H-HEY, RED...
TALK LATER!
FSSSHH

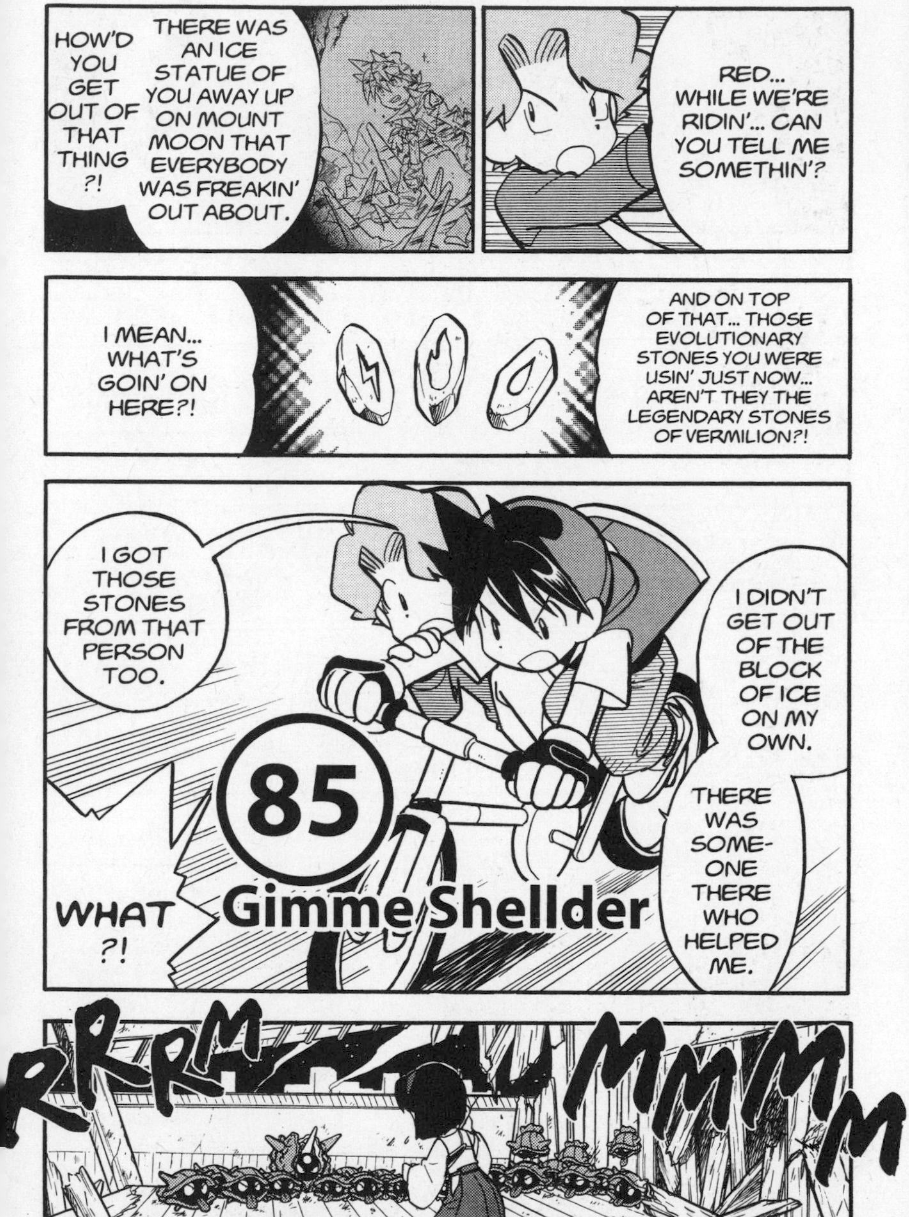
RED... WHILE WE'RE RIDIN'... CAN YOU TELL ME SOMETHIN'?
THERE WAS AN ICE STATUE OF YOU AWAY UP ON MOUNT MOON THAT EVERYBODY WAS FREAKIN' OUT ABOUT.
HOW'D YOU GET OUT OF THAT THING?!
AND ON TOP OF THAT... THOSE EVOLUTIONARY STONES YOU WERE USIN' JUST NOW... AREN'T THEY THE LEGENDARY STONES OF VERMILION?!
I MEAN... WHAT'S GOIN' ON HERE?!
I DIDN'T GET OUT OF THE BLOCK OF ICE ON MY OWN.
THERE WAS SOMEONE THERE WHO HELPED ME.
I GOT THOSE STONES FROM THAT PERSON TOO.
WHAT?!
85
Gimme Shellder
RRRM MMMMM

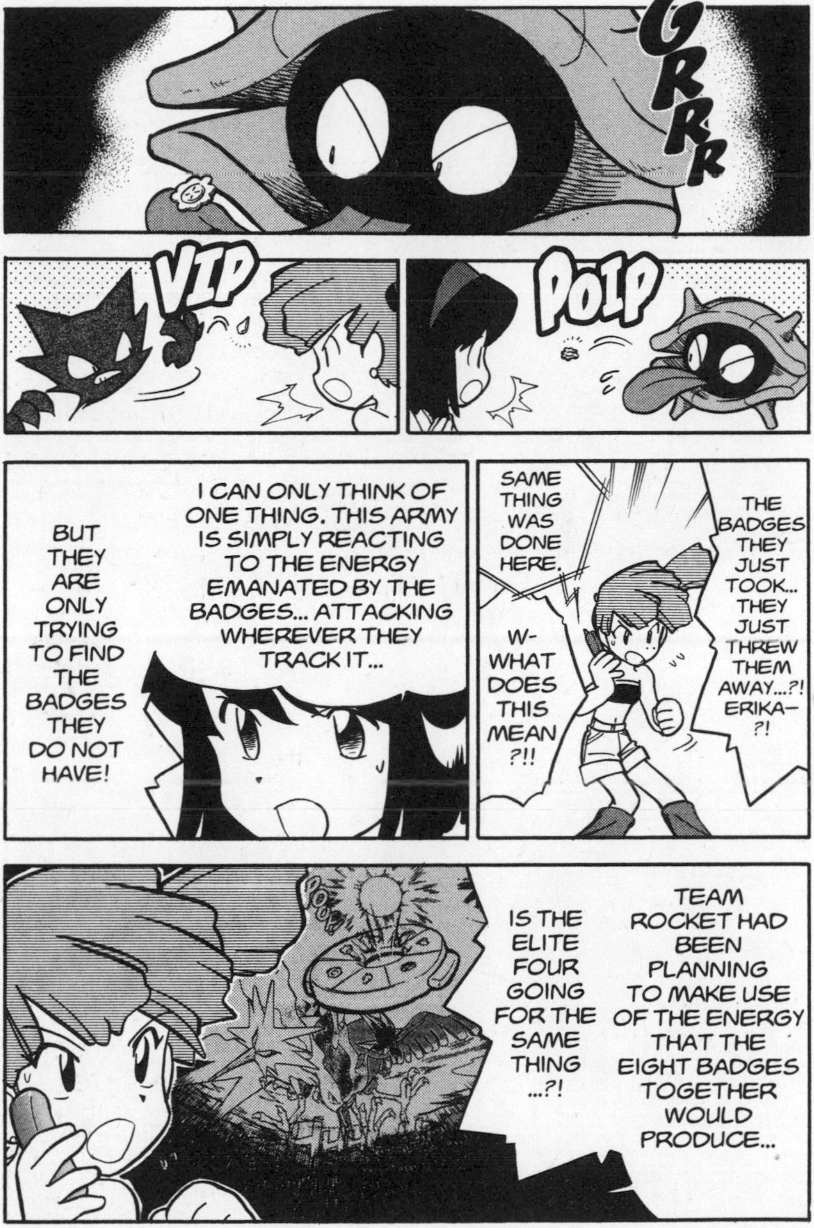
GRRR
POIP
VIP
THE BADGES THEY JUST TOOK... THEY JUST THREW THEM AWAY...?! ERIKA—?!
SAME THING WAS DONE HERE.
W-WHAT DOES THIS MEAN?!!
I CAN ONLY THINK OF ONE THING. THIS ARMY IS SIMPLY REACTING TO THE ENERGY EMANATED BY THE BADGES... ATTACKING WHEREVER THEY TRACK IT...
BUT THEY ARE ONLY TRYING TO FIND THE BADGES THEY DO NOT HAVE!
TEAM ROCKET HAD BEEN PLANNING TO MAKE USE OF THE ENERGY THAT THE EIGHT BADGES TOGETHER WOULD PRODUCE...
IS THE ELITE FOUR GOING FOR THE SAME THING...?!

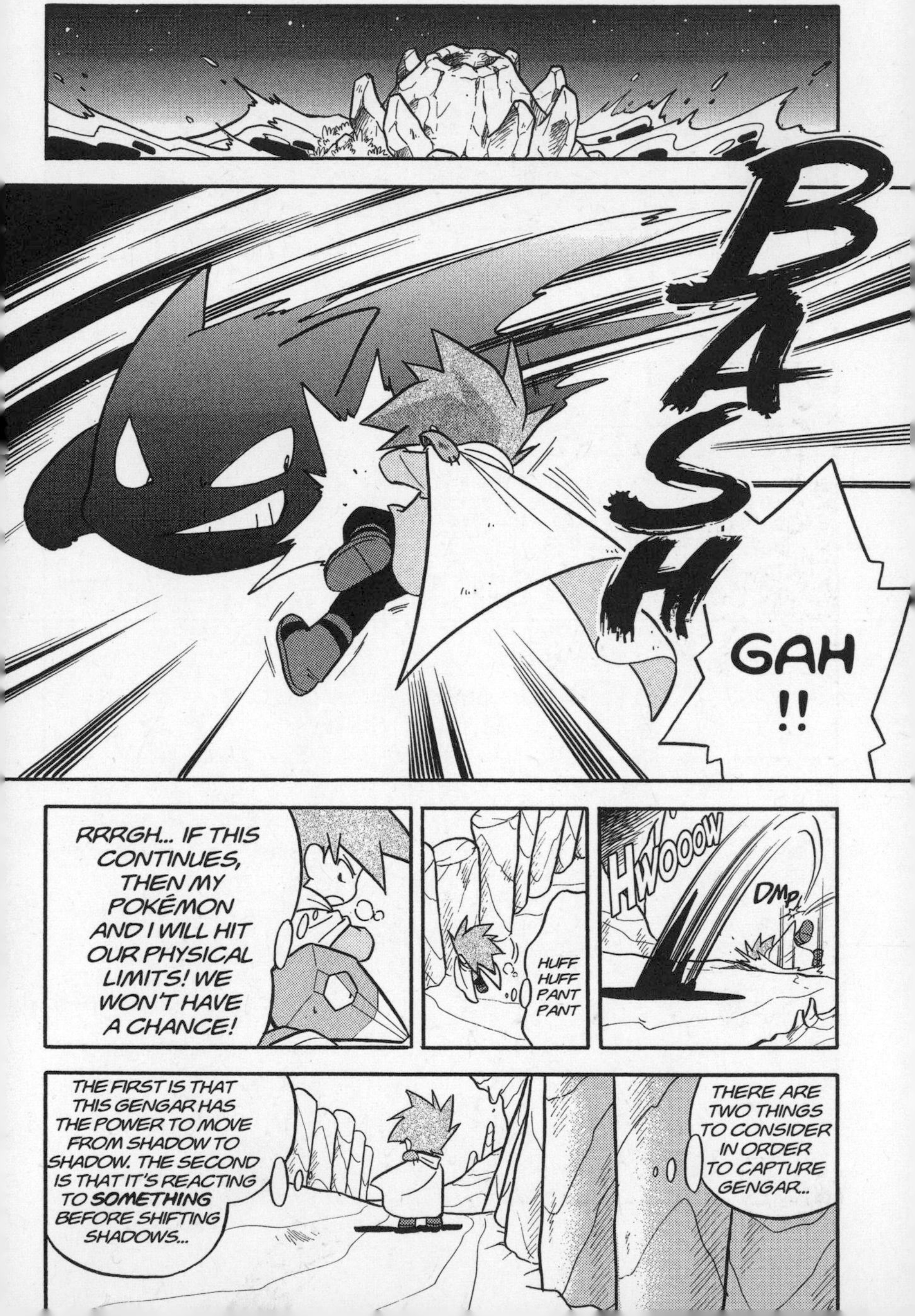
BASH
GAH!!
HWOOOW
DMP!
HUFF HUFF PANT PANT
RRRGH... IF THIS CONTINUES, THEN MY POKÉMON AND I WILL HIT OUR PHYSICAL LIMITS! WE WON'T HAVE A CHANCE!
THERE ARE TWO THINGS TO CONSIDER IN ORDER TO CAPTURE GENGAR...
THE FIRST IS THAT THIS GENGAR HAS THE POWER TO MOVE FROM SHADOW TO SHADOW. THE SECOND IS THAT IT'S REACTING TO **SOMETHING** BEFORE SHIFTING SHADOWS...

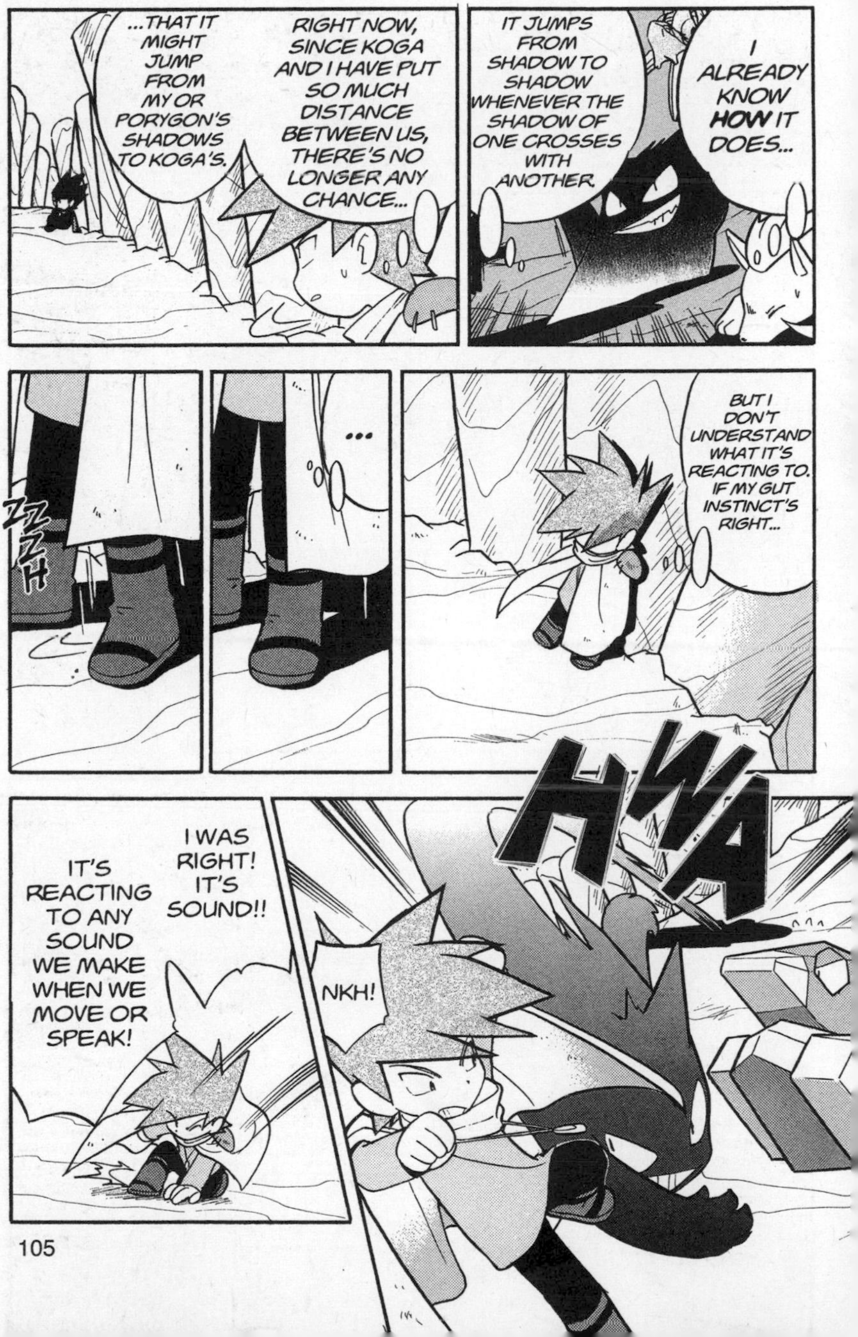
I ALREADY KNOW **HOW** IT DOES...
IT JUMPS FROM SHADOW TO SHADOW WHENEVER THE SHADOW OF ONE CROSSES WITH ANOTHER.
RIGHT NOW, SINCE KOGA AND I HAVE PUT SO MUCH DISTANCE BETWEEN US, THERE'S NO LONGER ANY CHANCE...
...THAT IT MIGHT JUMP FROM MY OR PORYGON'S SHADOWS TO KOGA'S.
BUT I DON'T UNDERSTAND WHAT IT'S REACTING TO. IF MY GUT INSTINCT'S RIGHT...
...
ZZZH
HWA
NKH!
I WAS RIGHT! IT'S SOUND!!
IT'S REACTING TO ANY SOUND WE MAKE WHEN WE MOVE OR SPEAK!

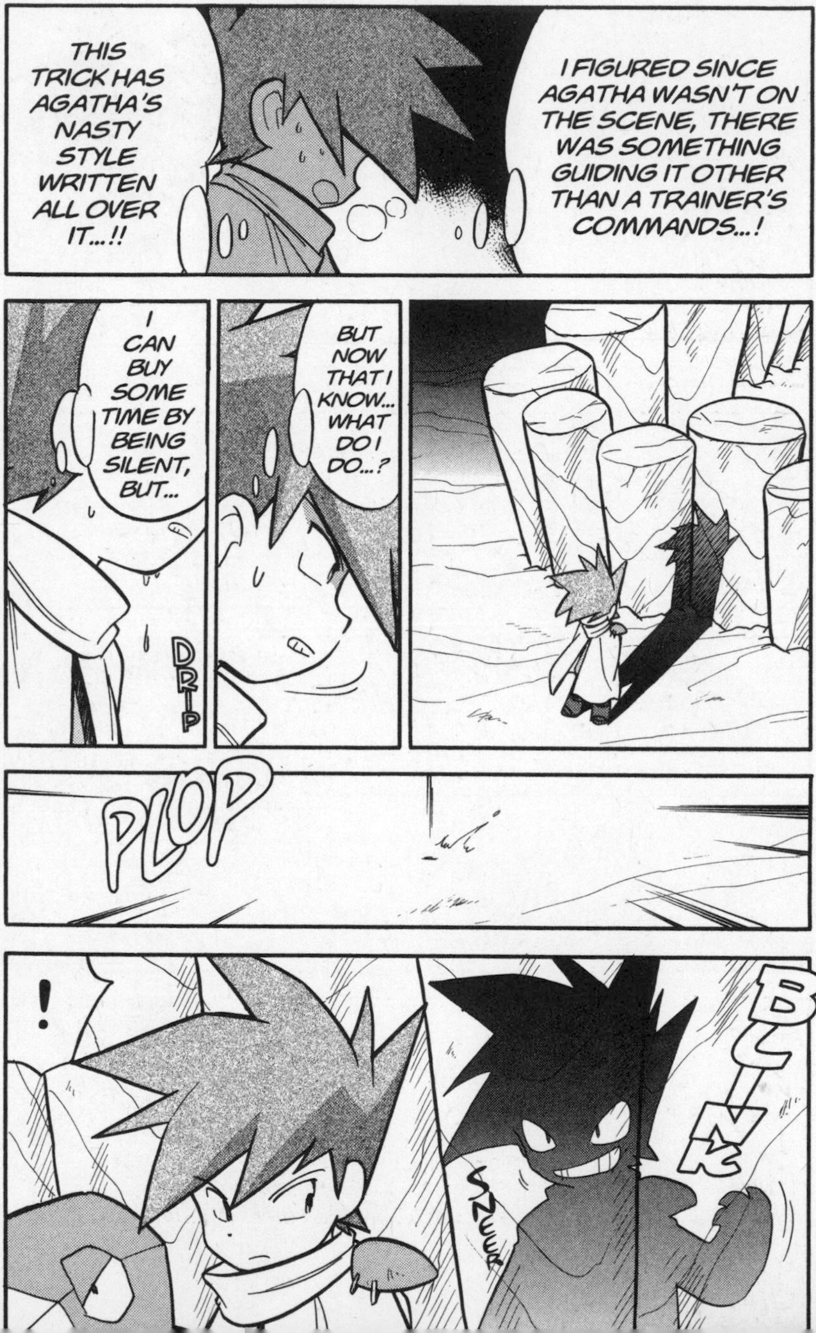
I FIGURED SINCE AGATHA WASN'T ON THE SCENE, THERE WAS SOMETHING GUIDING IT OTHER THAN A TRAINER'S COMMANDS...!
THIS TRICK HAS AGATHA'S NASTY STYLE WRITTEN ALL OVER IT...!!
BUT NOW THAT I KNOW... WHAT DO I DO...?
I CAN BUY SOME TIME BY BEING SILENT, BUT...
DRIP
PLOP
BLINK
SNEER
!

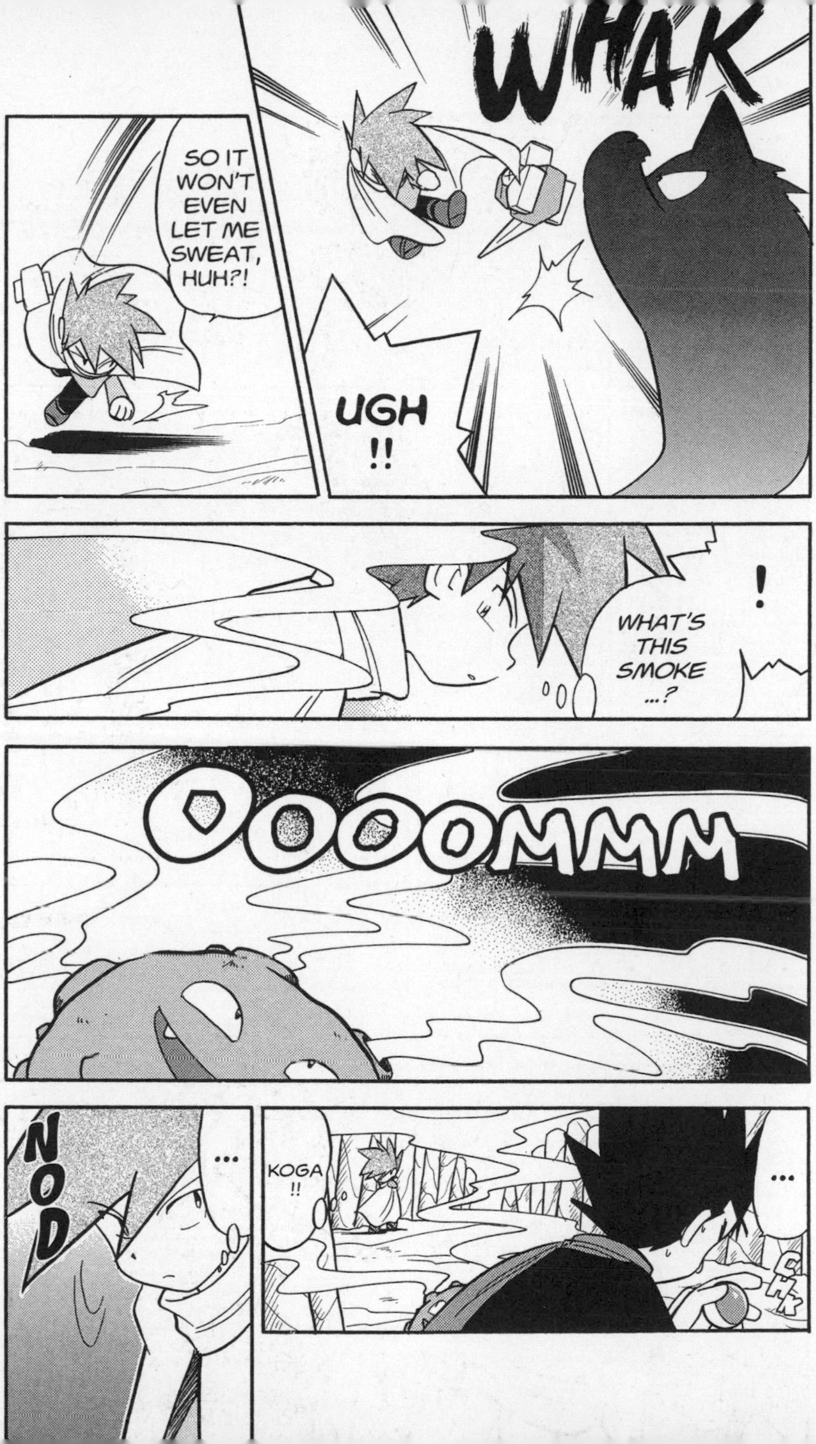
WHAK
UGH !!
SO IT WON'T EVEN LET ME SWEAT, HUH?!
!
WHAT'S THIS SMOKE ...?
OOOOMMMM
...
CHK
KOGA !!
...
NOD

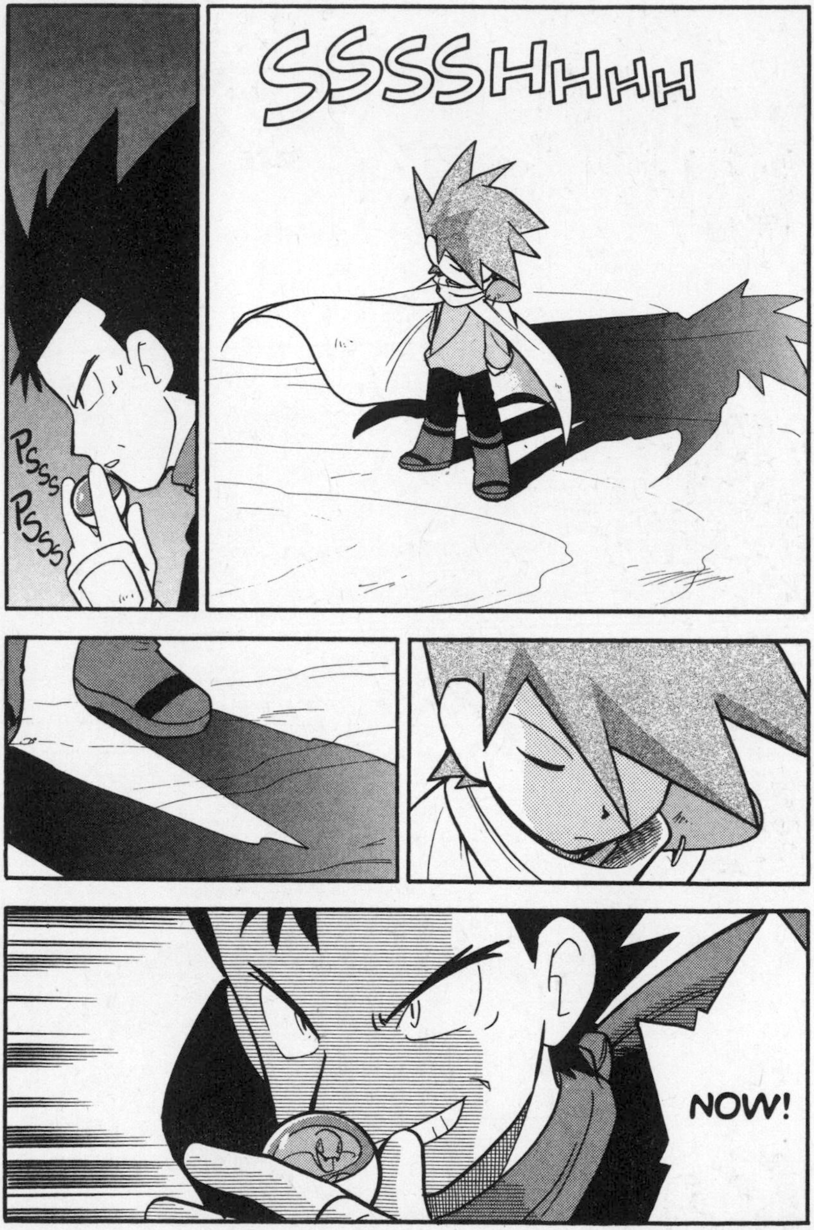
SSSSHHHH
PSSSS PSSSS
NOW!

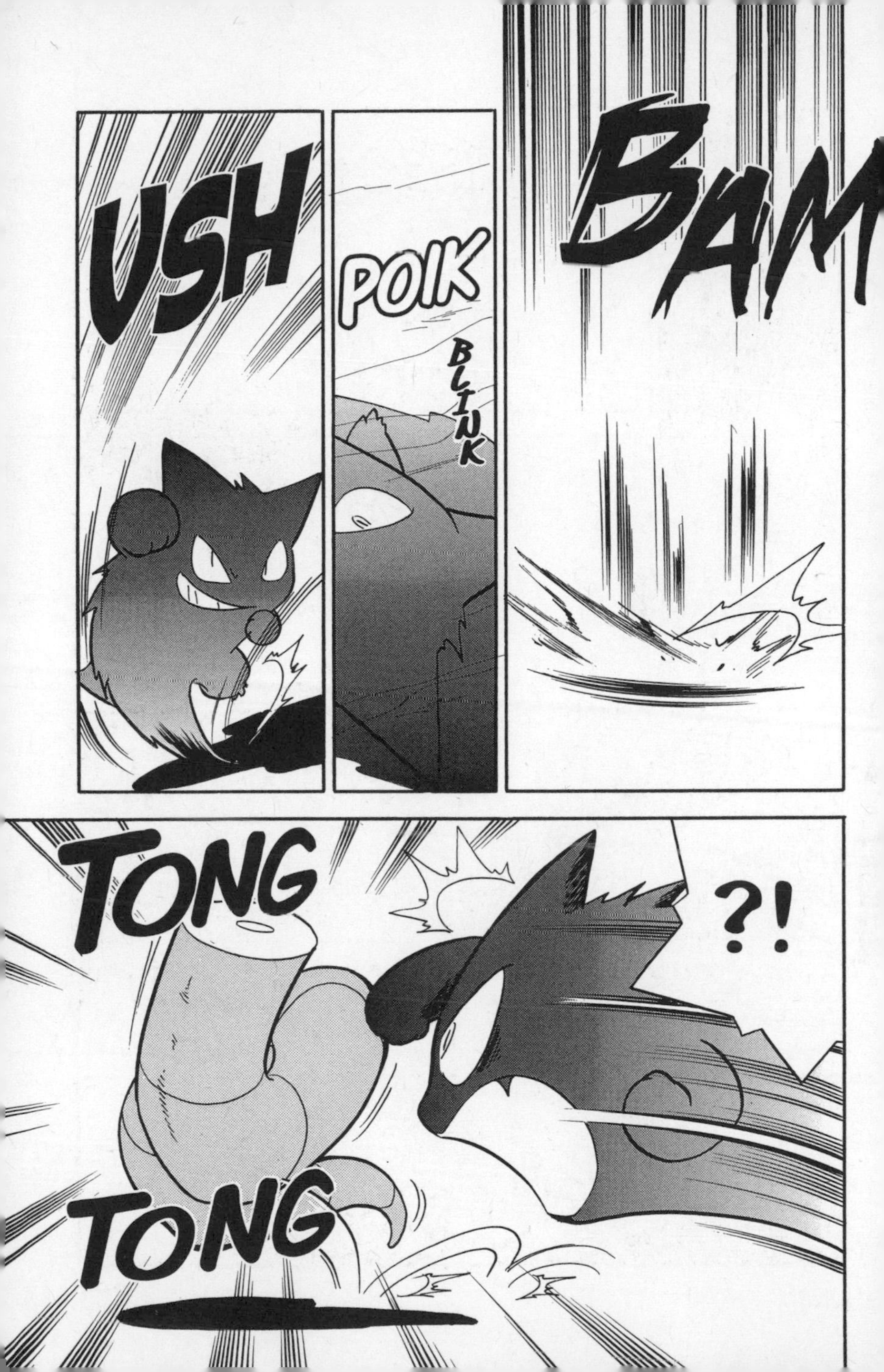

BAM
POIK
BLINK
USH
?!
TONG
TONG

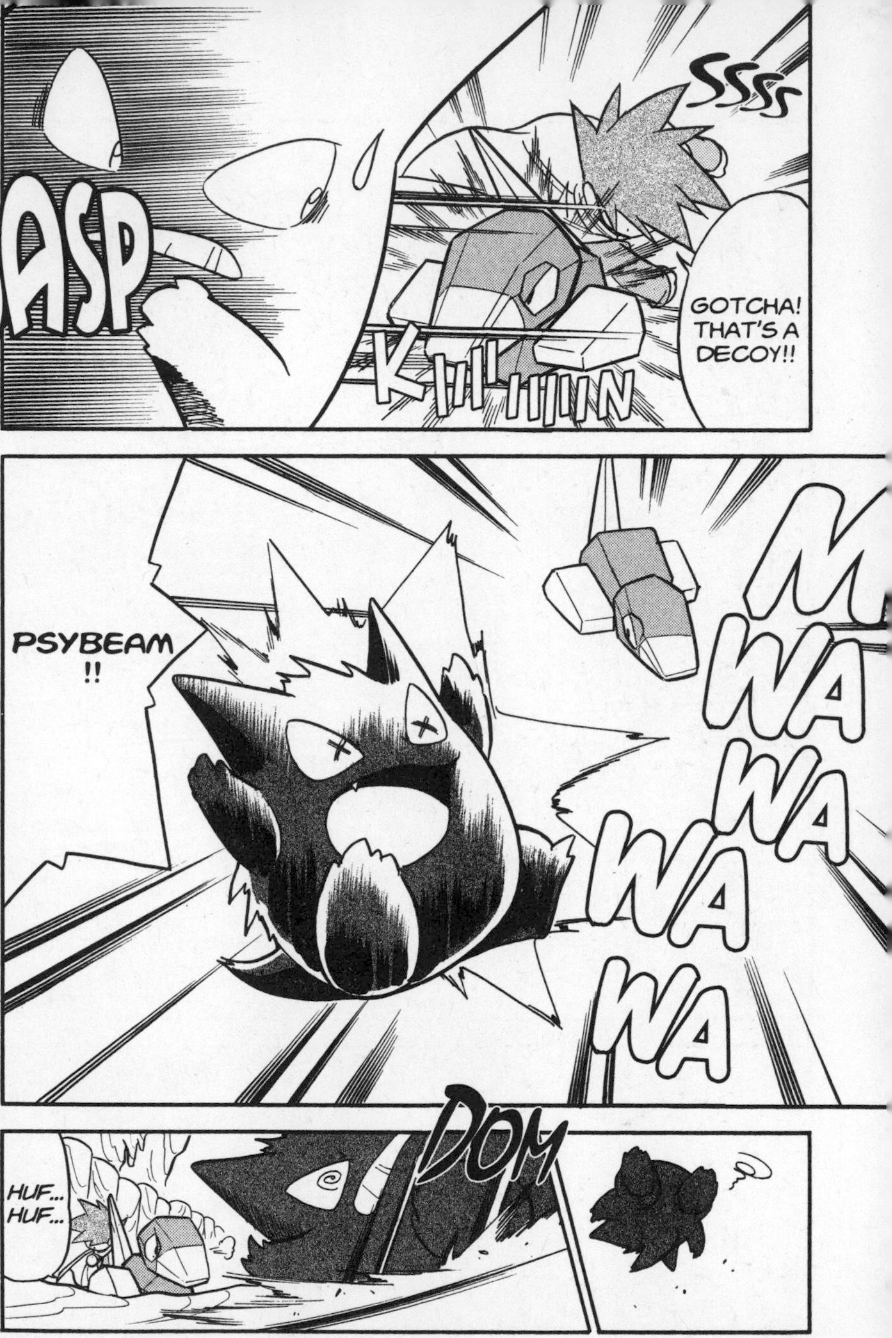
SSSS
GOTCHA! THAT'S A DECOY!!
KIIIIIIIN
GASP
MWA WA WA WA WA
PSYBEAM !!
DOM
HUF... HUF...

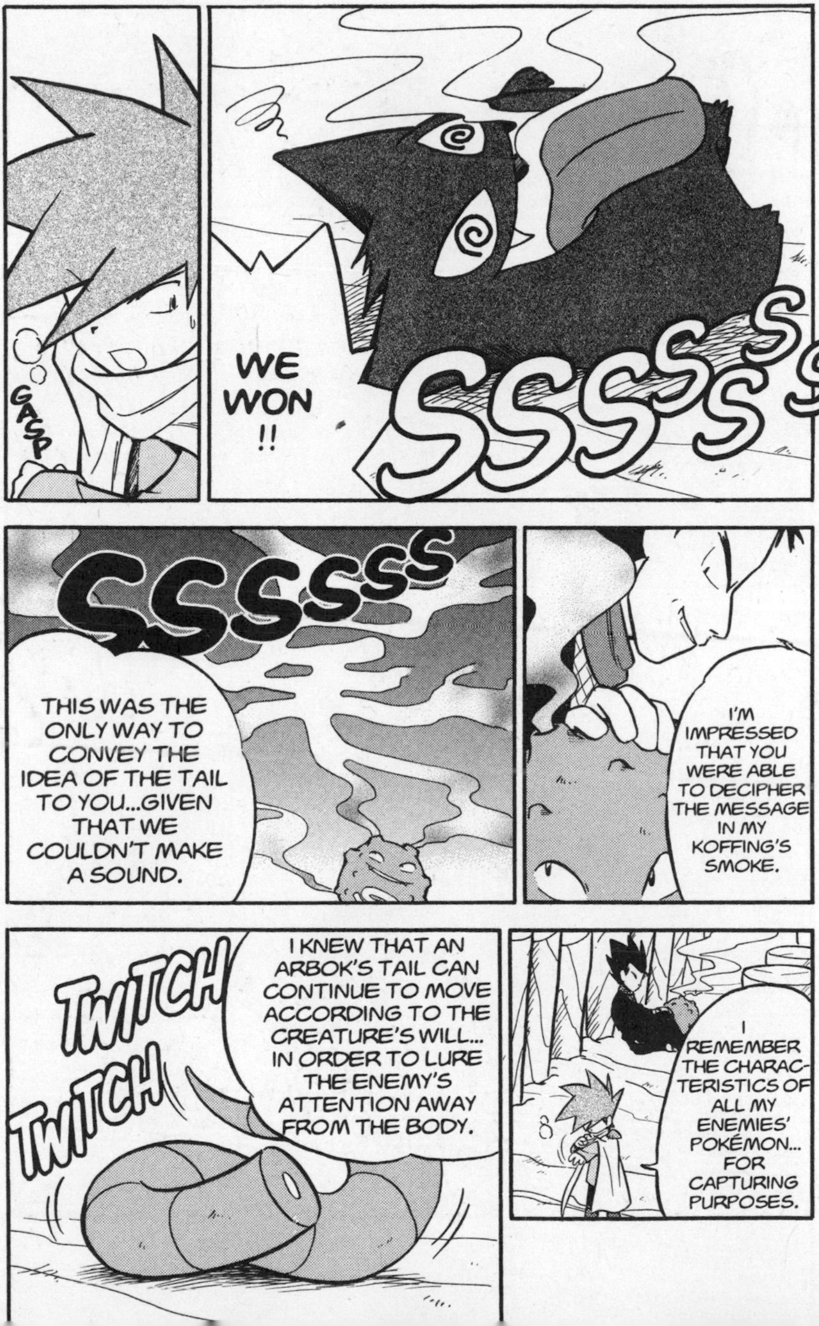
SSSSSSS
WE WON !!
GASP
I'M IMPRESSED THAT YOU WERE ABLE TO DECIPHER THE MESSAGE IN MY KOFFING'S SMOKE.
SSSSSS
THIS WAS THE ONLY WAY TO CONVEY THE IDEA OF THE TAIL TO YOU...GIVEN THAT WE COULDN'T MAKE A SOUND.
I REMEMBER THE CHARACTERISTICS OF ALL MY ENEMIES' POKÉMON... FOR CAPTURING PURPOSES.
I KNEW THAT AN ARBOK'S TAIL CAN CONTINUE TO MOVE ACCORDING TO THE CREATURE'S WILL... IN ORDER TO LURE THE ENEMY'S ATTENTION AWAY FROM THE BODY.
TWITCH
TWITCH

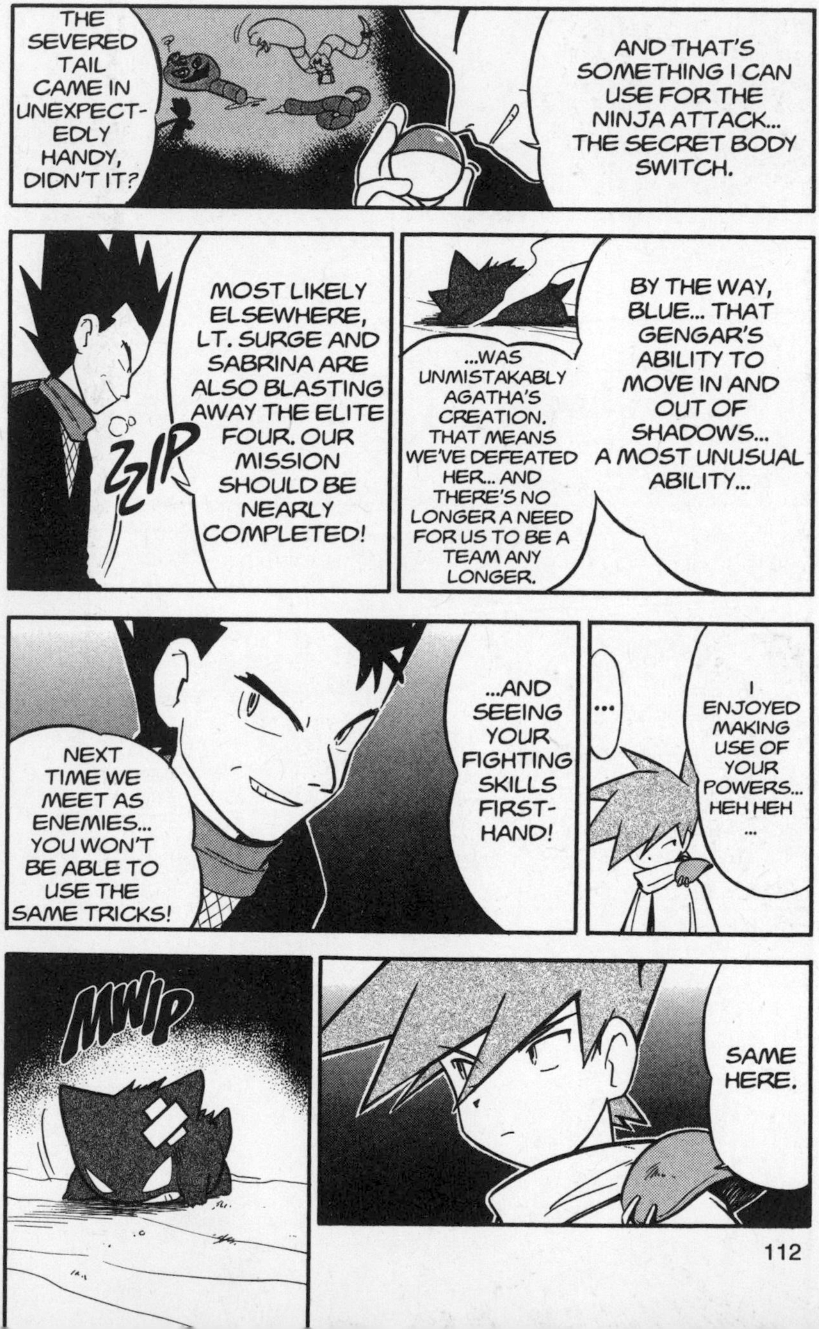
AND THAT'S SOMETHING I CAN USE FOR THE NINJA ATTACK... THE SECRET BODY SWITCH.
THE SEVERED TAIL CAME IN UNEXPECT-EDLY HANDY, DIDN'T IT?
BY THE WAY, BLUE... THAT GENGAR'S ABILITY TO MOVE IN AND OUT OF SHADOWS... A MOST UNUSUAL ABILITY...
...WAS UNMISTAKABLY AGATHA'S CREATION. THAT MEANS WE'VE DEFEATED HER... AND THERE'S NO LONGER A NEED FOR US TO BE A TEAM ANY LONGER.
MOST LIKELY ELSEWHERE, LT. SURGE AND SABRINA ARE ALSO BLASTING AWAY THE ELITE FOUR. OUR MISSION SHOULD BE NEARLY COMPLETED!
ZZIP
I ENJOYED MAKING USE OF YOUR POWERS... HEH HEH ...
...
...AND SEEING YOUR FIGHTING SKILLS FIRST-HAND!
NEXT TIME WE MEET AS ENEMIES... YOU WON'T BE ABLE TO USE THE SAME TRICKS!
SAME HERE.
MWIP

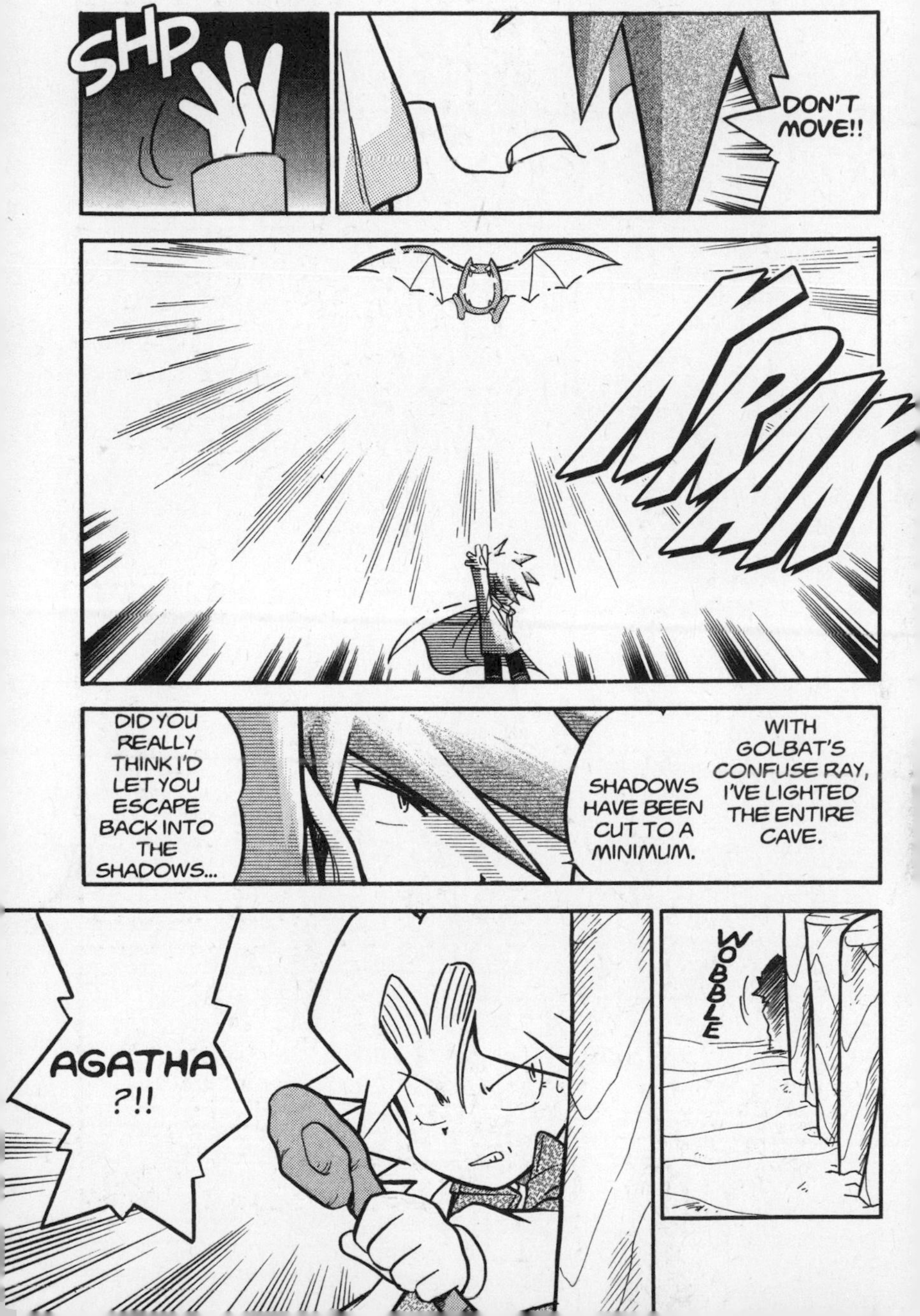
DON'T MOVE!!
SHP
WITH GOLBAT'S CONFUSE RAY, I'VE LIGHTED THE ENTIRE CAVE.
SHADOWS HAVE BEEN CUT TO A MINIMUM.
DID YOU REALLY THINK I'D LET YOU ESCAPE BACK INTO THE SHADOWS...
WOBBLE
AGATHA ?!!

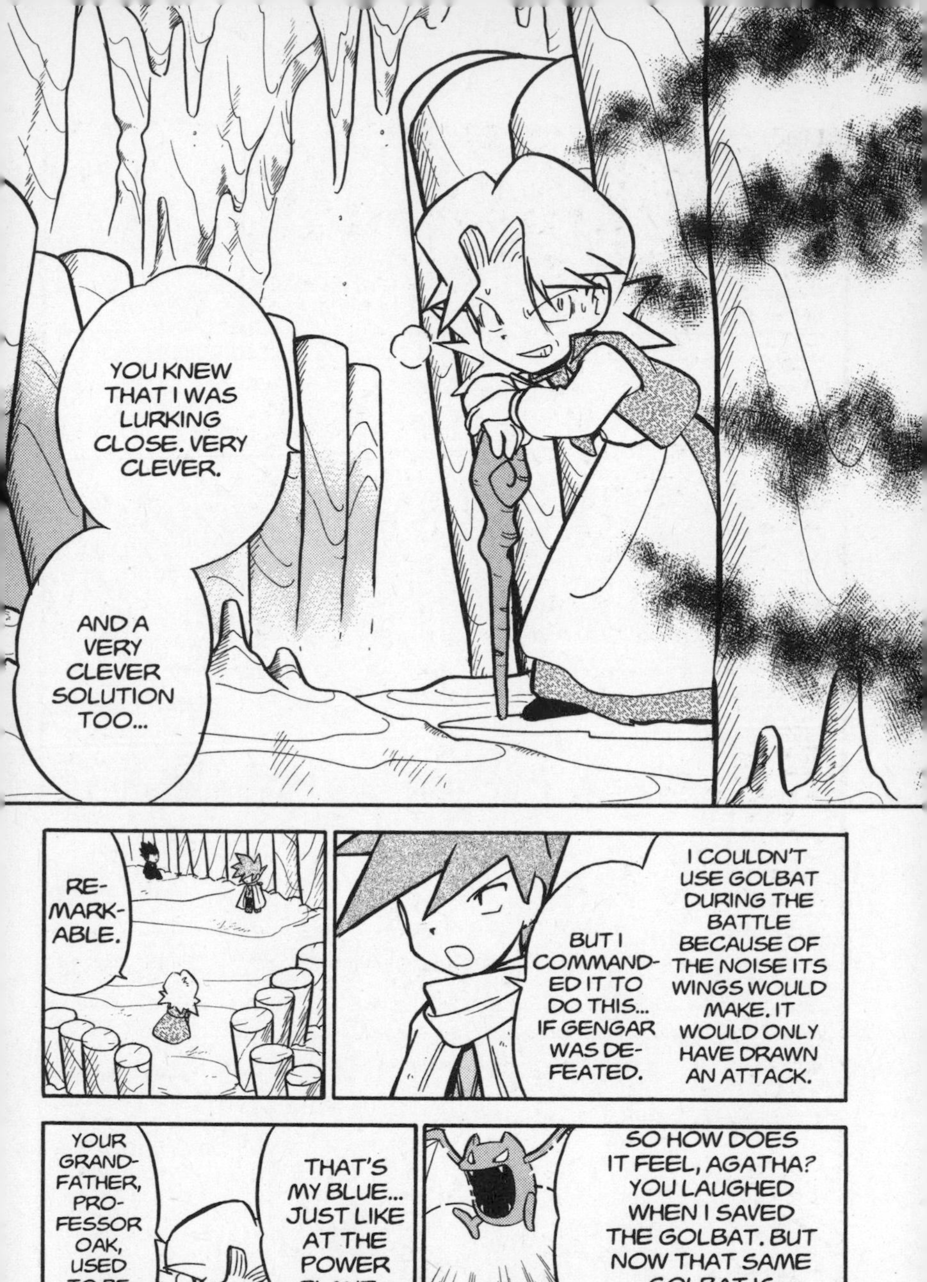
YOU KNEW THAT I WAS LURKING CLOSE. VERY CLEVER.
AND A VERY CLEVER SOLUTION TOO...
I COULDN'T USE GOLBAT DURING THE BATTLE BECAUSE OF THE NOISE ITS WINGS WOULD MAKE. IT WOULD ONLY HAVE DRAWN AN ATTACK.
BUT I COMMAND-ED IT TO DO THIS... IF GENGAR WAS DE-FEATED.
RE-MARK-ABLE.
SO HOW DOES IT FEEL, AGATHA? YOU LAUGHED WHEN I SAVED THE GOLBAT. BUT NOW THAT SAME GOLBAT IS PREVENTING YOU FROM MOVING.
THAT'S MY BLUE... JUST LIKE AT THE POWER PLANT...
YOUR GRAND-FATHER, PRO-FESSOR OAK, USED TO BE SUCH A MAN...

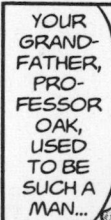

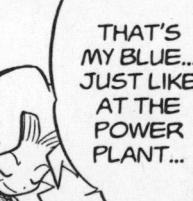

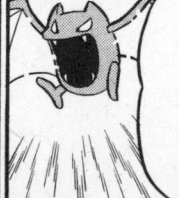

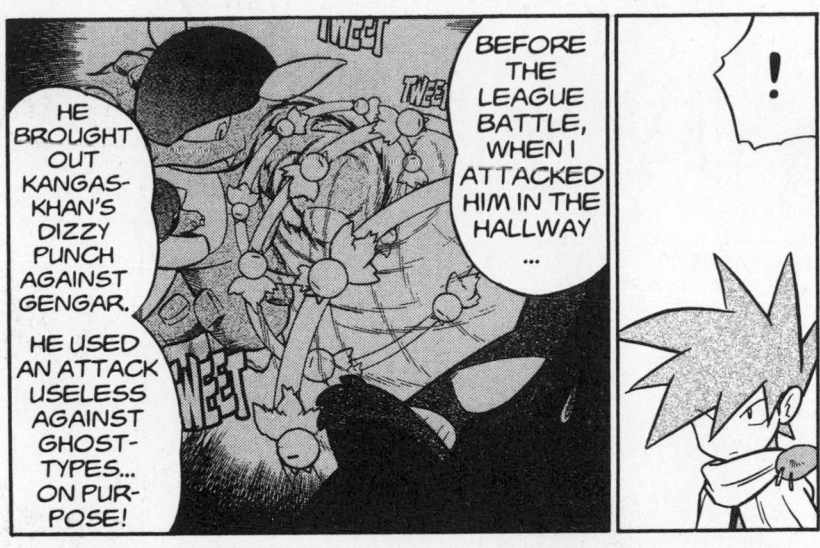

!
BEFORE THE LEAGUE BATTLE, WHEN I ATTACKED HIM IN THE HALLWAY ...
TWEET
TWEET
HE BROUGHT OUT KANGAS-KHAN'S DIZZY PUNCH AGAINST GENGAR.
HE USED AN ATTACK USELESS AGAINST GHOST-TYPES... ON PUR-POSE!
TWEET
I SHOULDN'T HAVE LET IT GET TO ME, BUT... WELL... I'M SUCH A SOFTY... HEH HEH HEH...
...
HE WAS GOOD...AND BRAVE...AND STRONG, THEN! HE ISN'T EVEN A SHADOW OF HIMSELF ANYMORE! MAKING SILLY LITTLE TOYS LIKE THE POKÉDEX! FEH!
OH, BY THE WAY, BLUE. BY LIGHTING THE PLACE FROM ABOVE... AREN'T YOU OVERLOOKING SOMETHING VERY IMPOR-TANT?
THAT BEING ...? GASP

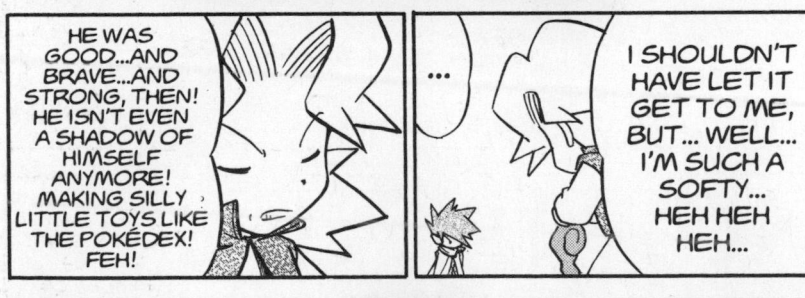

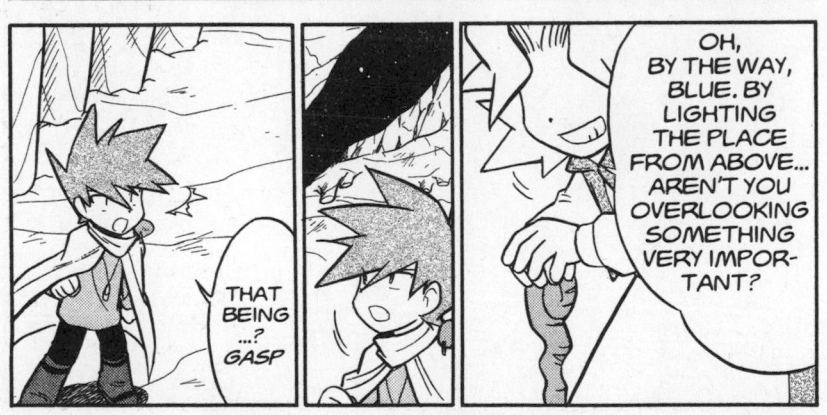

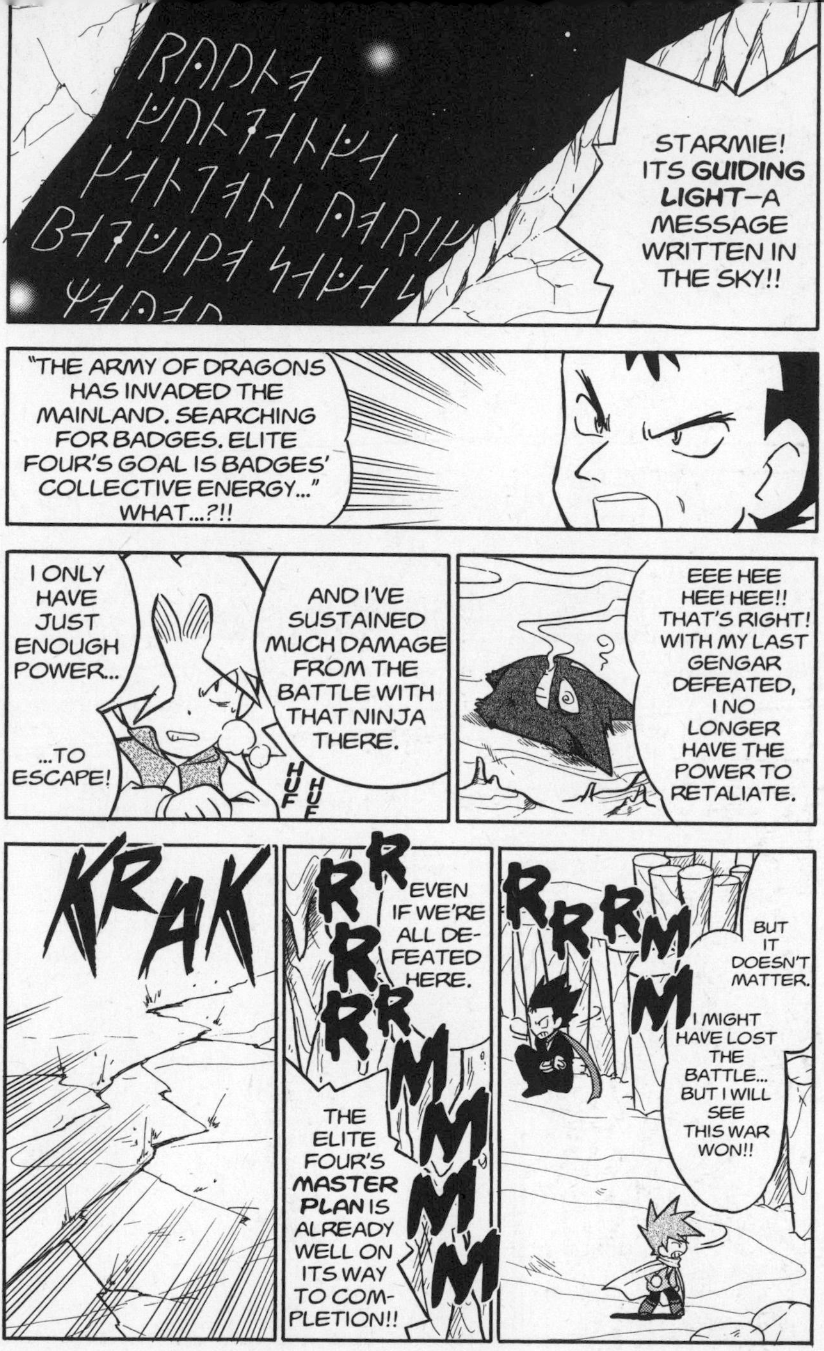
STARMIE! ITS **GUIDING LIGHT**—A MESSAGE WRITTEN IN THE SKY!!
"THE ARMY OF DRAGONS HAS INVADED THE MAINLAND. SEARCHING FOR BADGES. ELITE FOUR'S GOAL IS BADGES' COLLECTIVE ENERGY..." WHAT...?!!
EEE HEE HEE HEE!! THAT'S RIGHT! WITH MY LAST GENGAR DEFEATED, I NO LONGER HAVE THE POWER TO RETALIATE.
AND I'VE SUSTAINED MUCH DAMAGE FROM THE BATTLE WITH THAT NINJA THERE.
I ONLY HAVE JUST ENOUGH POWER...
...TO ESCAPE!
HUF HUF
RRRRMM
BUT IT DOESN'T MATTER.
I MIGHT HAVE LOST THE BATTLE... BUT I WILL SEE THIS WAR WON!!
RRRRRRMMMMM
EVEN IF WE'RE ALL DEFEATED HERE.
THE ELITE FOUR'S **MASTER PLAN** IS ALREADY WELL ON ITS WAY TO COMPLETION!!
KRAK

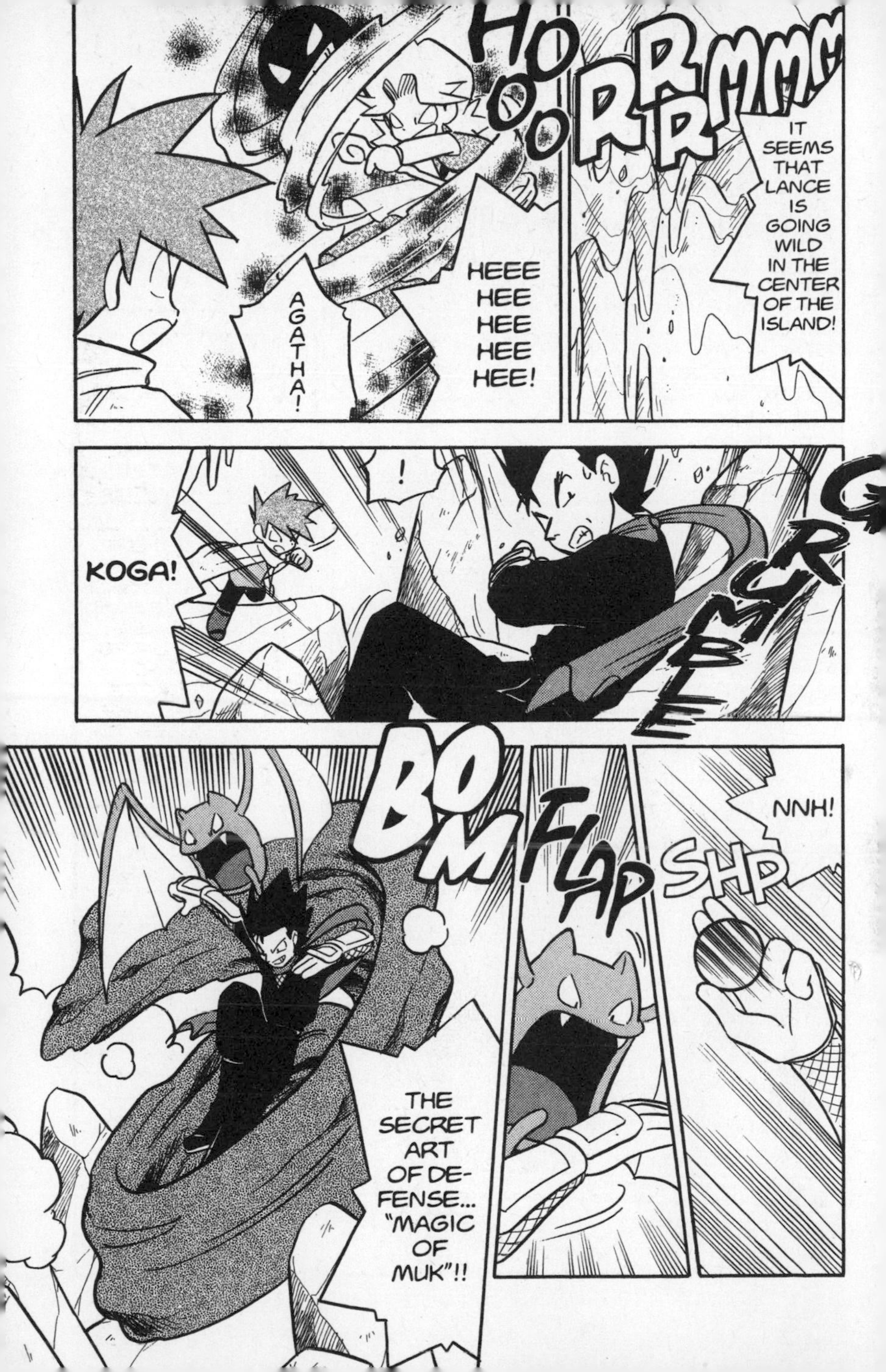
HOOORRRMMM
IT SEEMS THAT LANCE IS GOING WILD IN THE CENTER OF THE ISLAND!
HEEEE HEE HEE HEE HEE!
AGATHA!
GRUMBLE
!
KOGA!
NNH!
SHP
FLAP
BOM
THE SECRET ART OF DE-FENSE... "MAGIC OF MUK"!!

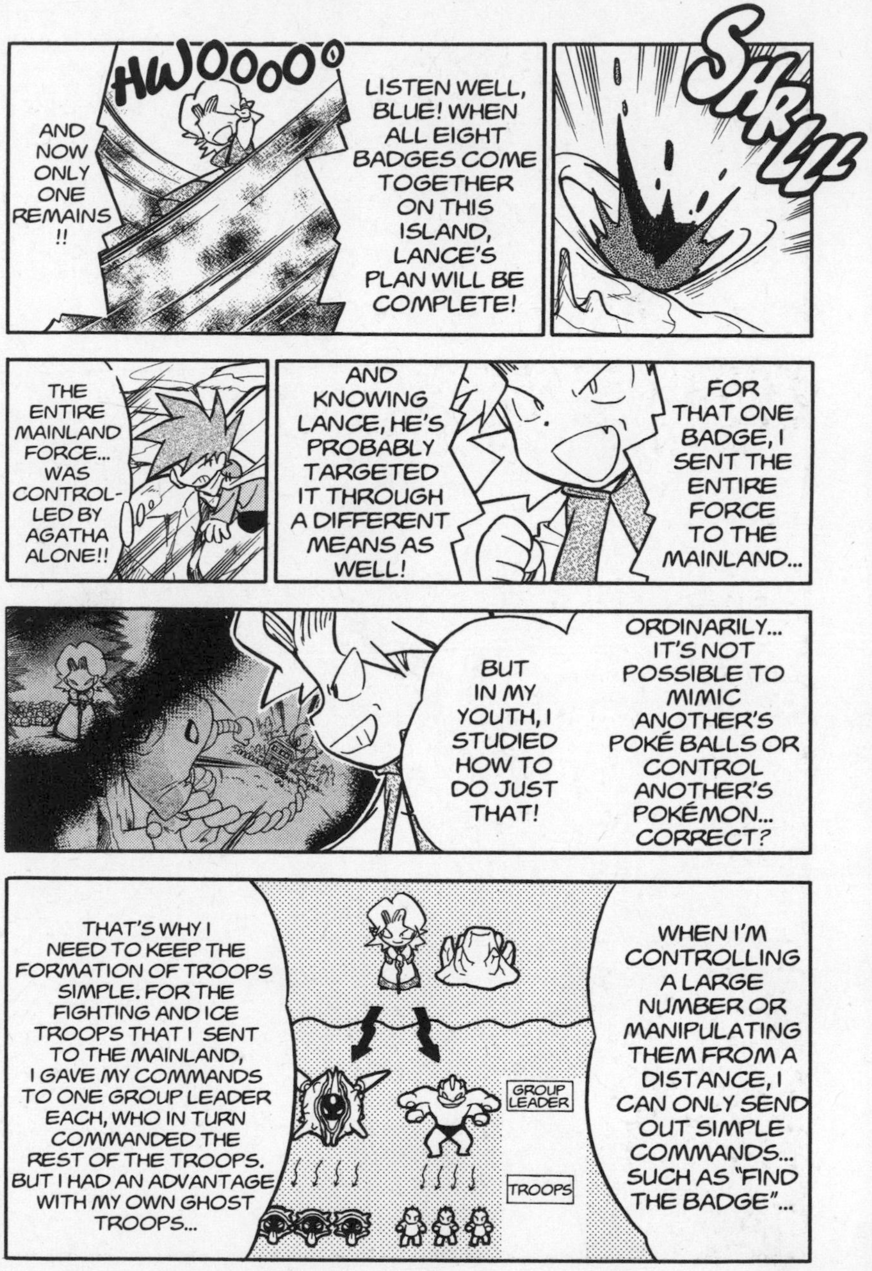
SHRIII
HWOOOOO
LISTEN WELL, BLUE! WHEN ALL EIGHT BADGES COME TOGETHER ON THIS ISLAND, LANCE'S PLAN WILL BE COMPLETE!
AND NOW ONLY ONE REMAINS!!
FOR THAT ONE BADGE, I SENT THE ENTIRE FORCE TO THE MAINLAND...
AND KNOWING LANCE, HE'S PROBABLY TARGETED IT THROUGH A DIFFERENT MEANS AS WELL!
THE ENTIRE MAINLAND FORCE... WAS CONTROL-LED BY AGATHA ALONE!!
ORDINARILY... IT'S NOT POSSIBLE TO MIMIC ANOTHER'S POKÉ BALLS OR CONTROL ANOTHER'S POKÉMON... CORRECT?
BUT IN MY YOUTH, I STUDIED HOW TO DO JUST THAT!
WHEN I'M CONTROLLING A LARGE NUMBER OR MANIPULATING THEM FROM A DISTANCE, I CAN ONLY SEND OUT SIMPLE COMMANDS... SUCH AS "FIND THE BADGE"...
THAT'S WHY I NEED TO KEEP THE FORMATION OF TROOPS SIMPLE. FOR THE FIGHTING AND ICE TROOPS THAT I SENT TO THE MAINLAND, I GAVE MY COMMANDS TO ONE GROUP LEADER EACH, WHO IN TURN COMMANDED THE REST OF THE TROOPS. BUT I HAD AN ADVANTAGE WITH MY OWN GHOST TROOPS...
GROUP LEADER
TROOPS

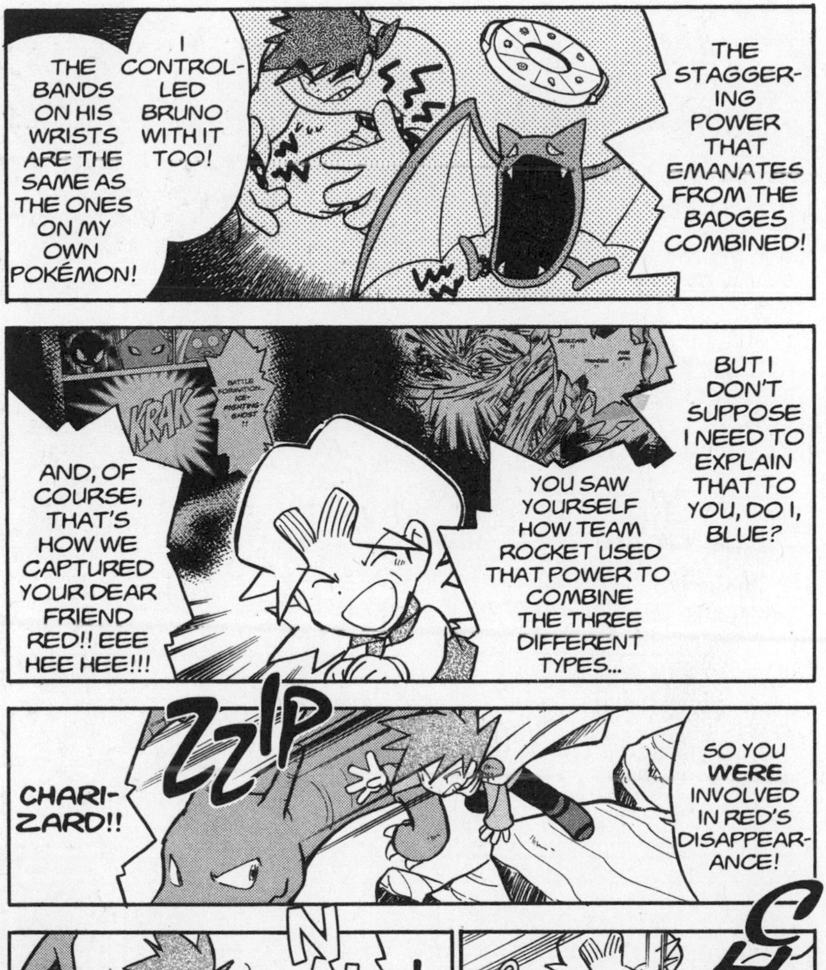

THE STAGGERING POWER THAT EMANATES FROM THE BADGES COMBINED!
I CONTROLLED BRUNO WITH IT TOO!
THE BANDS ON HIS WRISTS ARE THE SAME AS THE ONES ON MY OWN POKÉMON!
BUT I DON'T SUPPOSE I NEED TO EXPLAIN THAT TO YOU, DO I, BLUE?
YOU SAW YOURSELF HOW TEAM ROCKET USED THAT POWER TO COMBINE THE THREE DIFFERENT TYPES...
BATTLE FORMATION: ICE-FIGHTING-GHOST!!
KRAK
AND, OF COURSE, THAT'S HOW WE CAPTURED YOUR DEAR FRIEND RED!! EEE HEE HEE!!!
SO YOU **WERE** INVOLVED IN RED'S DISAPPEARANCE!
ZZIP
CHARIZARD!!
CHARRR
HOOOSH
!
NNN??

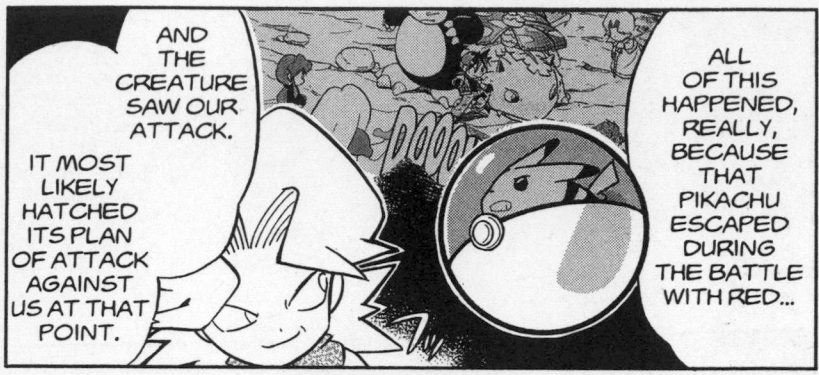

ALL OF THIS HAPPENED, REALLY, BECAUSE THAT PIKACHU ESCAPED DURING THE BATTLE WITH RED...
DOOOO
AND THE CREATURE SAW OUR ATTACK.
IT MOST LIKELY HATCHED ITS PLAN OF ATTACK AGAINST US AT THAT POINT.
IT MUST HAVE REALIZED THAT IT'S IMPOSSIBLE TO RETURN ENERGY ALREADY RELEASED. IN ORDER TO OVERCOME THAT ENERGY, ONE CAN ONLY COUNTER WITH AN EVEN STRONGER FORCE...!
NOT THAT IT COULD DO ANYTHING LIKE THAT...
UNLESS IT HAD SOMETHING MORE POWERFUL THAN **THUNDERBOLT**!
I'VE TALKED... TOO LONG.
HWOOOO
BUT THEN... YOU ARE OAK'S GRANDSON...
EEE HEE HEE HEE.
AGATHA!!
!
KRAK

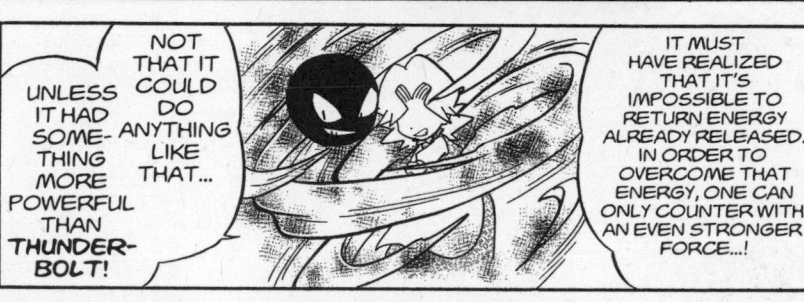

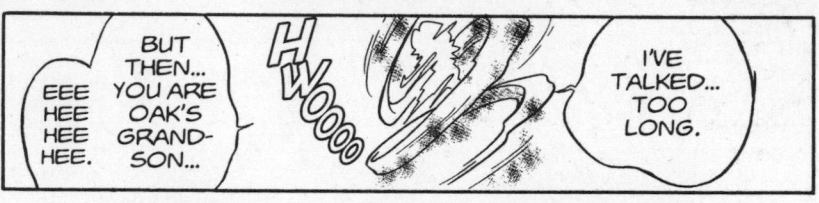

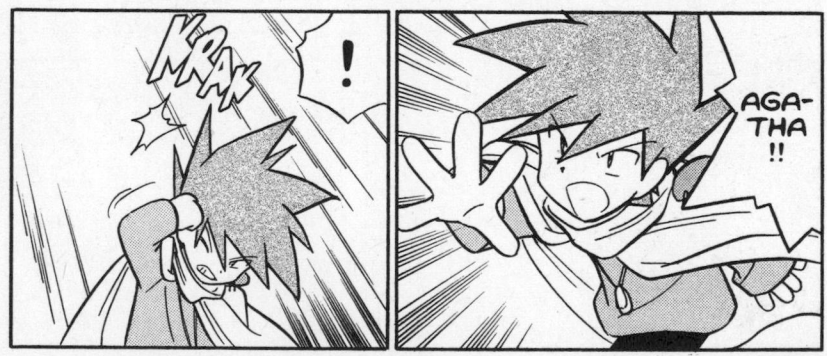

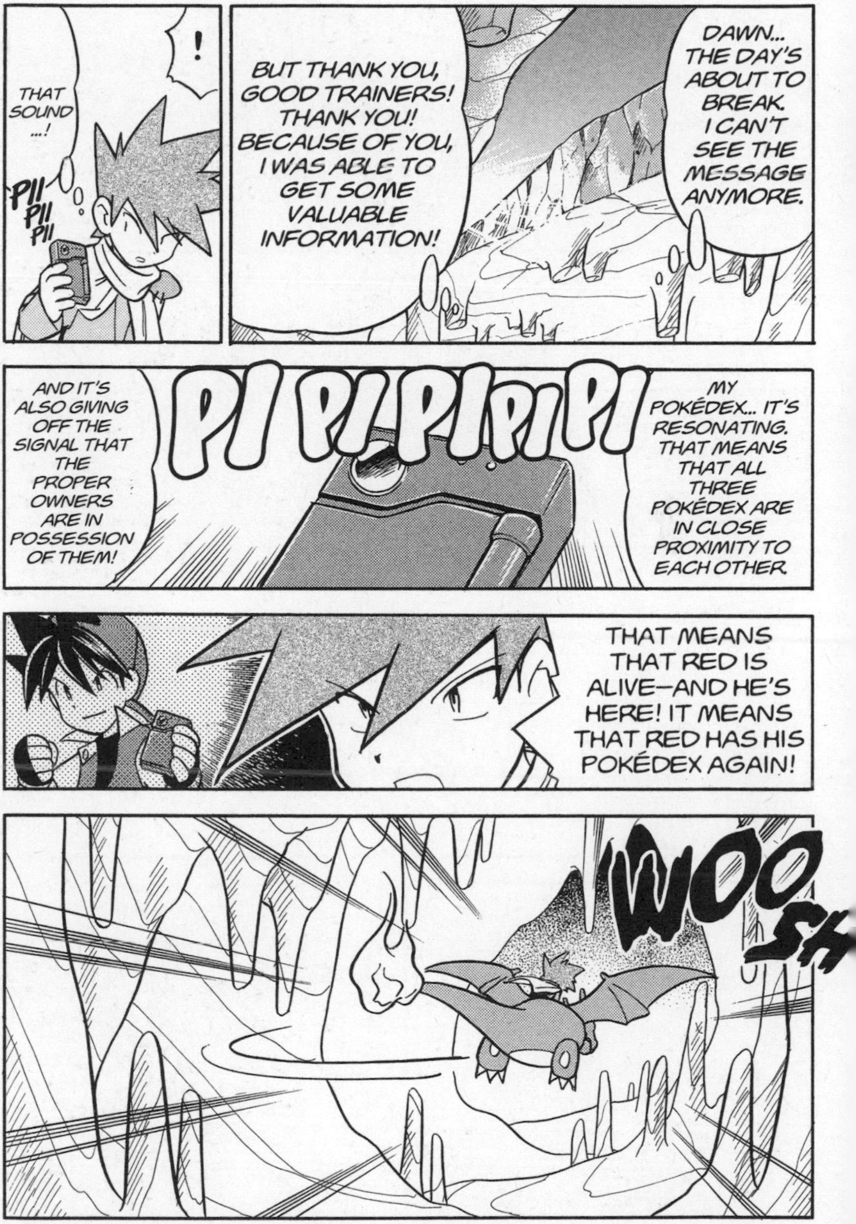
DAWN... THE DAY'S ABOUT TO BREAK. I CAN'T SEE THE MESSAGE ANYMORE.
BUT THANK YOU, GOOD TRAINERS! THANK YOU! BECAUSE OF YOU, I WAS ABLE TO GET SOME VALUABLE INFORMATION!
!
THAT SOUND ...!
PII PII PII
MY POKÉDEX... IT'S RESONATING. THAT MEANS THAT ALL THREE POKÉDEX ARE IN CLOSE PROXIMITY TO EACH OTHER.
PI PI PI PI PI
AND IT'S ALSO GIVING OFF THE SIGNAL THAT THE PROPER OWNERS ARE IN POSSESSION OF THEM!
THAT MEANS THAT RED IS ALIVE—AND HE'S HERE! IT MEANS THAT RED HAS HIS POKÉDEX AGAIN!
WOOSH

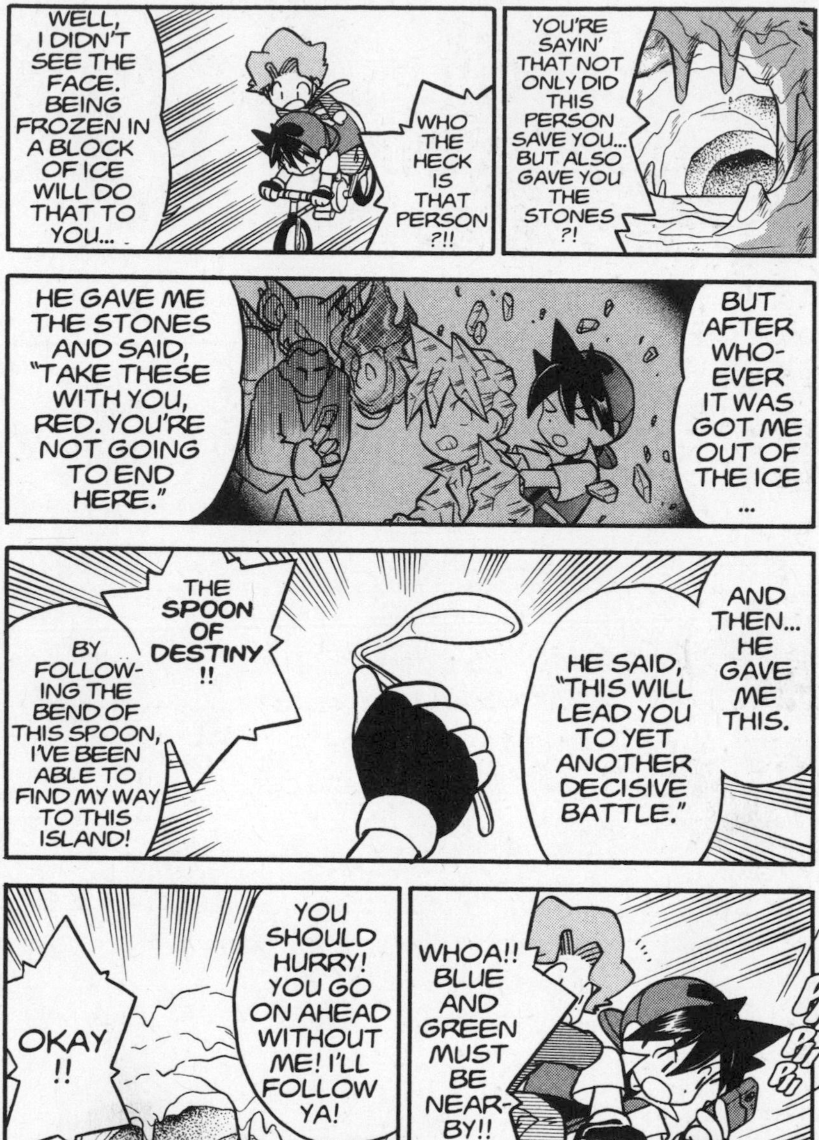
YOU'RE SAYIN' THAT NOT ONLY DID THIS PERSON SAVE YOU... BUT ALSO GAVE YOU THE STONES ?!
WHO THE HECK IS THAT PERSON ?!!
WELL, I DIDN'T SEE THE FACE. BEING FROZEN IN A BLOCK OF ICE WILL DO THAT TO YOU...
BUT AFTER WHO-EVER IT WAS GOT ME OUT OF THE ICE ...
HE GAVE ME THE STONES AND SAID, "TAKE THESE WITH YOU, RED. YOU'RE NOT GOING TO END HERE."
AND THEN... HE GAVE ME THIS.
HE SAID, "THIS WILL LEAD YOU TO YET ANOTHER DECISIVE BATTLE."
THE SPOON OF DESTINY !!
BY FOLLOW-ING THE BEND OF THIS SPOON, I'VE BEEN ABLE TO FIND MY WAY TO THIS ISLAND!
PI PI PI
WHOA!! BLUE AND GREEN MUST BE NEAR-BY!!
YOU SHOULD HURRY! YOU GO ON AHEAD WITHOUT ME! I'LL FOLLOW YA!
OKAY !!

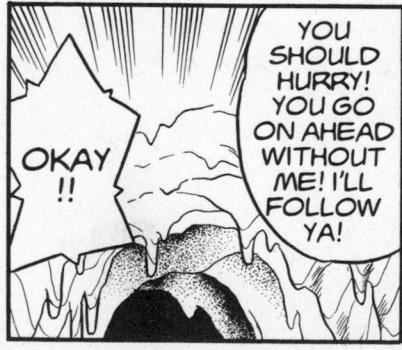

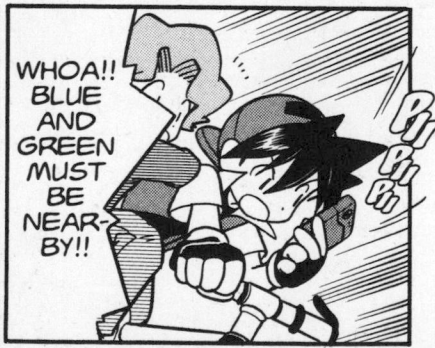

86 Double Dragonair

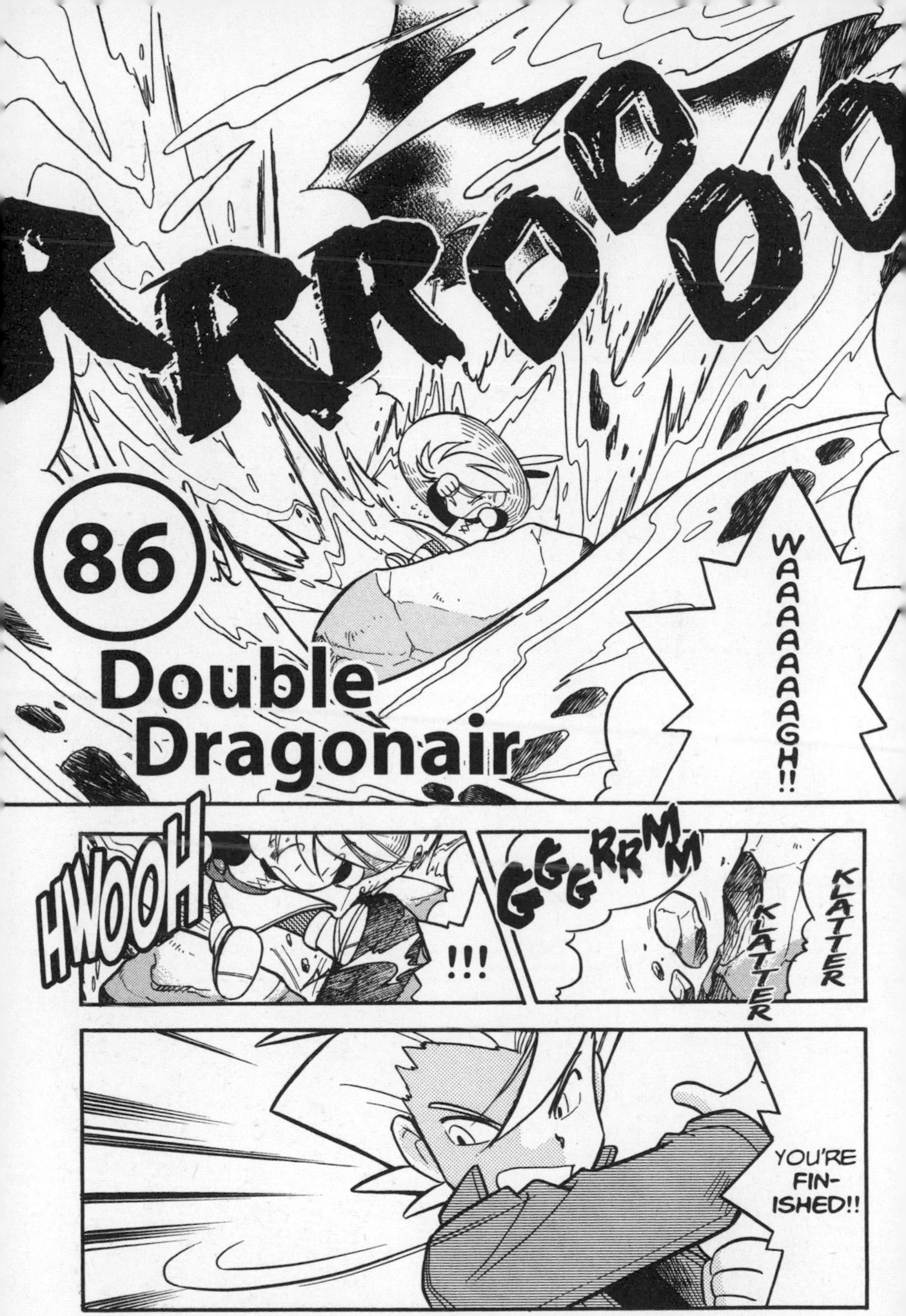
RRROOOOOO
WAAAAAAAAGH!!
GGGRRMM
KLATTER
KLATTER
HWOOH
!!!
YOU'RE FIN-ISHED!!

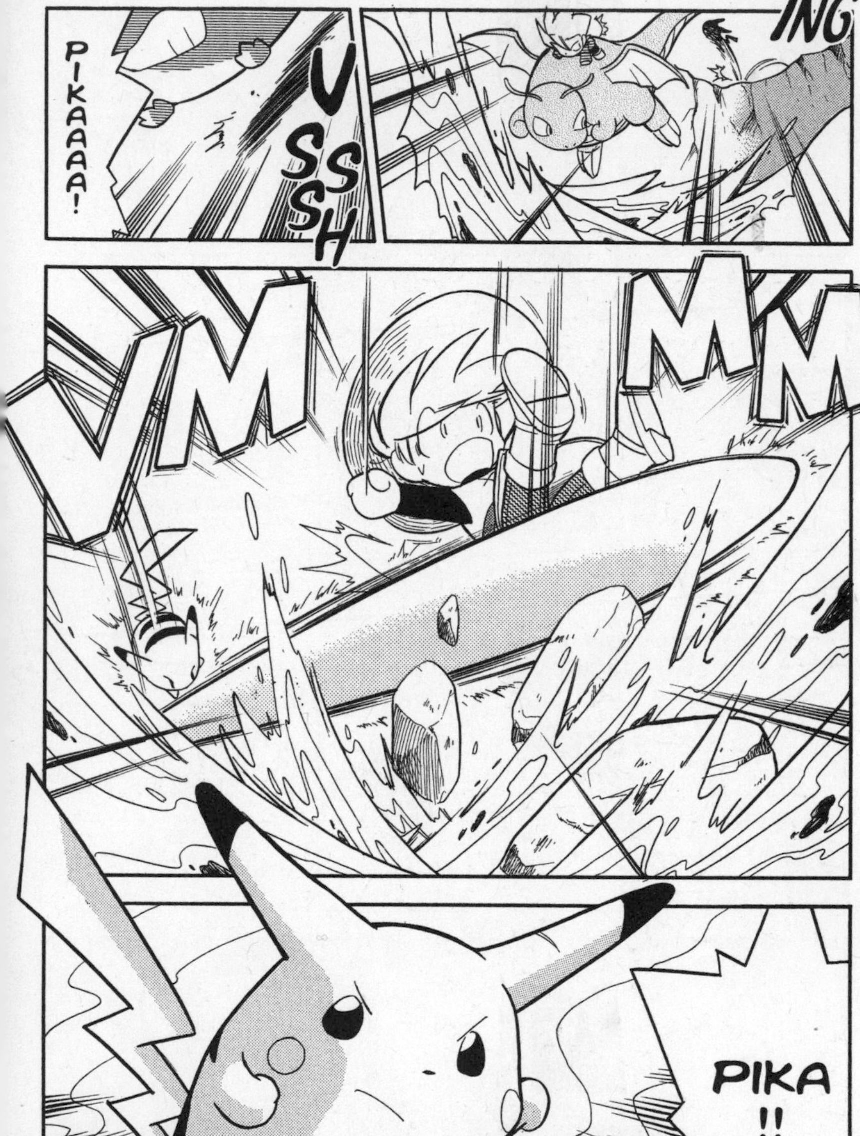
TNG
VSSSH
PIKAAAA!
VMMMM
PIKA!!

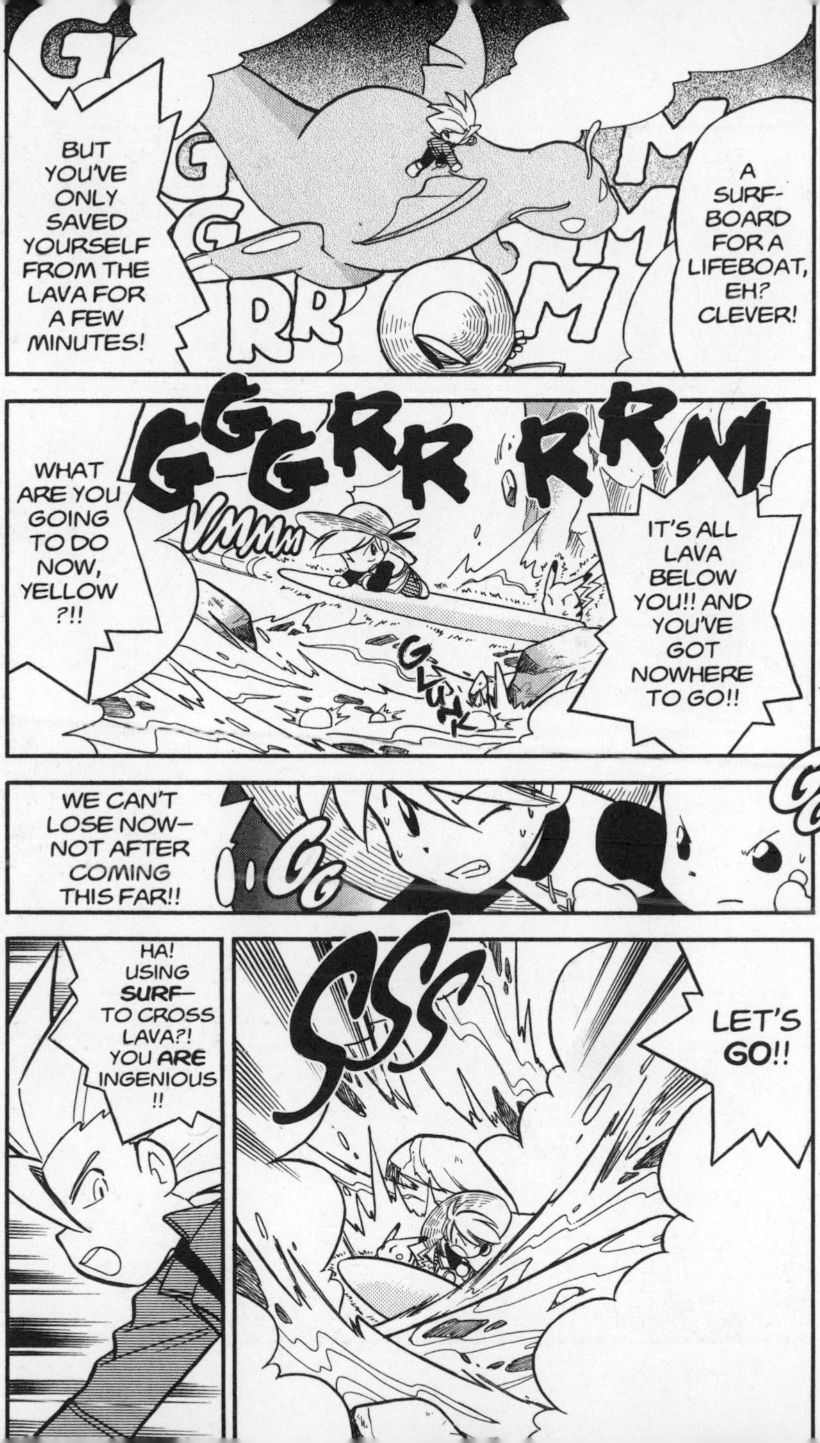
A SURF-BOARD FOR A LIFEBOAT, EH? CLEVER!
GGGRROMMM
BUT YOU'VE ONLY SAVED YOURSELF FROM THE LAVA FOR A FEW MINUTES!
GGGRRR RRRM
IT'S ALL LAVA BELOW YOU!! AND YOU'VE GOT NOWHERE TO GO!!
GLUNK
VMMM
WHAT ARE YOU GOING TO DO NOW, YELLOW?!!
GG
GG
WE CAN'T LOSE NOW—NOT AFTER COMING THIS FAR!!
LET'S GO!!
SSS
HA! USING **SURF** TO CROSS LAVA?! YOU **ARE** INGENIOUS!!

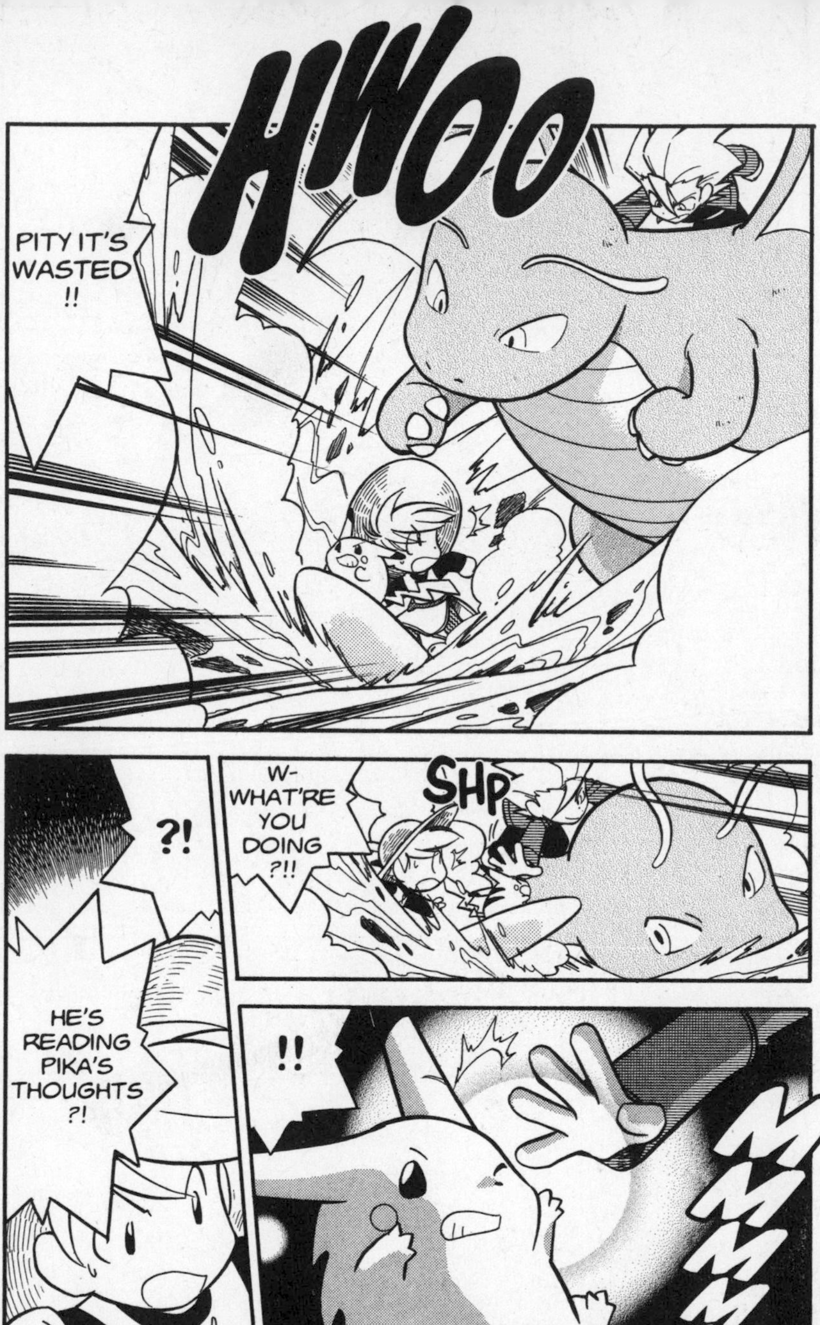
HWOO
PITY IT'S WASTED !!
SHP
W-WHAT'RE YOU DOING ?!!
!!
MMMMMM
?!
HE'S READING PIKA'S THOUGHTS ?!

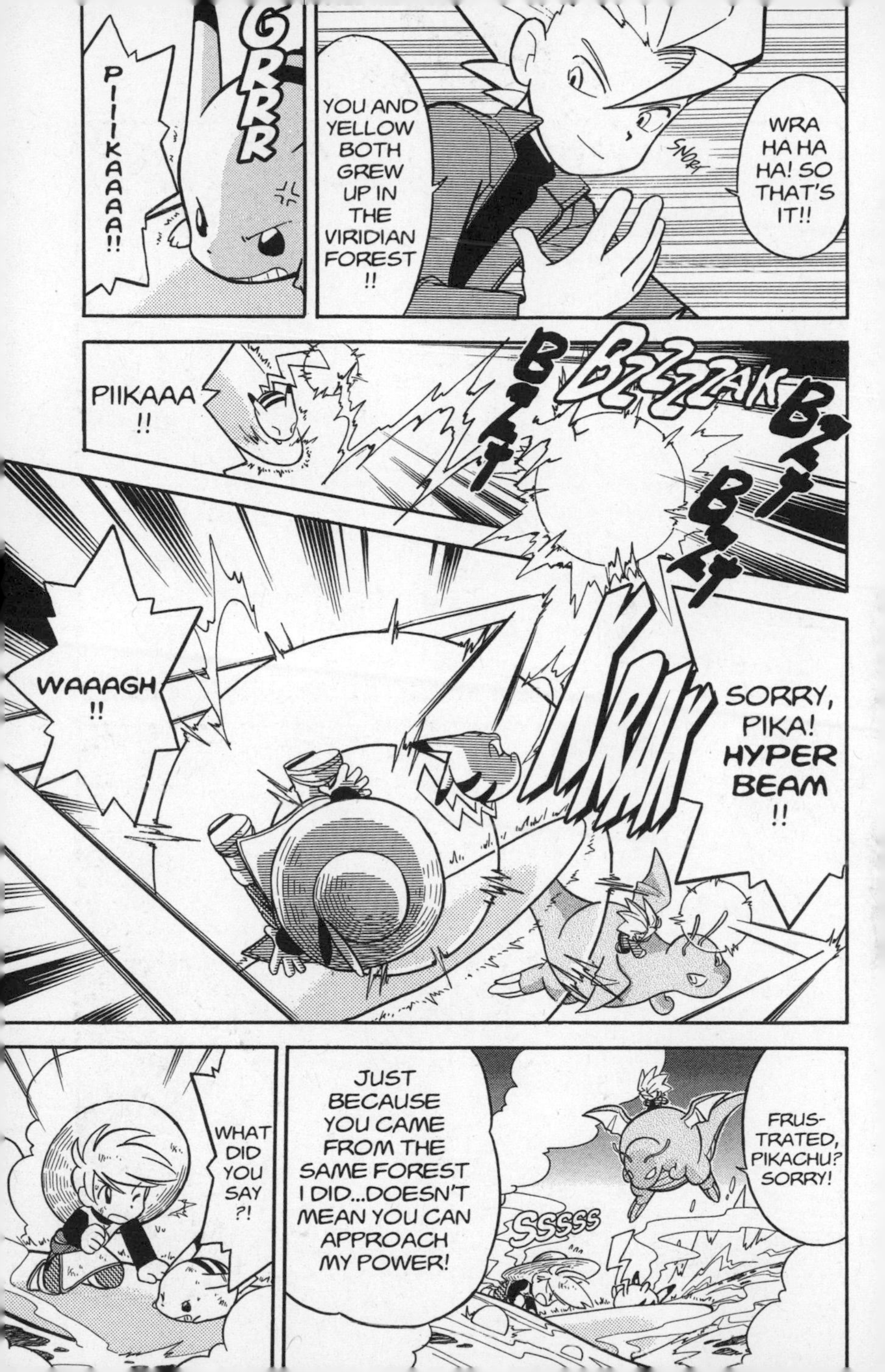
WRA HA HA HA! SO THAT'S IT!!
SNORT
YOU AND YELLOW BOTH GREW UP IN THE VIRIDIAN FOREST!!
GRRR
PIIIKAAAA!!
BZZZZAK
PIIKAAA!!
SORRY, PIKA! HYPER BEAM!!
WAAAGH!!
FRUS-TRATED, PIKACHU? SORRY!
SSSSS
JUST BECAUSE YOU CAME FROM THE SAME FOREST I DID...DOESN'T MEAN YOU CAN APPROACH MY POWER!
WHAT DID YOU SAY?!

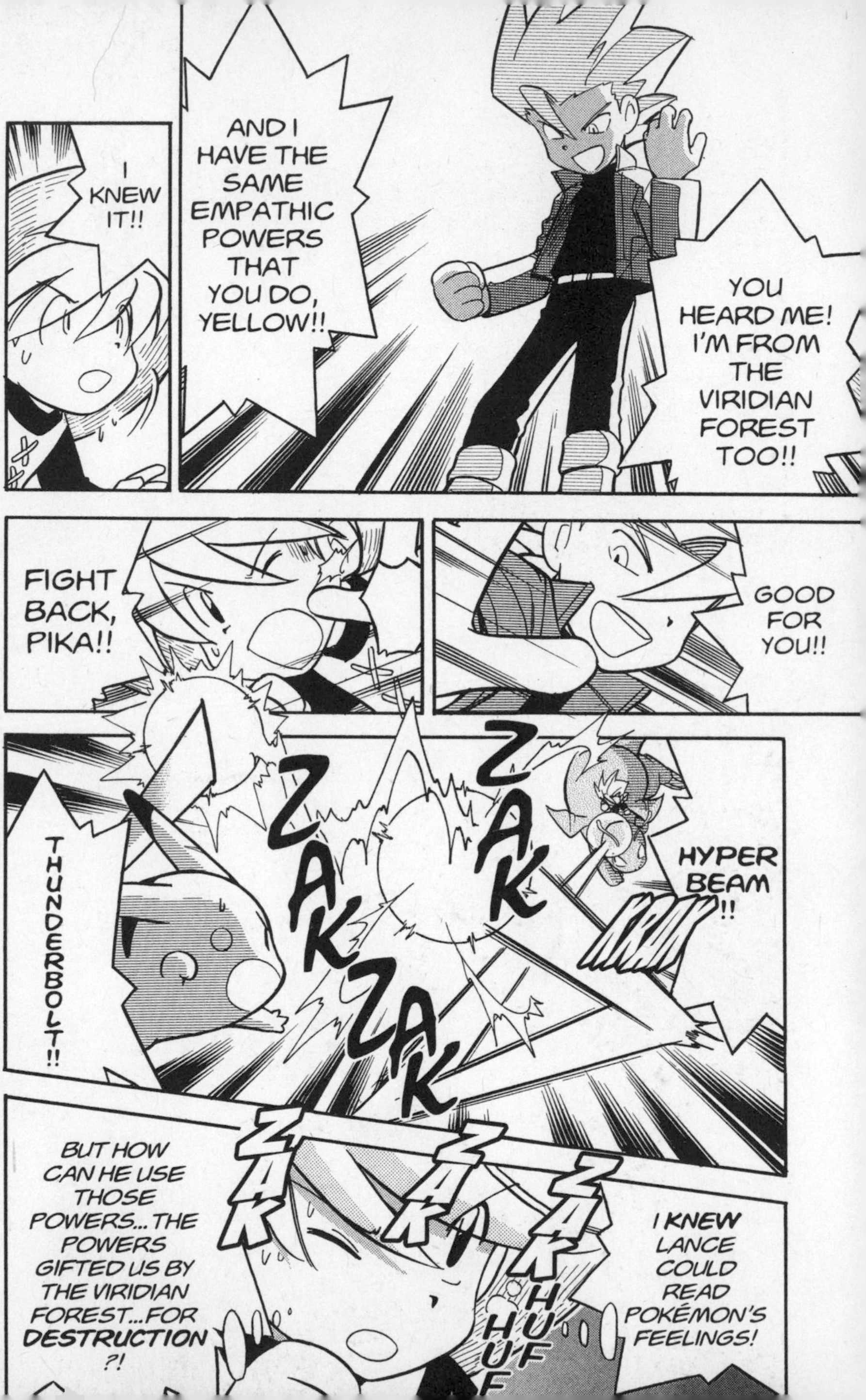
YOU HEARD ME! I'M FROM THE VIRIDIAN FOREST TOO!!
AND I HAVE THE SAME EMPATHIC POWERS THAT YOU DO, YELLOW!!
I KNEW IT!!
GOOD FOR YOU!!
FIGHT BACK, PIKA!!
HYPER BEAM!!
ZAK
ZAK
THUNDERBOLT!!
ZAK
ZAK
I KNEW LANCE COULD READ POKÉMON'S FEELINGS!
ZAK
HUF HUF
ZAK
ZAK
BUT HOW CAN HE USE THOSE POWERS... THE POWERS GIFTED US BY THE VIRIDIAN FOREST... FOR **DESTRUCTION**?!

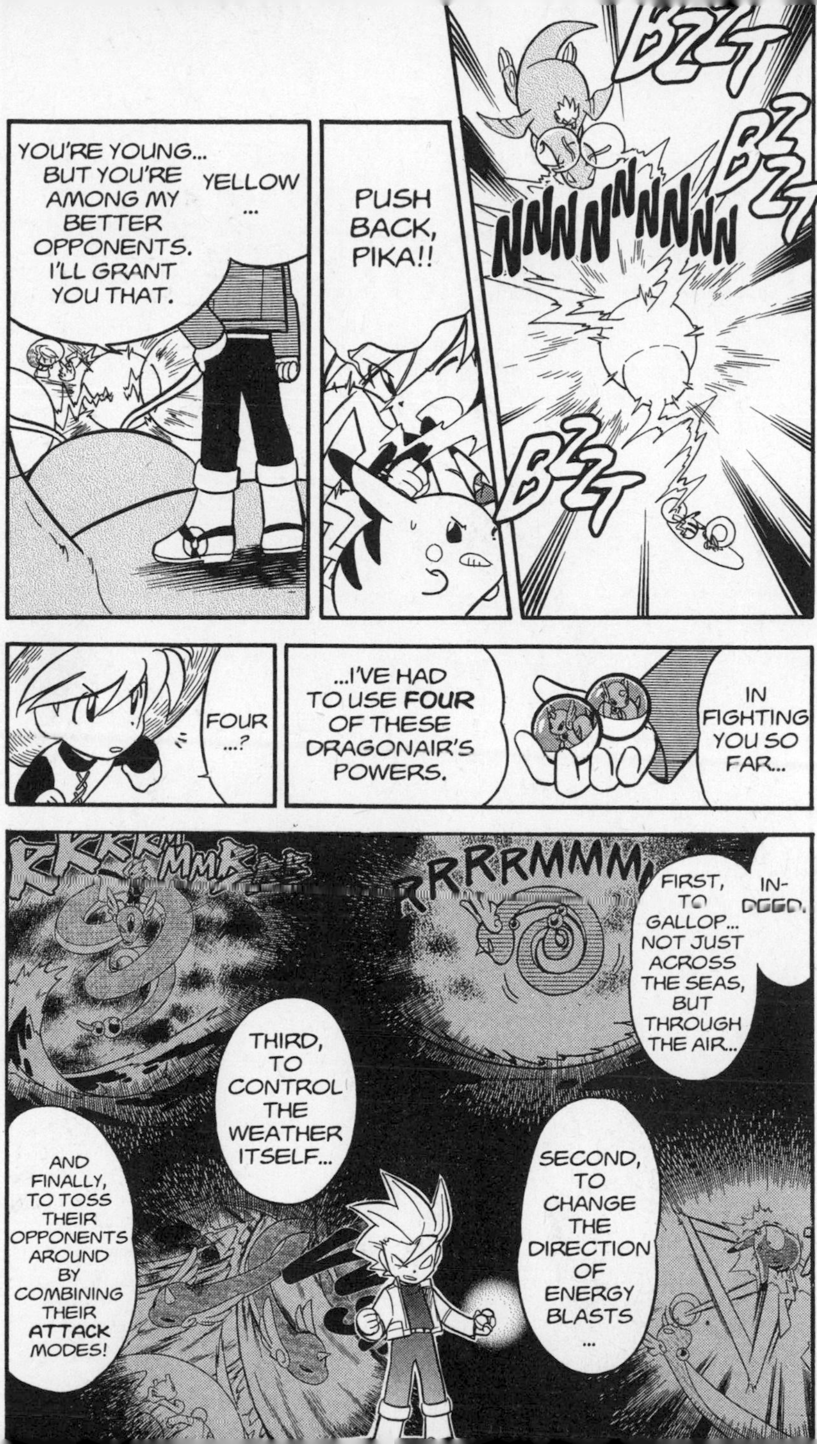
BZZT
BZZT
NNNNNNNNN
BZZT
PUSH BACK, PIKA!!
YELLOW ...
YOU'RE YOUNG... BUT YOU'RE AMONG MY BETTER OPPONENTS. I'LL GRANT YOU THAT.
IN FIGHTING YOU SO FAR...
...I'VE HAD TO USE FOUR OF THESE DRAGONAIR'S POWERS.
FOUR ...?
RRRRMMM
IN-DEED.
FIRST, TO GALLOP... NOT JUST ACROSS THE SEAS, BUT THROUGH THE AIR...
SECOND, TO CHANGE THE DIRECTION OF ENERGY BLASTS ...
THIRD, TO CONTROL THE WEATHER ITSELF...
AND FINALLY, TO TOSS THEIR OPPONENTS AROUND BY COMBINING THEIR ATTACK MODES!

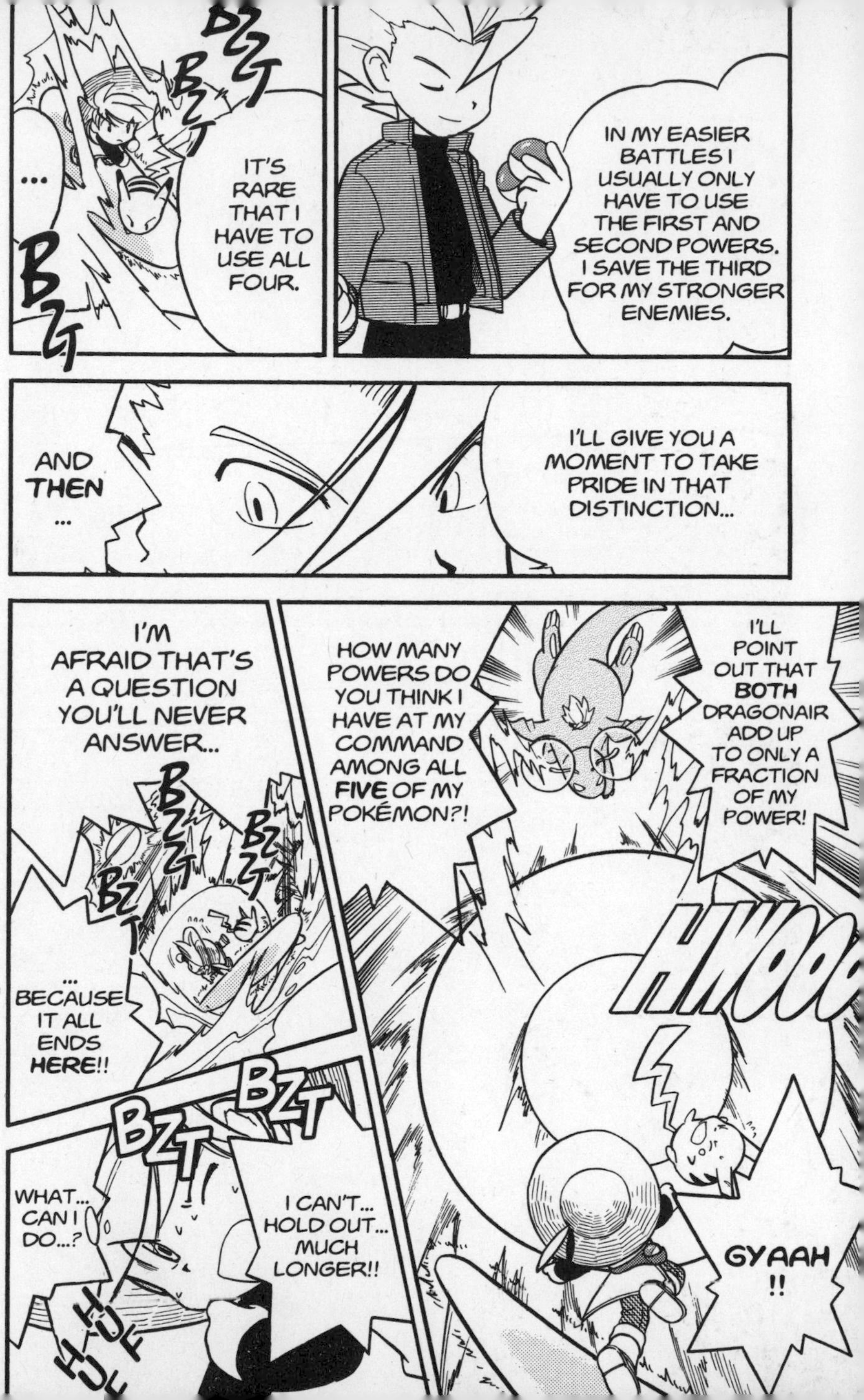

DZZT
BZZT
IN MY EASIER BATTLES I USUALLY ONLY HAVE TO USE THE FIRST AND SECOND POWERS. I SAVE THE THIRD FOR MY STRONGER ENEMIES.
IT'S RARE THAT I HAVE TO USE ALL FOUR.
...
BZZT
I'LL GIVE YOU A MOMENT TO TAKE PRIDE IN THAT DISTINCTION...
AND **THEN** ...
I'LL POINT OUT THAT **BOTH** DRAGONAIR ADD UP TO ONLY A FRACTION OF MY POWER!
HOW MANY POWERS DO YOU THINK I HAVE AT MY COMMAND AMONG ALL **FIVE** OF MY POKÉMON?!
I'M AFRAID THAT'S A QUESTION YOU'LL NEVER ANSWER...
BZZZT
BZZT
BZT
... BECAUSE IT ALL ENDS **HERE**!!
HWOOO
GYAAH!!
BZT
BZT
I CAN'T... HOLD OUT... MUCH LONGER!!
WHAT... CAN I DO...?
HUF HUF

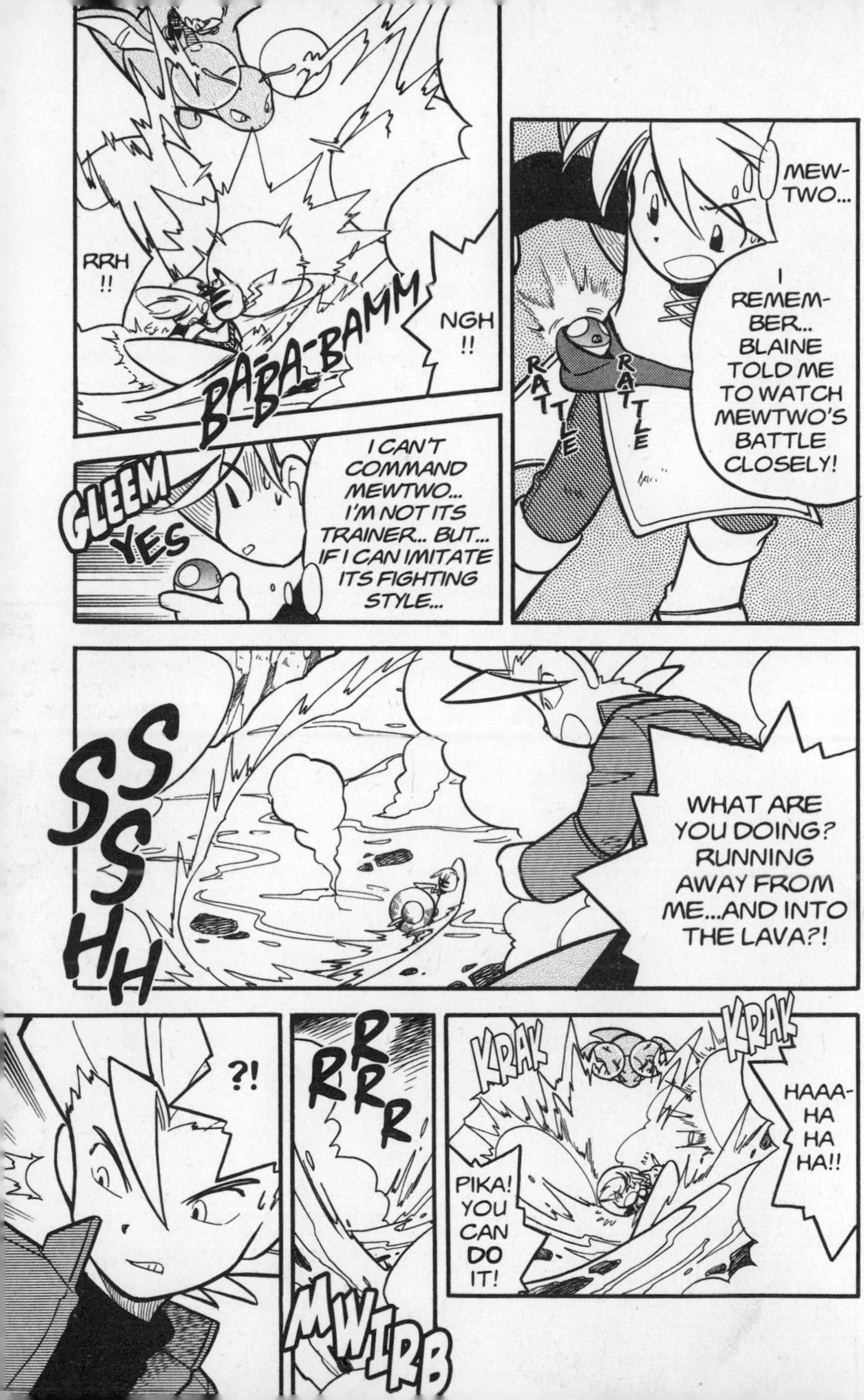
MEW-TWO...
I REMEMBER... BLAINE TOLD ME TO WATCH MEWTWO'S BATTLE CLOSELY!
RATTLE
RATTLE
NGH!!
BA-BA-BAMM
RRH!!
I CAN'T COMMAND MEWTWO... I'M NOT ITS TRAINER... BUT... IF I CAN IMITATE ITS FIGHTING STYLE...
GLEEM
YES
WHAT ARE YOU DOING? RUNNING AWAY FROM ME...AND INTO THE LAVA?!
SSSHH
KRAK
HAAA-HA HA HA!!
PIKA! YOU CAN DO IT!
KRAK
RRRRR
MWIRB
?!

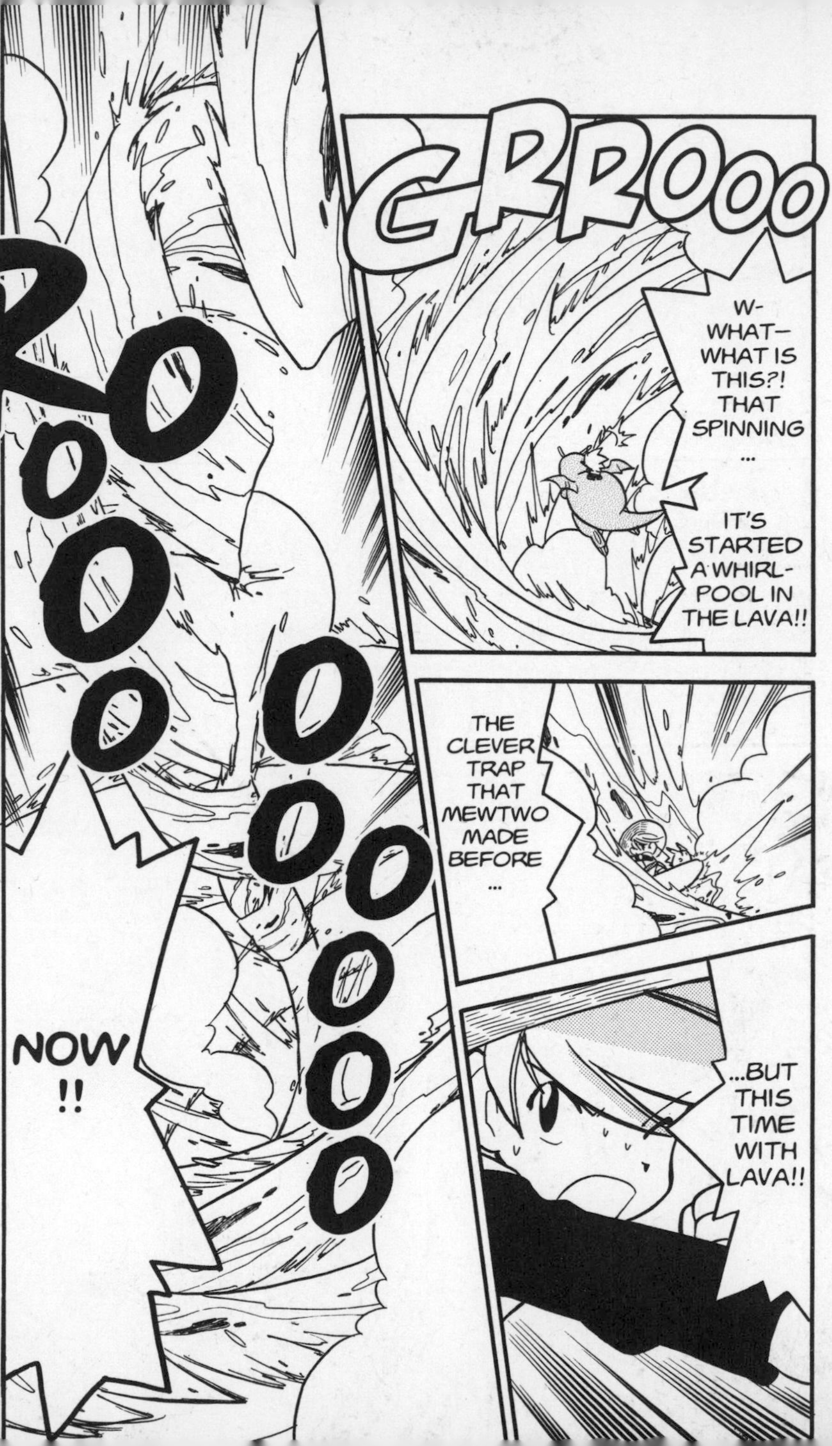
GRROOO
W-WHAT—WHAT IS THIS?! THAT SPINNING...
IT'S STARTED A WHIRLPOOL IN THE LAVA!!
THE CLEVER TRAP THAT MEWTWO MADE BEFORE...
...BUT THIS TIME WITH LAVA!!
ROOOOOOOOOOO
NOW!!

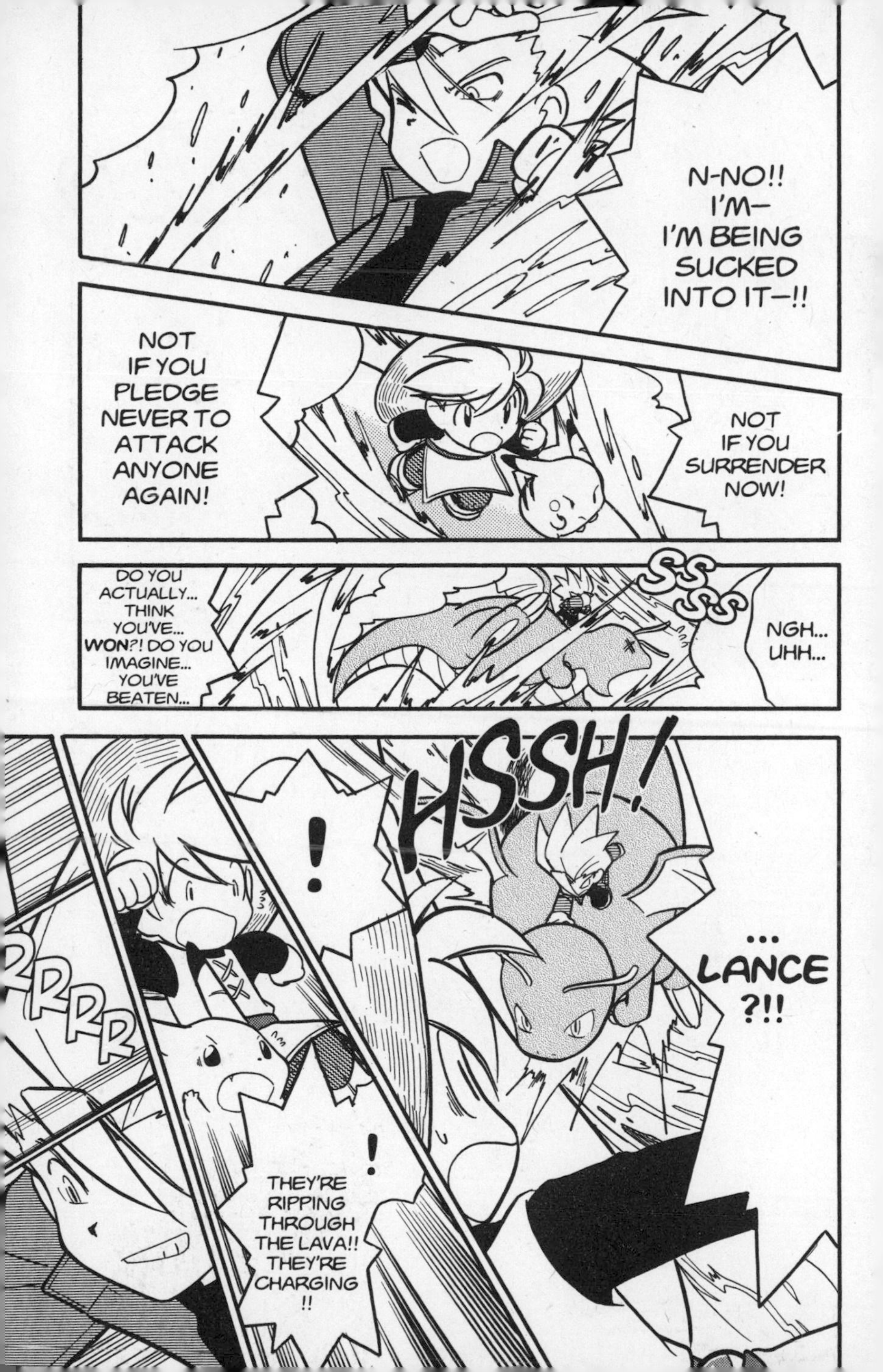
N-NO!! I'M— I'M BEING SUCKED INTO IT—!!
NOT IF YOU SURRENDER NOW!
NOT IF YOU PLEDGE NEVER TO ATTACK ANYONE AGAIN!
SSSSS
NGH... UHH...
DO YOU ACTUALLY... THINK YOU'VE... WON?! DO YOU IMAGINE... YOU'VE BEATEN...
HSSH!
...LANCE ?!!
!
RRRR
!
THEY'RE RIPPING THROUGH THE LAVA!! THEY'RE CHARGING !!

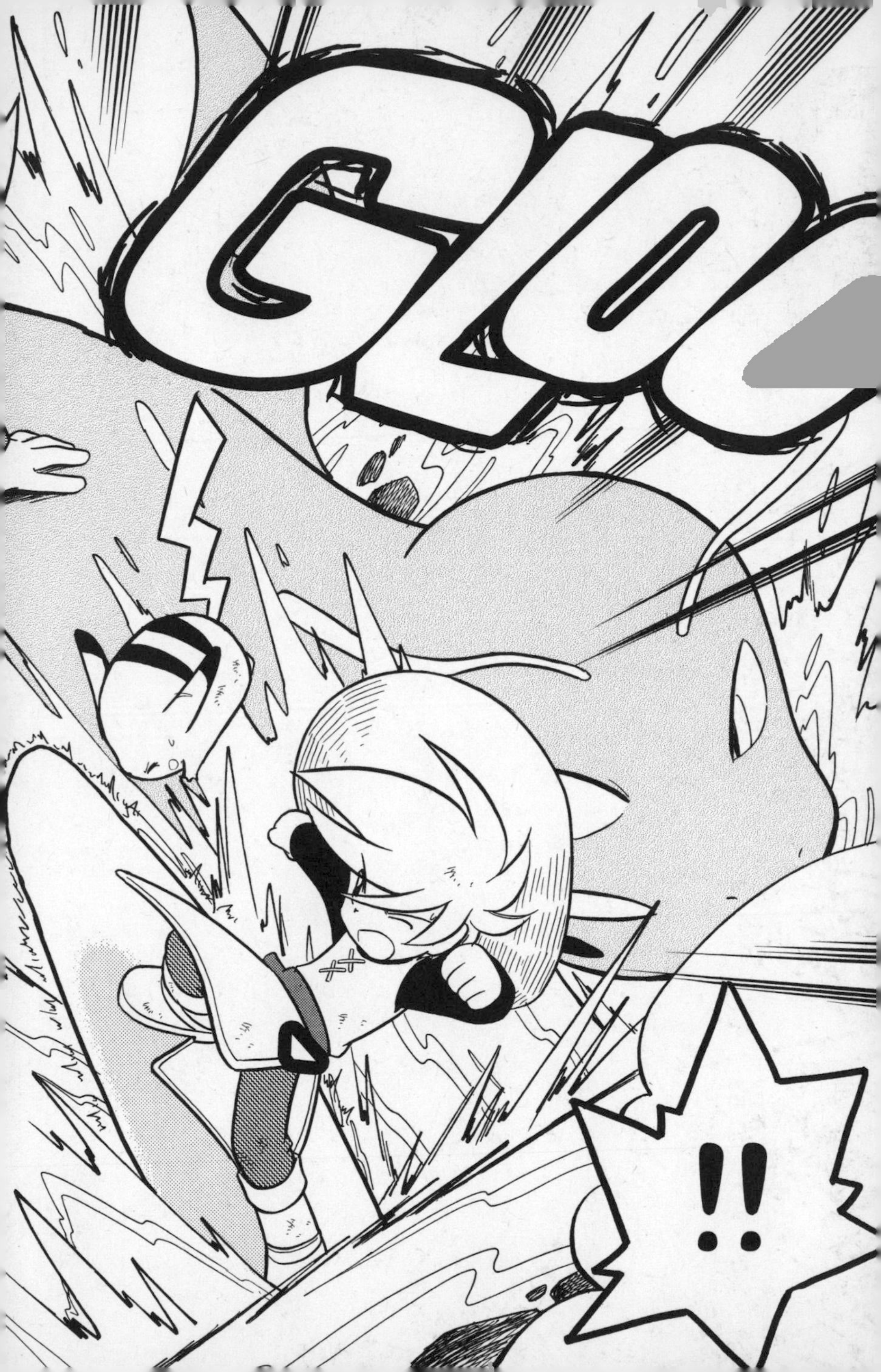
GO
!!

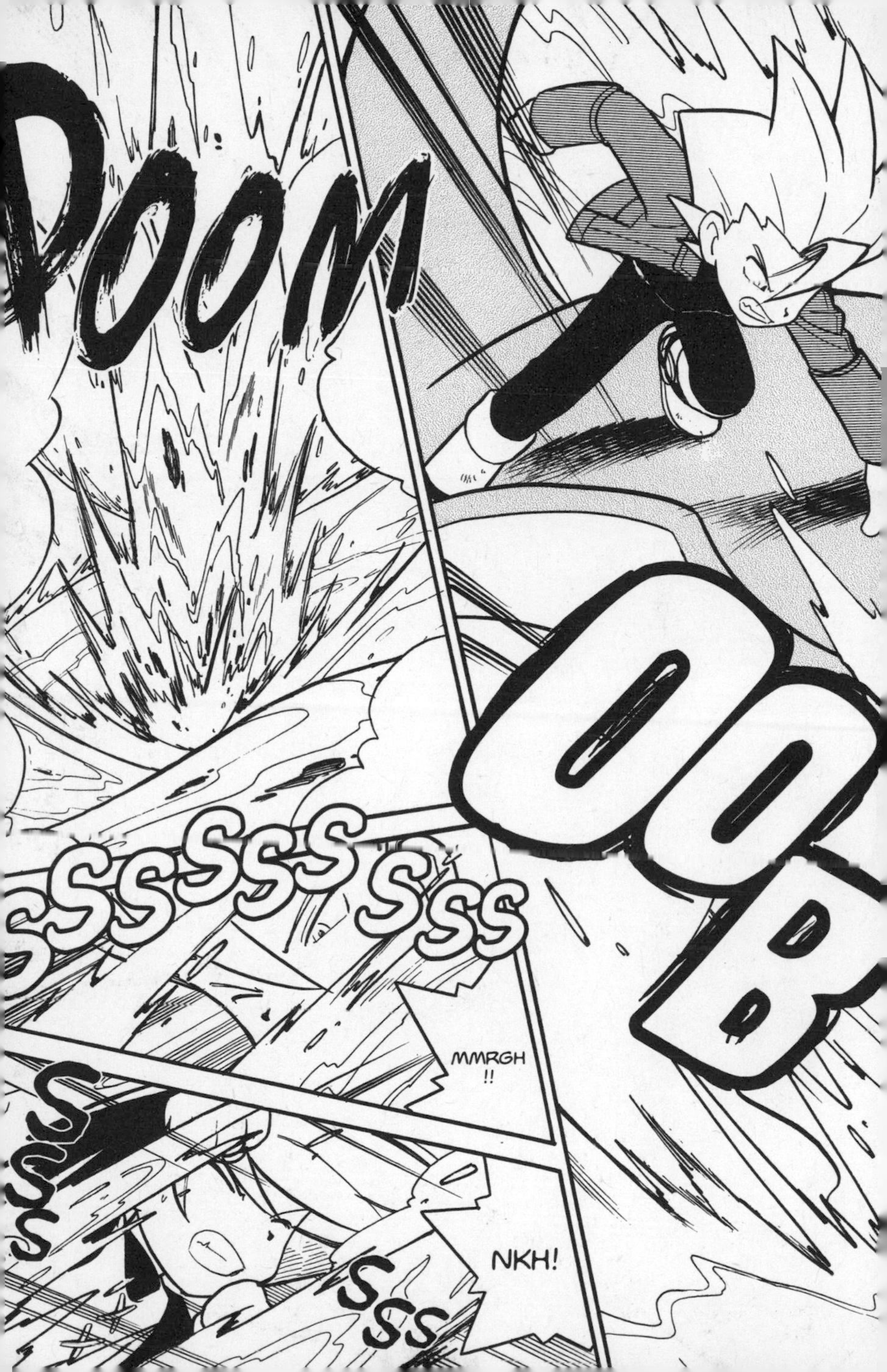
DOOM
BOO
SSSSSSSSS
MMRGH !!
NKH!
SSSS
SSS

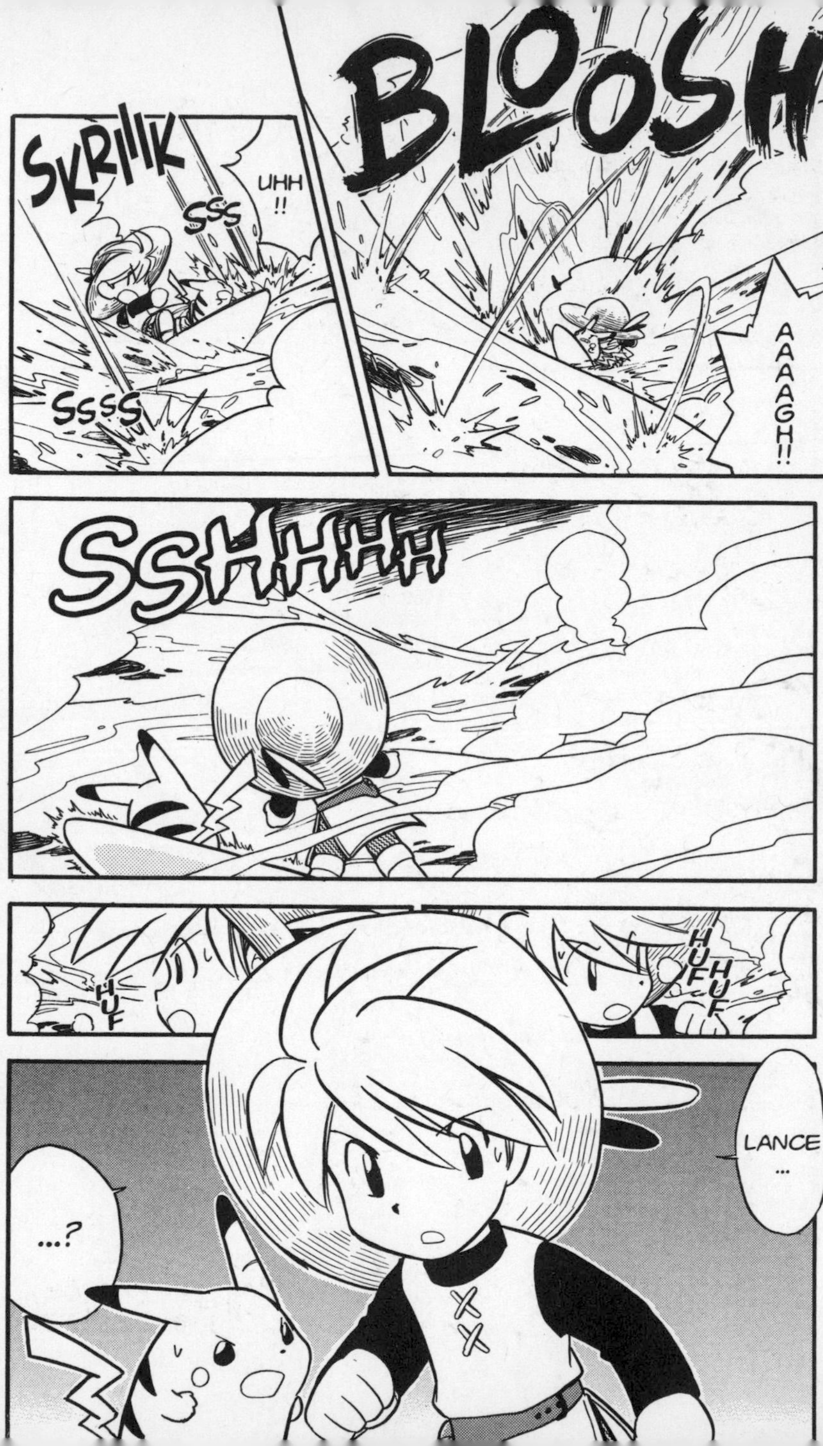
BLOOSH
AAAAGH!!
SKRIIIK
UHH!!
SSS
SSSS
SSHHHH
HUF HUF
HUF
LANCE...
...?

87 Rhyhorn Rising

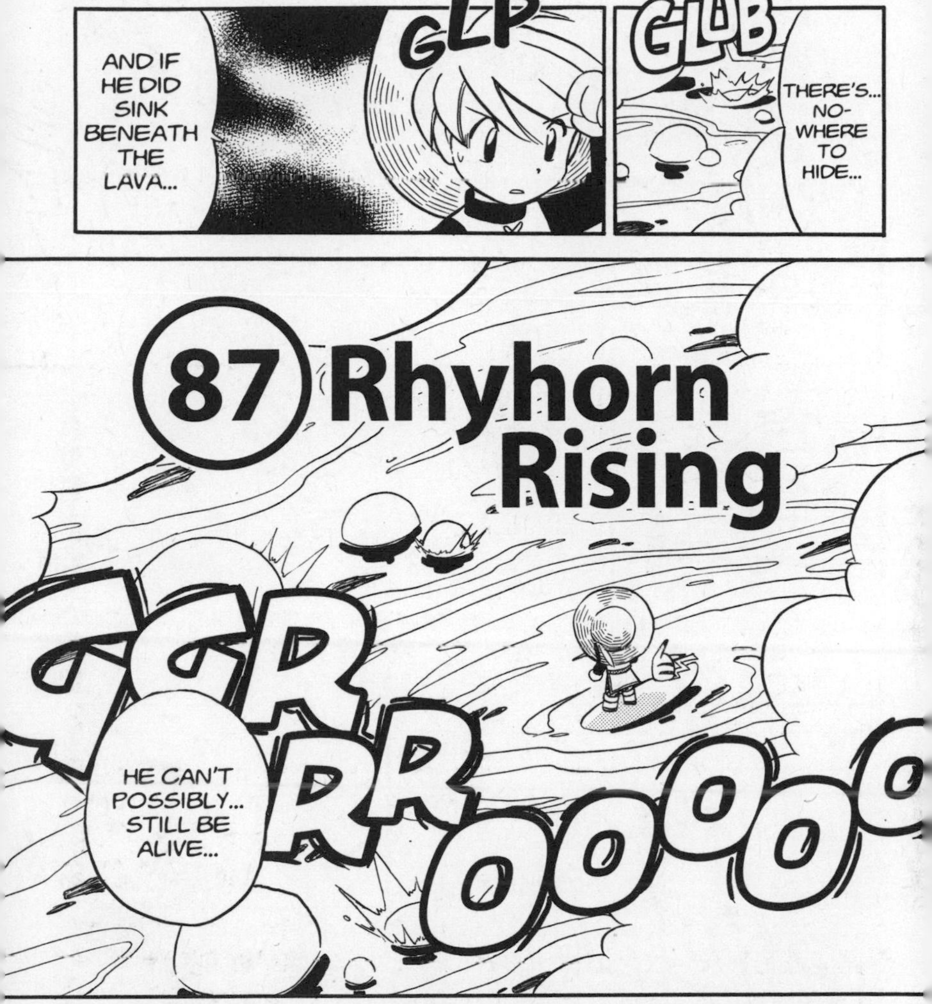

GLUB
THERE'S... NO-WHERE TO HIDE...
GLP
AND IF HE DID SINK BENEATH THE LAVA...
GRRROOOOO
HE CAN'T POSSIBLY... STILL BE ALIVE...
WE...CAN'T STAY HERE. IT'S DANGEROUS. WE HAVE TO FIND RATTY AND THE OTHERS...

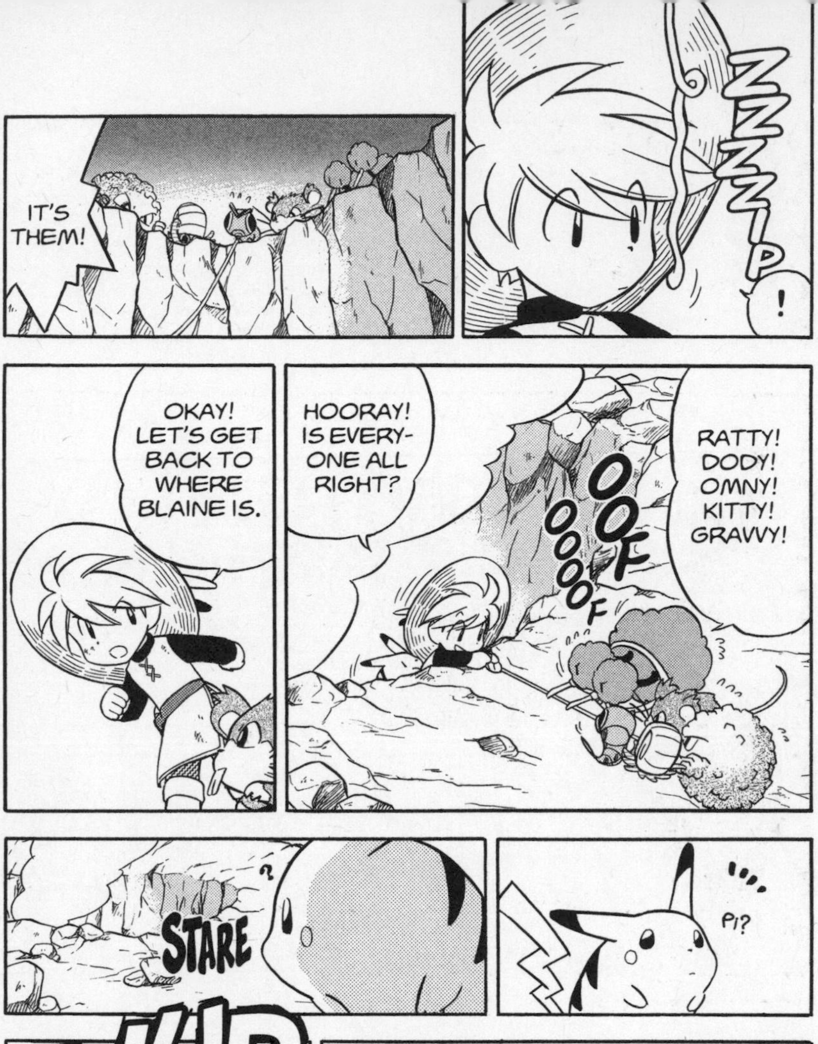
ZZZZIP
!
IT'S THEM!
RATTY! DODY! OMNY! KITTY! GRAVVY!
OOOF
OOOOOF
HOORAY! IS EVERY-ONE ALL RIGHT?
OKAY! LET'S GET BACK TO WHERE BLAINE IS.
PI?
STARE
WHRRR
TMTMTM
GLUP

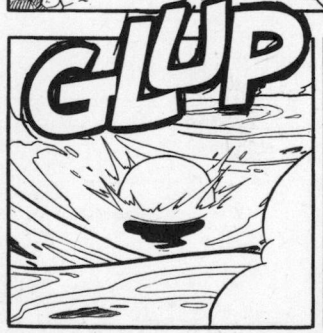

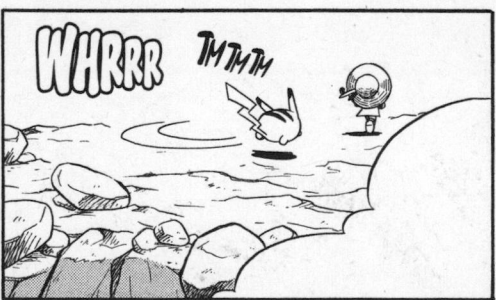

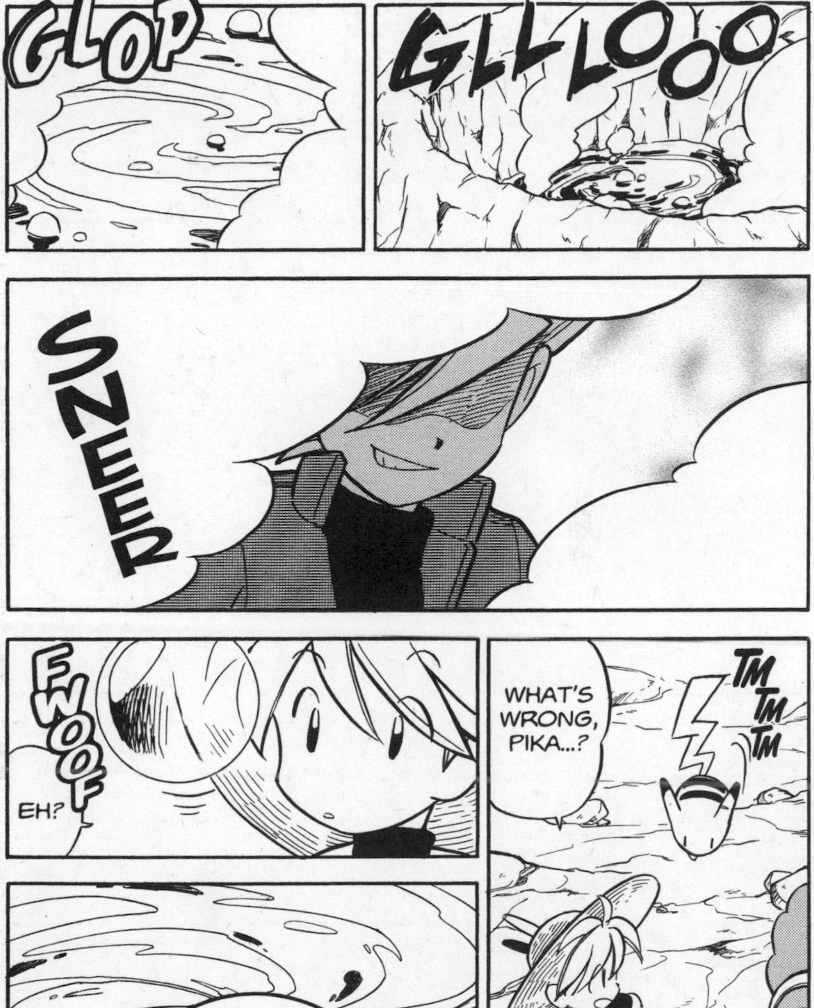
GLLOOO
GLOP
SNEER
TM TM TM
WHAT'S WRONG, PIKA...?
FWOOF
EH?
GLLLLRRR

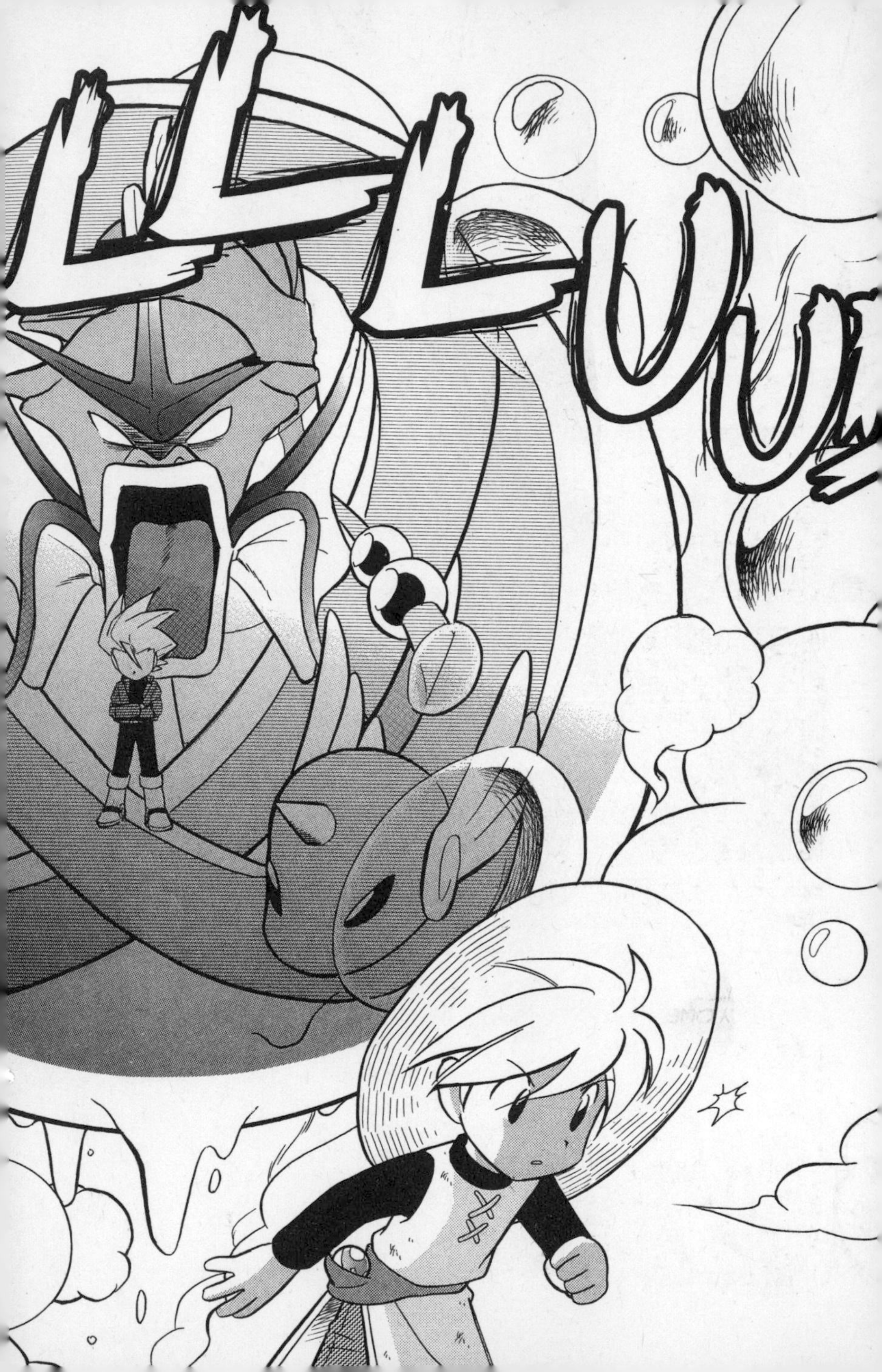

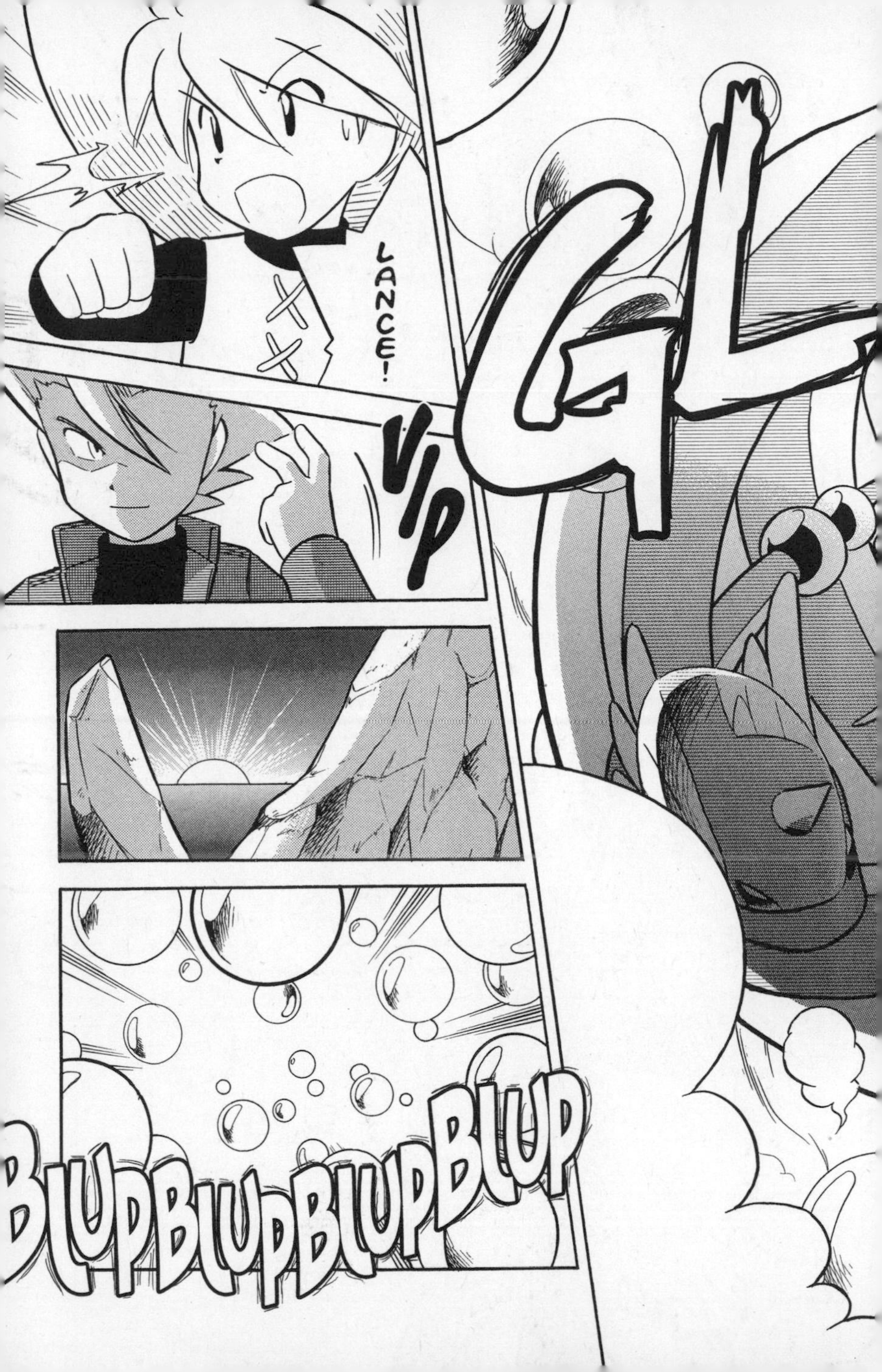
GL
LANCE!
VIP
BLUPBLUPBLUPBLUP

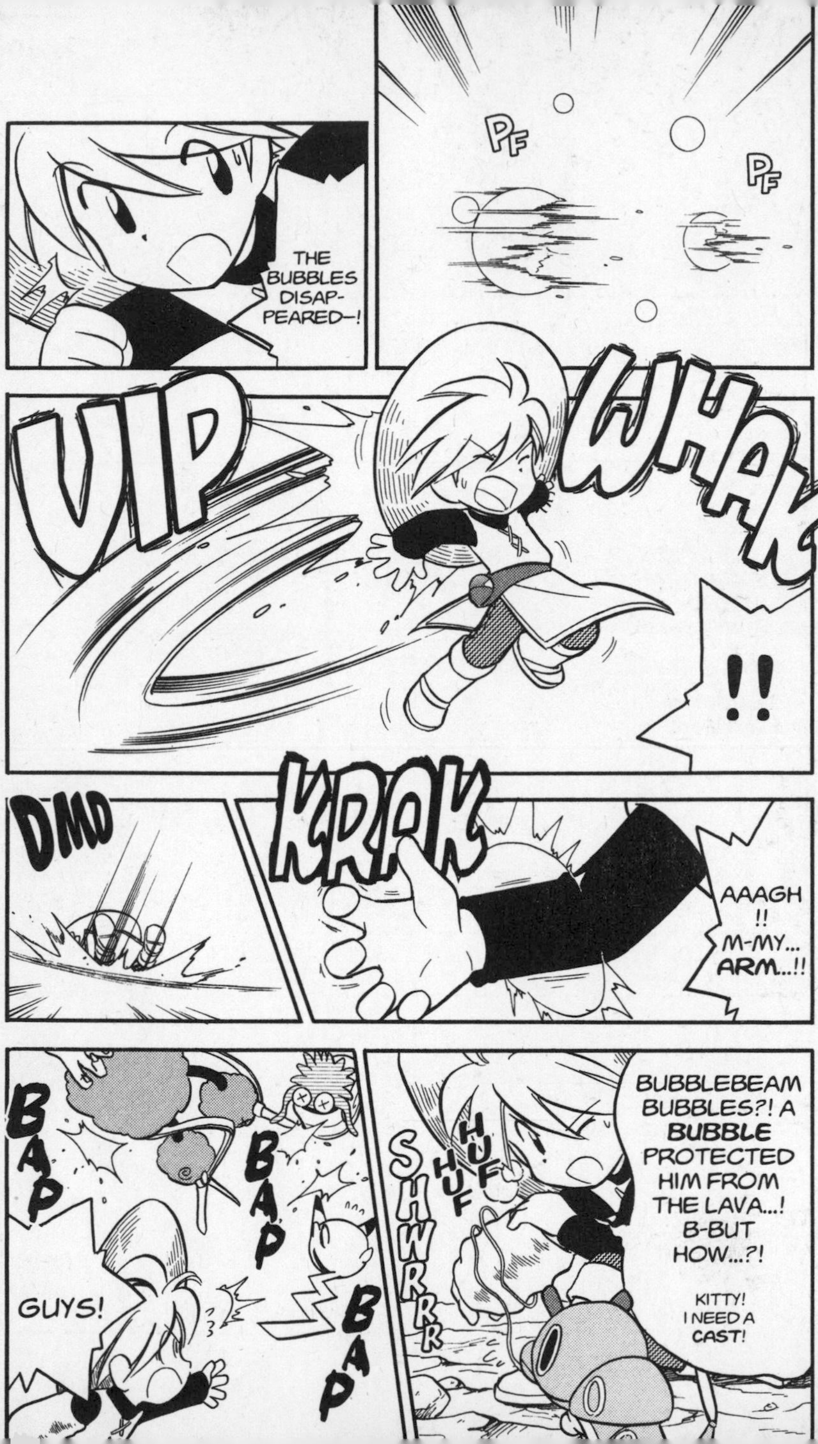
PF
PF
THE BUBBLES DISAP-PEARED—!
WHAK
VIP
!!
KRAK
AAAGH !! M-MY... ARM...!!
DMD
BUBBLEBEAM BUBBLES?! A BUBBLE PROTECTED HIM FROM THE LAVA...! B-BUT HOW...?!
HUF HUF
SHWRRR
KITTY! I NEED A CAST!
BAP
BAP
BAP
GUYS!

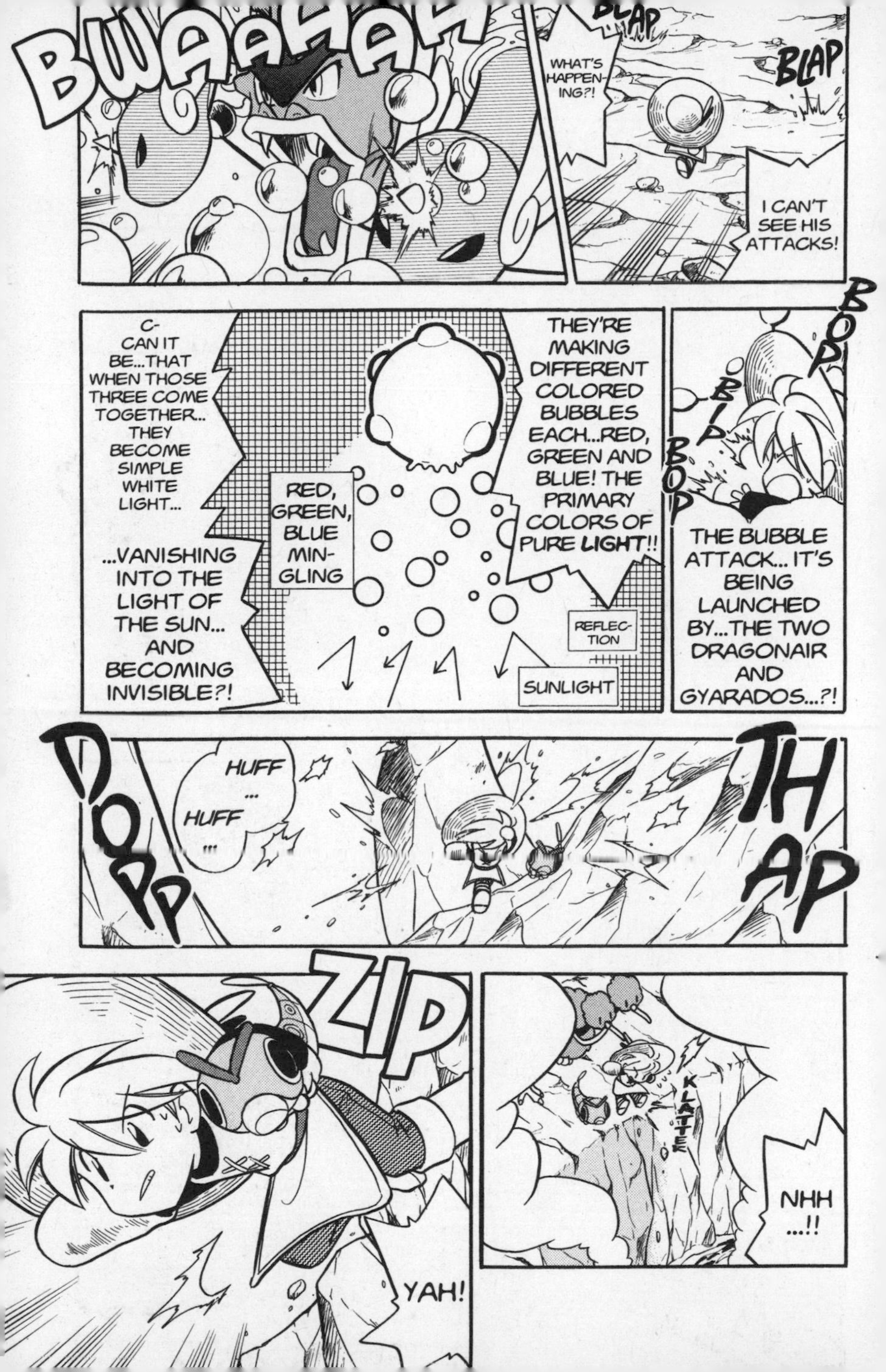
BLAP
BLAP
WHAT'S HAPPENING?!
I CAN'T SEE HIS ATTACKS!
BWAAHAH
BOP
BIP
BOP
THE BUBBLE ATTACK... IT'S BEING LAUNCHED BY...THE TWO DRAGONAIR AND GYARADOS...?!
THEY'RE MAKING DIFFERENT COLORED BUBBLES EACH...RED, GREEN AND BLUE! THE PRIMARY COLORS OF PURE LIGHT!!
RED, GREEN, BLUE MINGLING
C-CAN IT BE...THAT WHEN THOSE THREE COME TOGETHER... THEY BECOME SIMPLE WHITE LIGHT...
...VANISHING INTO THE LIGHT OF THE SUN... AND BECOMING INVISIBLE?!
REFLECTION
SUNLIGHT
THAP
HUFF ... HUFF ...
DOPP
KLATTER
NHH ...!!
ZIP
YAH!

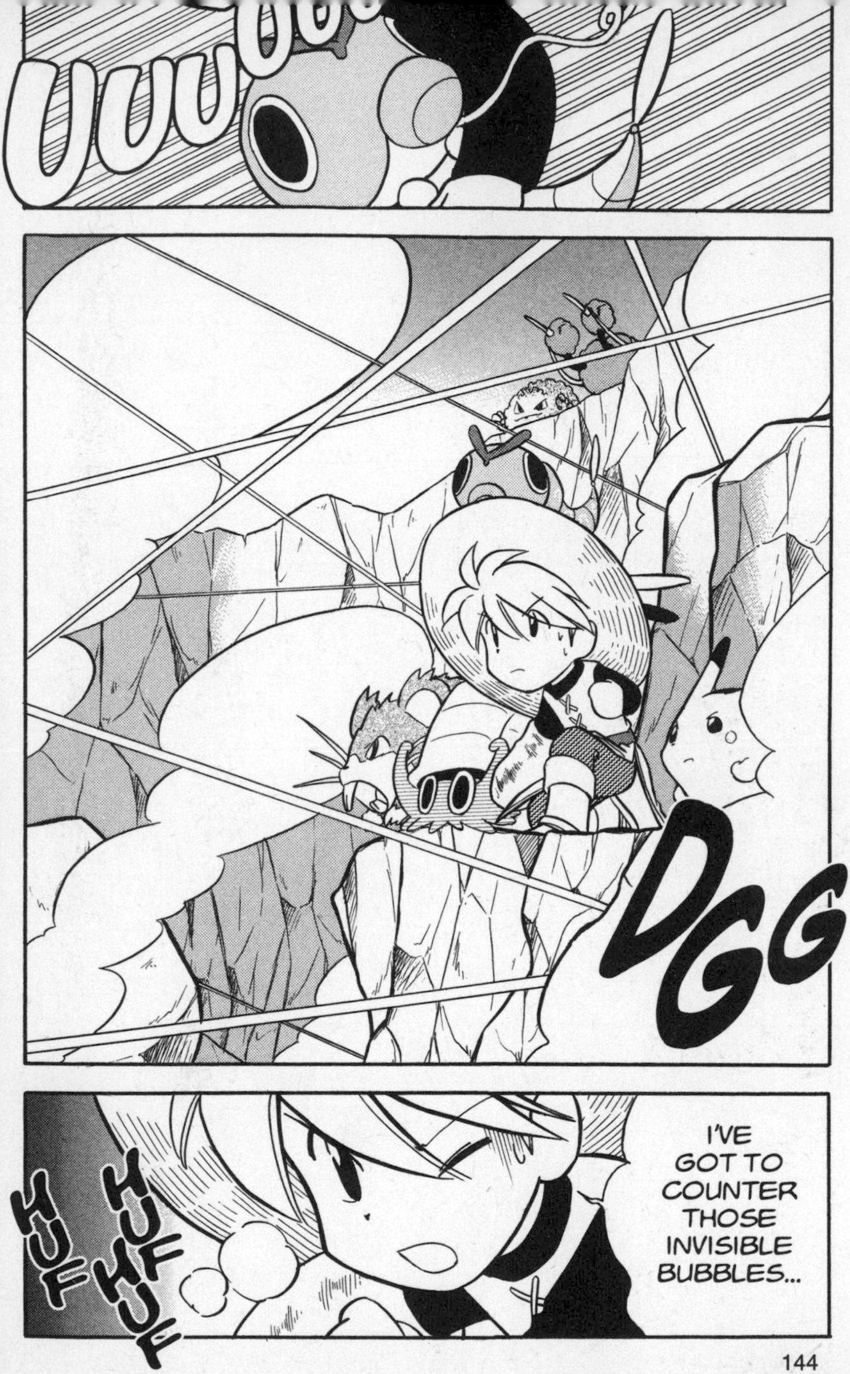
UUUOOO
DGG
I'VE GOT TO COUNTER THOSE INVISIBLE BUBBLES...
HUF HUF
HUF HUF

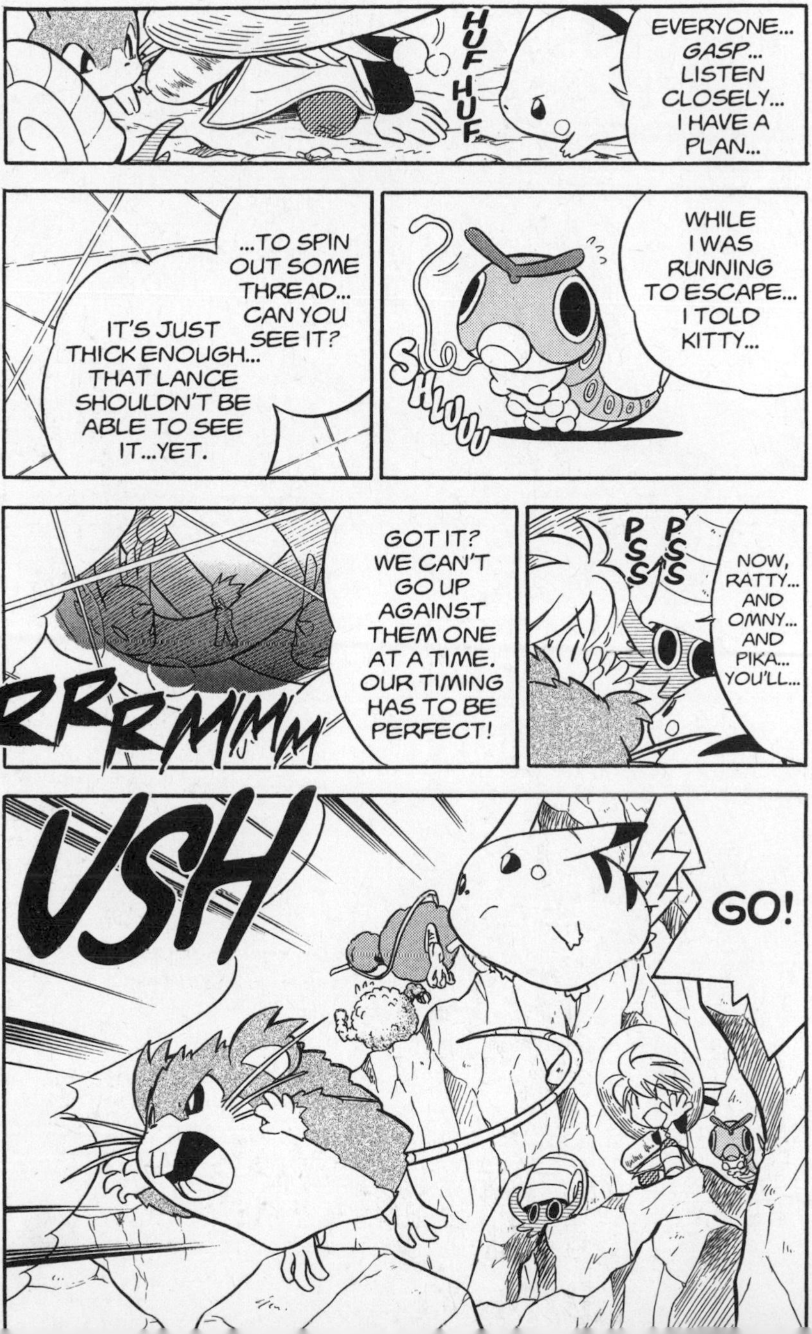
EVERYONE... GASP... LISTEN CLOSELY... I HAVE A PLAN...
HUF HUF
WHILE I WAS RUNNING TO ESCAPE... I TOLD KITTY...
SHWUUU
...TO SPIN OUT SOME THREAD... CAN YOU SEE IT?
IT'S JUST THICK ENOUGH... THAT LANCE SHOULDN'T BE ABLE TO SEE IT...YET.
PSS PSS
NOW, RATTY... AND OMNY... AND PIKA... YOU'LL...
GOT IT? WE CAN'T GO UP AGAINST THEM ONE AT A TIME. OUR TIMING HAS TO BE PERFECT!
RRRMMMM
GO!
VSH

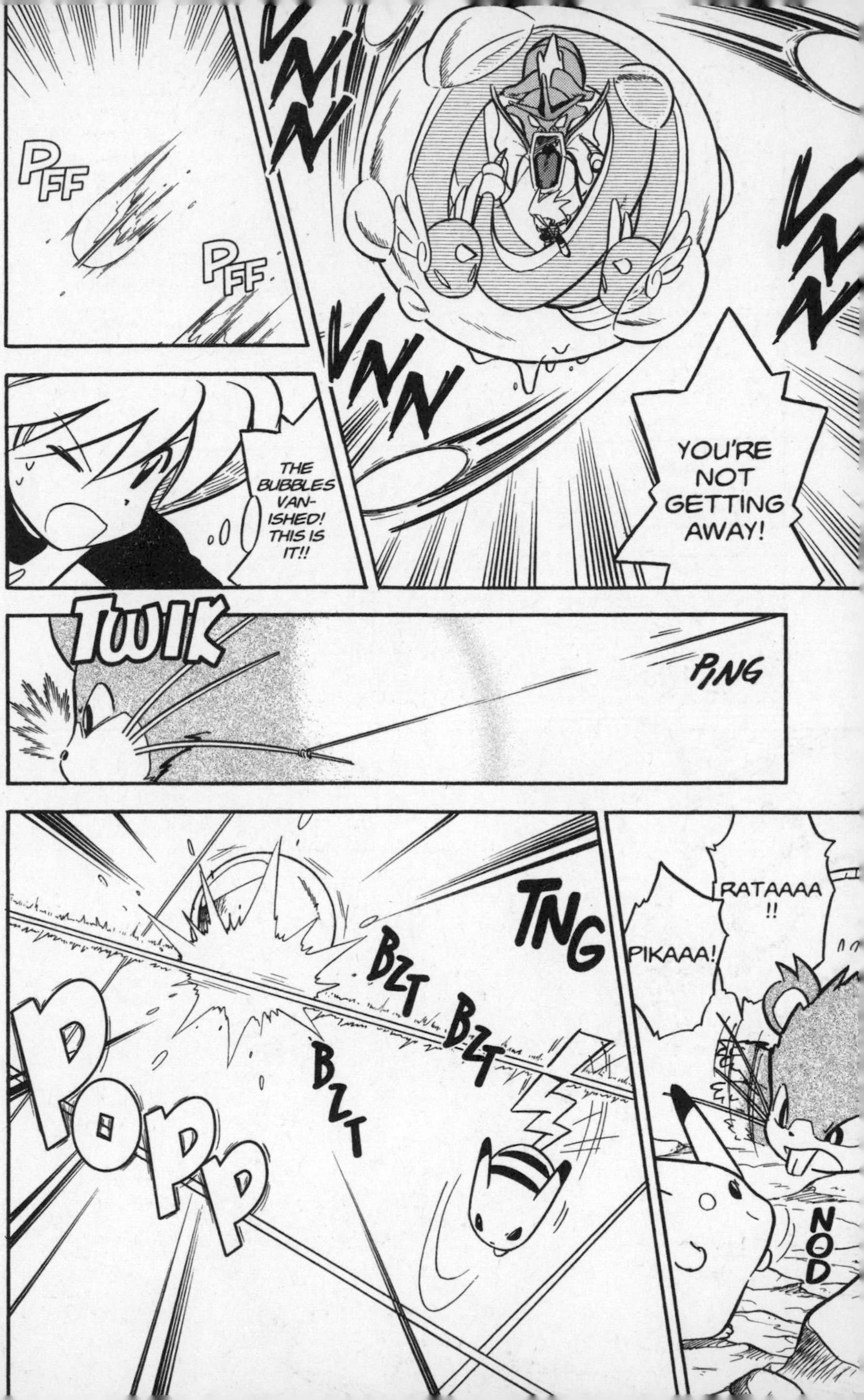
VNNN
VNNN
VNN
YOU'RE NOT GETTING AWAY!
PFF
PFF
THE BUBBLES VAN-ISHED! THIS IS IT!!
TWIK
PING
RATAAAA!!
PIKAAA!
NOD
TNG
BZT
BZT
BZT
POPP

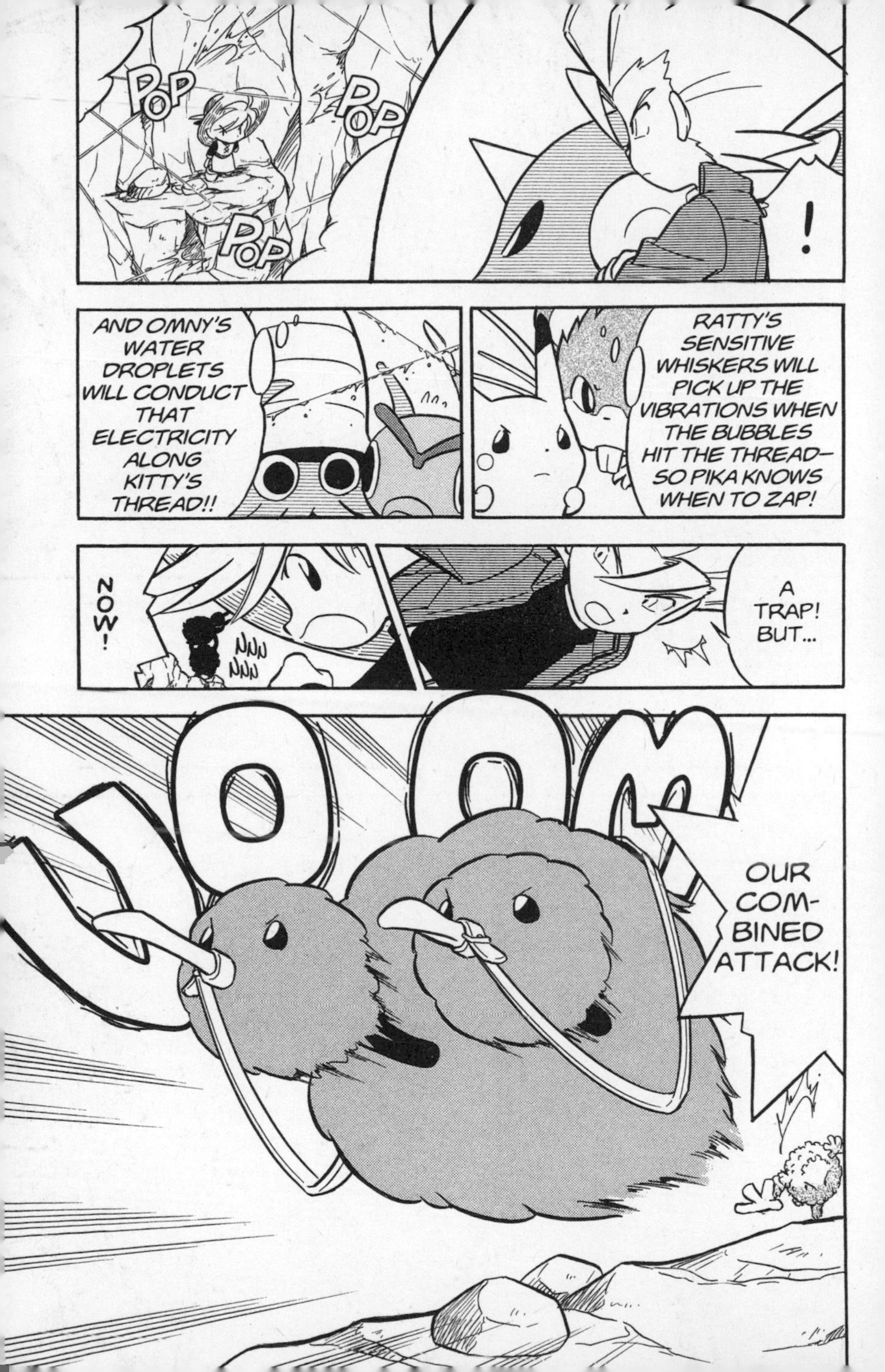
!
POP
POP
POP
RATTY'S SENSITIVE WHISKERS WILL PICK UP THE VIBRATIONS WHEN THE BUBBLES HIT THE THREAD— SO PIKA KNOWS WHEN TO ZAP!
AND OMNY'S WATER DROPLETS WILL CONDUCT THAT ELECTRICITY ALONG KITTY'S THREAD!!
A TRAP! BUT...
NOW!
NNN NNN
VOOM
OUR COM-BINED ATTACK!

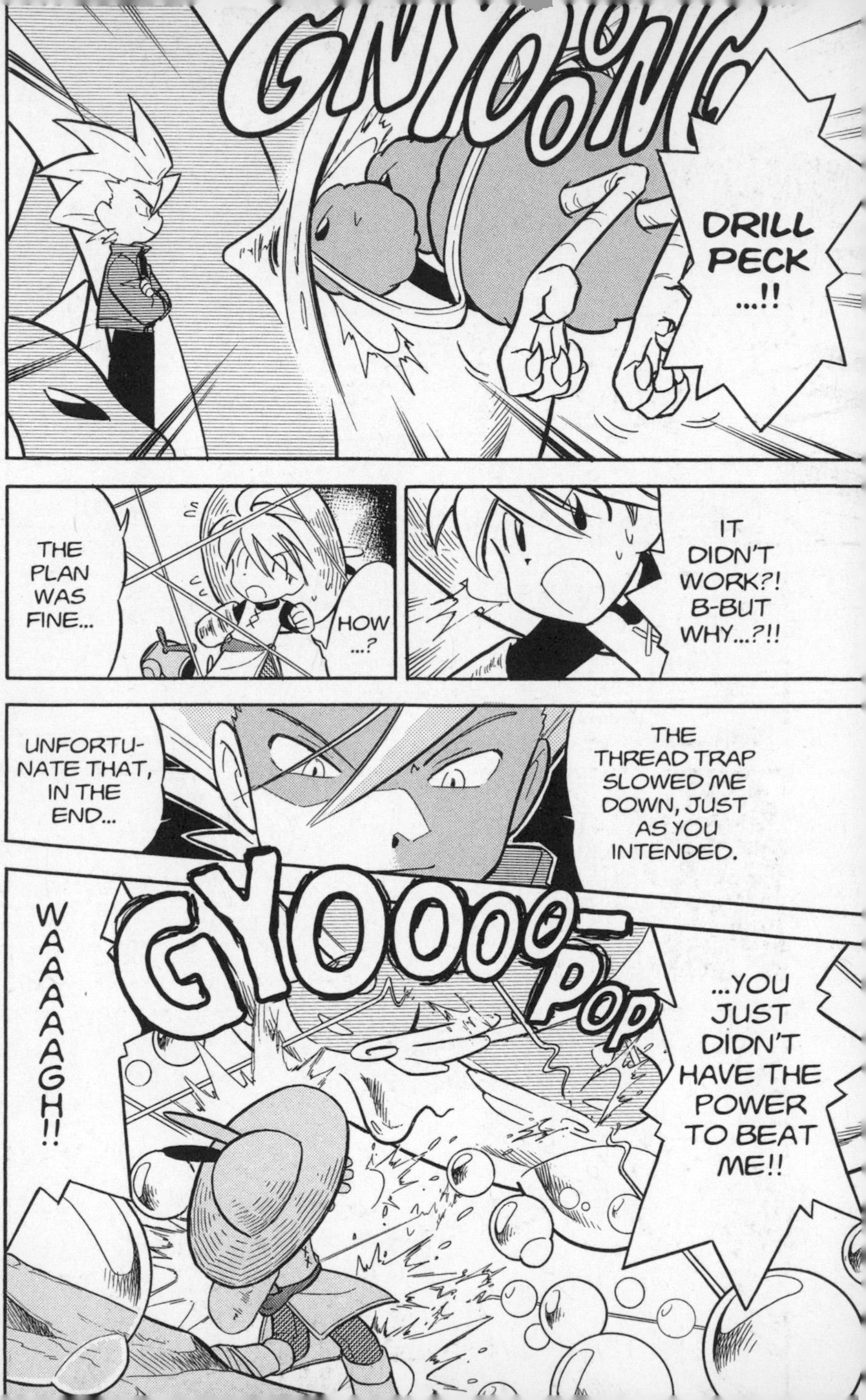
DRILL PECK ...!!
IT DIDN'T WORK?! B-BUT WHY...?!!
HOW ...?
THE PLAN WAS FINE...
THE THREAD TRAP SLOWED ME DOWN, JUST AS YOU INTENDED.
UNFORTU-NATE THAT, IN THE END...
GYOOOO-POP
...YOU JUST DIDN'T HAVE THE POWER TO BEAT ME!!
WAAAAAAGH!!

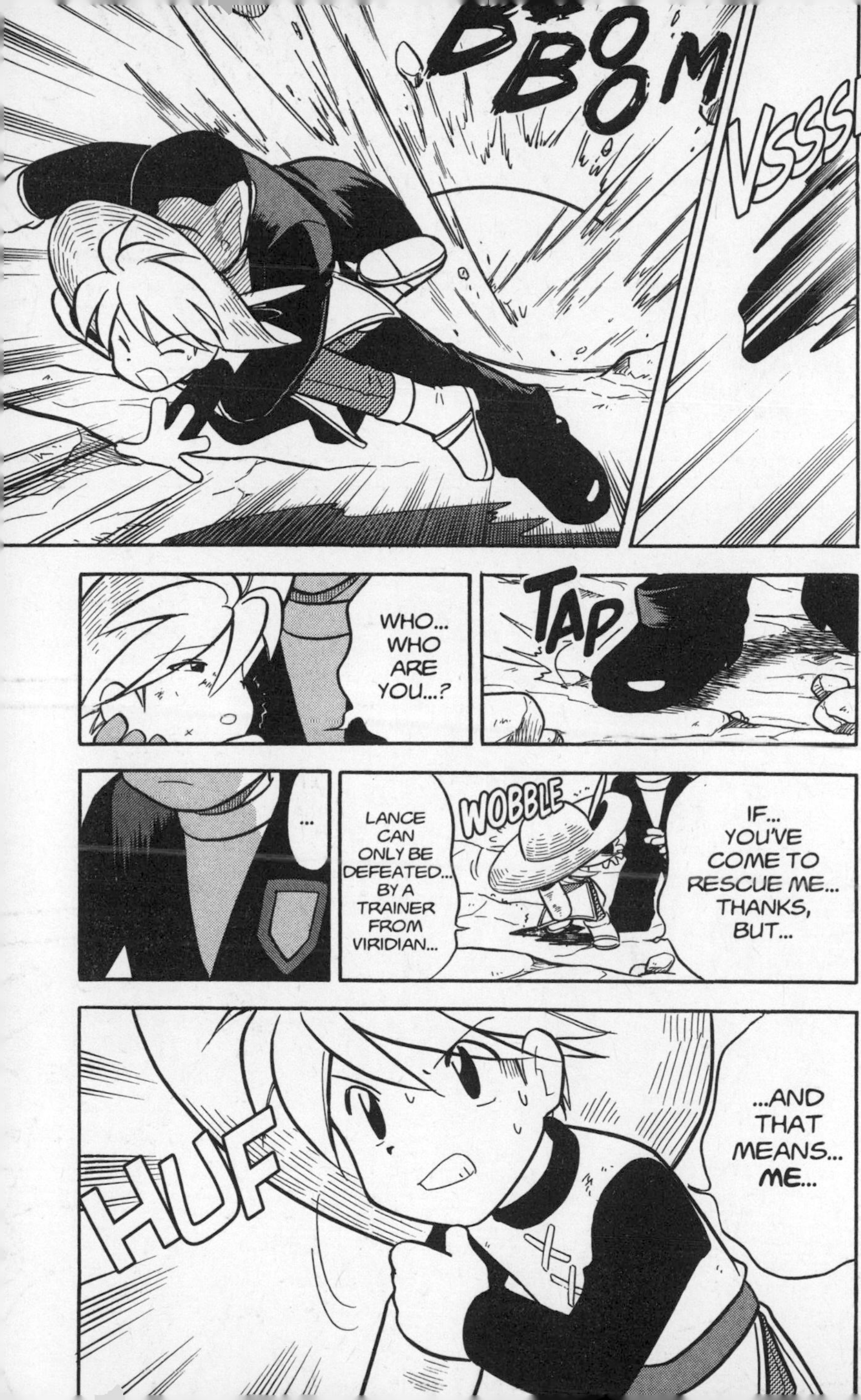
VSSSH
DBOOM
TAP
WHO... WHO ARE YOU...?
IF... YOU'VE COME TO RESCUE ME... THANKS, BUT...
WOBBLE
LANCE CAN ONLY BE DEFEATED... BY A TRAINER FROM VIRIDIAN...
...
...AND THAT MEANS... ME...
HUF

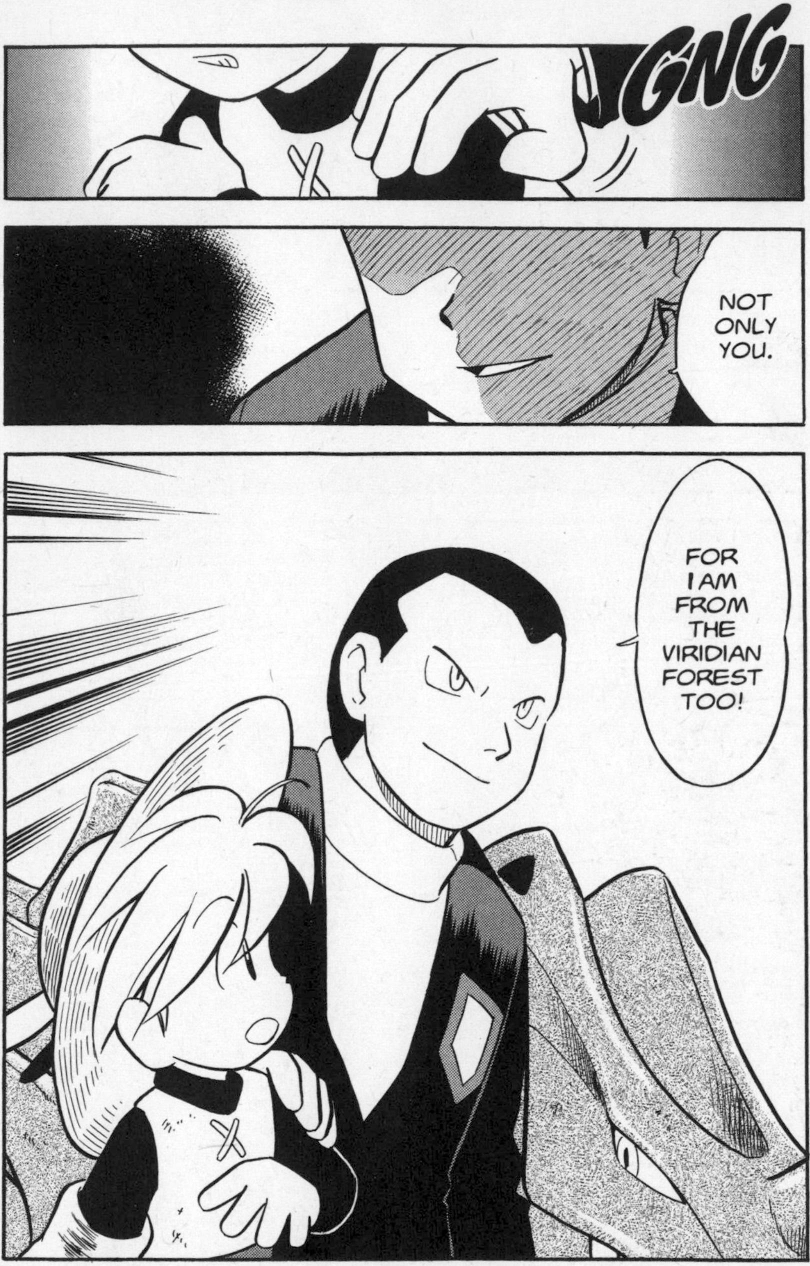
GNG
NOT ONLY YOU.
FOR I AM FROM THE VIRIDIAN FOREST TOO!

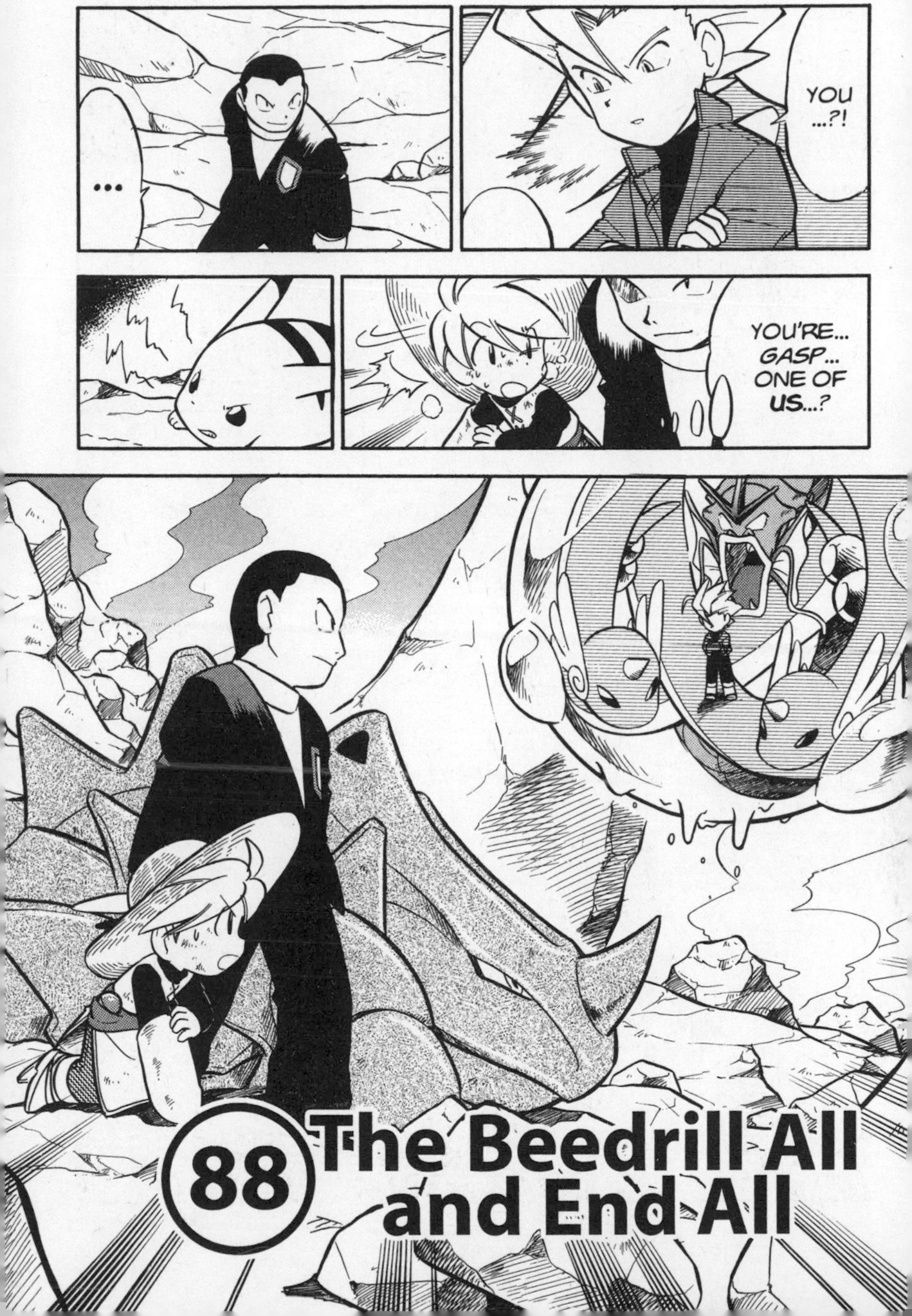
YOU ...?!
...
YOU'RE... GASP... ONE OF US...?
88 The Beedrill All and End All

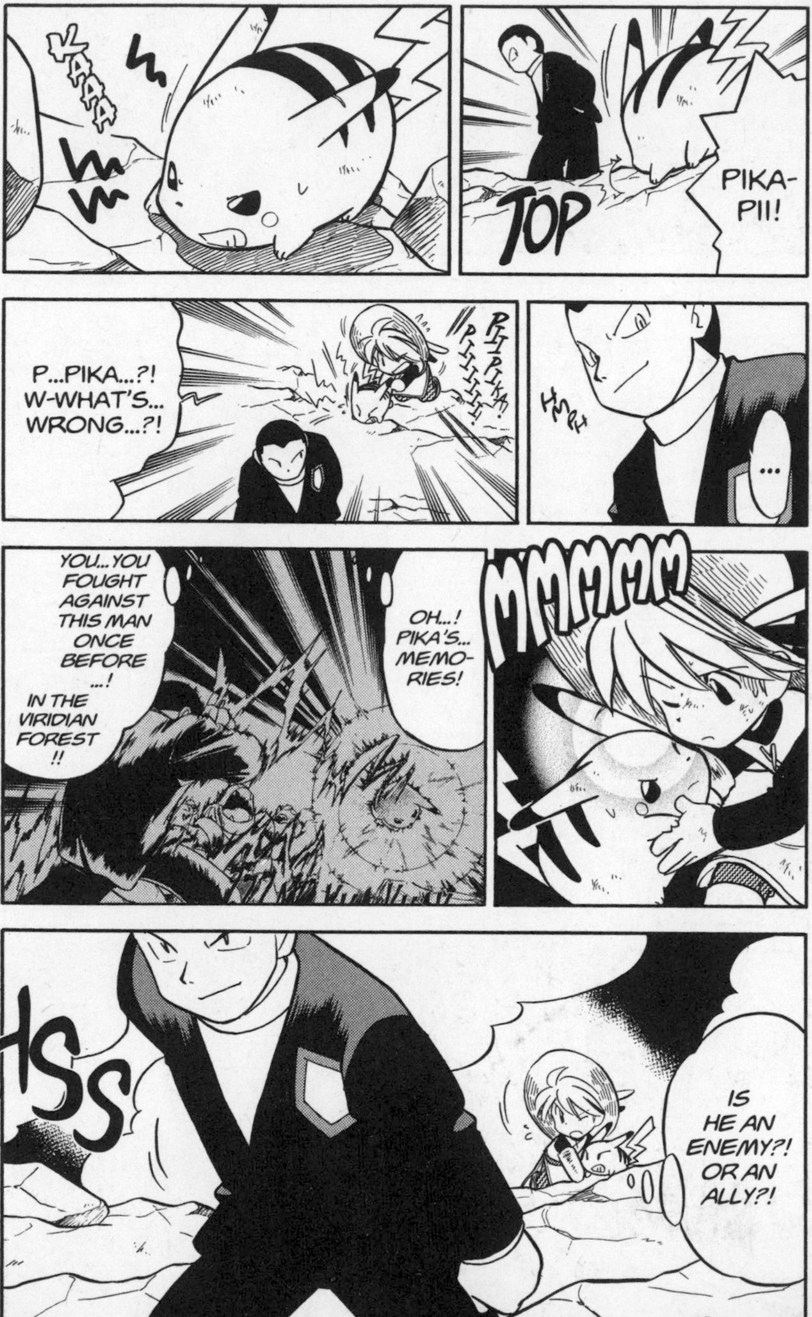
TOP
PIKA-PII!
KAAAA
HMPH
...
P...PIKA...?! W-WHAT'S... WRONG...?!
PIIIPIKA! PIIIIIII!
MMMMMM
OH...! PIKA'S... MEMORIES!
YOU...YOU FOUGHT AGAINST THIS MAN ONCE BEFORE ...!
IN THE VIRIDIAN FOREST !!
IS HE AN ENEMY?! OR AN ALLY?!
HSS

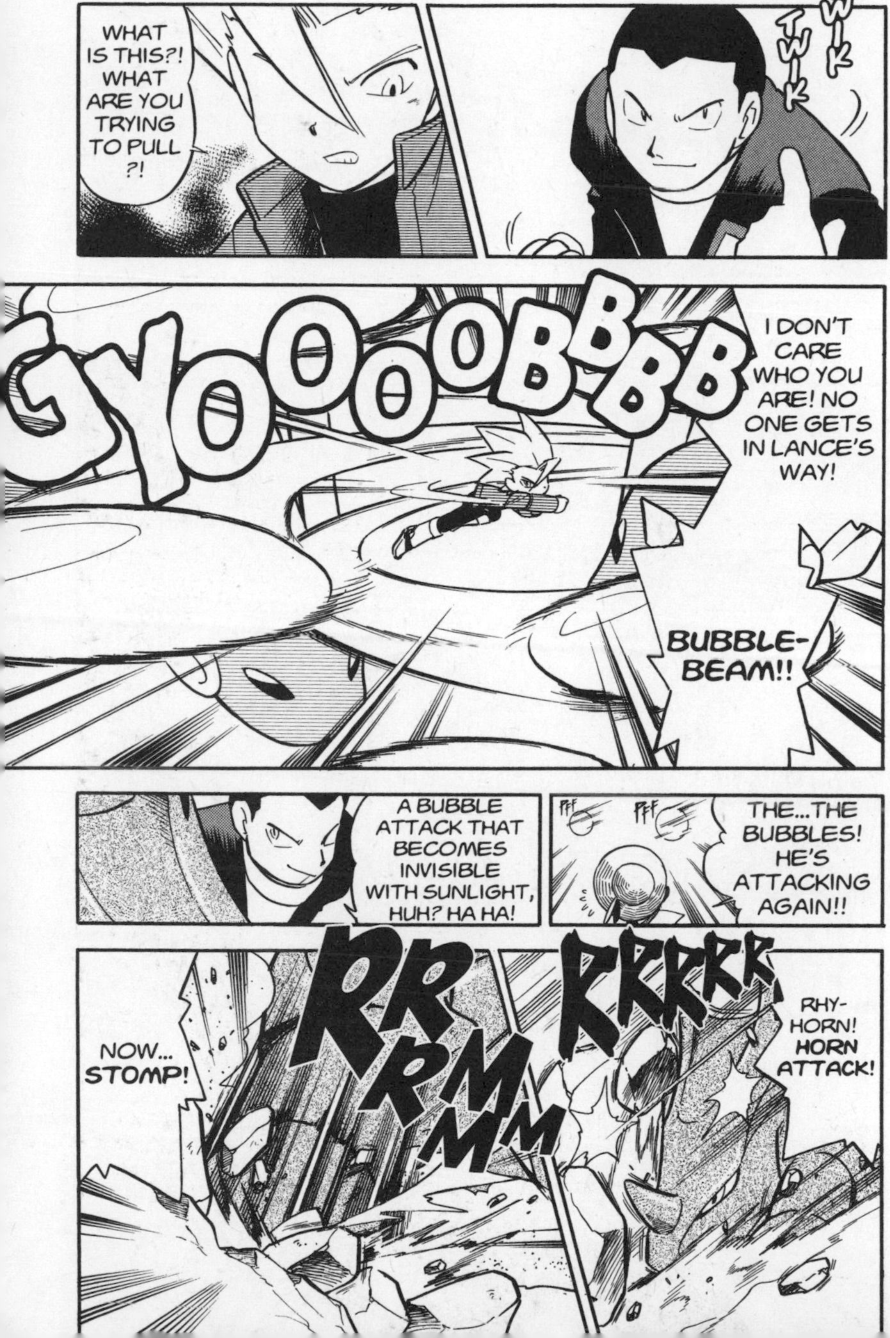
TWIK TWIK
WHAT IS THIS?! WHAT ARE YOU TRYING TO PULL?!
I DON'T CARE WHO YOU ARE! NO ONE GETS IN LANCE'S WAY!
GYOOOOBBBB
BUBBLE-BEAM!!
PFF
PFF
THE...THE BUBBLES! HE'S ATTACKING AGAIN!!
A BUBBLE ATTACK THAT BECOMES INVISIBLE WITH SUNLIGHT, HUH? HA HA!
RHY-HORN! HORN ATTACK!
RRRRR
RRRMMMM
NOW... STOMP!

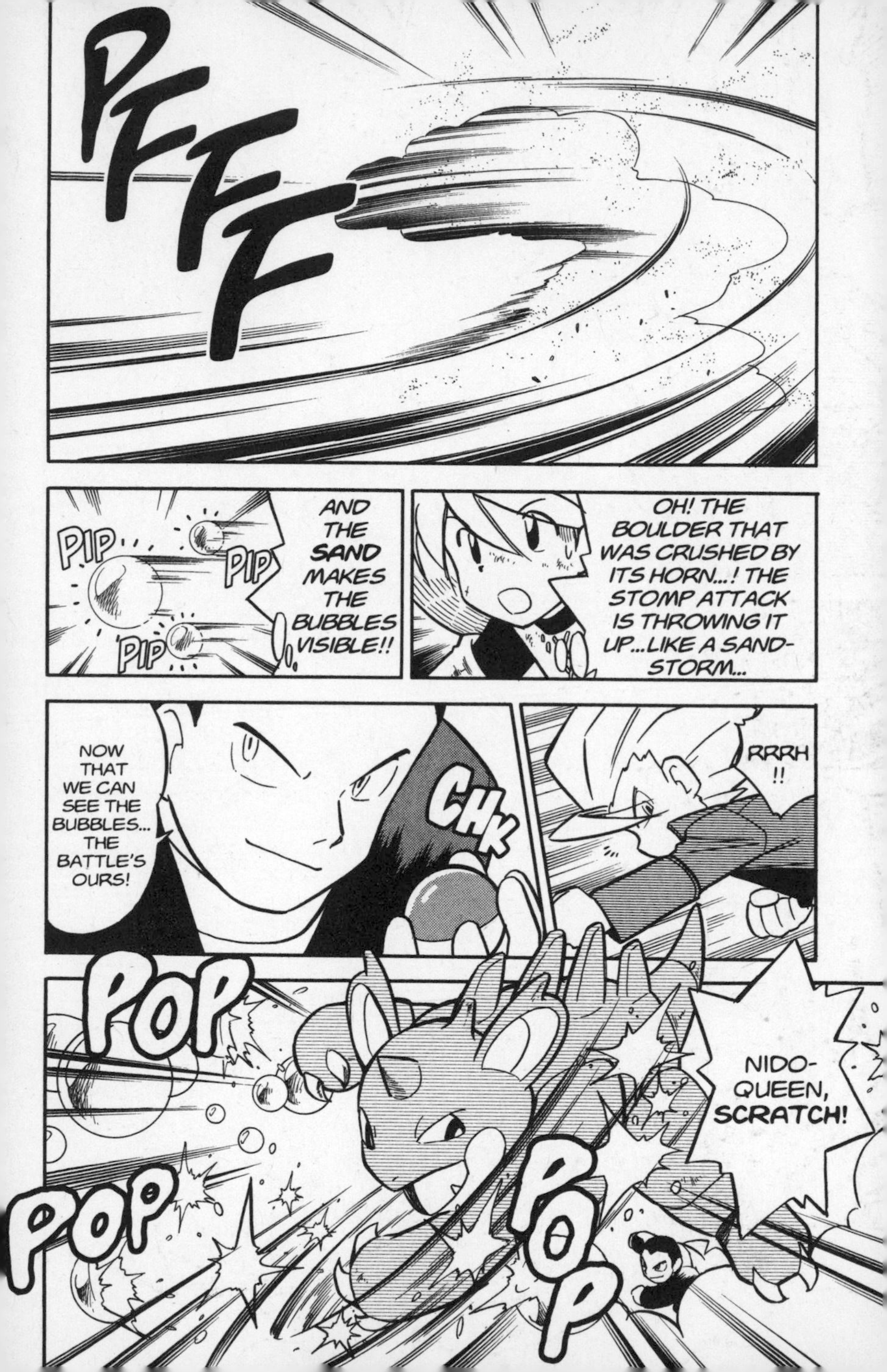
PFFFF
OH! THE BOULDER THAT WAS CRUSHED BY ITS HORN...! THE STOMP ATTACK IS THROWING IT UP...LIKE A SAND-STORM...
PIP
PIP
PIP
AND THE SAND MAKES THE BUBBLES VISIBLE!!
RRRH !!
NOW THAT WE CAN SEE THE BUBBLES... THE BATTLE'S OURS!
CHK
NIDO-QUEEN, SCRATCH!
POP
POP
POP

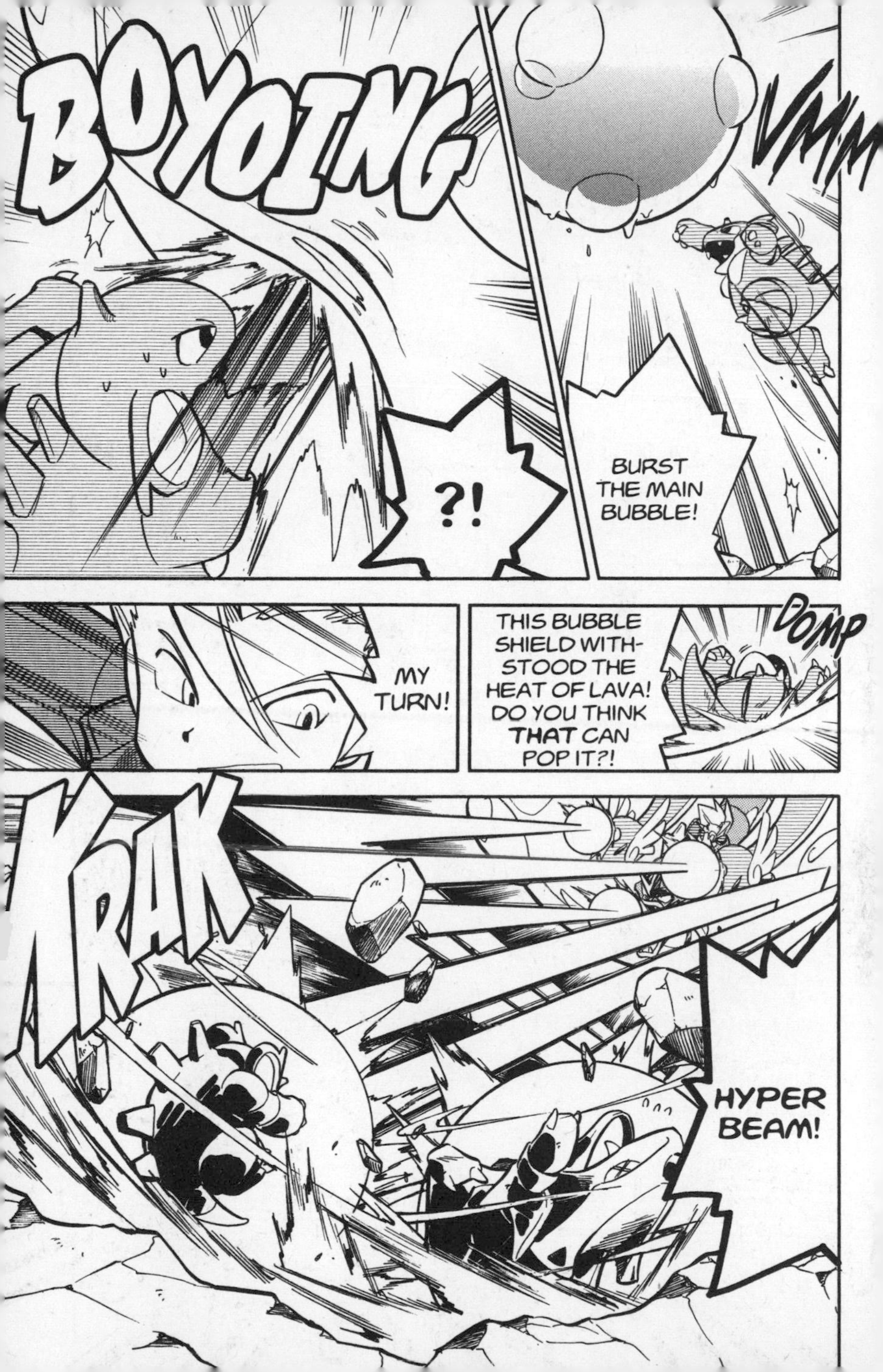
VMMM
BURST THE MAIN BUBBLE!
BOYOING
?!
DOMP
THIS BUBBLE SHIELD WITHSTOOD THE HEAT OF LAVA! DO YOU THINK THAT CAN POP IT?!
MY TURN!
HYPER BEAM!
KRAK

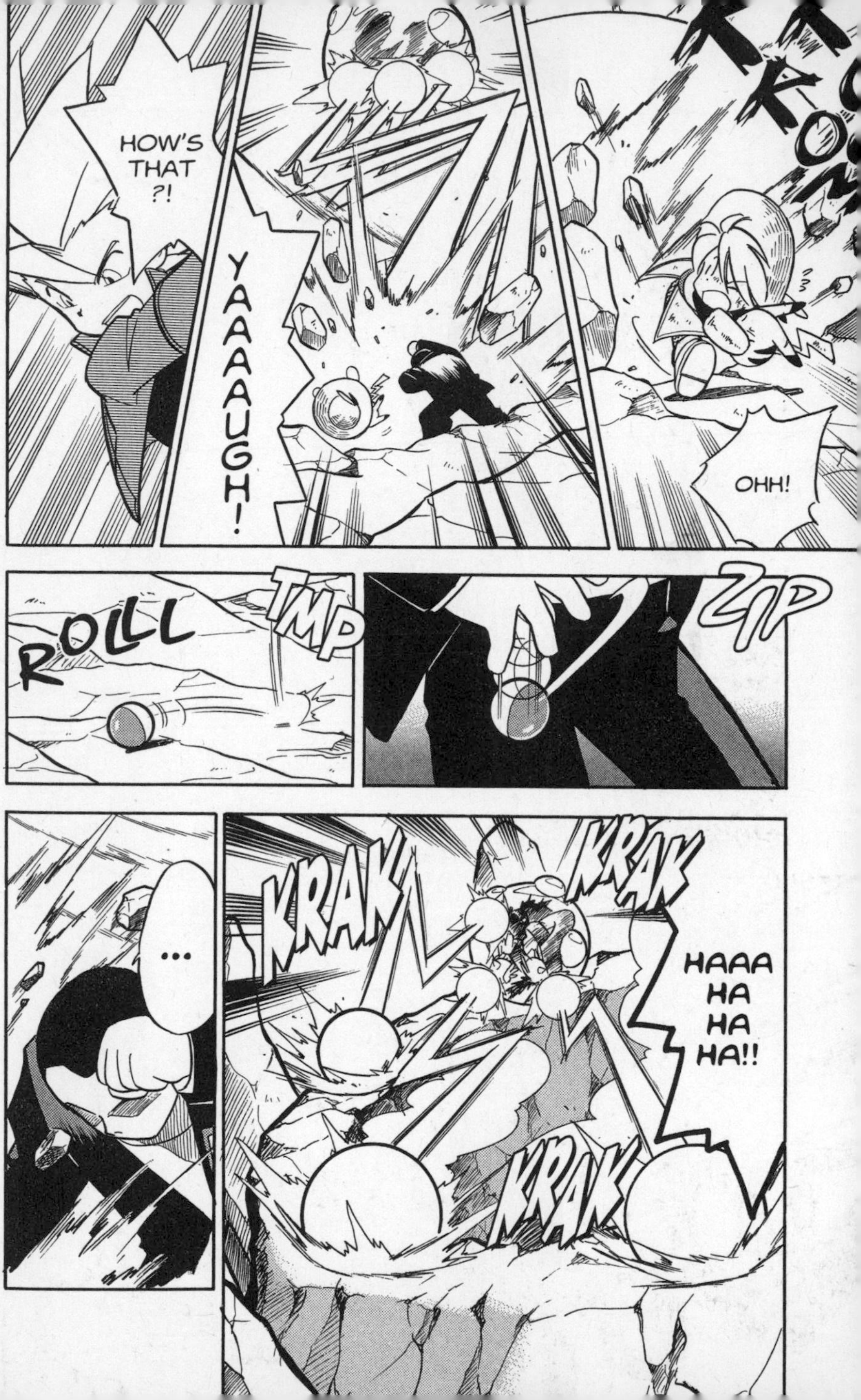
OHH!
YAAAAAUGH!
HOW'S THAT ?!
ZIP
TMP
ROLLL
KRAK
KRAK
HAAA HA HA HA!!
KRAK
...

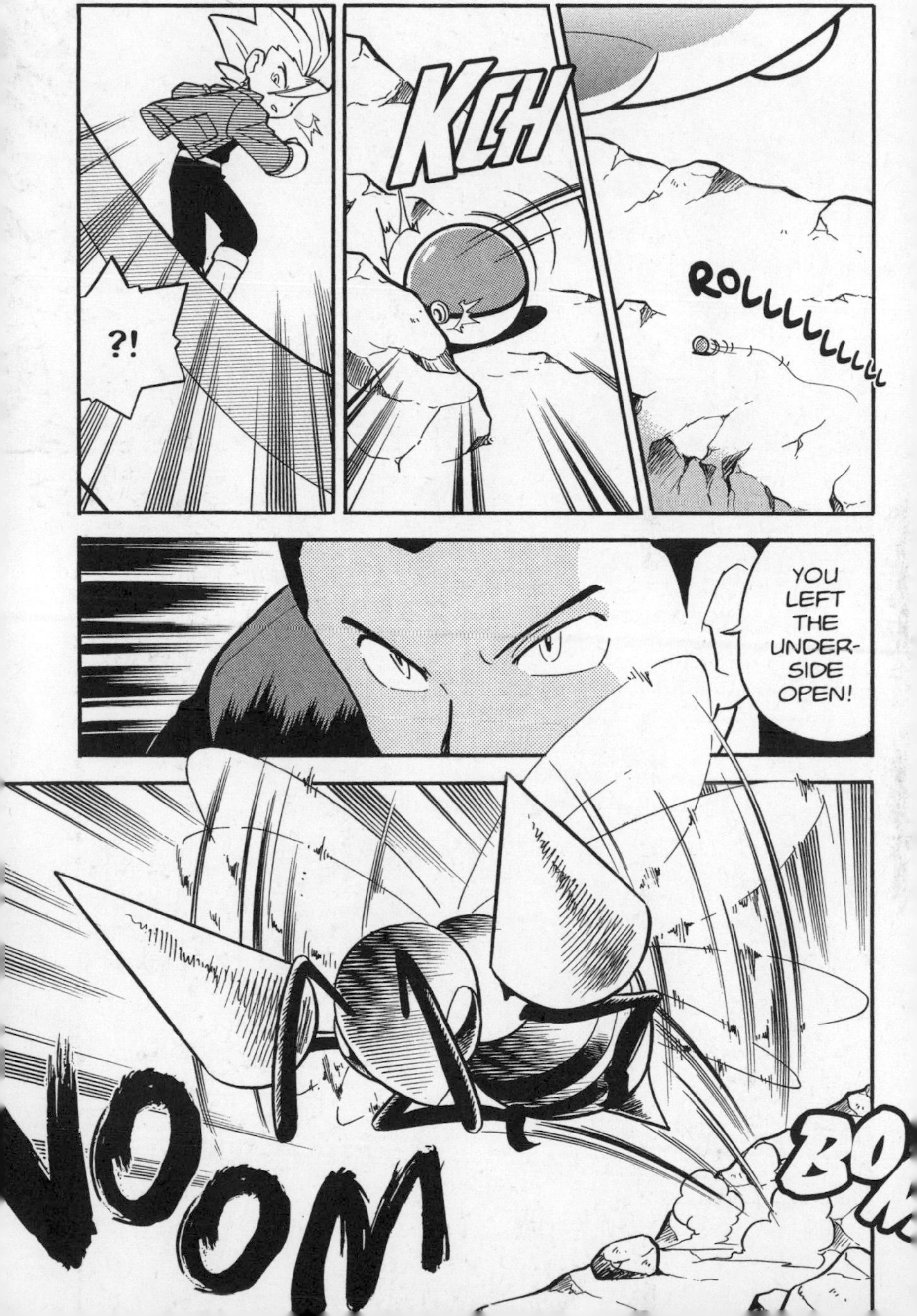
ROLLLLLLLLLLL
KCH
?!
YOU LEFT THE UNDER-SIDE OPEN!
BO

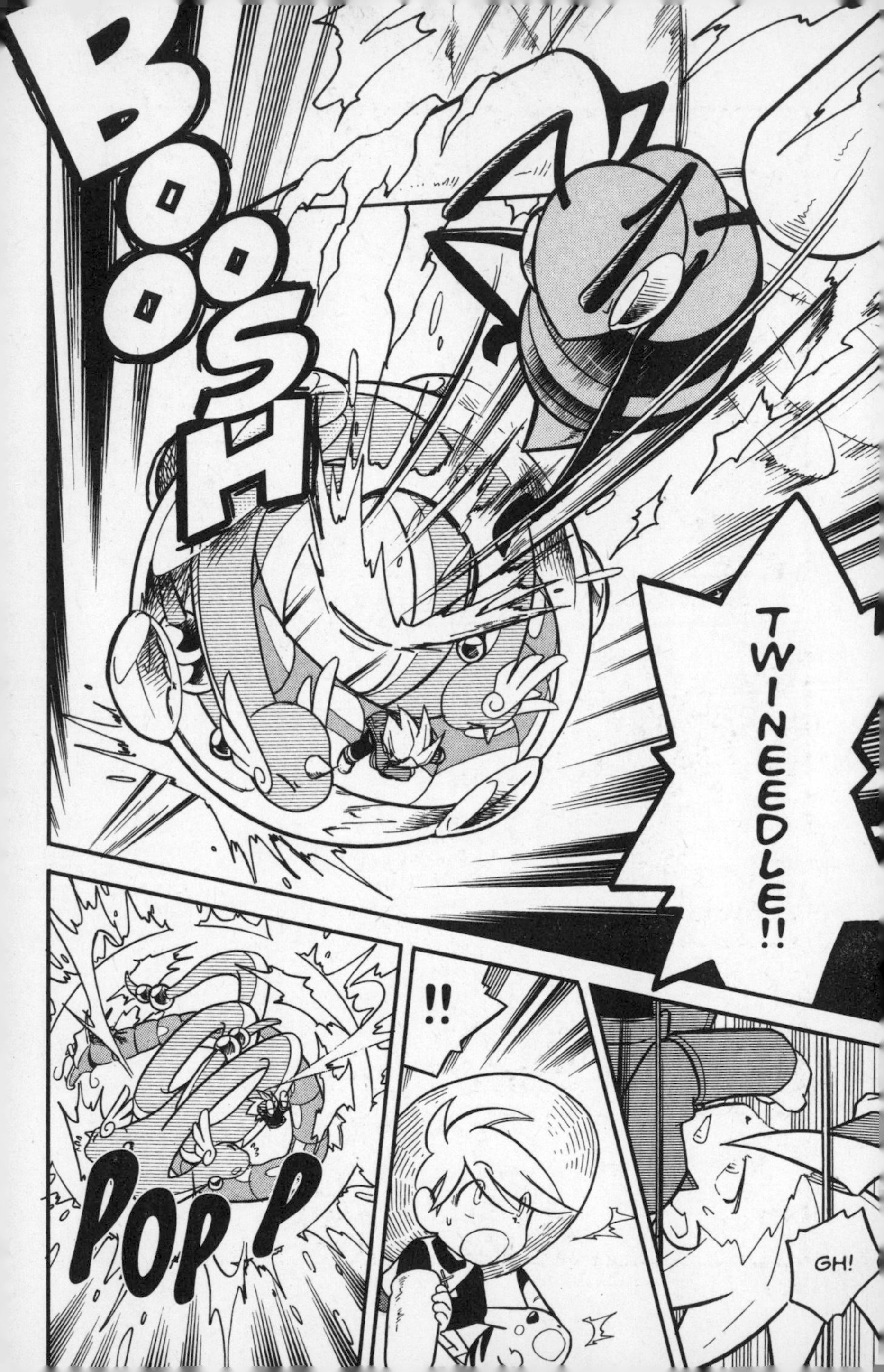
BOOOSH
TWINEEDLE!!
GH!
!!
POPP

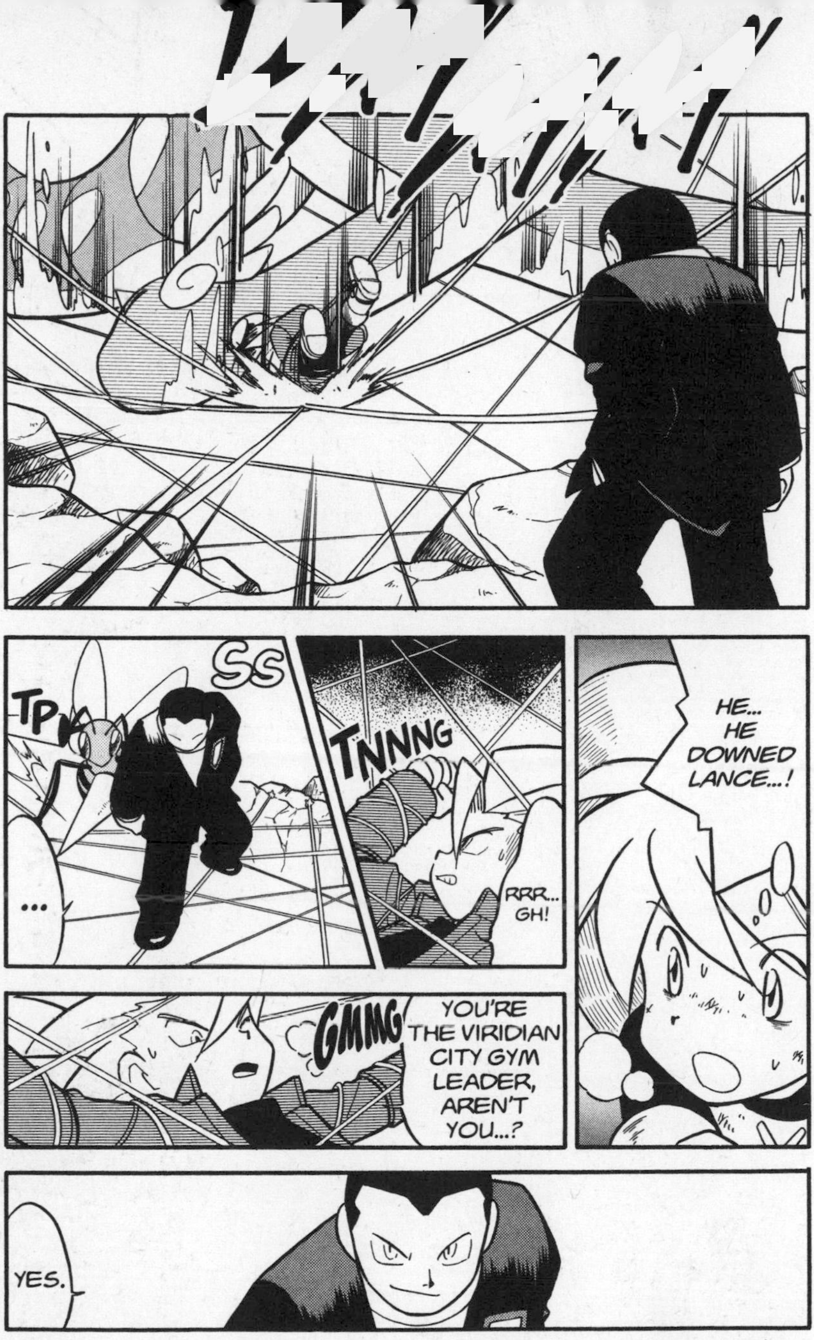
HE... HE DOWNED LANCE...!
TNNNG
RRR... GH!
Ss
TP
...
GMMG
YOU'RE THE VIRIDIAN CITY GYM LEADER, AREN'T YOU...?
YES.

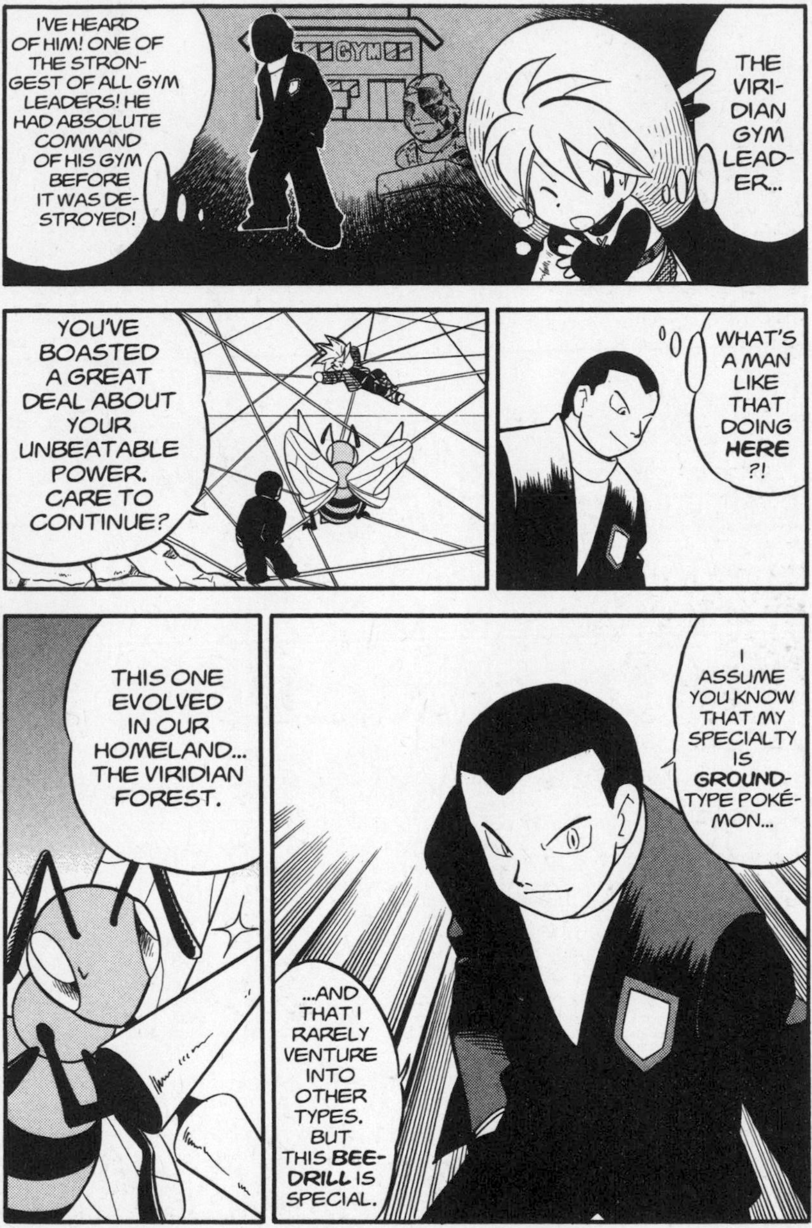
THE VIRIDIAN GYM LEADER...
I'VE HEARD OF HIM! ONE OF THE STRONGEST OF ALL GYM LEADERS! HE HAD ABSOLUTE COMMAND OF HIS GYM BEFORE IT WAS DESTROYED!
WHAT'S A MAN LIKE THAT DOING **HERE**?!
YOU'VE BOASTED A GREAT DEAL ABOUT YOUR UNBEATABLE POWER. CARE TO CONTINUE?
I ASSUME YOU KNOW THAT MY SPECIALTY IS **GROUND**-TYPE POKÉMON...
...AND THAT I RARELY VENTURE INTO OTHER TYPES. BUT THIS **BEEDRILL** IS SPECIAL.
THIS ONE EVOLVED IN OUR HOMELAND... THE VIRIDIAN FOREST.

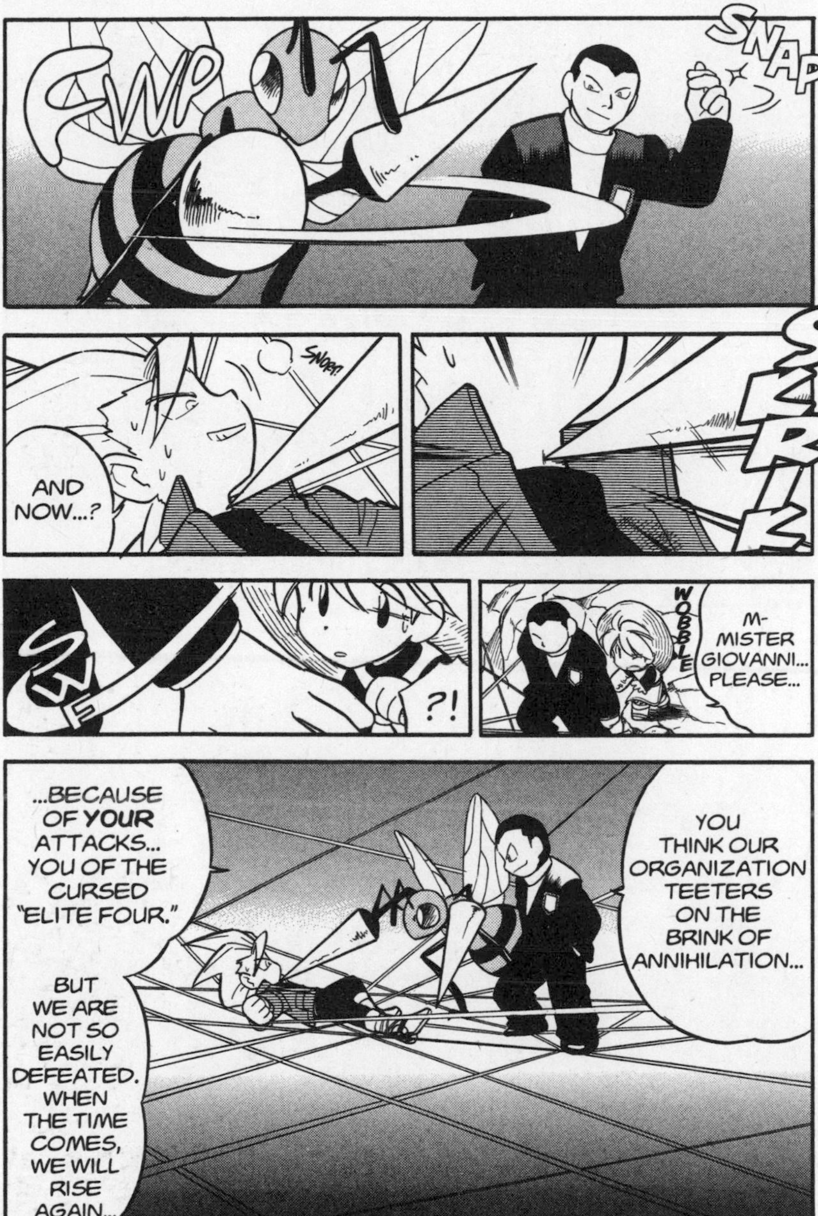
SNAP
SWP
SKRIK
AND NOW...?
WOBBLE
M-MISTER GIOVANNI... PLEASE...
?!
SWF
YOU THINK OUR ORGANIZATION TEETERS ON THE BRINK OF ANNIHILATION...
...BECAUSE OF **YOUR** ATTACKS... YOU OF THE CURSED "ELITE FOUR."
BUT WE ARE NOT SO EASILY DEFEATED. WHEN THE TIME COMES, WE WILL RISE AGAIN...

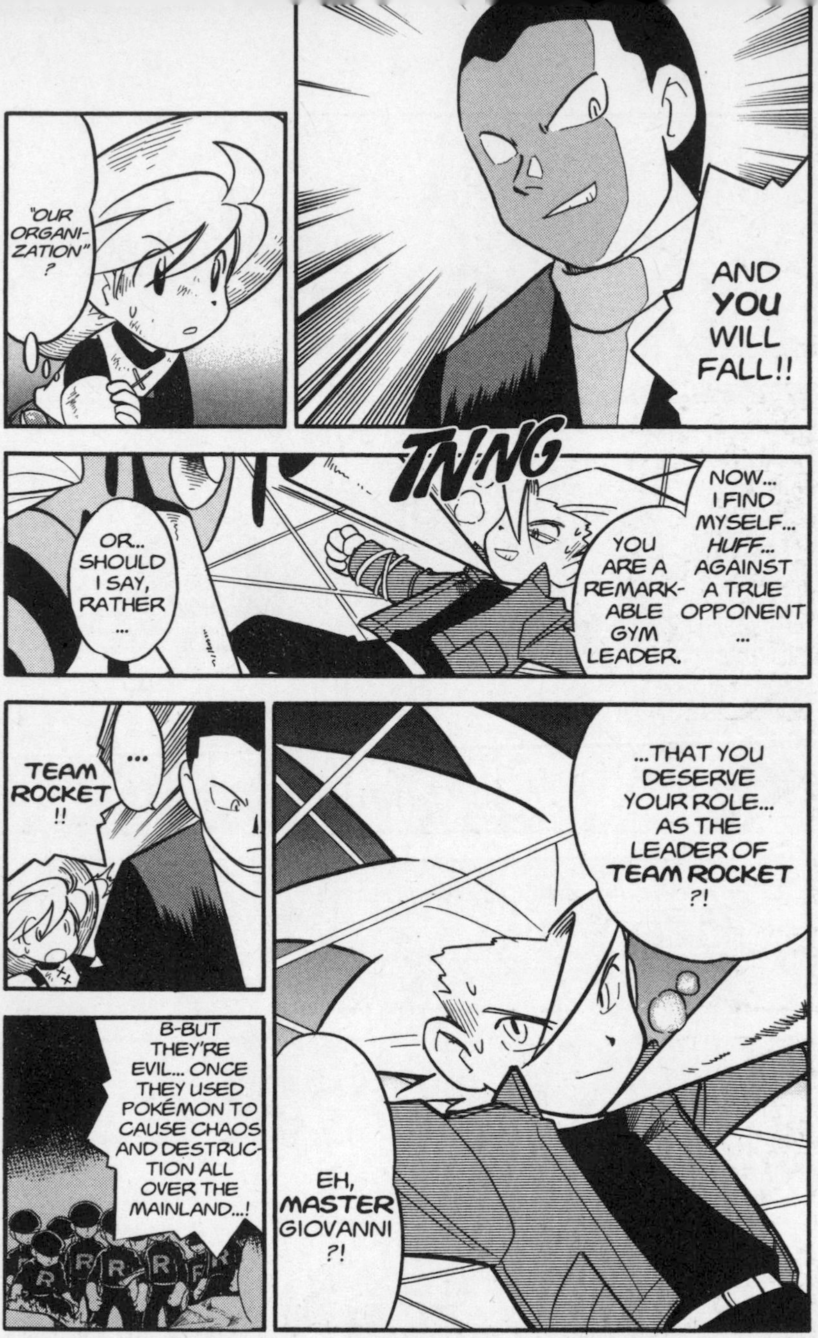
AND YOU WILL FALL!!
"OUR ORGANIZATION"?
TNNG
NOW... I FIND MYSELF... HUFF... AGAINST A TRUE OPPONENT...
YOU ARE A REMARKABLE GYM LEADER.
OR... SHOULD I SAY, RATHER...
...THAT YOU DESERVE YOUR ROLE... AS THE LEADER OF TEAM ROCKET?!
EH, MASTER GIOVANNI?!
...
TEAM ROCKET!!
B-BUT THEY'RE EVIL... ONCE THEY USED POKÉMON TO CAUSE CHAOS AND DESTRUCTION ALL OVER THE MAINLAND...!

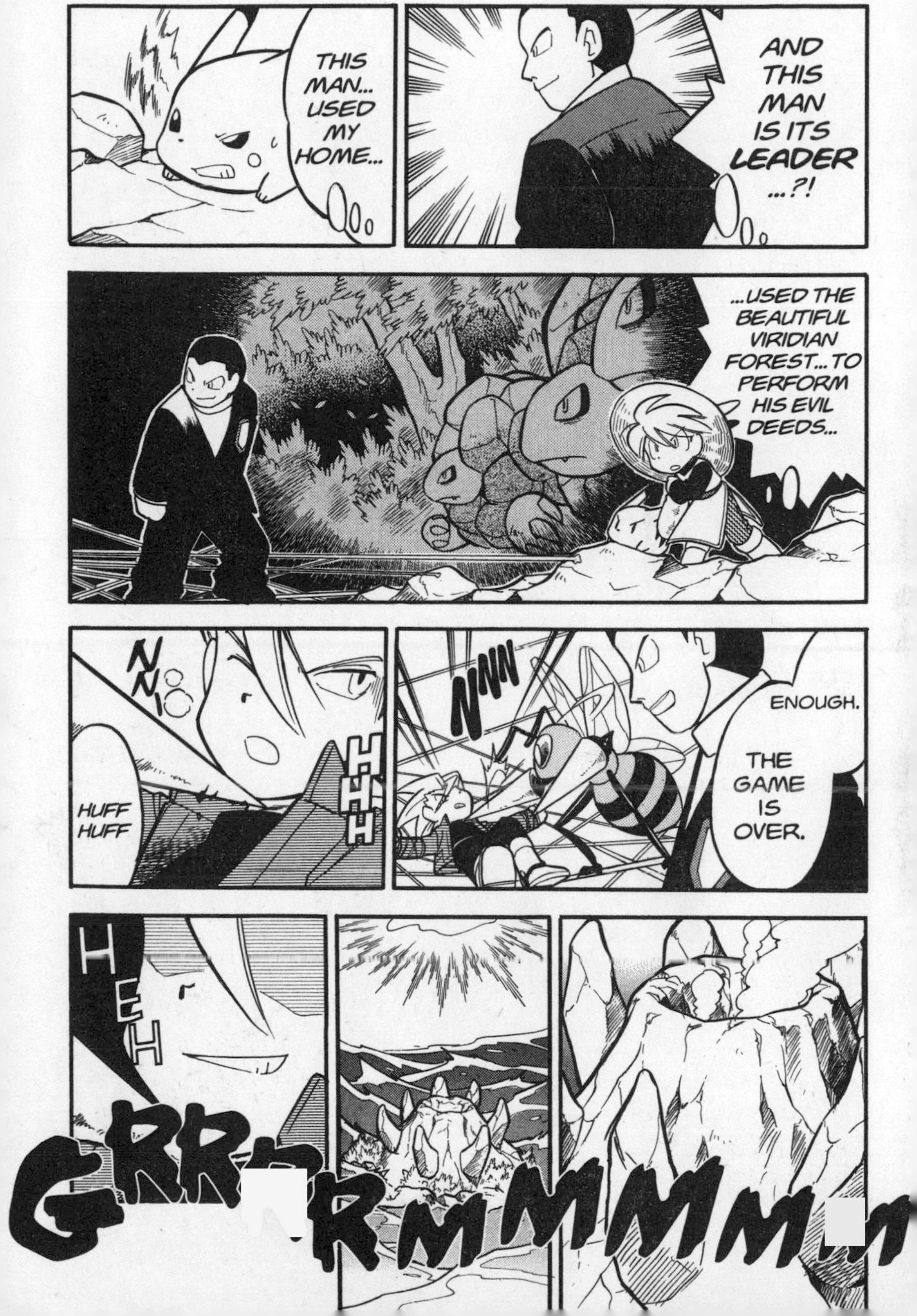
AND THIS MAN IS ITS LEADER ...?!
THIS MAN... USED MY HOME...
...USED THE BEAUTIFUL VIRIDIAN FOREST...TO PERFORM HIS EVIL DEEDS...
NNN
ENOUGH.
THE GAME IS OVER.
NN
HHHH
HUFF HUFF
HEH
GRR
RMMMMM

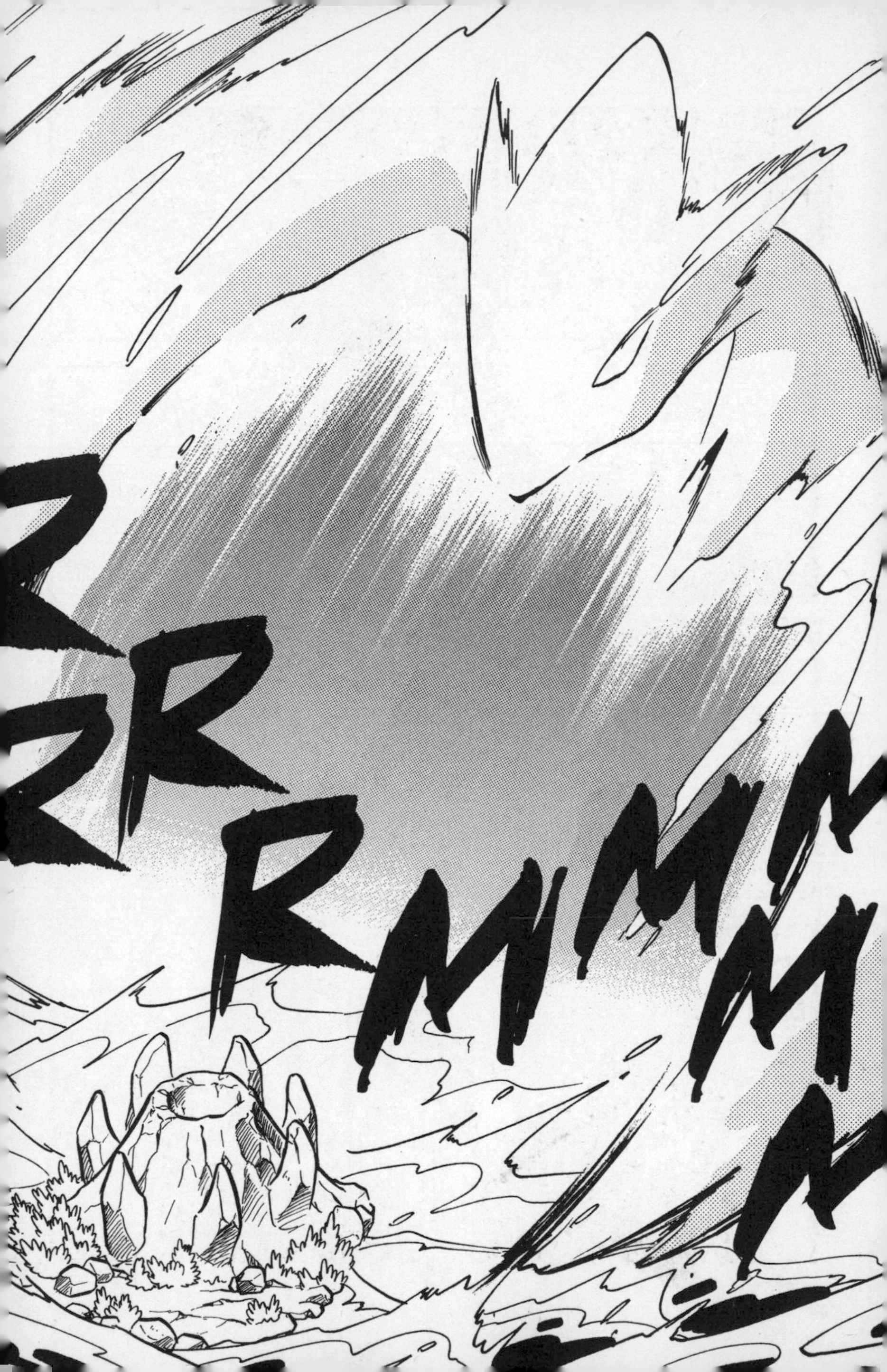
RRRMMMM

HA HA HA HA HA... WRA-HA-HAA!!!

?!

EH...? HEH... HEH-HEH...

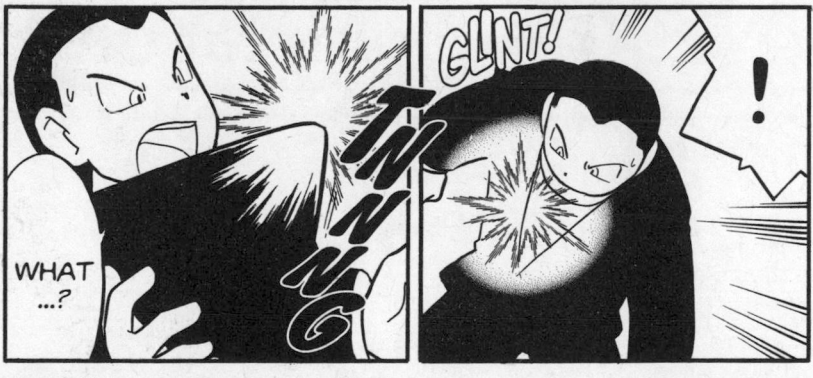

WHAT ...?

TINNNG

GLINT!

!

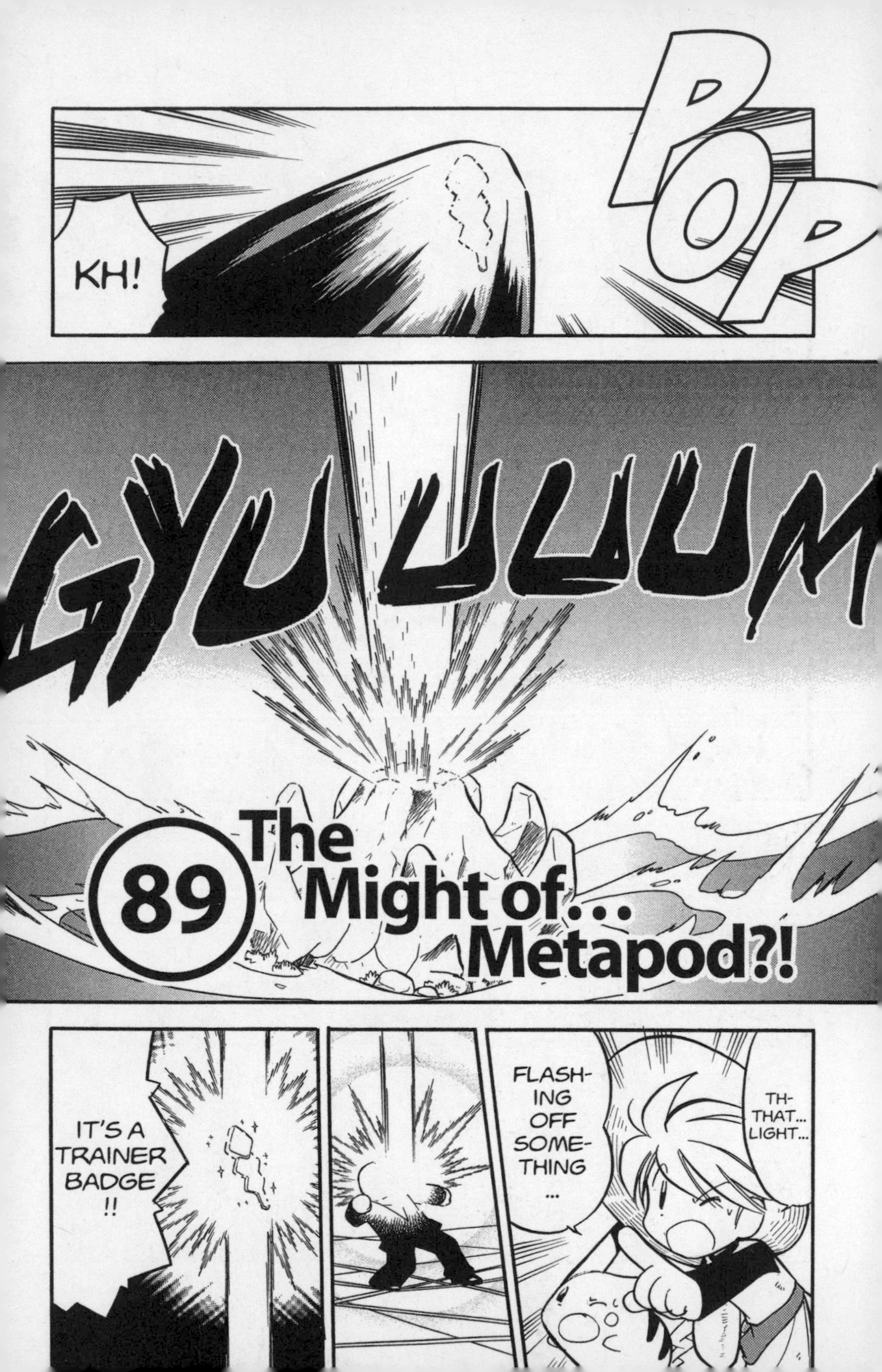
POP
KH!
GYUUUM
89 The Might of... Metapod?!
TH- THAT... LIGHT...
FLASHING OFF SOMETHING ...
IT'S A TRAINER BADGE !!

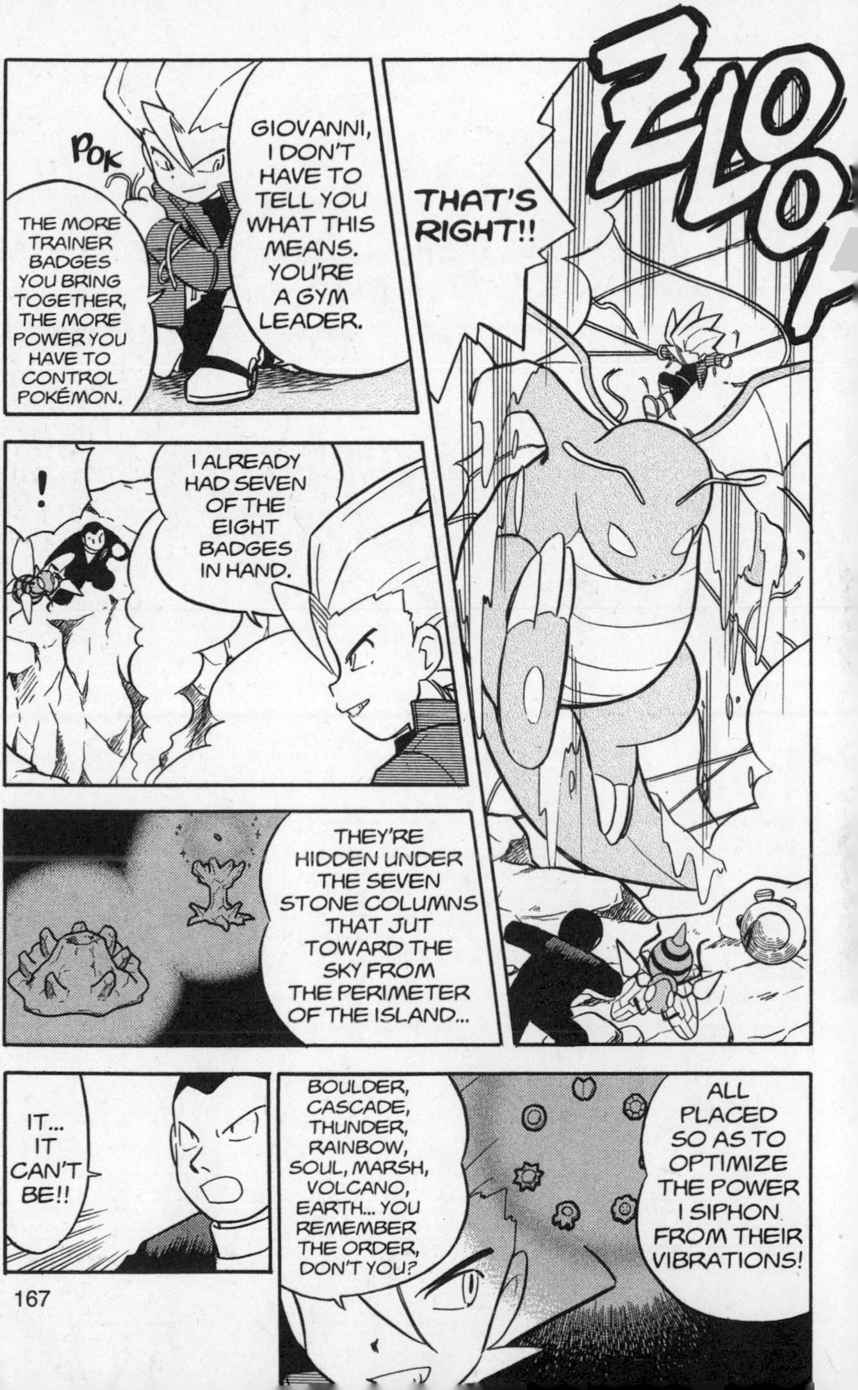
ZLOOO
THAT'S RIGHT!!
GIOVANNI, I DON'T HAVE TO TELL YOU WHAT THIS MEANS. YOU'RE A GYM LEADER.
POK
THE MORE TRAINER BADGES YOU BRING TOGETHER, THE MORE POWER YOU HAVE TO CONTROL POKÉMON.
I ALREADY HAD SEVEN OF THE EIGHT BADGES IN HAND.
!
THEY'RE HIDDEN UNDER THE SEVEN STONE COLUMNS THAT JUT TOWARD THE SKY FROM THE PERIMETER OF THE ISLAND...
ALL PLACED SO AS TO OPTIMIZE THE POWER I SIPHON FROM THEIR VIBRATIONS!
BOULDER, CASCADE, THUNDER, RAINBOW, SOUL, MARSH, VOLCANO, EARTH... YOU REMEMBER THE ORDER, DON'T YOU?
IT... IT CAN'T BE!!

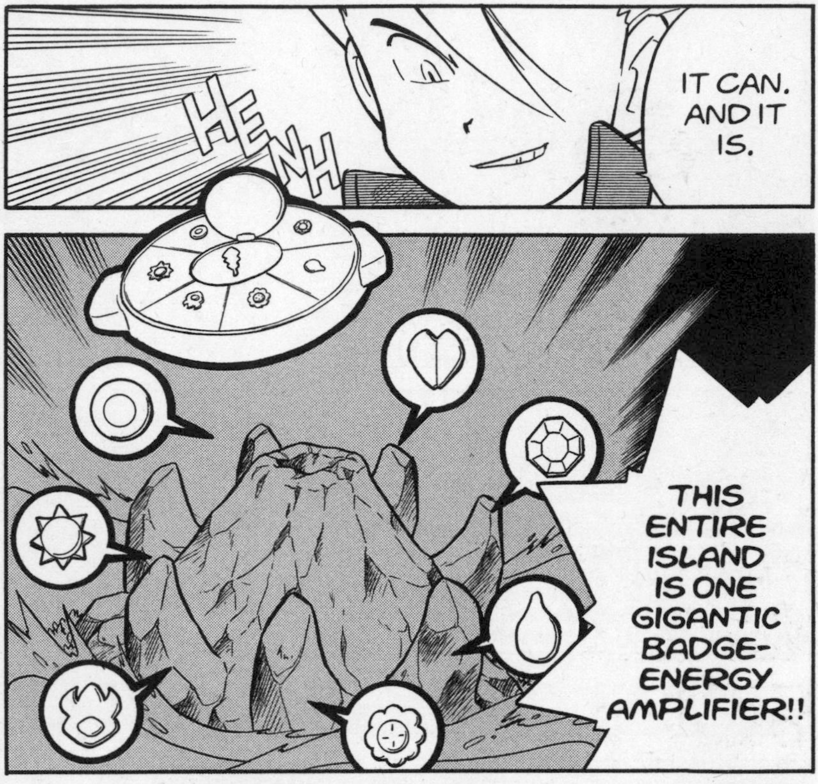

IT CAN. AND IT IS.
HENNH
THIS ENTIRE ISLAND IS ONE GIGANTIC BADGE-ENERGY AMPLIFIER!!
THE ONE THAT JUST FLEW FROM YOUR CHEST AND STARTED TO GLOW WAS THE LAST ONE! THE ONE I'VE BEEN SEARCHING FOR!
THIS "AMPLIFIER" IS LAID OUT SO THAT MERELY BRINGING THE BADGE TO ITS MIDPOINT...
...WOULD AUTOMAT-ICALLY RELEASE ITS ENERGY!
YOU THOUGHT THAT YOU WERE PUSHING ME TO THE EDGE?! HA!
I WAS IN COMMAND!
I LURED YOU TO THE CENTER OF THE ISLAND!
...

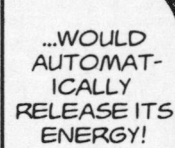

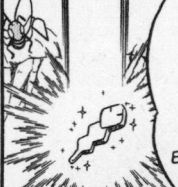

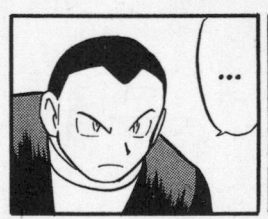

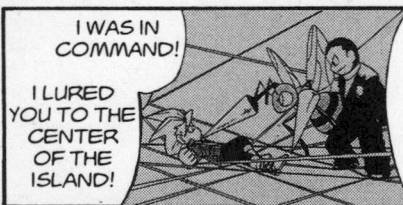

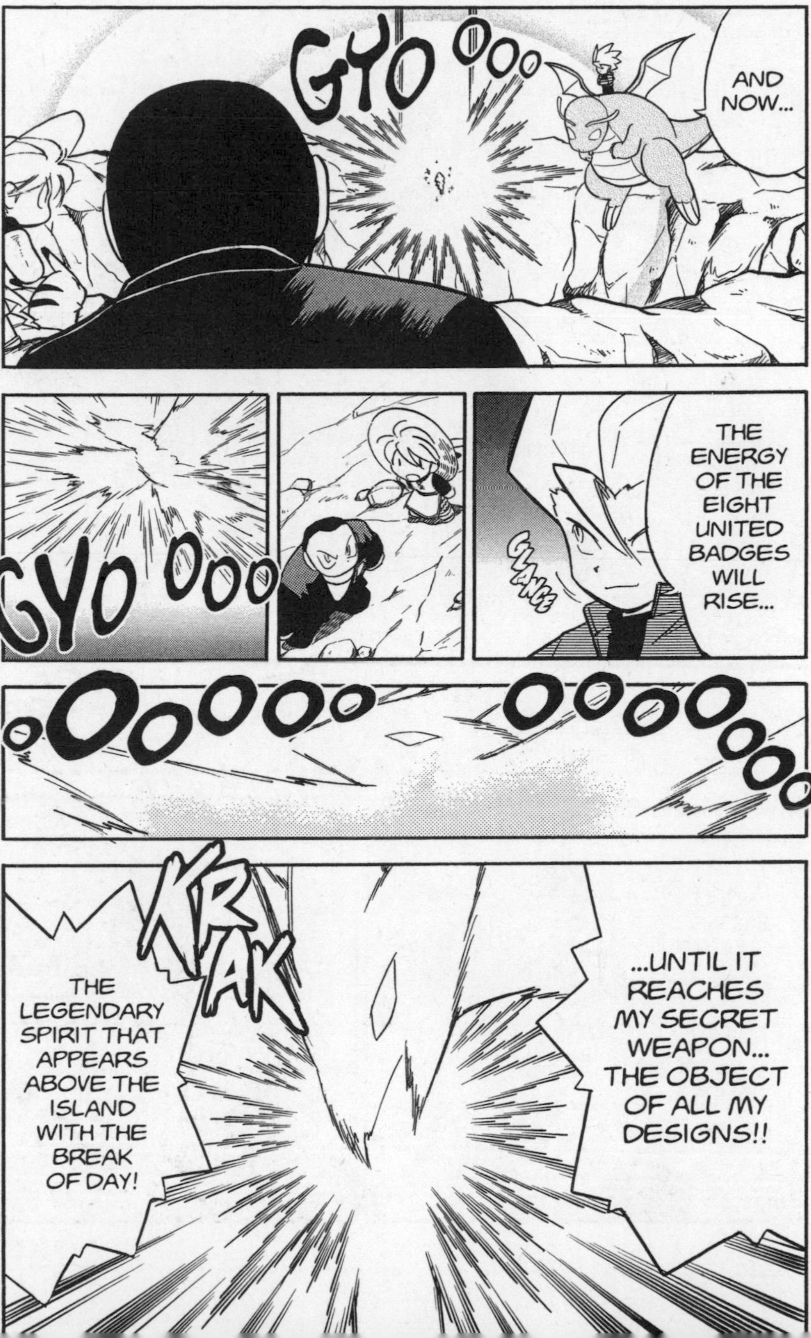
AND NOW...
GYO OOO
THE ENERGY OF THE EIGHT UNITED BADGES WILL RISE...
GLANCE
GYO OOO
OOOOOO OOOOOOOOO
...UNTIL IT REACHES MY SECRET WEAPON... THE OBJECT OF ALL MY DESIGNS!!
KRAK
THE LEGENDARY SPIRIT THAT APPEARS ABOVE THE ISLAND WITH THE BREAK OF DAY!

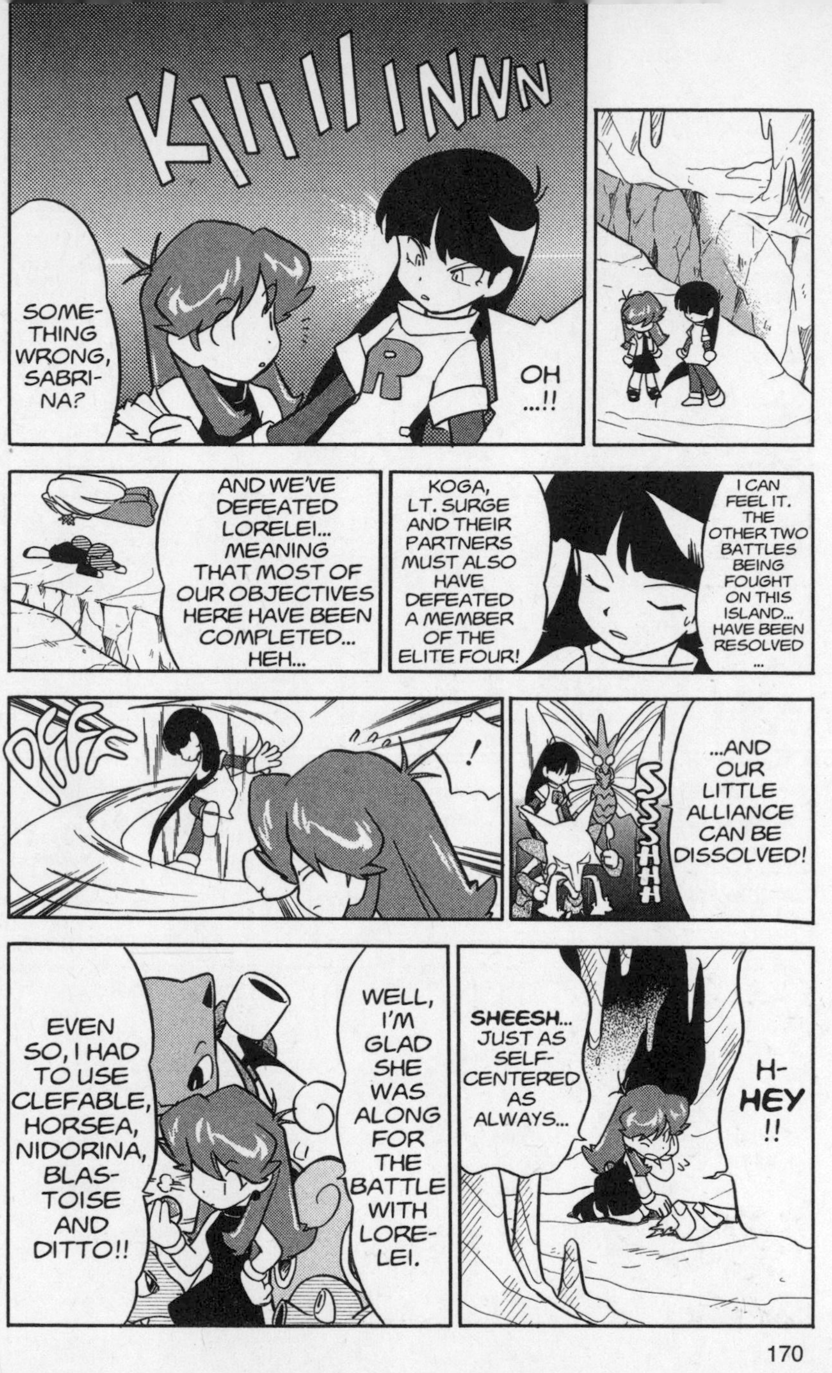
KIIIIIINNNN
OH ...!!
SOMETHING WRONG, SABRINA?
I CAN FEEL IT. THE OTHER TWO BATTLES BEING FOUGHT ON THIS ISLAND... HAVE BEEN RESOLVED ...
KOGA, LT. SURGE AND THEIR PARTNERS MUST ALSO HAVE DEFEATED A MEMBER OF THE ELITE FOUR!
AND WE'VE DEFEATED LORELEI... MEANING THAT MOST OF OUR OBJECTIVES HERE HAVE BEEN COMPLETED... HEH...
...AND OUR LITTLE ALLIANCE CAN BE DISSOLVED!
SSSHHH
!
PFFF
H-HEY !!
SHEESH... JUST AS SELF-CENTERED AS ALWAYS...
WELL, I'M GLAD SHE WAS ALONG FOR THE BATTLE WITH LORELEI.
EVEN SO, I HAD TO USE CLEFABLE, HORSEA, NIDORINA, BLASTOISE AND DITTO!!

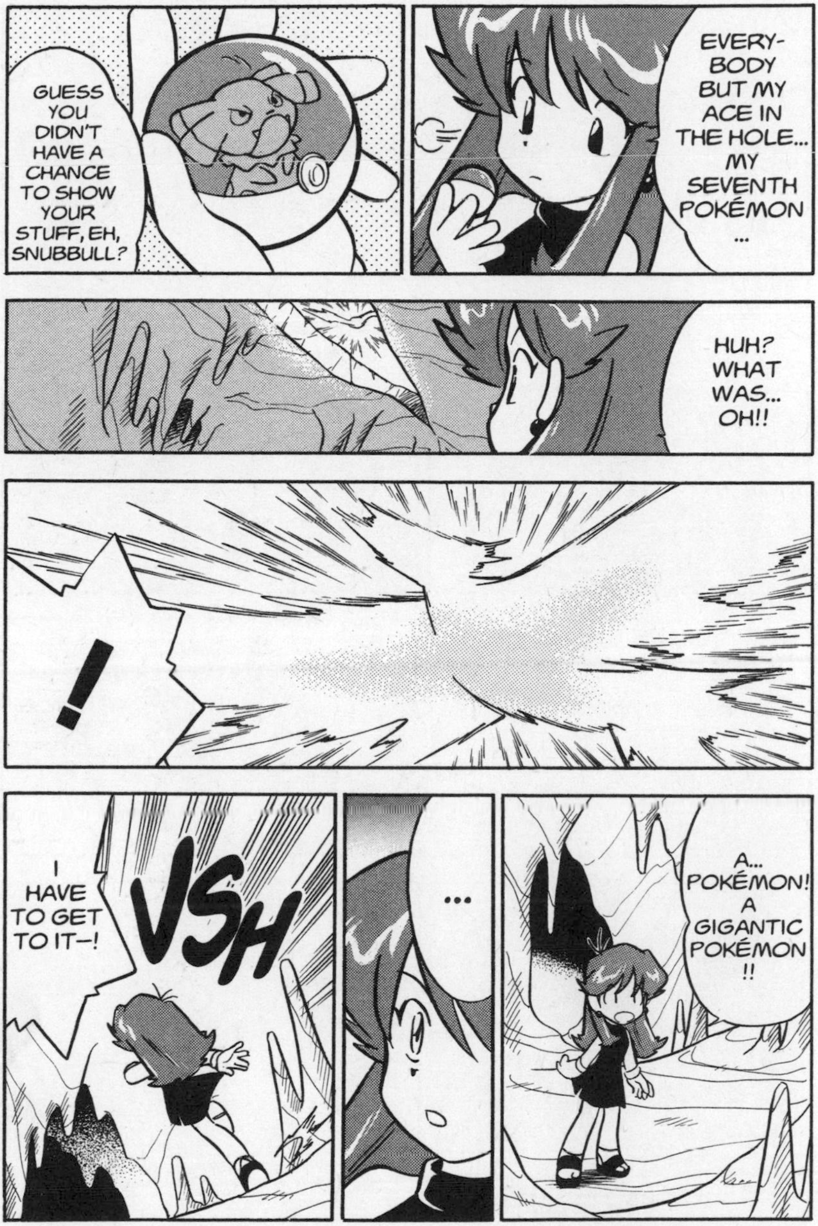
EVERY-BODY BUT MY ACE IN THE HOLE... MY SEVENTH POKÉMON ...
GUESS YOU DIDN'T HAVE A CHANCE TO SHOW YOUR STUFF, EH, SNUBBULL?
HUH? WHAT WAS... OH!!
!
A... POKÉMON! A GIGANTIC POKÉMON !!
...
VSH
I HAVE TO GET TO IT–!

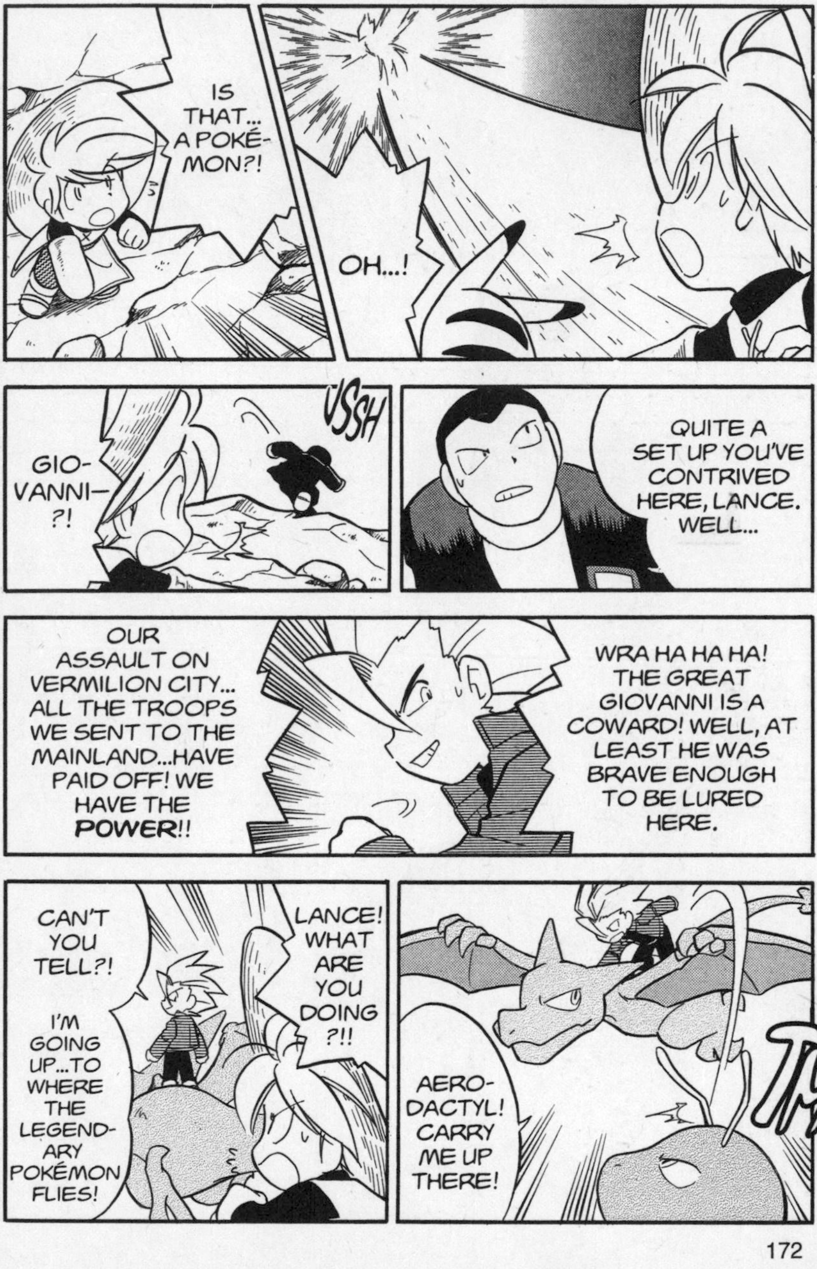
OH...!
IS THAT... A POKÉ-MON?!
QUITE A SET UP YOU'VE CONTRIVED HERE, LANCE. WELL...
VSSH
GIO-VANNI-?!
WRA HA HA HA! THE GREAT GIOVANNI IS A COWARD! WELL, AT LEAST HE WAS BRAVE ENOUGH TO BE LURED HERE.
OUR ASSAULT ON VERMILION CITY... ALL THE TROOPS WE SENT TO THE MAINLAND...HAVE PAID OFF! WE HAVE THE **POWER**!!
AERO-DACTYL! CARRY ME UP THERE!
LANCE! WHAT ARE YOU DOING?!!
CAN'T YOU TELL?!
I'M GOING UP...TO WHERE THE LEGEND-ARY POKÉMON FLIES!

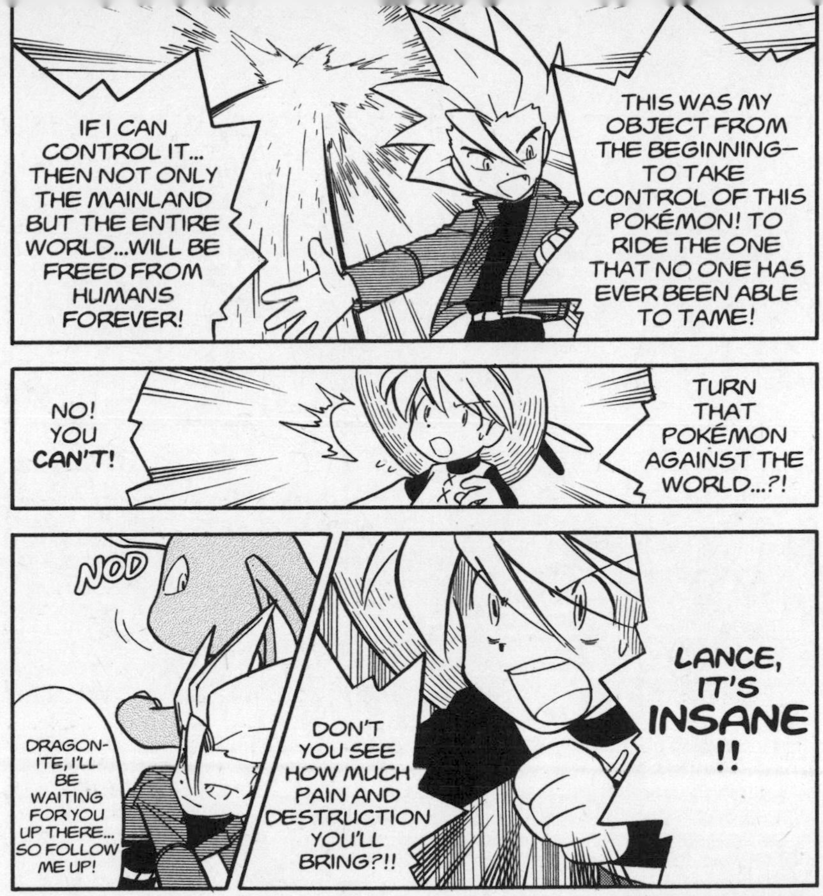

THIS WAS MY OBJECT FROM THE BEGINNING—TO TAKE CONTROL OF THIS POKÉMON! TO RIDE THE ONE THAT NO ONE HAS EVER BEEN ABLE TO TAME!
IF I CAN CONTROL IT... THEN NOT ONLY THE MAINLAND BUT THE ENTIRE WORLD...WILL BE FREED FROM HUMANS FOREVER!
TURN THAT POKÉMON AGAINST THE WORLD...?!
NO! YOU CAN'T!
LANCE, IT'S INSANE!!
DON'T YOU SEE HOW MUCH PAIN AND DESTRUCTION YOU'LL BRING?!!
NOD
DRAGON-ITE, I'LL BE WAITING FOR YOU UP THERE... SO FOLLOW ME UP!
GRRN
HWOOO
NKH!
VIIIN

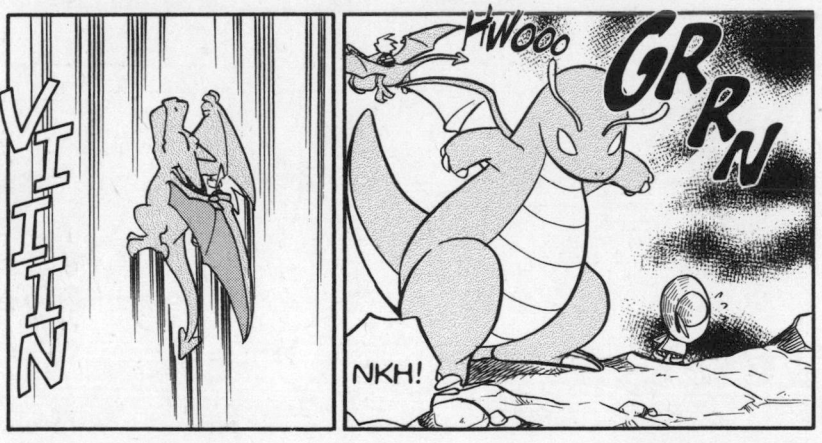

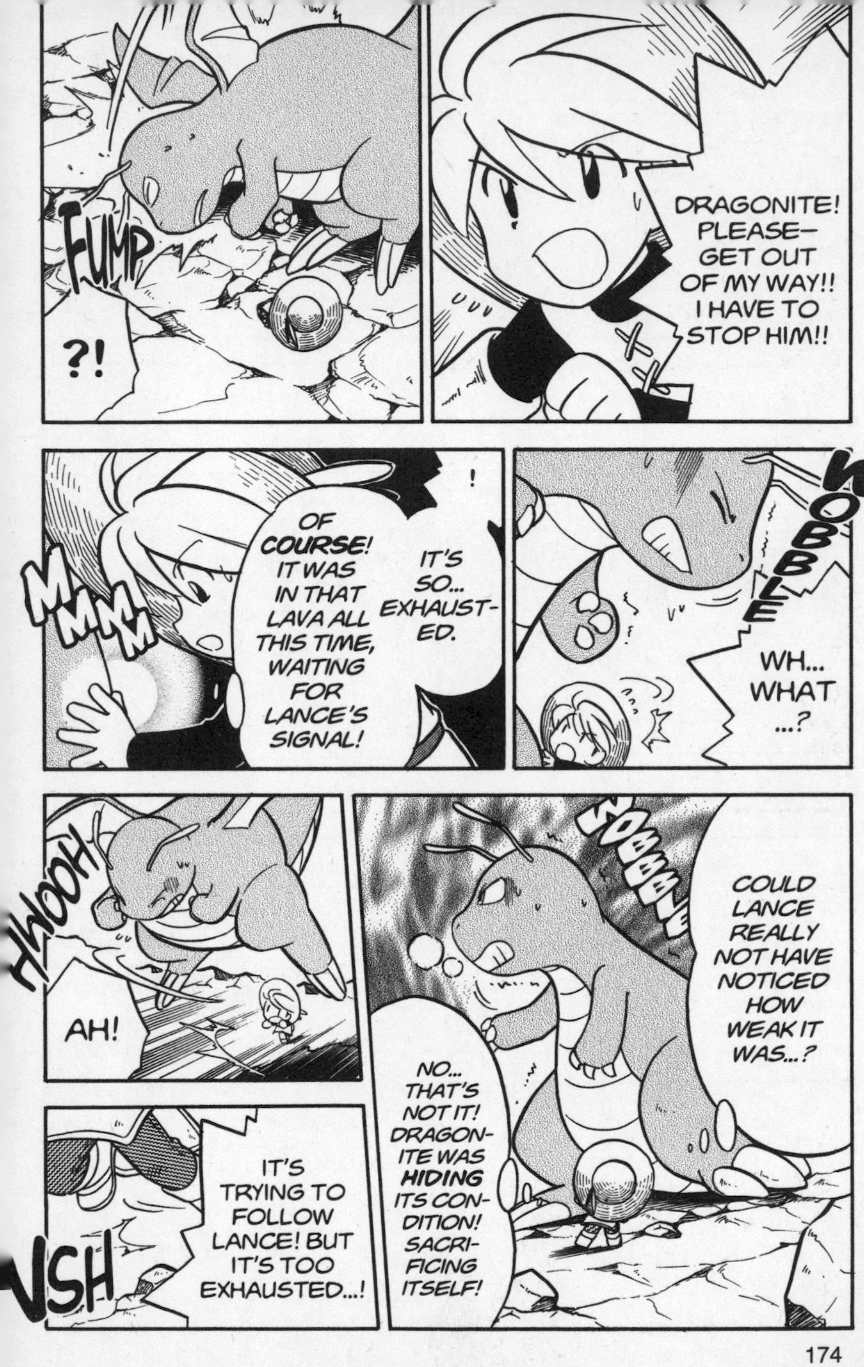
DRAGONITE! PLEASE— GET OUT OF MY WAY!! I HAVE TO STOP HIM!!
FUMP
?!
WOBBLE
WH... WHAT ...?
!
IT'S SO... EXHAUST-ED.
OF COURSE! IT WAS IN THAT LAVA ALL THIS TIME, WAITING FOR LANCE'S SIGNAL!
MMMM
WOBBLE
COULD LANCE REALLY NOT HAVE NOTICED HOW WEAK IT WAS...?
NO... THAT'S NOT IT! DRAGON-ITE WAS HIDING ITS CON-DITION! SACRI-FICING ITSELF!
HWOOH
AH!
IT'S TRYING TO FOLLOW LANCE! BUT IT'S TOO EXHAUSTED...!
WSH

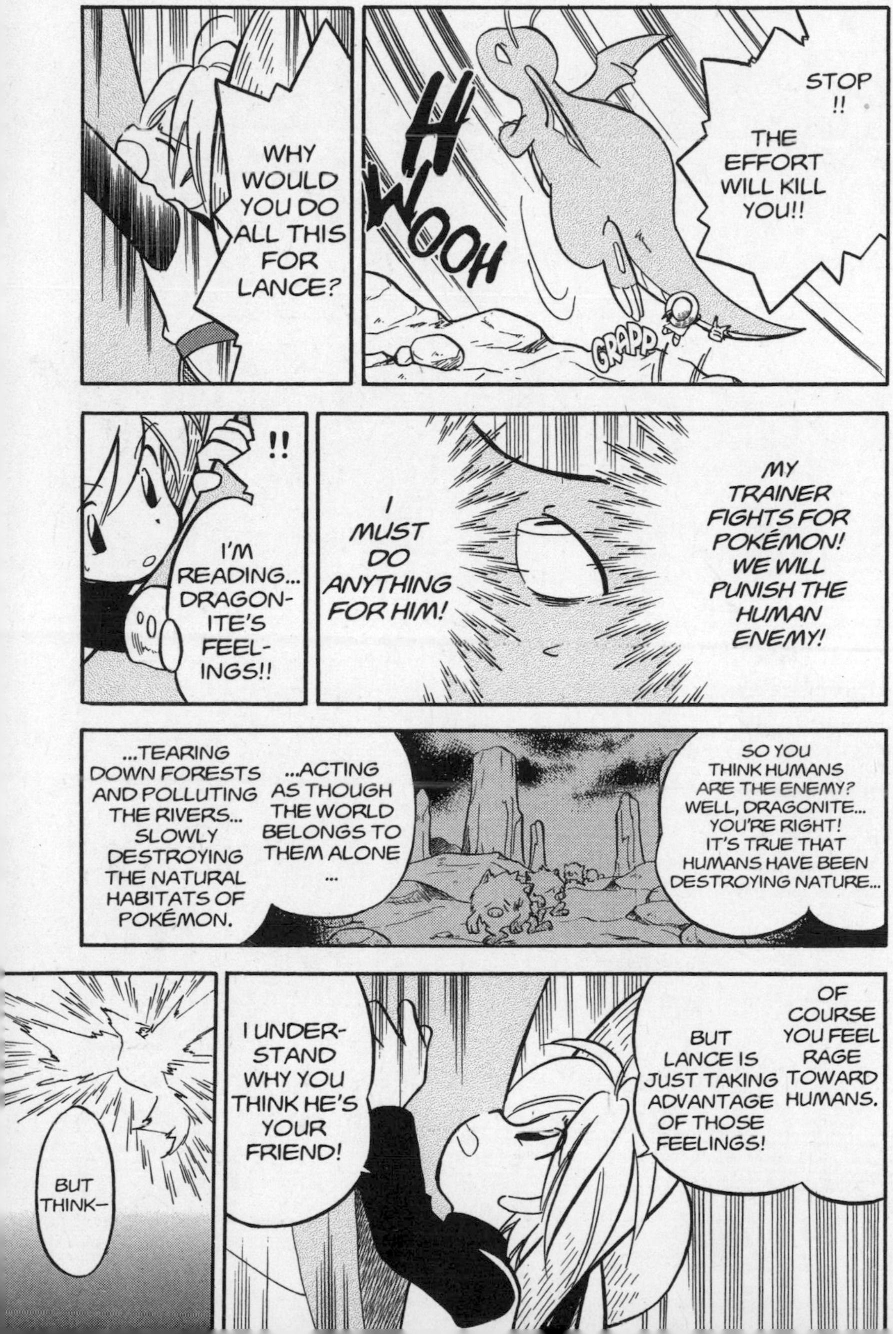
HWOOH
STOP !!
THE EFFORT WILL KILL YOU!!
GRAPP
WHY WOULD YOU DO ALL THIS FOR LANCE?
MY TRAINER FIGHTS FOR POKÉMON! WE WILL PUNISH THE HUMAN ENEMY!
I MUST DO ANYTHING FOR HIM!
!!
I'M READING... DRAGON-ITE'S FEEL-INGS!!
SO YOU THINK HUMANS ARE THE ENEMY? WELL, DRAGONITE... YOU'RE RIGHT! IT'S TRUE THAT HUMANS HAVE BEEN DESTROYING NATURE...
...ACTING AS THOUGH THE WORLD BELONGS TO THEM ALONE ...
...TEARING DOWN FORESTS AND POLLUTING THE RIVERS... SLOWLY DESTROYING THE NATURAL HABITATS OF POKÉMON.
OF COURSE YOU FEEL RAGE TOWARD HUMANS.
BUT LANCE IS JUST TAKING ADVANTAGE OF THOSE FEELINGS!
I UNDER-STAND WHY YOU THINK HE'S YOUR FRIEND!
BUT THINK—

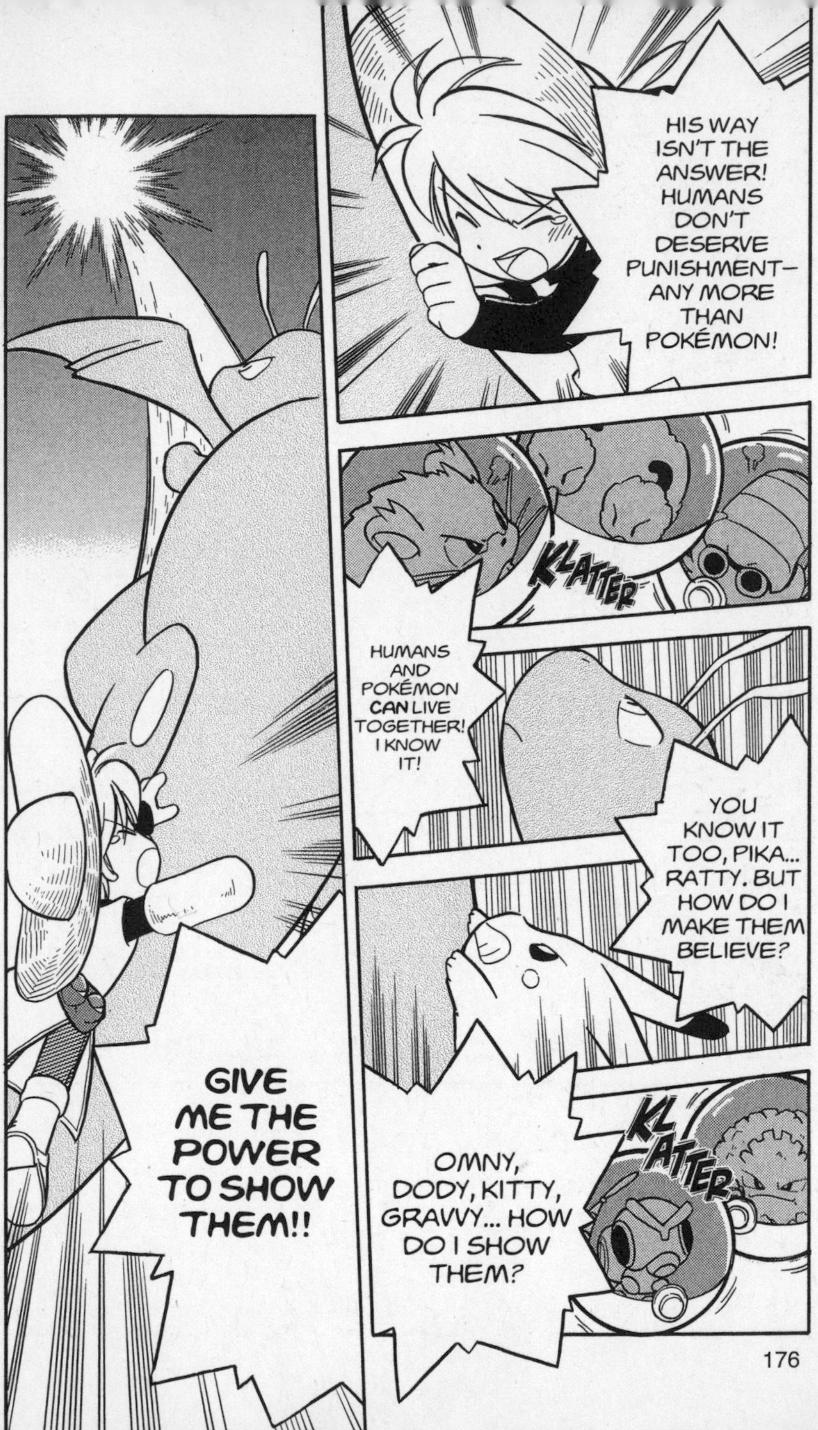
HIS WAY ISN'T THE ANSWER! HUMANS DON'T DESERVE PUNISHMENT— ANY MORE THAN POKÉMON!
KLATTER
HUMANS AND POKÉMON **CAN** LIVE TOGETHER! I KNOW IT!
YOU KNOW IT TOO, PIKA... RATTY. BUT HOW DO I MAKE THEM BELIEVE?
KLATTER
OMNY, DODY, KITTY, GRAVVY... HOW DO I SHOW THEM?
GIVE ME THE POWER TO SHOW THEM!!

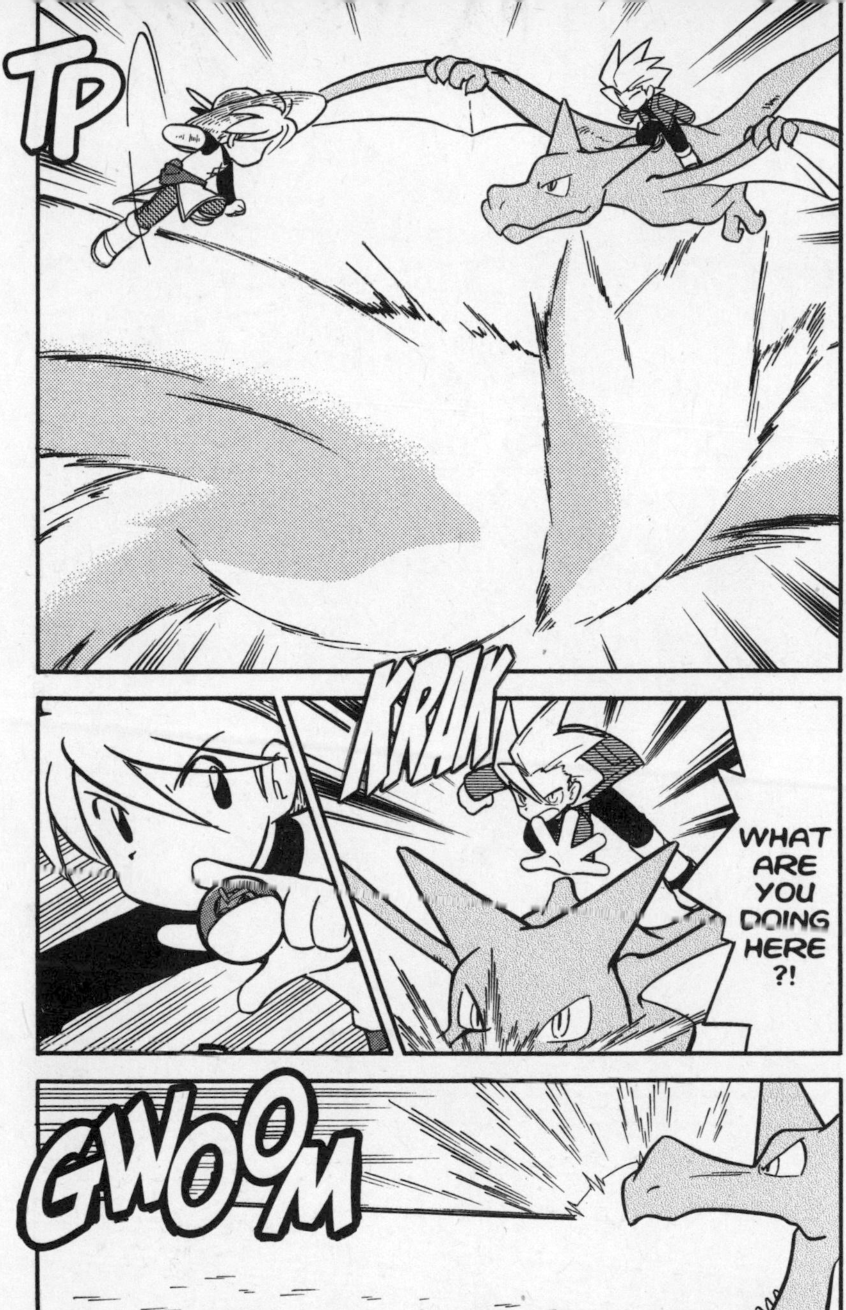
TP
KRAK
WHAT ARE YOU DOING HERE ?!
GWOOM

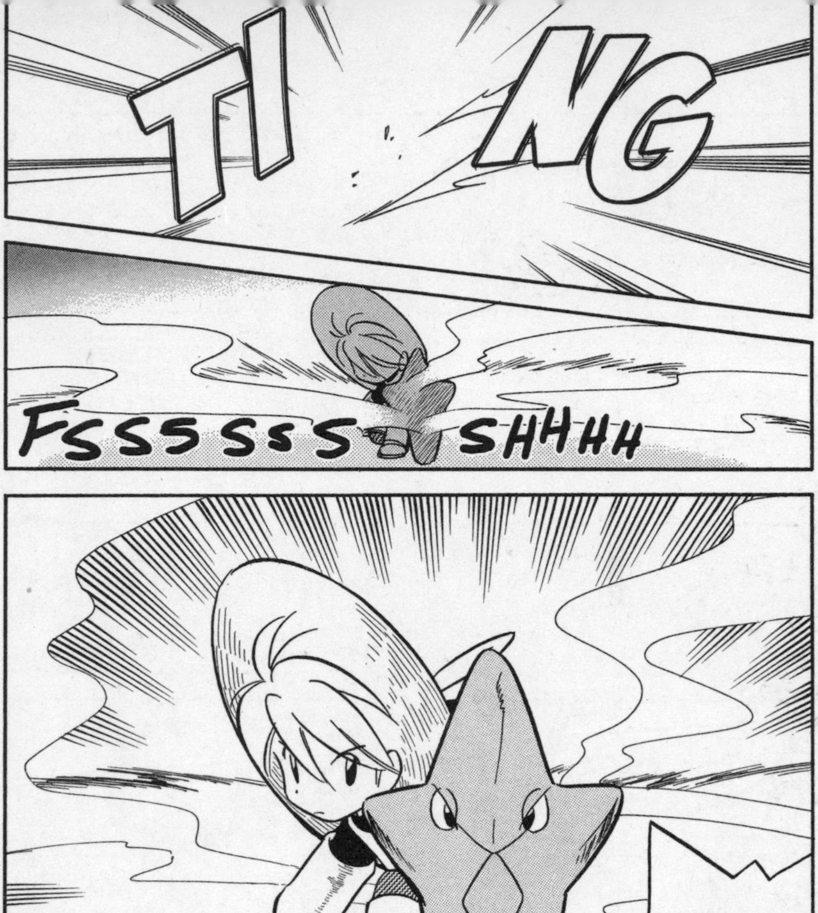
TI NG
FSSSSSS SHHHH
!
A METAPOD ?!

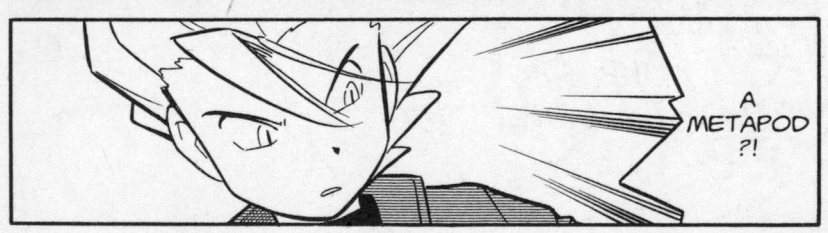

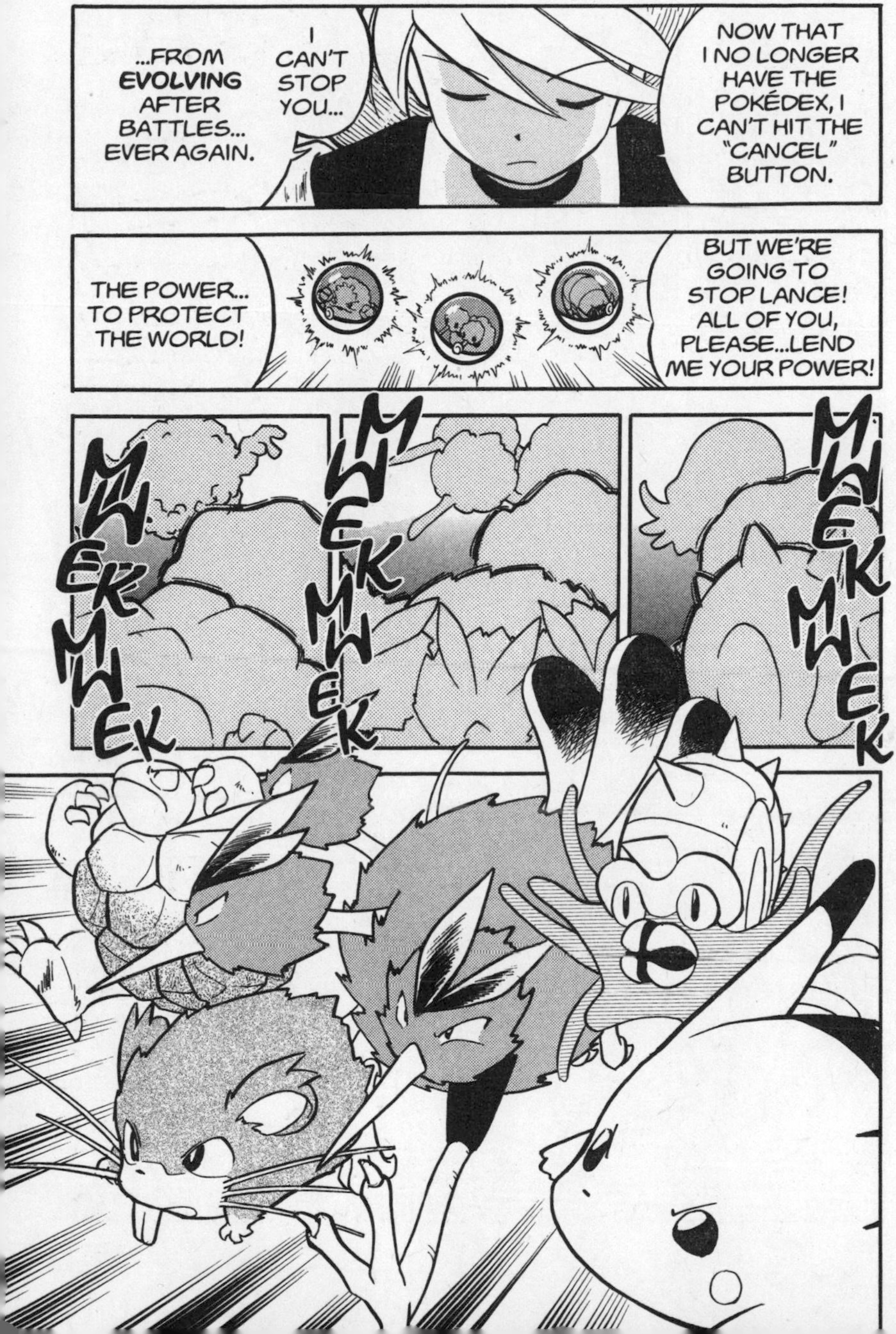
NOW THAT I NO LONGER HAVE THE POKÉDEX, I CAN'T HIT THE "CANCEL" BUTTON.
I CAN'T STOP YOU...
...FROM **EVOLVING** AFTER BATTLES... EVER AGAIN.
BUT WE'RE GOING TO STOP LANCE! ALL OF YOU, PLEASE...LEND ME YOUR POWER!
THE POWER... TO PROTECT THE WORLD!
MWEK MWEK
MWEK MWEK
MWEK MWEK

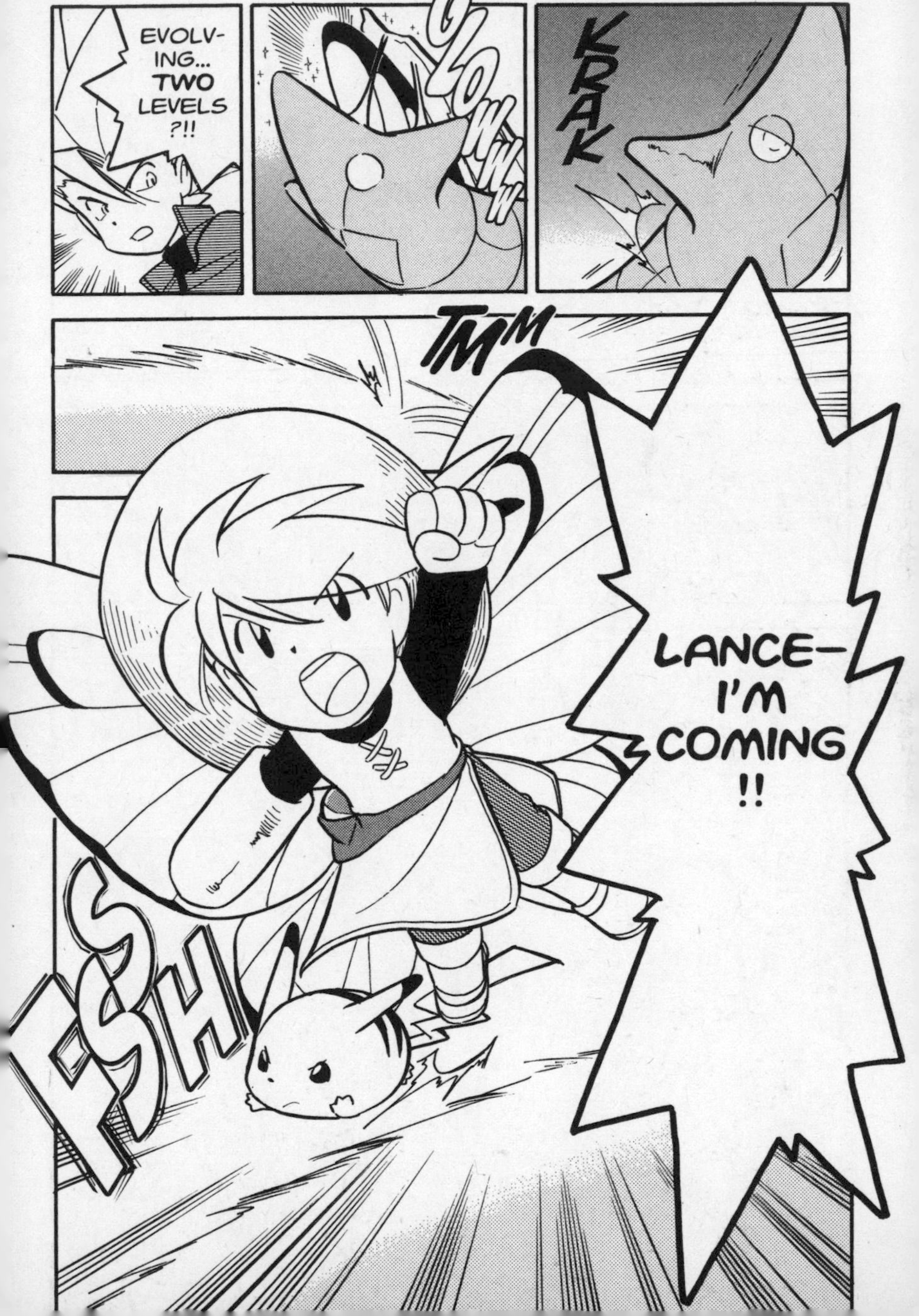
KRAK
GLOWWW
EVOLV-ING... TWO LEVELS ?!!
TMM
LANCE— I'M COMING !!
FSSH

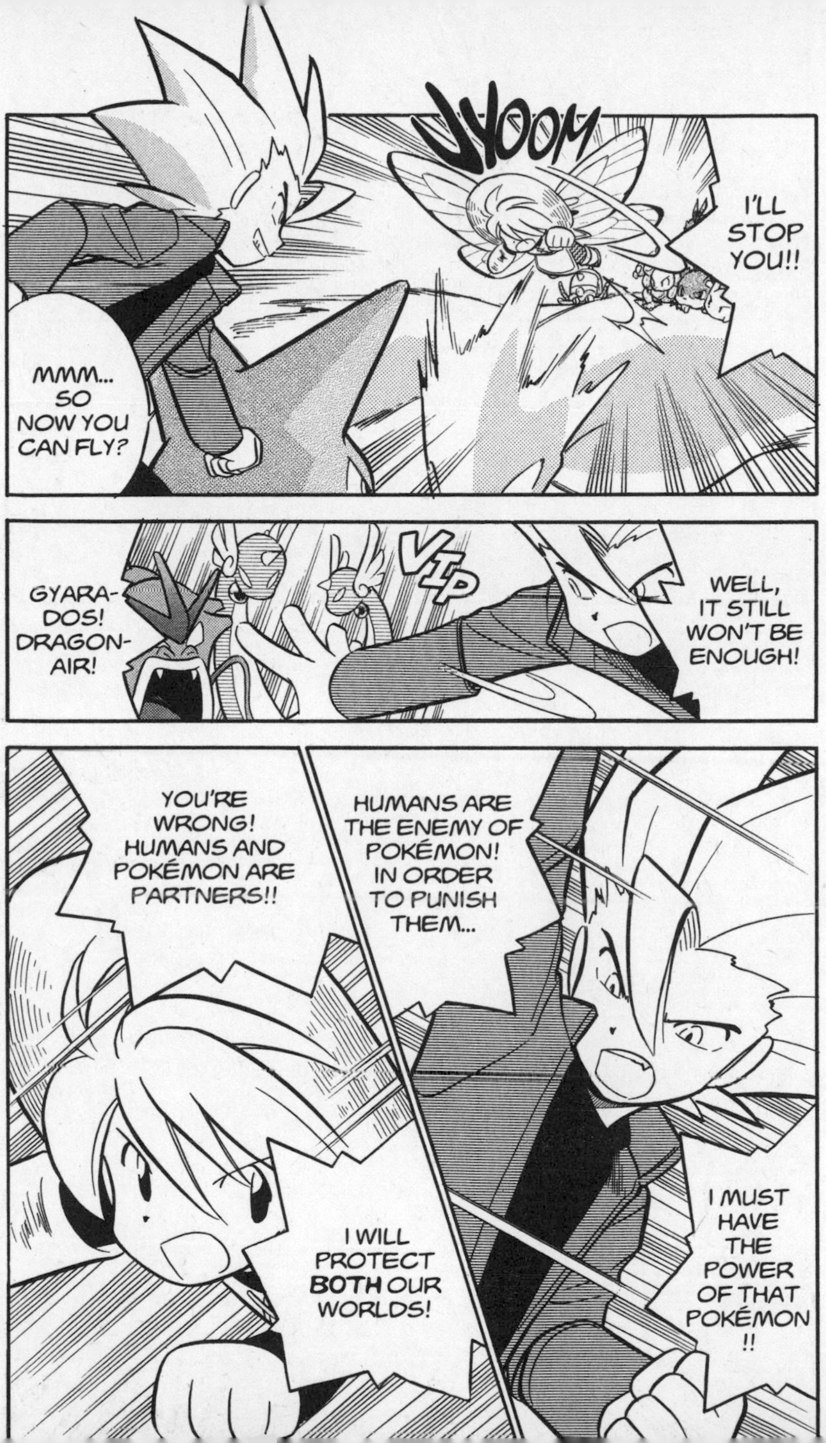
I'LL STOP YOU!!
JYOOM
MMM... SO NOW YOU CAN FLY?
WELL, IT STILL WON'T BE ENOUGH!
VIP
GYARA-DOS! DRAGON-AIR!
HUMANS ARE THE ENEMY OF POKÉMON! IN ORDER TO PUNISH THEM...
I MUST HAVE THE POWER OF THAT POKÉMON !!
YOU'RE WRONG! HUMANS AND POKÉMON ARE PARTNERS!!
I WILL PROTECT **BOTH** OUR WORLDS!

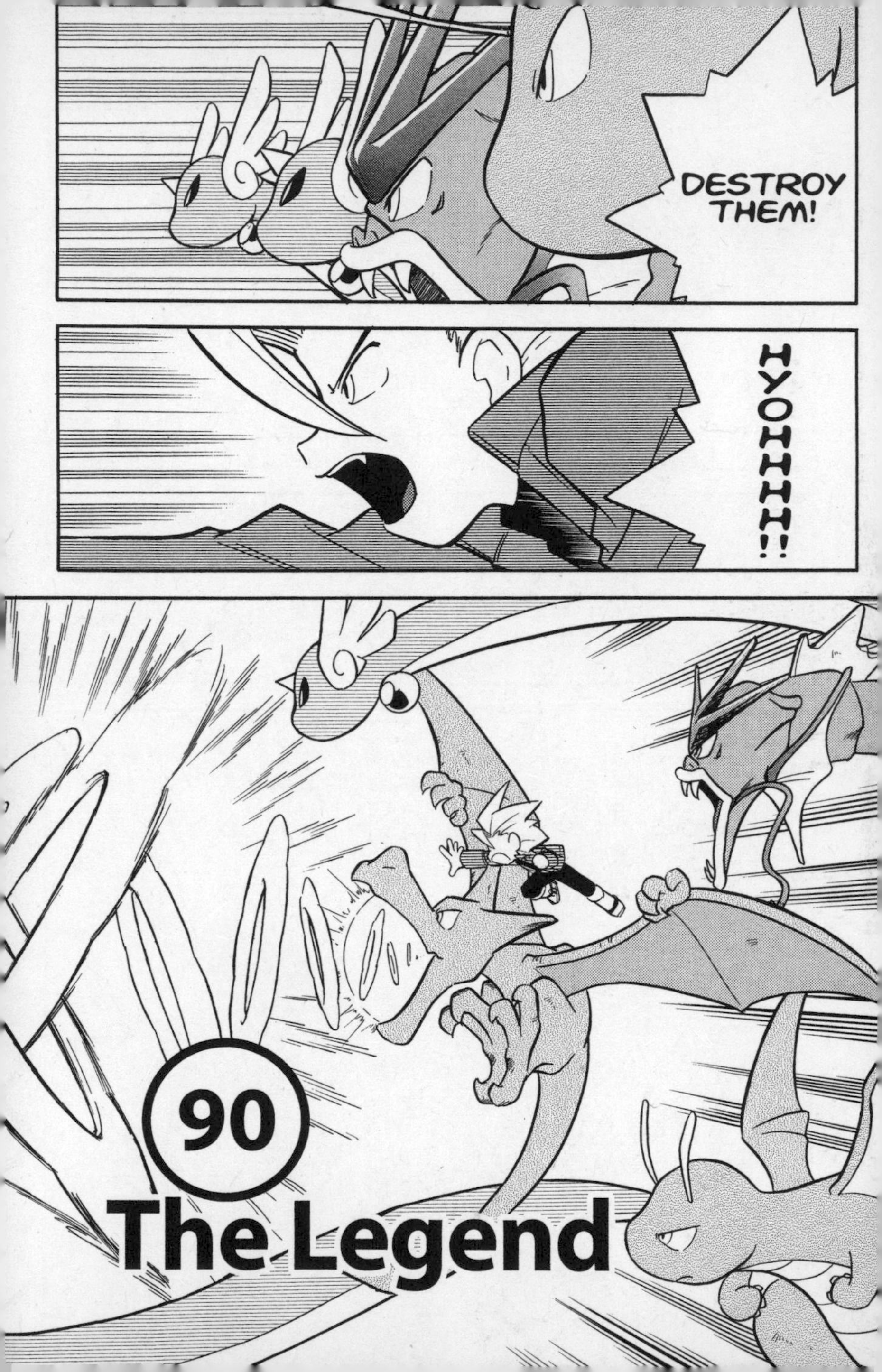
DESTROY THEM!
HYOHHHH!!
90
The Legend

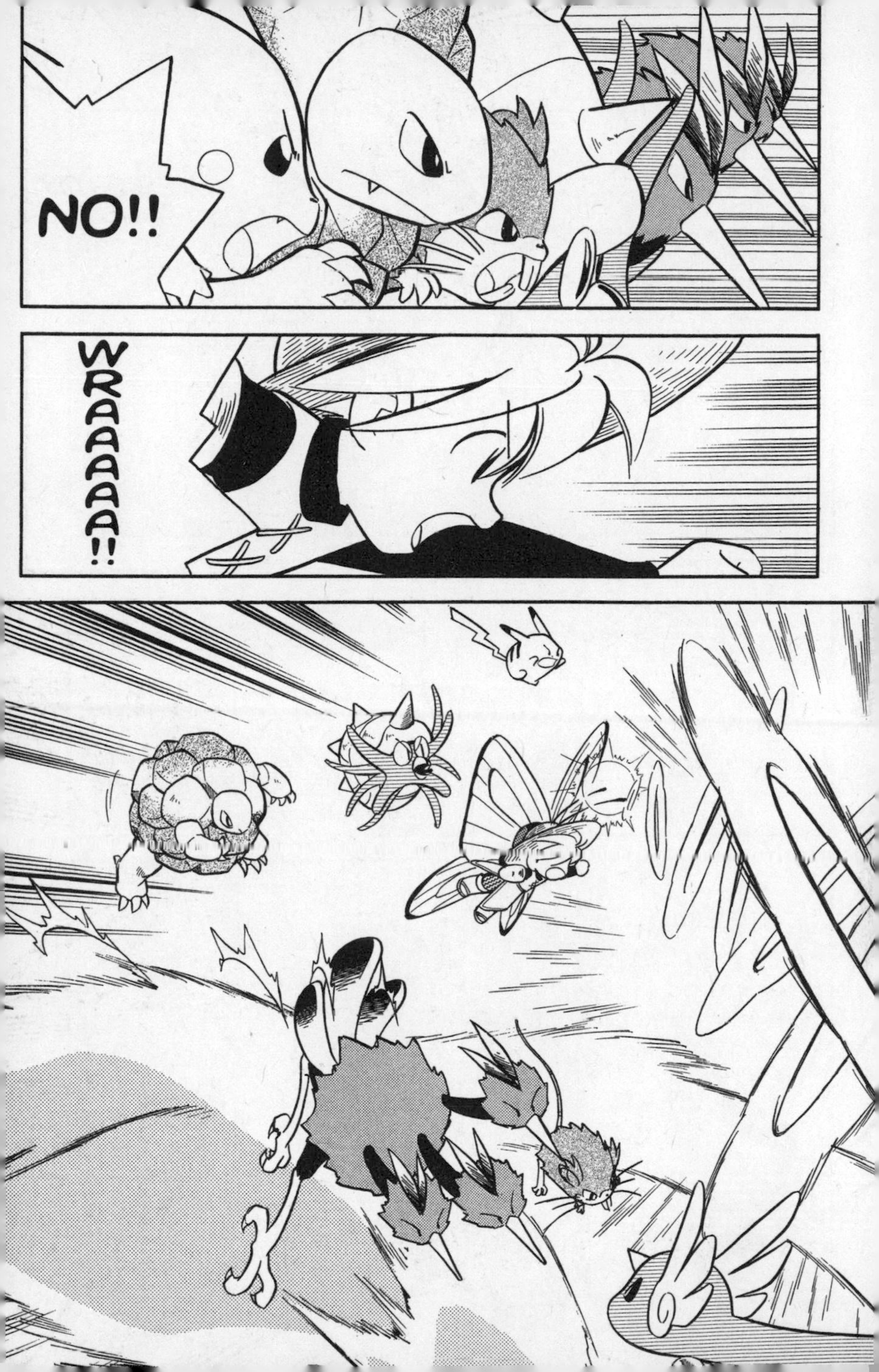

NO!!
WRAAAAAA!!

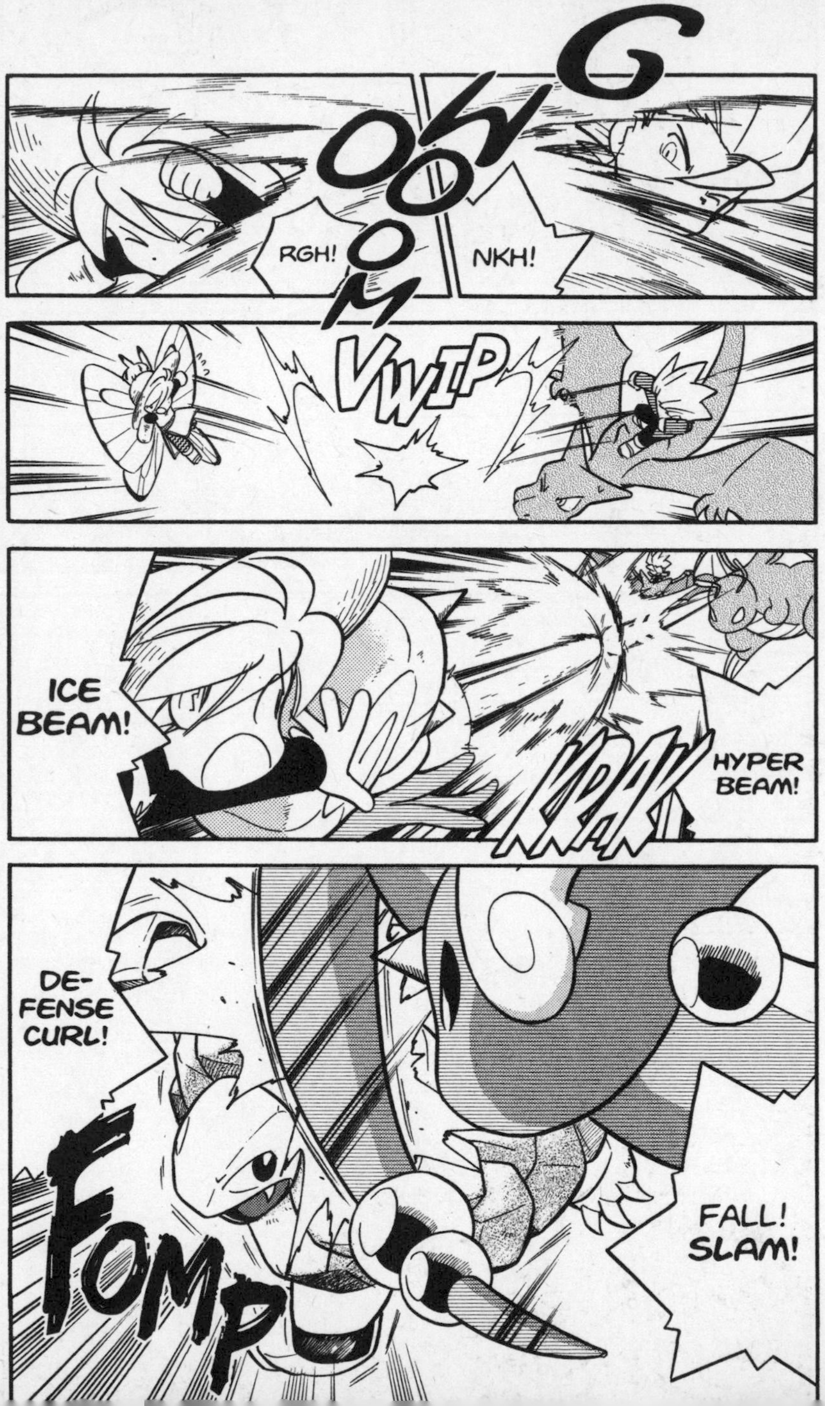
NKH!
RGH!
VWIP
HYPER BEAM!
KRAK
ICE BEAM!
FALL! SLAM!
DE-FENSE CURL!
FOMP

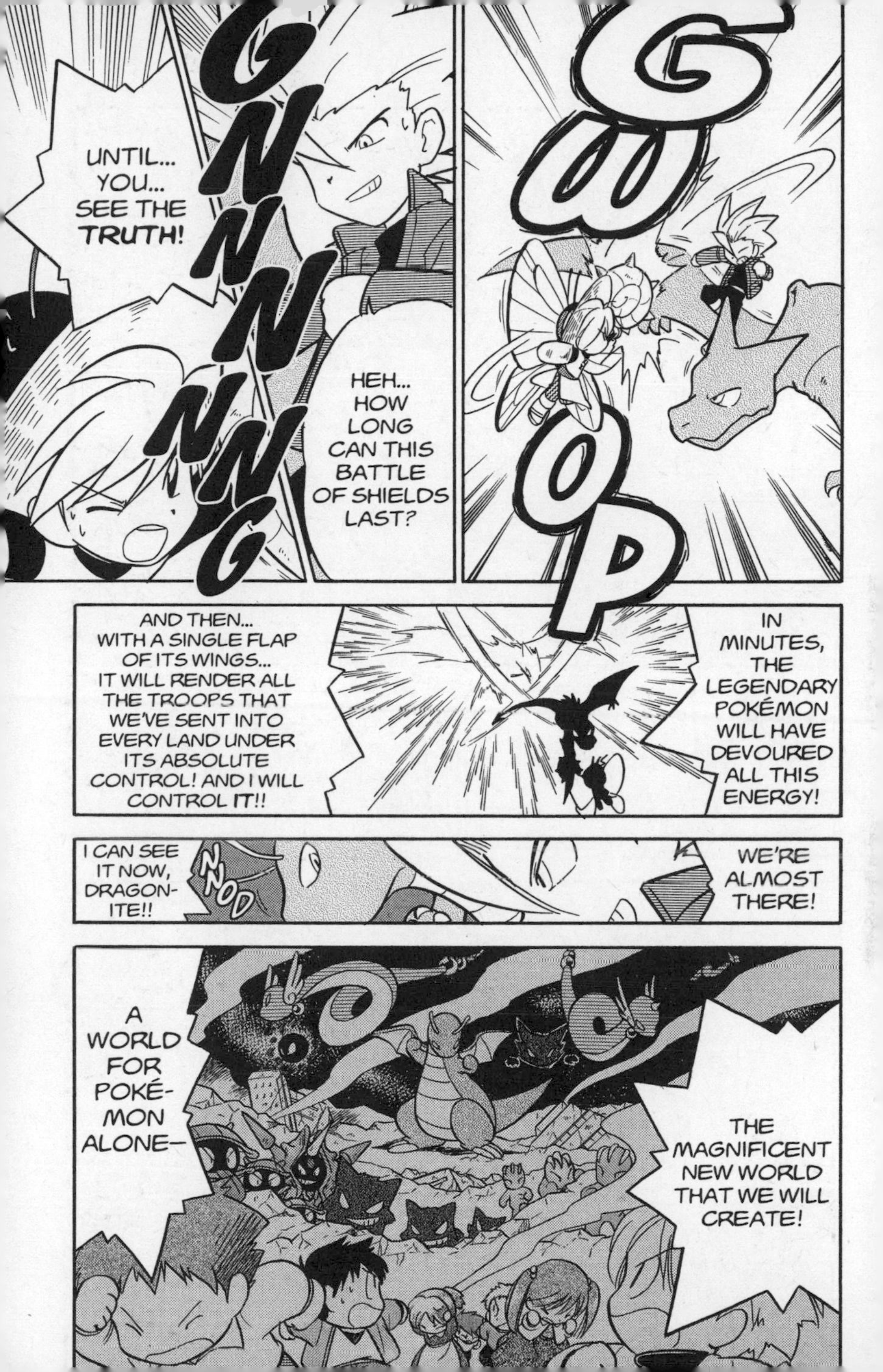
GWOOP
GNNNNNG
UNTIL... YOU... SEE THE TRUTH!
HEH... HOW LONG CAN THIS BATTLE OF SHIELDS LAST?
IN MINUTES, THE LEGENDARY POKÉMON WILL HAVE DEVOURED ALL THIS ENERGY!
AND THEN... WITH A SINGLE FLAP OF ITS WINGS... IT WILL RENDER ALL THE TROOPS THAT WE'VE SENT INTO EVERY LAND UNDER ITS ABSOLUTE CONTROL! AND I WILL CONTROL IT!!
WE'RE ALMOST THERE!
NNOD
I CAN SEE IT NOW, DRAGON-ITE!!
THE MAGNIFICENT NEW WORLD THAT WE WILL CREATE!
A WORLD FOR POKÉ-MON ALONE—

FREE FROM HUMANS!

HKK!

SHJJJ SHJJ

PA-THET-IC!!

BWAP

BZZZ BZZZ

BM BM

PIKA!

RAGE!

BIDE!

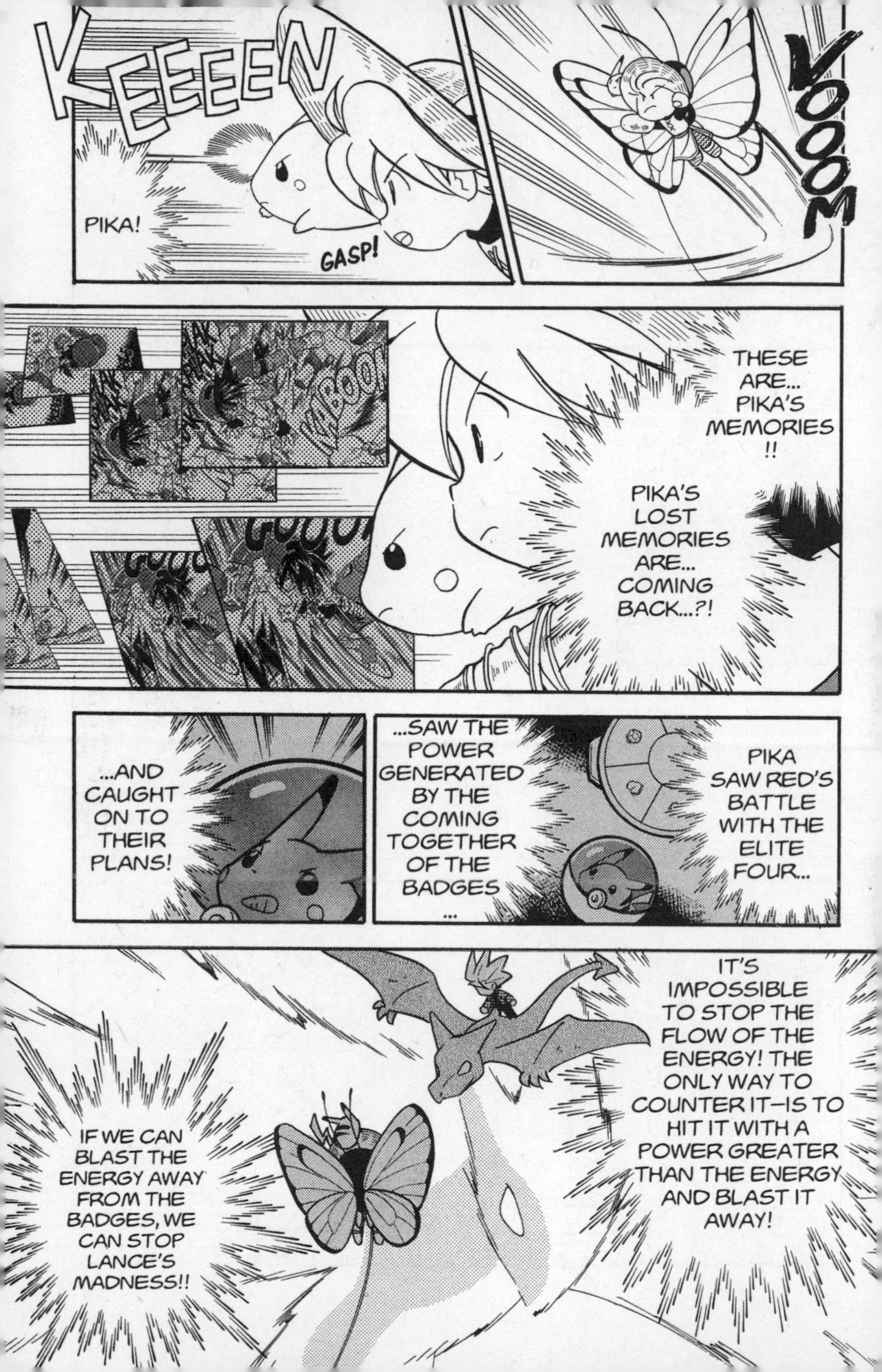
VOOOOM
KEEEEN
PIKA!
GASP!
THESE ARE... PIKA'S MEMORIES !!
PIKA'S LOST MEMORIES ARE... COMING BACK...?!
PIKA SAW RED'S BATTLE WITH THE ELITE FOUR...
...SAW THE POWER GENERATED BY THE COMING TOGETHER OF THE BADGES ...
...AND CAUGHT ON TO THEIR PLANS!
IT'S IMPOSSIBLE TO STOP THE FLOW OF THE ENERGY! THE ONLY WAY TO COUNTER IT—IS TO HIT IT WITH A POWER GREATER THAN THE ENERGY AND BLAST IT AWAY!
IF WE CAN BLAST THE ENERGY AWAY FROM THE BADGES, WE CAN STOP LANCE'S MADNESS!!

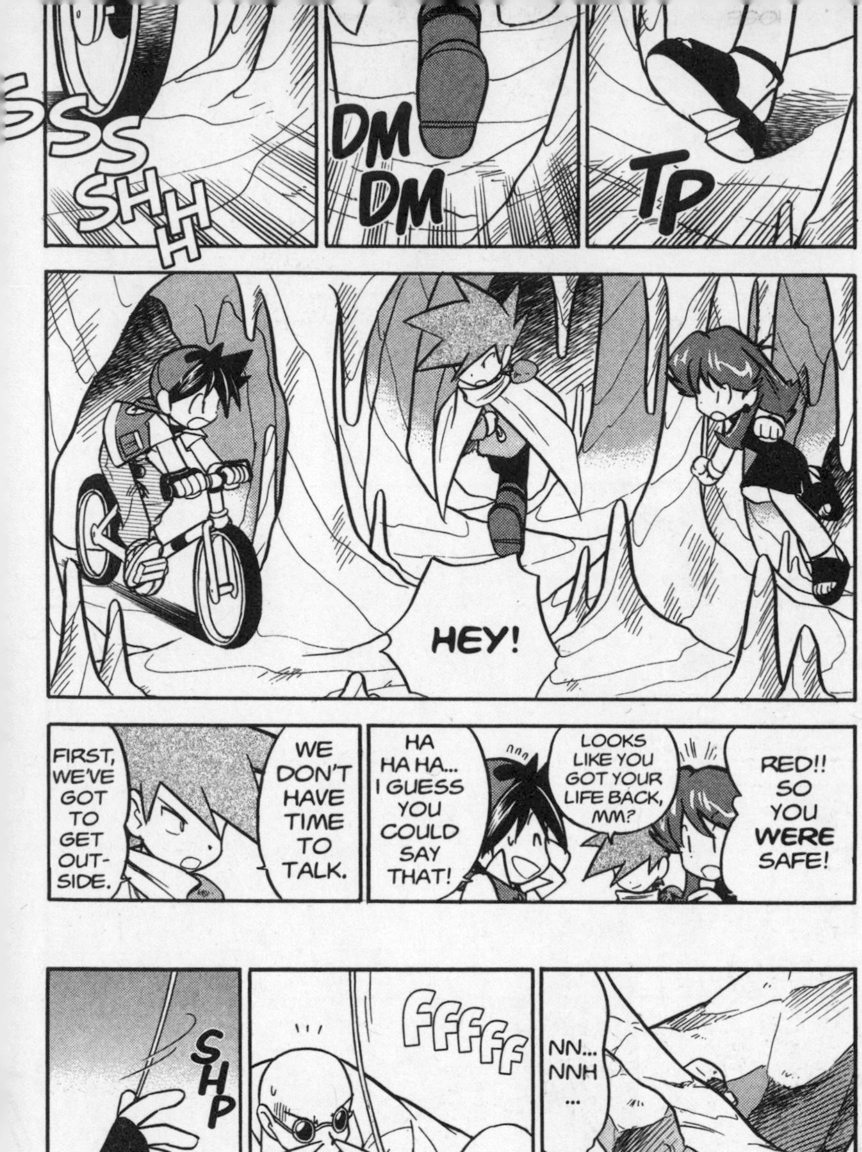
TP
DM DM
SSSHHH
HEY!
RED!! SO YOU WERE SAFE!
LOOKS LIKE YOU GOT YOUR LIFE BACK, MM?
HA HA HA... I GUESS YOU COULD SAY THAT!
WE DON'T HAVE TIME TO TALK.
FIRST, WE'VE GOT TO GET OUT-SIDE.
NN... NNH ...
FFFFF
THIS THREAD ...!
SHP
!

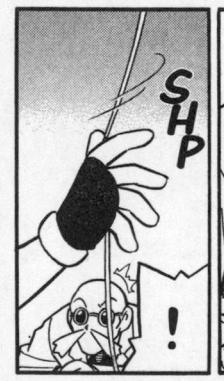

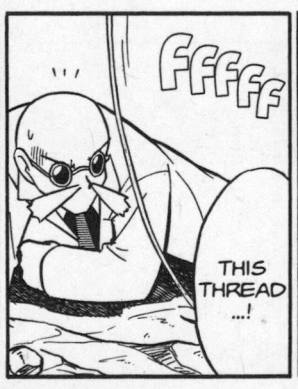

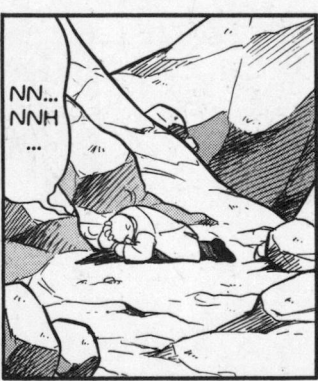

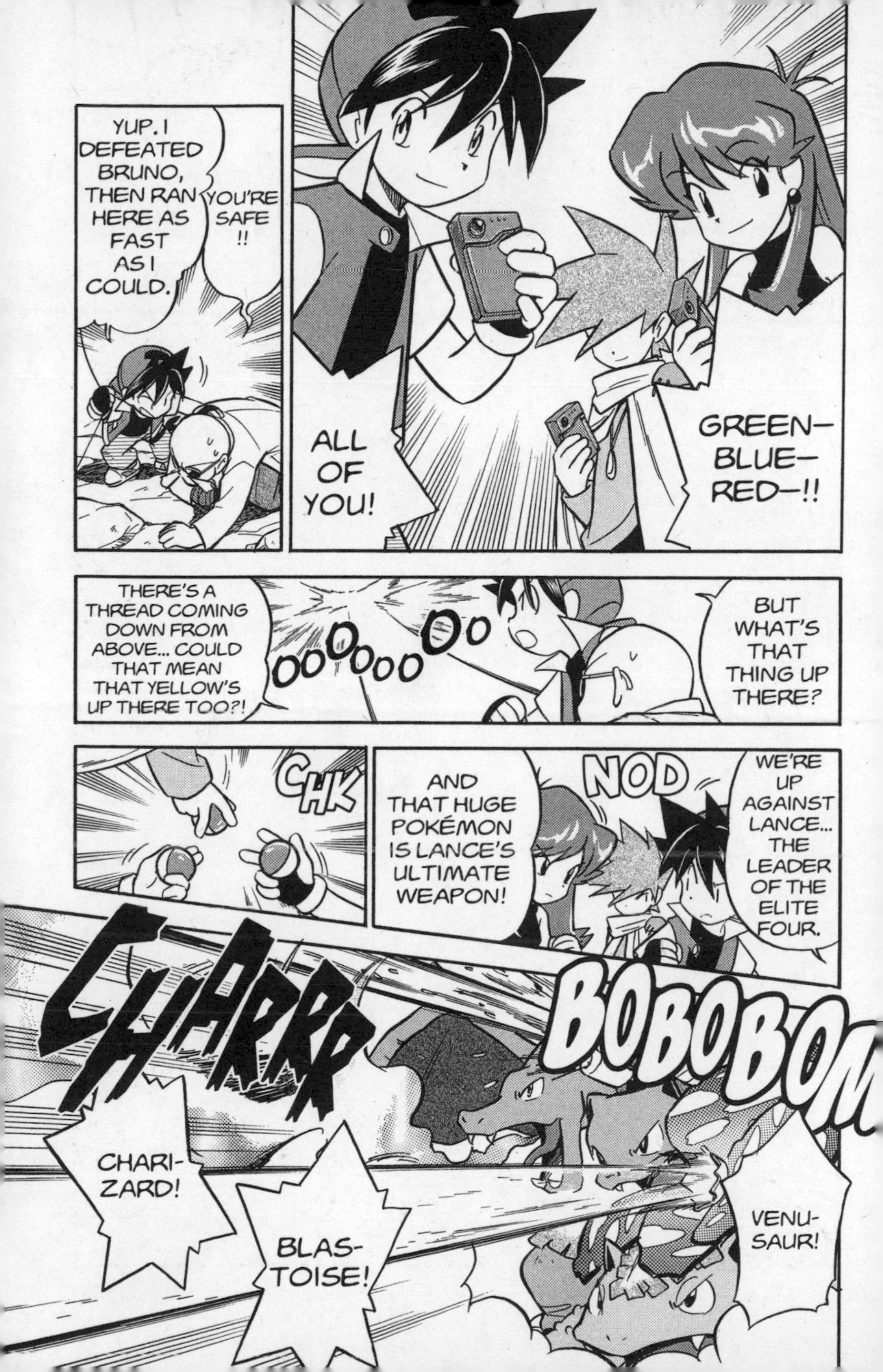
GREEN— BLUE— RED—!!
ALL OF YOU!
YOU'RE SAFE !!
YUP. I DEFEATED BRUNO, THEN RAN HERE AS FAST AS I COULD.
BUT WHAT'S THAT THING UP THERE?
OOOOOOOOO
THERE'S A THREAD COMING DOWN FROM ABOVE... COULD THAT MEAN THAT YELLOW'S UP THERE TOO?!
WE'RE UP AGAINST LANCE... THE LEADER OF THE ELITE FOUR.
NOD
AND THAT HUGE POKÉMON IS LANCE'S ULTIMATE WEAPON!
CHK
BOBOBOM
CHARRR
VENUSAUR!
CHARIZARD!
BLASTOISE!

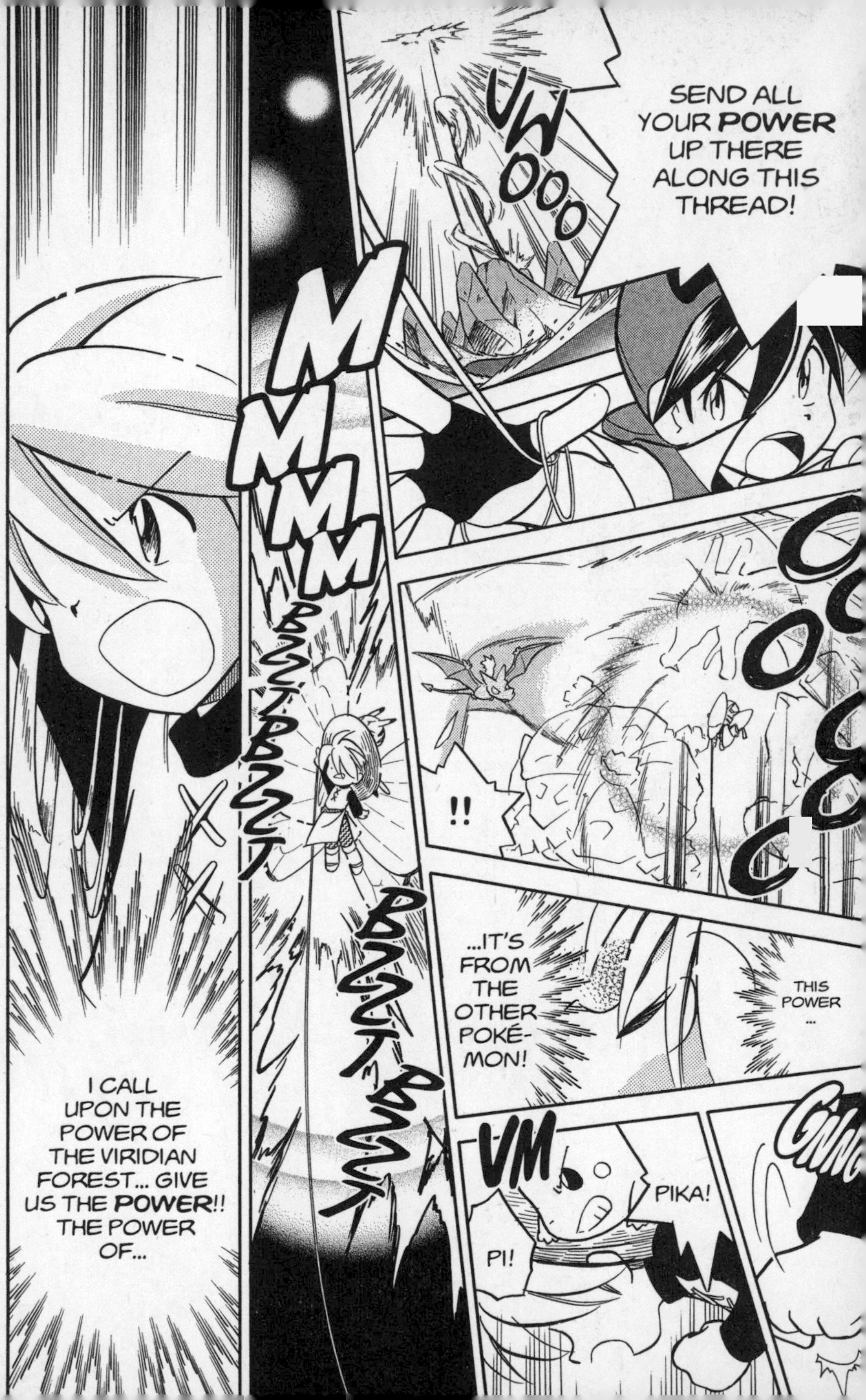
SEND ALL YOUR **POWER** UP THERE ALONG THIS THREAD!
UWOOO
!!
THIS POWER...
...IT'S FROM THE OTHER POKÉ-MON!
PIKA!
VM
PI!
MMMMM
I CALL UPON THE POWER OF THE VIRIDIAN FOREST... GIVE US THE **POWER**!! THE POWER OF...

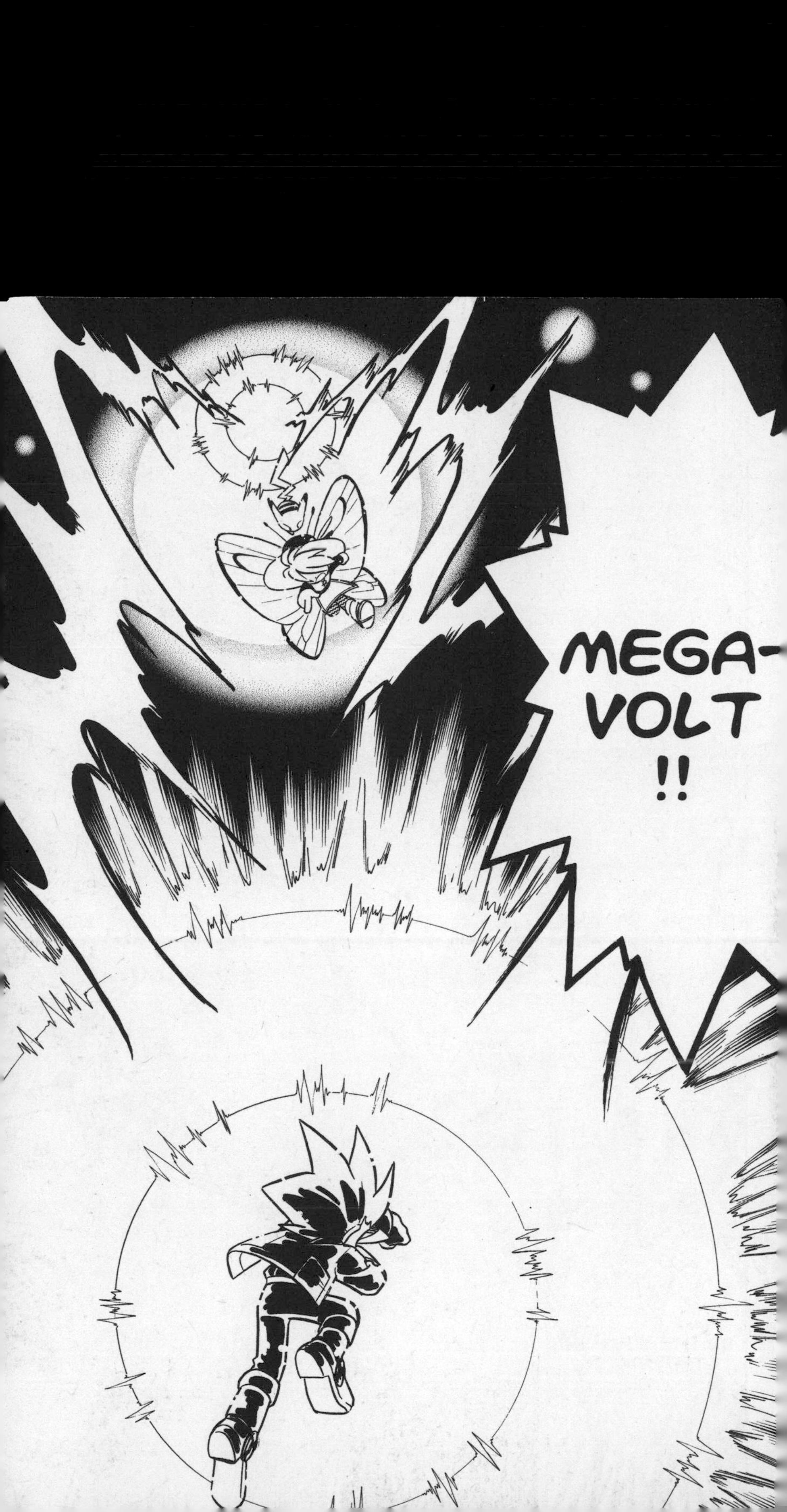
MEGA-
VOLT
!!

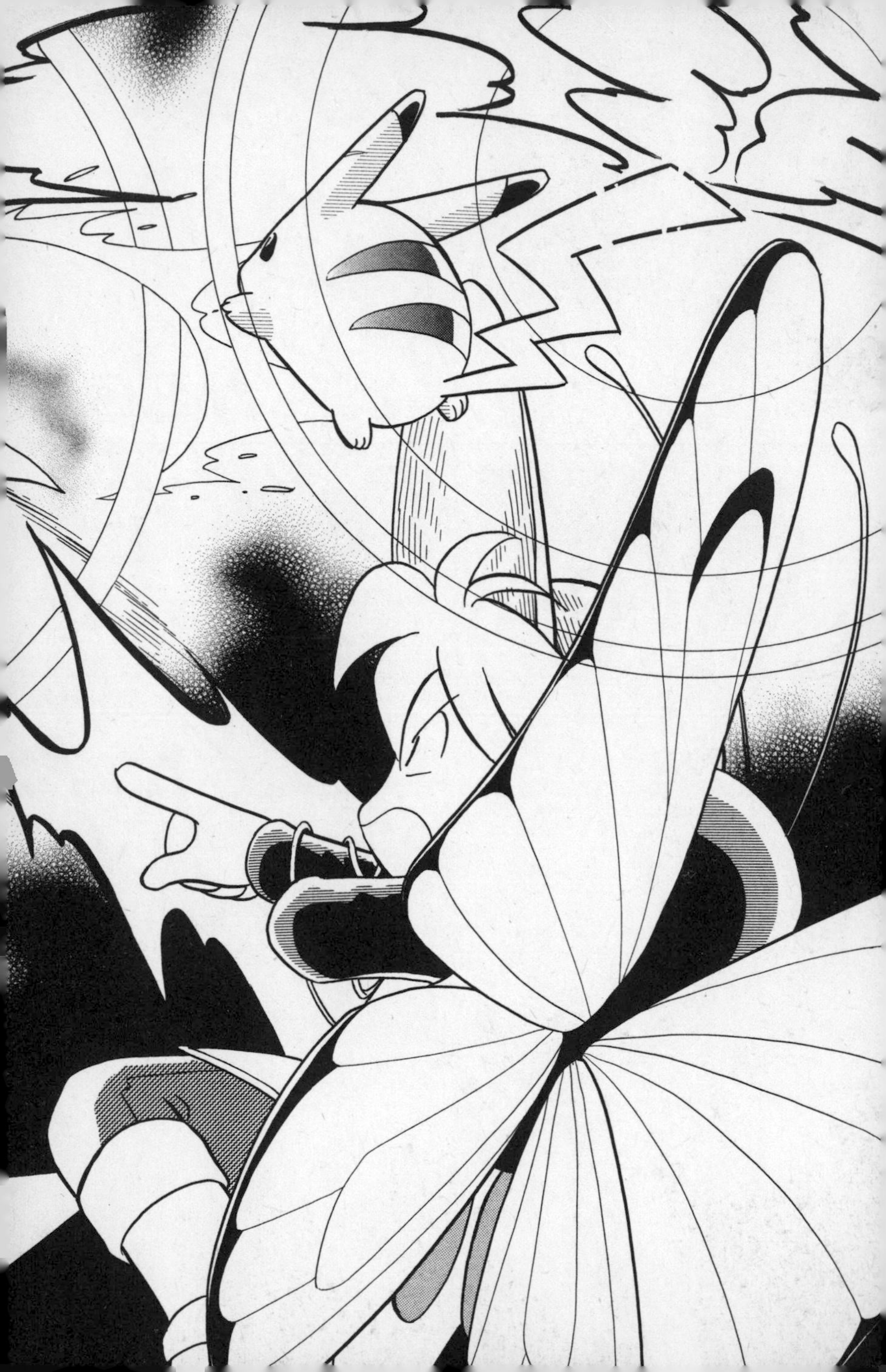

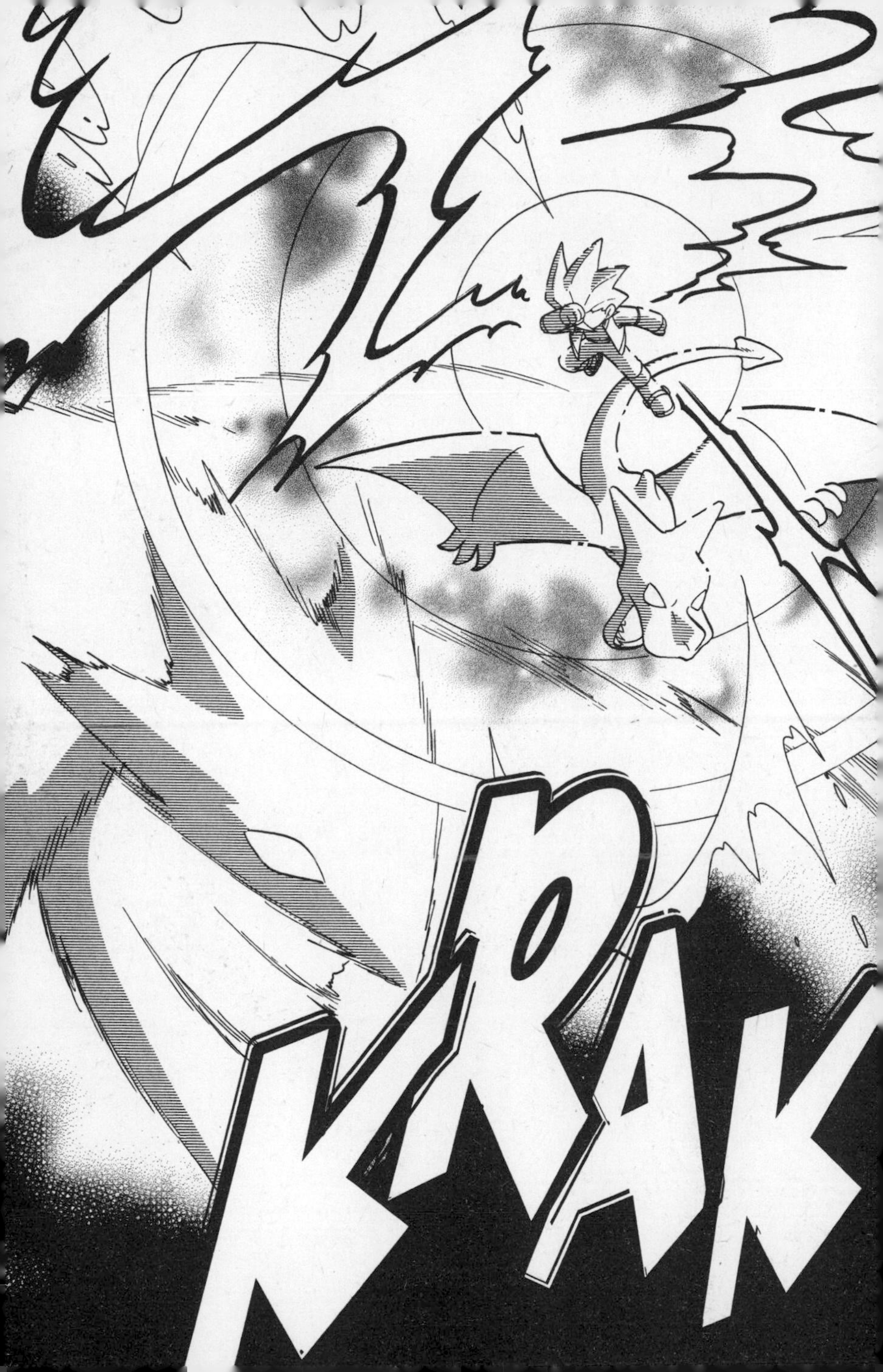
KRAK

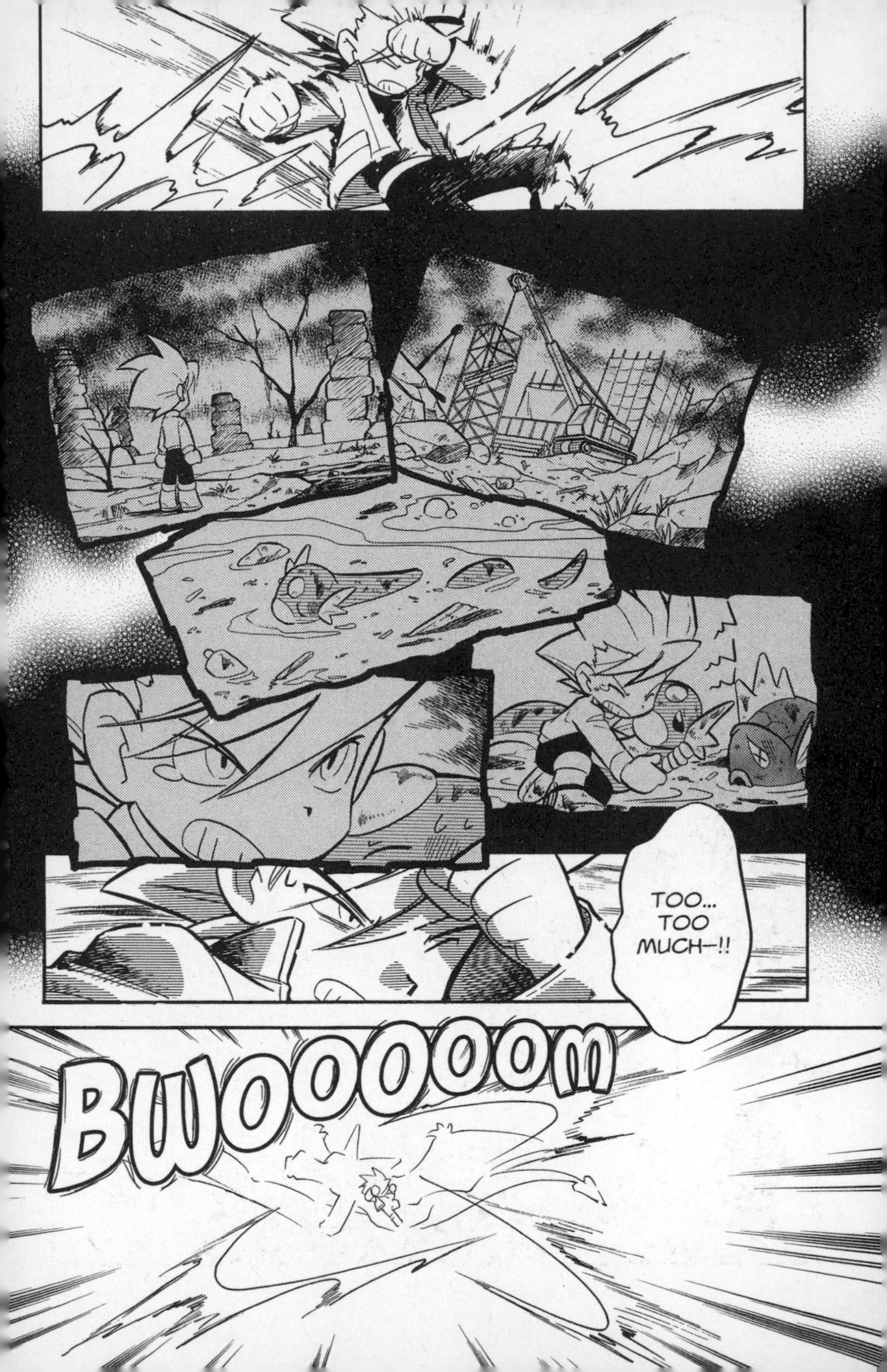
TOO... TOO MUCH—!!
BWOOOOOOM

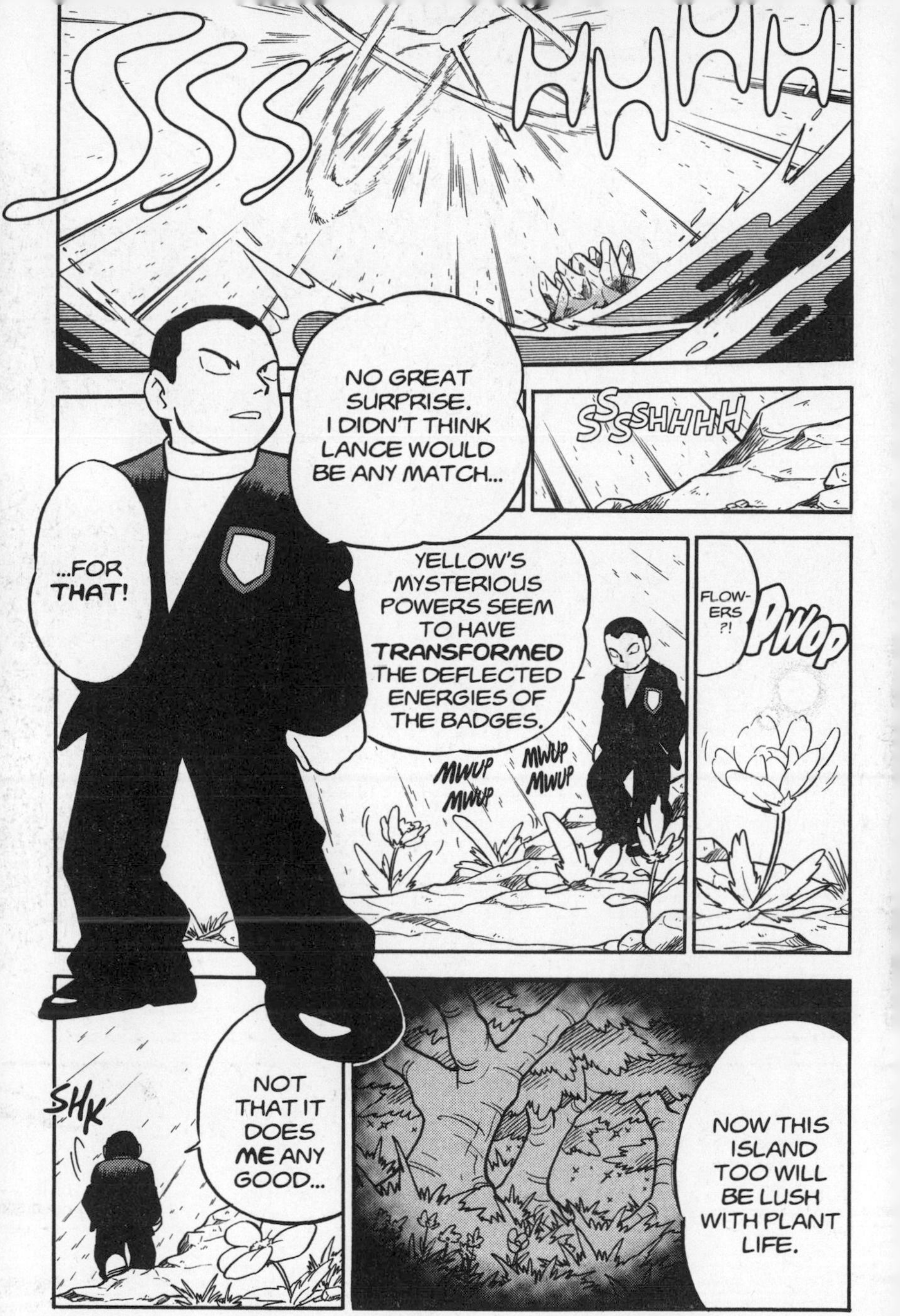
SSSSHHHHH
SSSHHHHH
NO GREAT SURPRISE. I DIDN'T THINK LANCE WOULD BE ANY MATCH...
...FOR THAT!
FLOW-ERS?!
PWOP
YELLOW'S MYSTERIOUS POWERS SEEM TO HAVE **TRANSFORMED** THE DEFLECTED ENERGIES OF THE BADGES.
MWUP MWUP
MWUP MWUP
NOW THIS ISLAND TOO WILL BE LUSH WITH PLANT LIFE.
NOT THAT IT DOES **ME** ANY GOOD...
SHK

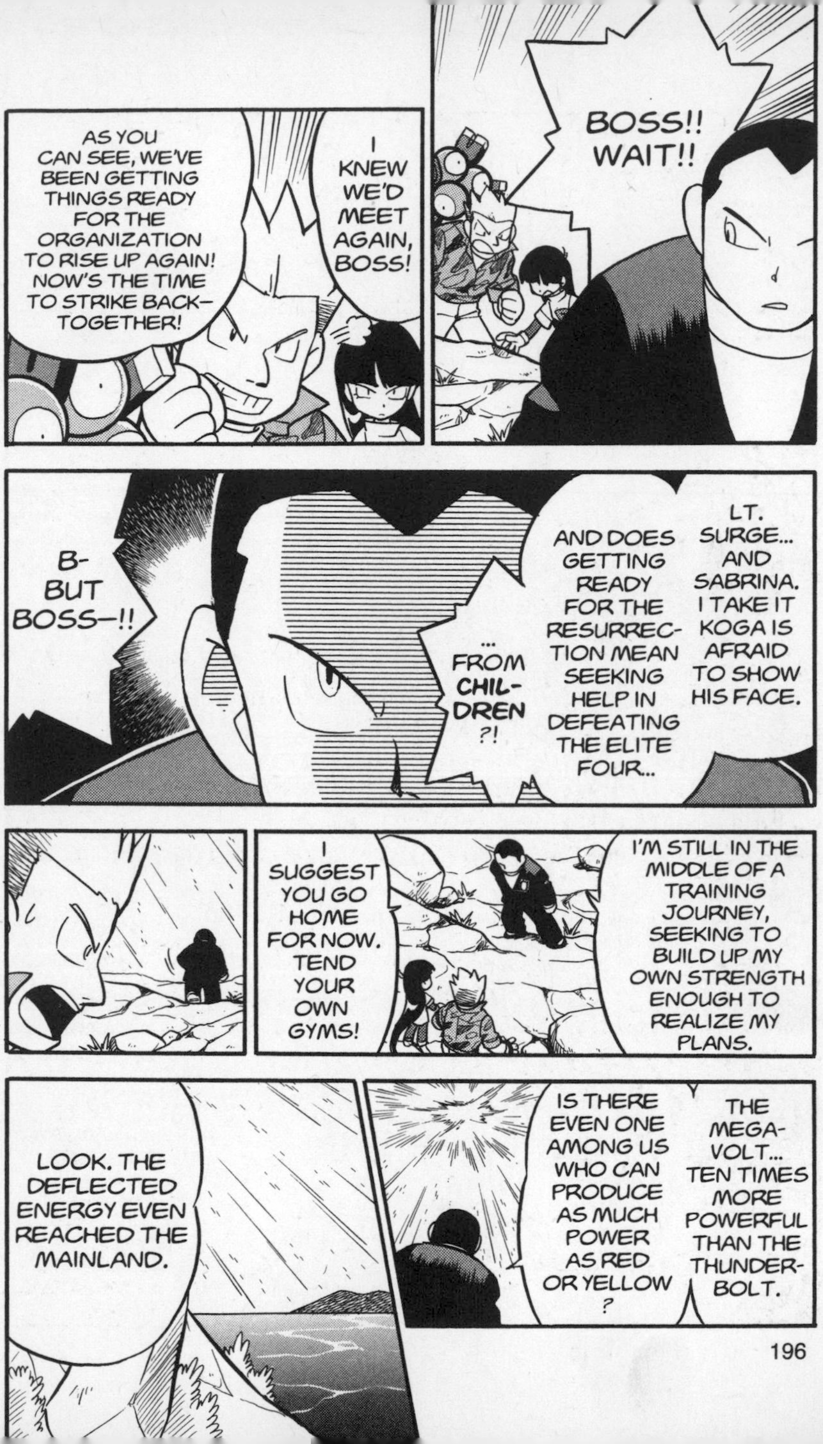
BOSS!! WAIT!!
I KNEW WE'D MEET AGAIN, BOSS!
AS YOU CAN SEE, WE'VE BEEN GETTING THINGS READY FOR THE ORGANIZATION TO RISE UP AGAIN! NOW'S THE TIME TO STRIKE BACK—TOGETHER!
LT. SURGE... AND SABRINA. I TAKE IT KOGA IS AFRAID TO SHOW HIS FACE.
AND DOES GETTING READY FOR THE RESURRECTION MEAN SEEKING HELP IN DEFEATING THE ELITE FOUR...
...FROM CHILDREN?!
B-BUT BOSS—!!
I'M STILL IN THE MIDDLE OF A TRAINING JOURNEY, SEEKING TO BUILD UP MY OWN STRENGTH ENOUGH TO REALIZE MY PLANS.
I SUGGEST YOU GO HOME FOR NOW. TEND YOUR OWN GYMS!
THE MEGA-VOLT... TEN TIMES MORE POWERFUL THAN THE THUNDERBOLT.
IS THERE EVEN ONE AMONG US WHO CAN PRODUCE AS MUCH POWER AS RED OR YELLOW?
LOOK. THE DEFLECTED ENERGY EVEN REACHED THE MAINLAND.

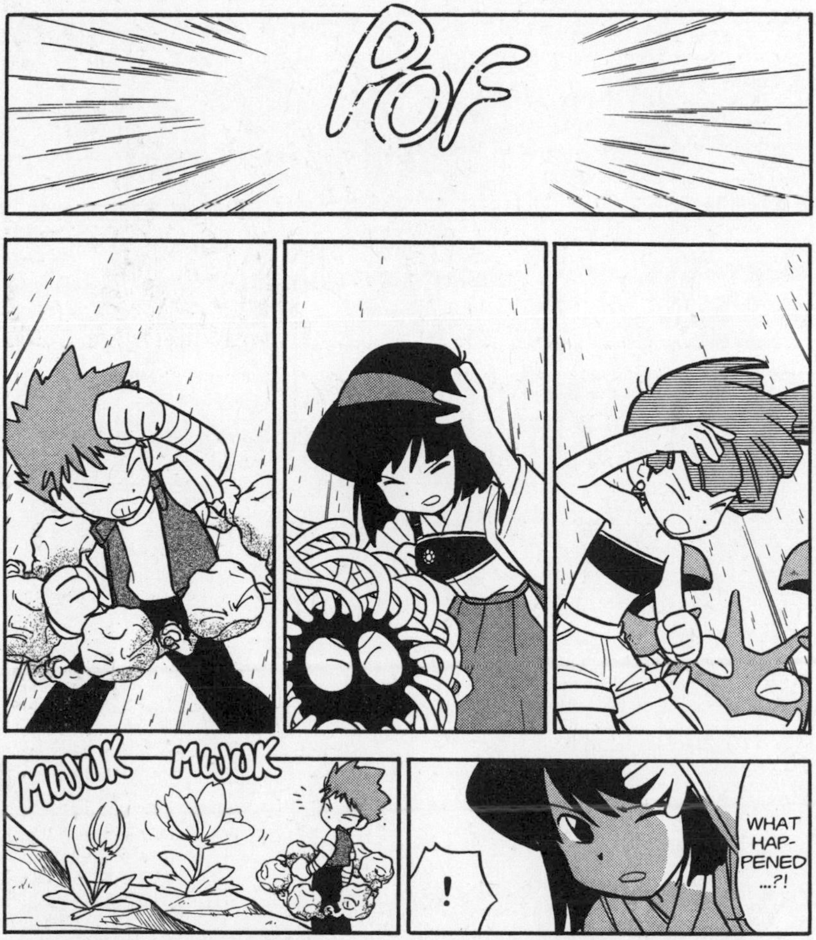
POF
WHAT HAP-PENED ...?!
!
MWOK
MWOK
IT... IT CAN'T BE...! THAT WHOLE RANGE FROM NORTHWEST CERULEAN TO THE ROCK MOUNTAINS HAD BEEN A WASTELAND FROM INDUSTRIAL RUINS...
MWOK
MWOK
MWOK

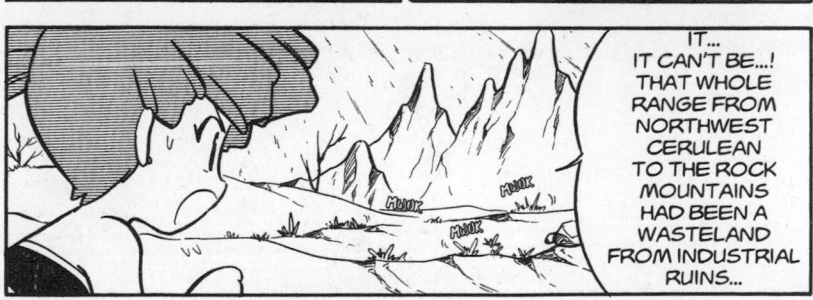

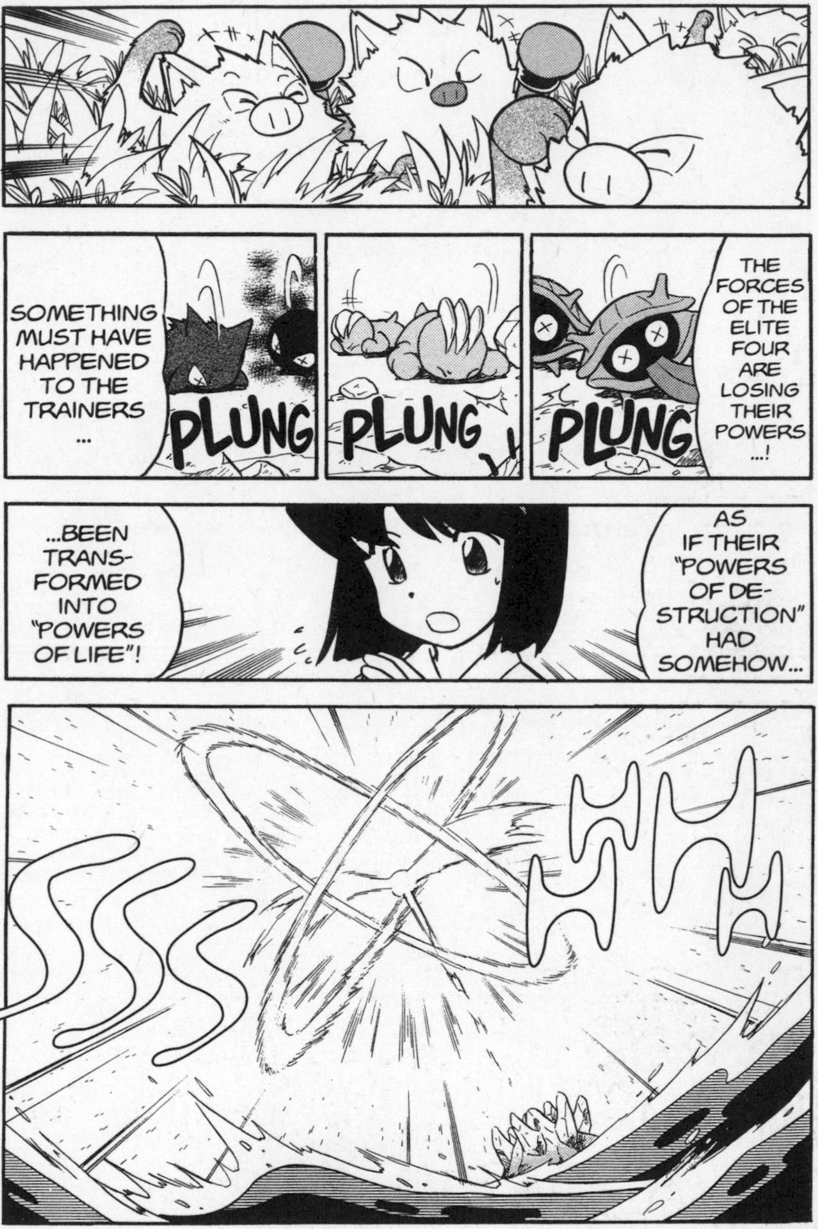
THE FORCES OF THE ELITE FOUR ARE LOSING THEIR POWERS ...!
PLUNG
PLUNG
PLUNG
SOMETHING MUST HAVE HAPPENED TO THE TRAINERS ...
AS IF THEIR "POWERS OF DE-STRUCTION" HAD SOMEHOW...
...BEEN TRANS-FORMED INTO "POWERS OF LIFE"!

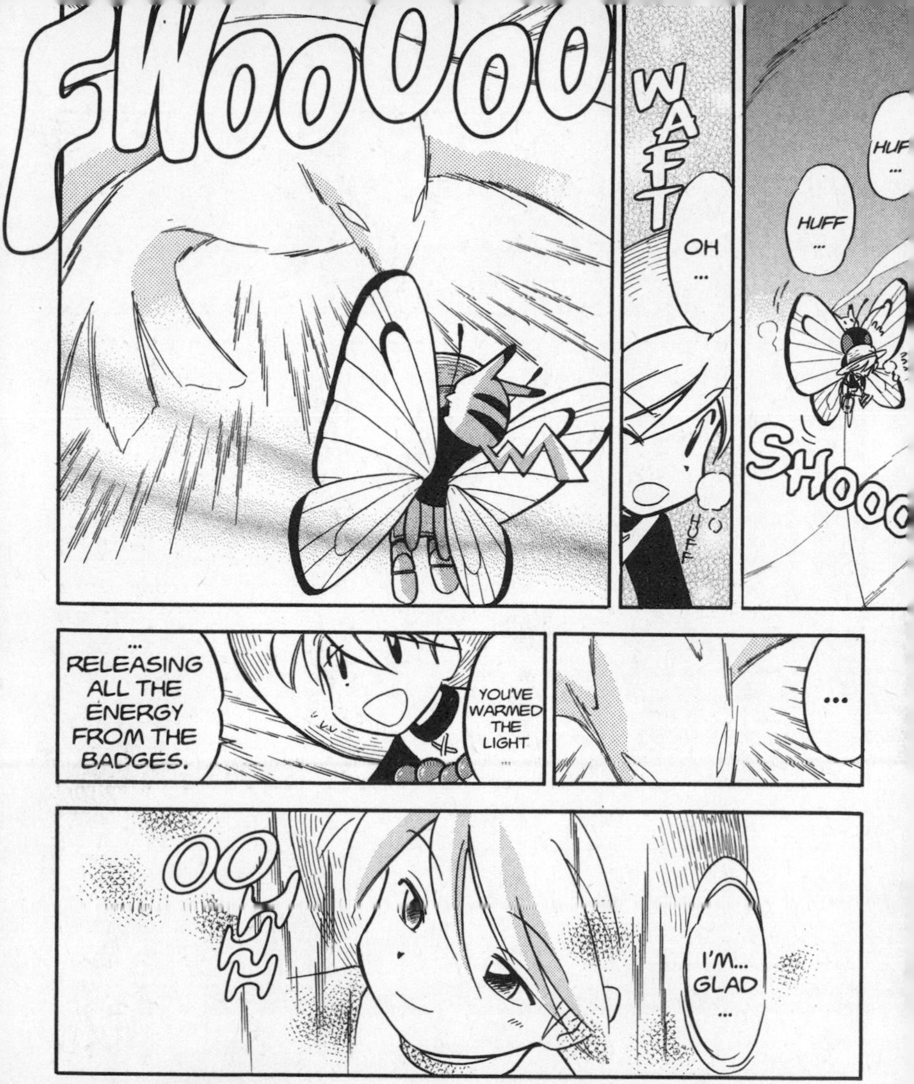
HUFF ...
SHOOO
WAFT
OH ...
HUFF HUFF
FWOOOOO
...
YOU'VE WARMED THE LIGHT ...
... RELEASING ALL THE ENERGY FROM THE BADGES.
I'M... GLAD ...
OO
FLAP FLAP
ZZZZZ

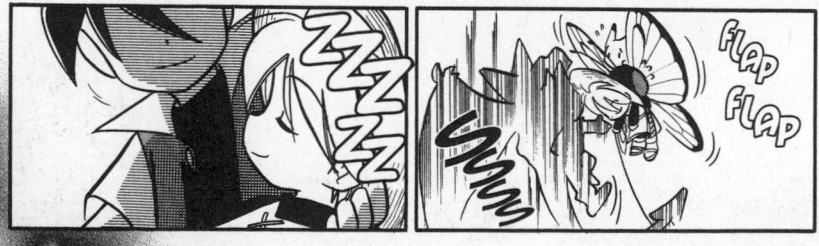

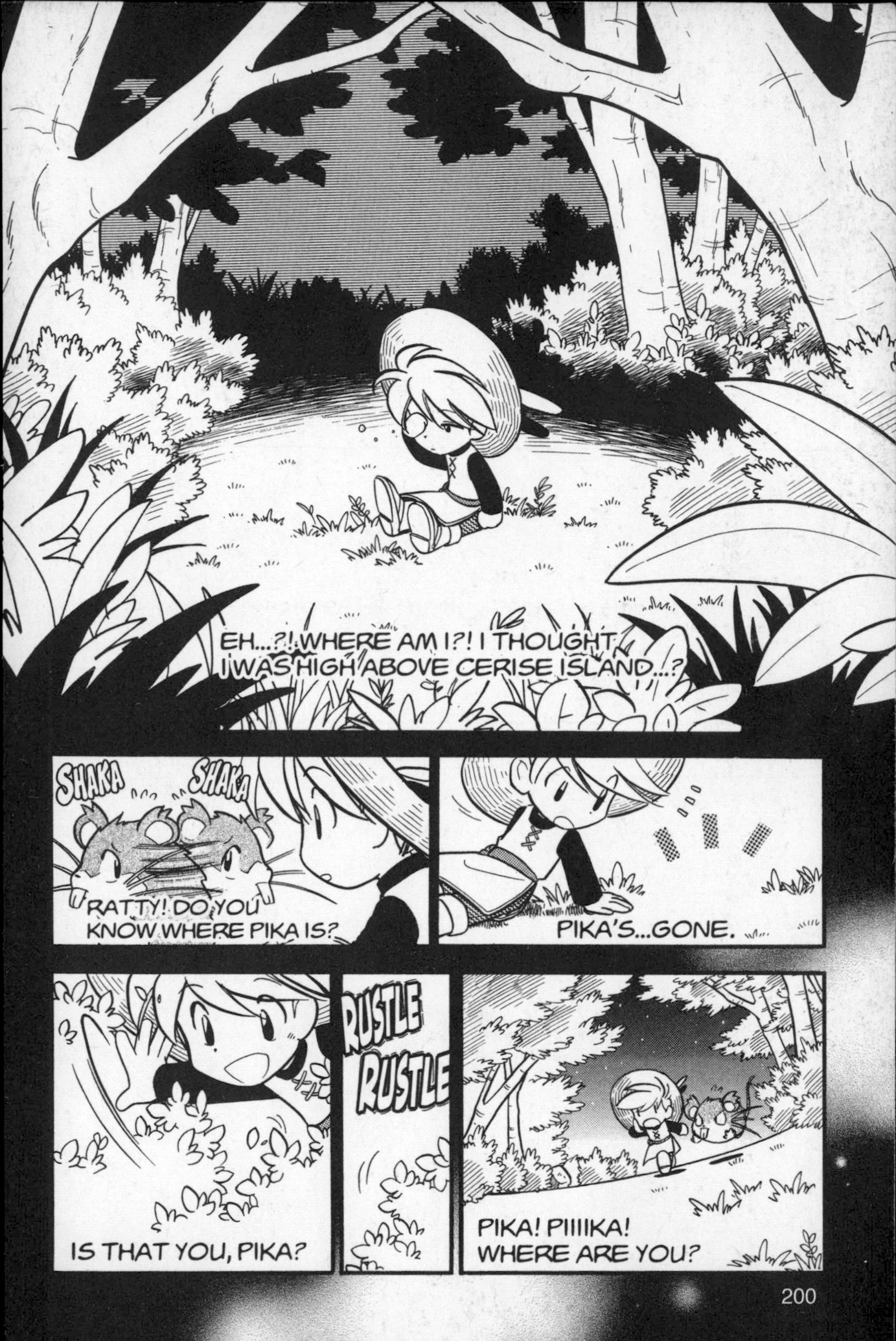
EH...?! WHERE AM I?! I THOUGHT I WAS HIGH ABOVE CERISE ISLAND...?
PIKA'S...GONE.
SHAKA SHAKA
RATTY! DO YOU KNOW WHERE PIKA IS?
PIKA! PIIIIKA! WHERE ARE YOU?
RUSTLE RUSTLE
IS THAT YOU, PIKA?

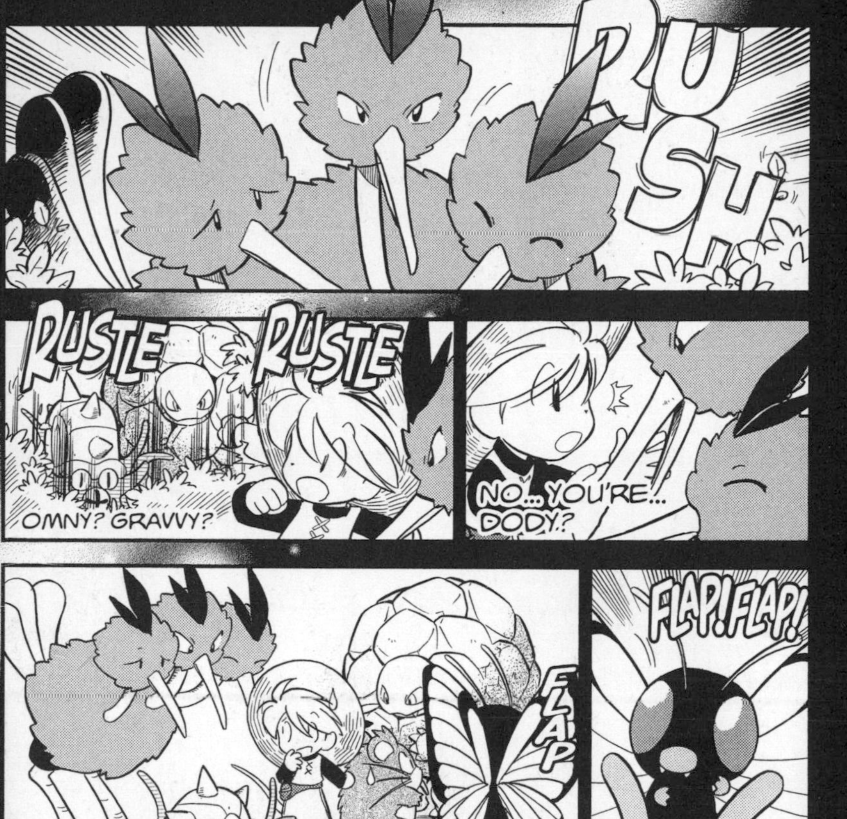
RUSH
NO... YOU'RE... DODY?
RUSTLE RUSTLE
OMNY? GRAVVY?
FLAP! FLAP!
AND...CAN IT BE? KITTY?!
FLAP FLAP
FLAP
YOU ALL LOOK SO DIFFERENT... OH. OF COURSE... YOU EVOLVED...
TUG TUG
YOU'RE TELLING ME TO COME OVER HERE?

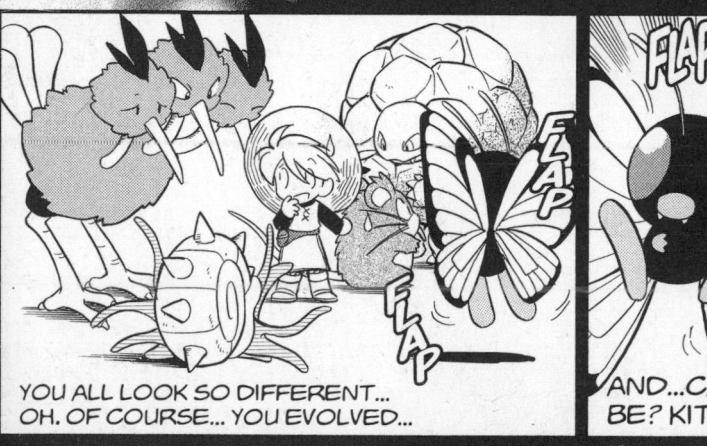

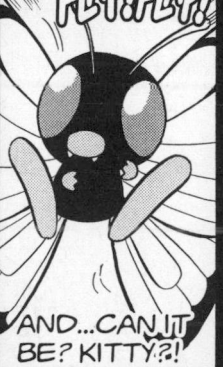

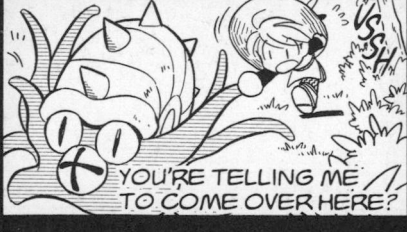

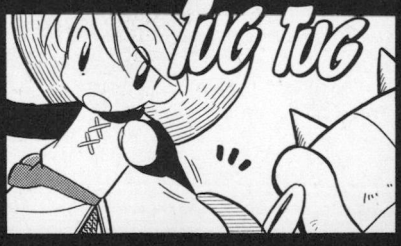

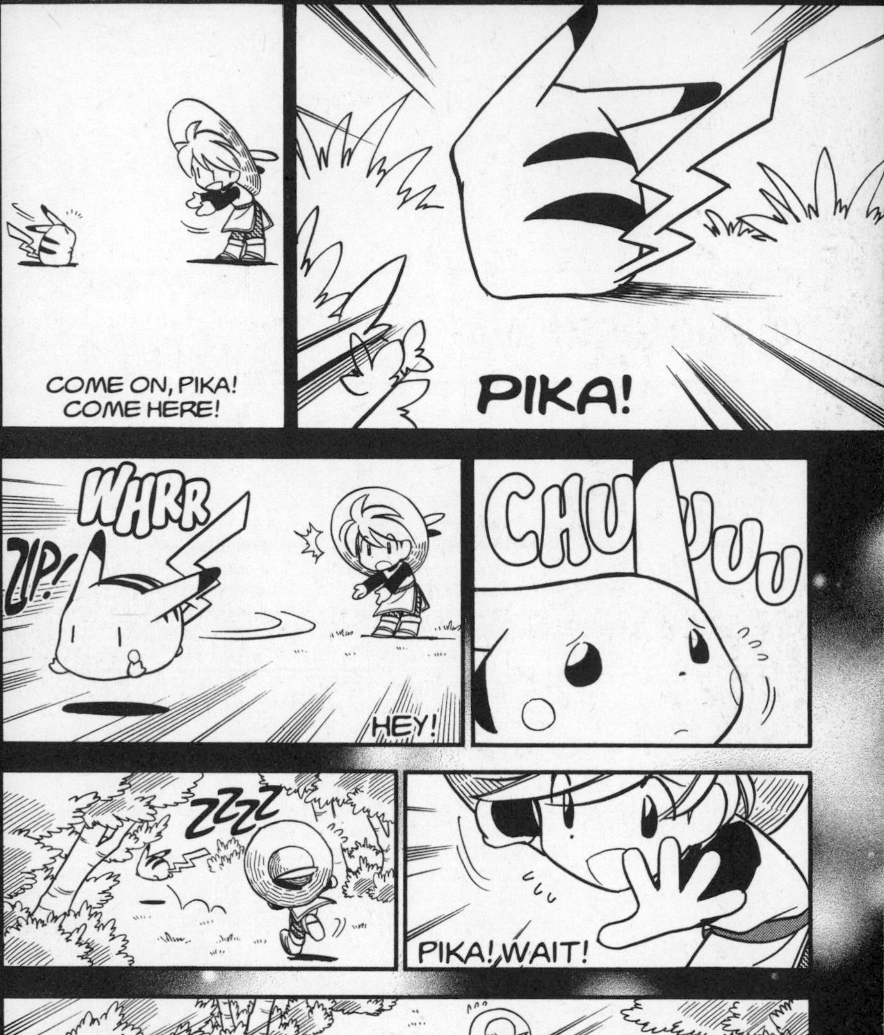
PIKA!
COME ON, PIKA!
COME HERE!
CHUUUUU
WHRR
ZIP!
HEY!
PIKA! WAIT!
ZZZZ
ZZZIP

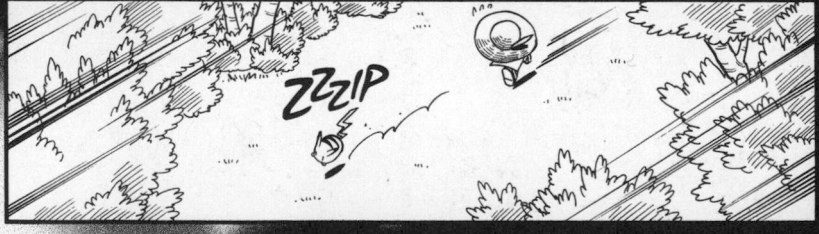

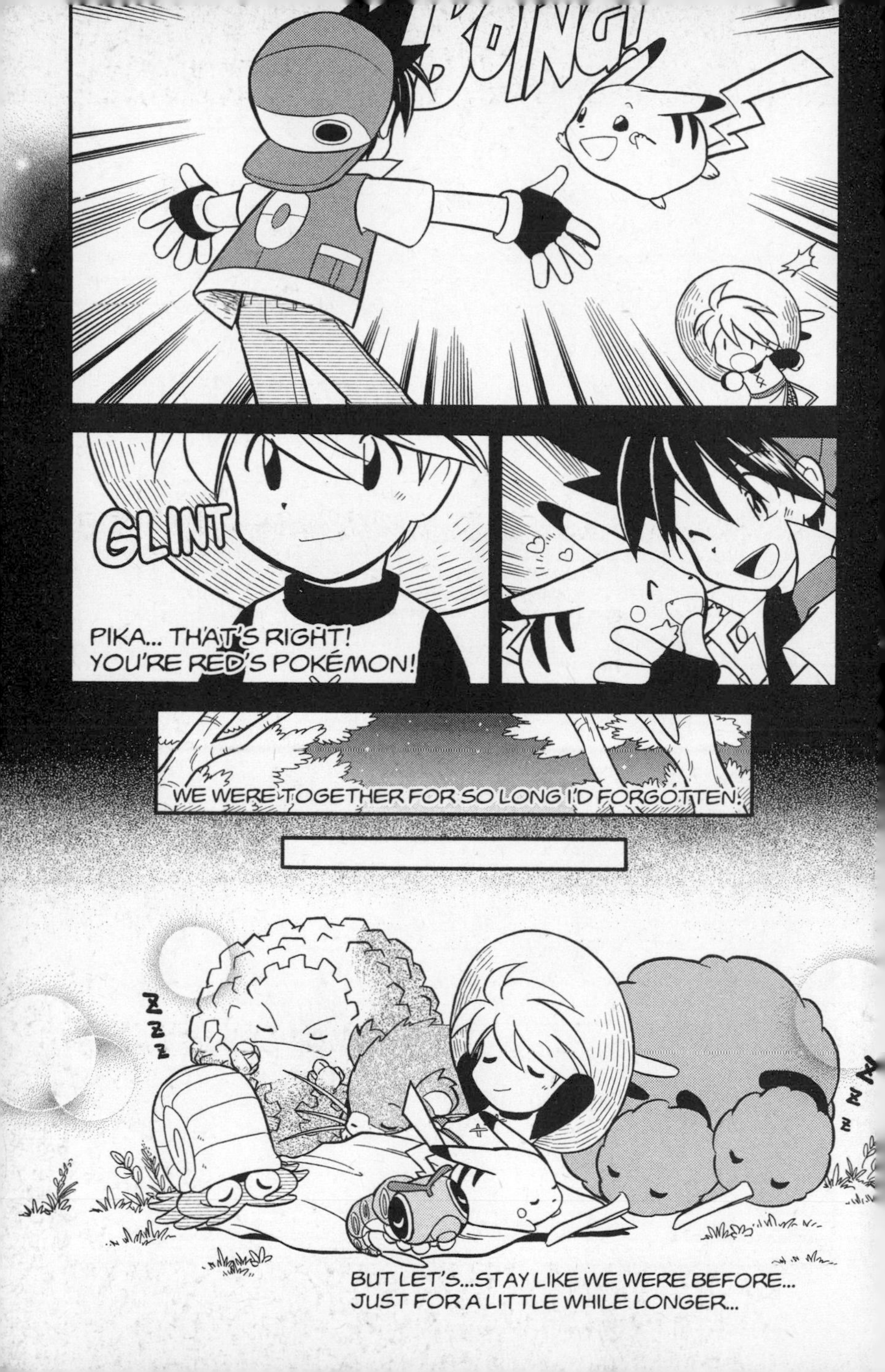
BOING!
GLINT
PIKA... THAT'S RIGHT!
YOU'RE RED'S POKÉMON!
WE WERE TOGETHER FOR SO LONG I'D FORGOTTEN!
BUT LET'S...STAY LIKE WE WERE BEFORE...
JUST FOR A LITTLE WHILE LONGER...

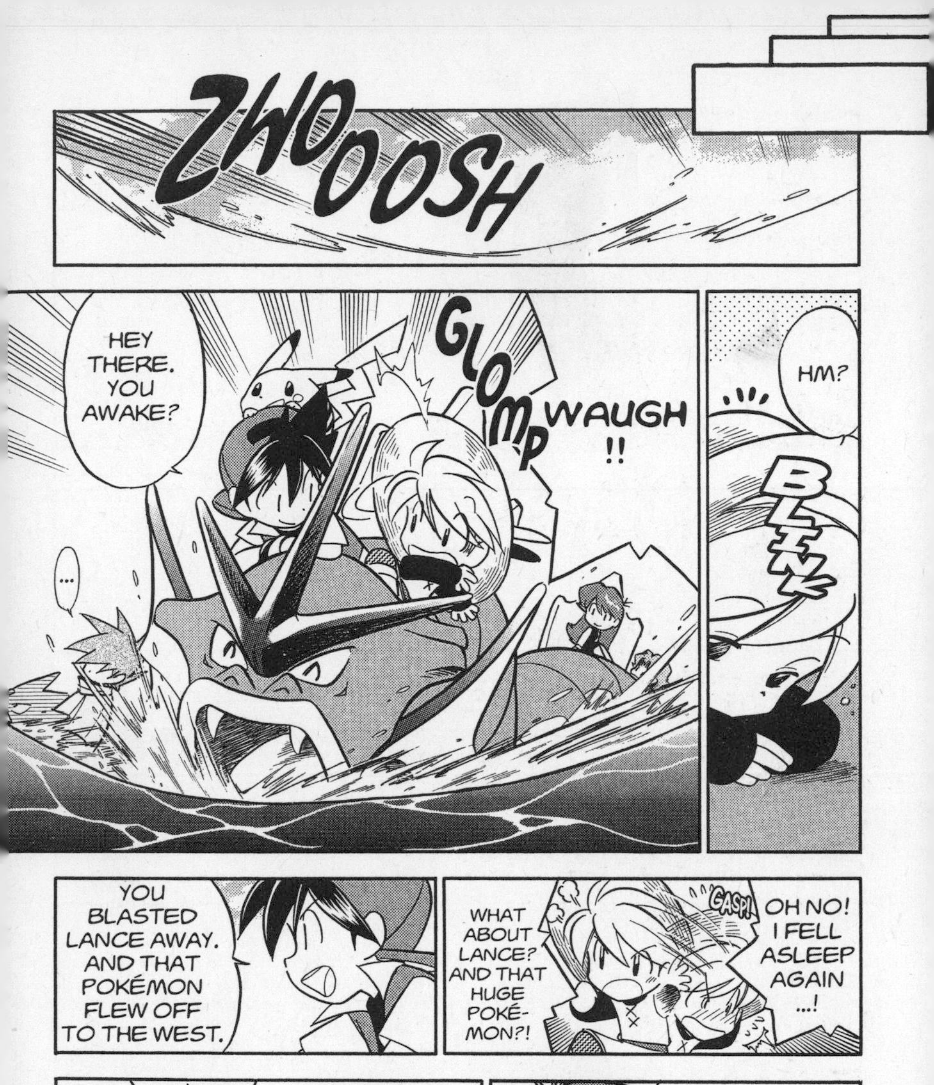
ZWOOOSH
HM?
BLINK
HEY THERE. YOU AWAKE?
GLOMP
WAUGH!!
...
OH NO! I FELL ASLEEP AGAIN ...!
GASP!
WHAT ABOUT LANCE? AND THAT HUGE POKÉ-MON?!
YOU BLASTED LANCE AWAY. AND THAT POKÉMON FLEW OFF TO THE WEST.
I JUST TALKED TO THE MAINLAND. APPARENTLY THE ELITE FOUR'S ARMY LOST ITS POWER AS SOON AS LANCE WAS OUT OF THE PICTURE!
PRRT
ALL QUITE REMARKABLE. YELLOW HAD CANCELED HER POKÉMON'S EVOLUTIONS AGAIN AND AGAIN... ONCE THEY WERE FINALLY ALLOWED TO EVOLVE, THE RESULT WAS MIRACULOUS.
Yes Yes ??
EVEN GOLEM, WHICH USUALLY ONLY EVOLVES WHEN TRADED ...

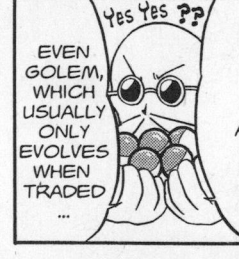

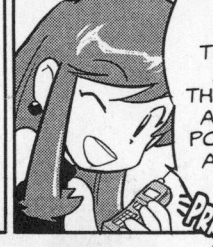

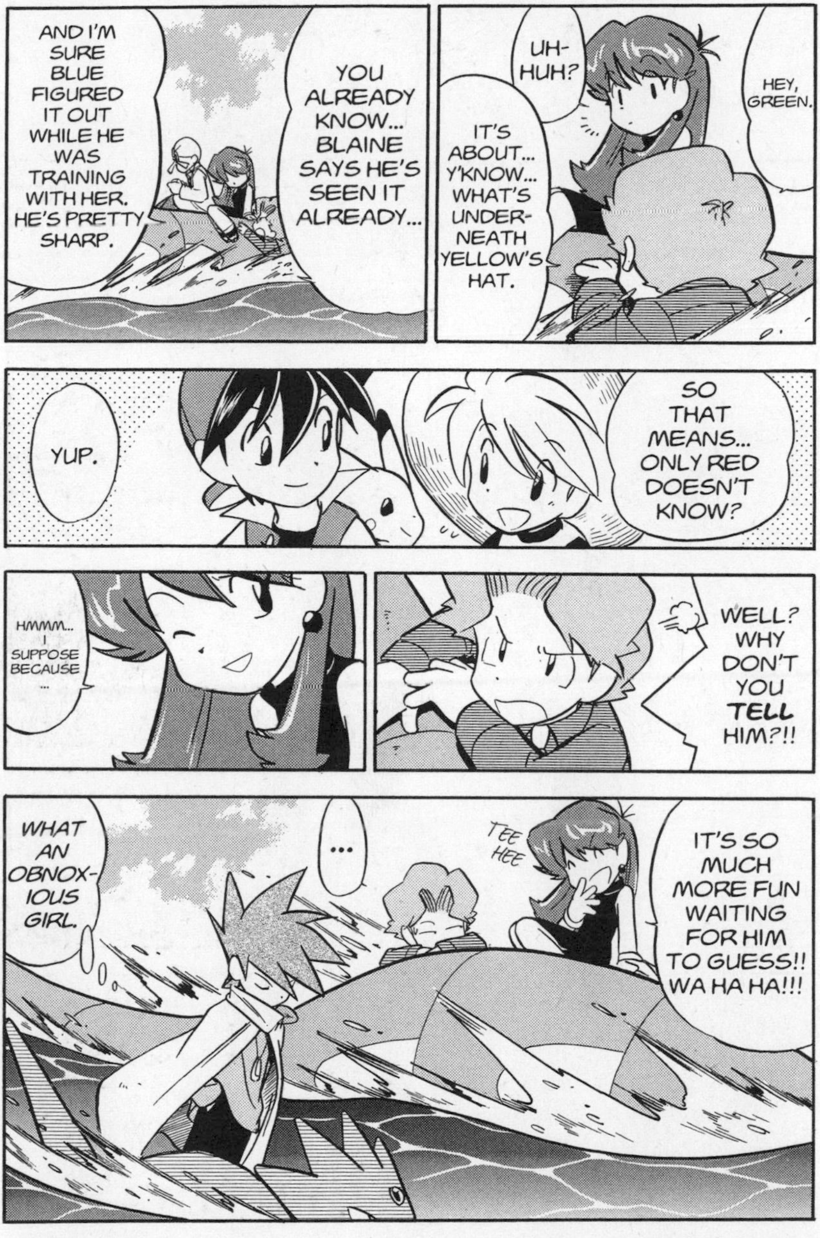
HEY, GREEN.
UH-HUH?
IT'S ABOUT... Y'KNOW... WHAT'S UNDER-NEATH YELLOW'S HAT.
YOU ALREADY KNOW... BLAINE SAYS HE'S SEEN IT ALREADY...
AND I'M SURE BLUE FIGURED IT OUT WHILE HE WAS TRAINING WITH HER. HE'S PRETTY SHARP.
SO THAT MEANS... ONLY RED DOESN'T KNOW?
YUP.
WELL? WHY DON'T YOU **TELL** HIM?!!
HMMM... I SUPPOSE BECAUSE ...
IT'S SO MUCH MORE FUN WAITING FOR HIM TO GUESS!! WA HA HA!!!
TEE HEE
...
WHAT AN OBNOX-IOUS GIRL.

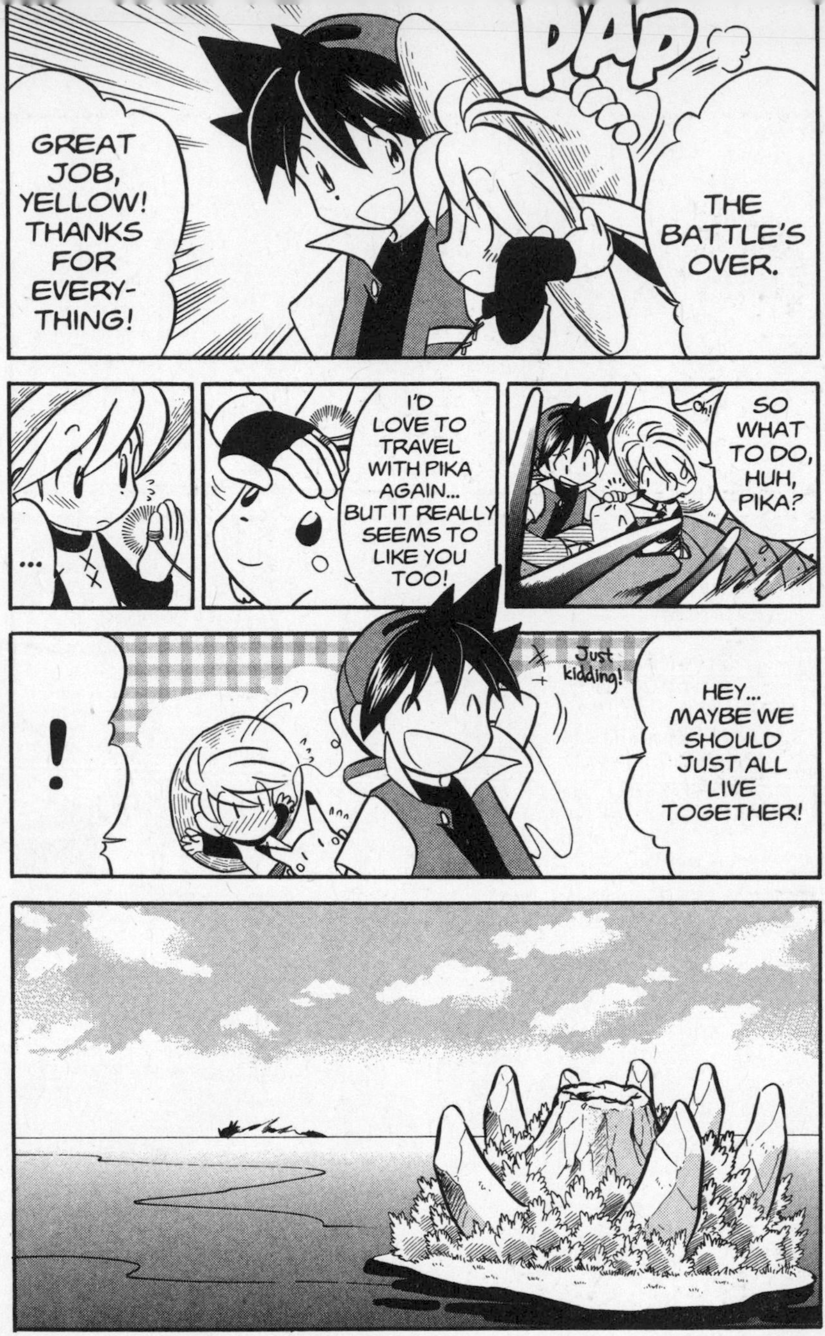
PAP
THE BATTLE'S OVER.
GREAT JOB, YELLOW! THANKS FOR EVERY-THING!
Oh!
SO WHAT TO DO, HUH, PIKA?
I'D LOVE TO TRAVEL WITH PIKA AGAIN... BUT IT REALLY SEEMS TO LIKE YOU TOO!
...
HEY... MAYBE WE SHOULD JUST ALL LIVE TOGETHER!
Just kidding!
!

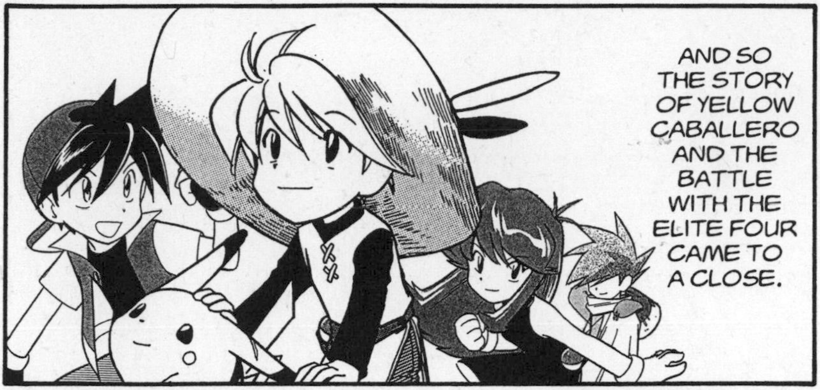
AND SO THE STORY OF YELLOW CABALLERO AND THE BATTLE WITH THE ELITE FOUR CAME TO A CLOSE.

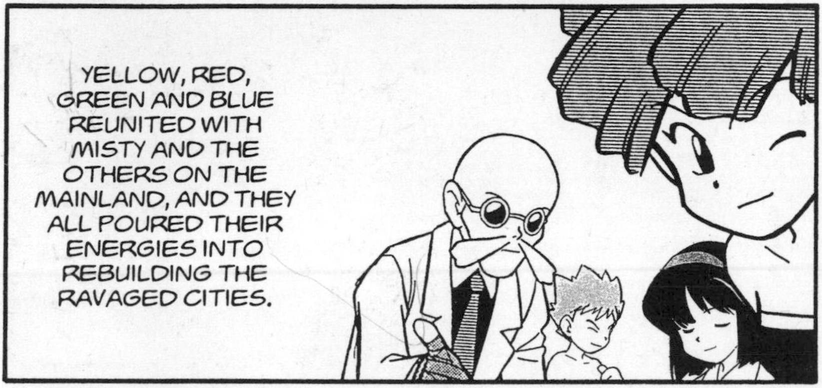
YELLOW, RED, GREEN AND BLUE REUNITED WITH MISTY AND THE OTHERS ON THE MAINLAND, AND THEY ALL POURED THEIR ENERGIES INTO REBUILDING THE RAVAGED CITIES.

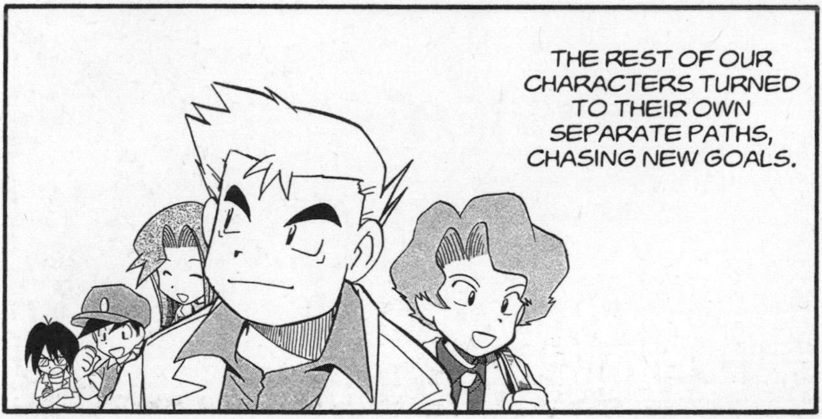
THE REST OF OUR CHARACTERS TURNED TO THEIR OWN SEPARATE PATHS, CHASING NEW GOALS.

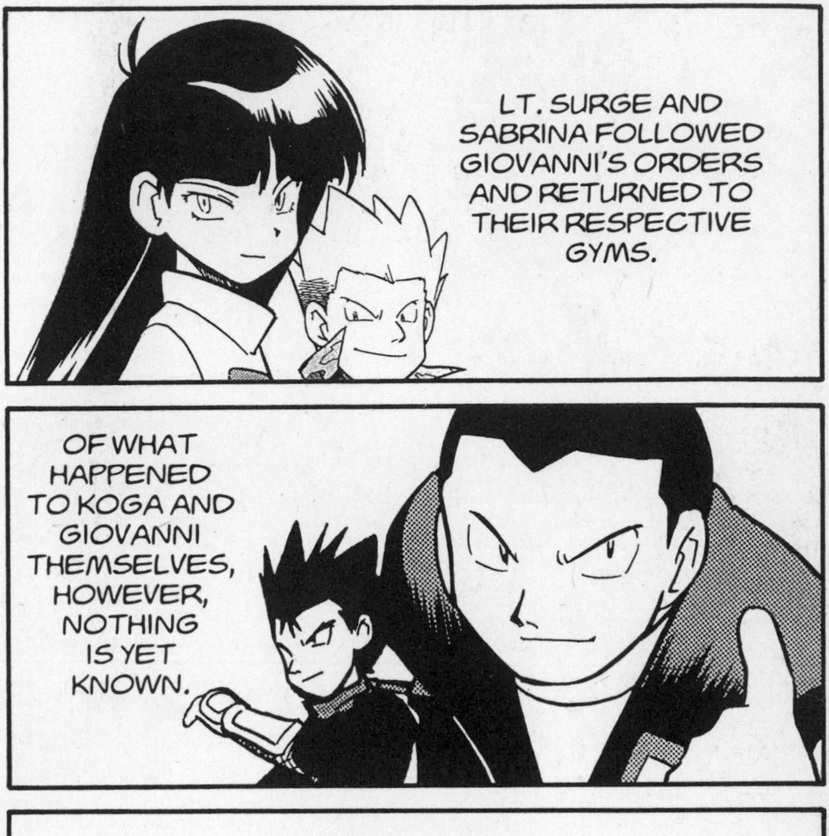
LT. SURGE AND SABRINA FOLLOWED GIOVANNI'S ORDERS AND RETURNED TO THEIR RESPECTIVE GYMS.
OF WHAT HAPPENED TO KOGA AND GIOVANNI THEMSELVES, HOWEVER, NOTHING IS YET KNOWN.
SO TIME FLOWS, AND THE STORIES NEVER TRULY END...

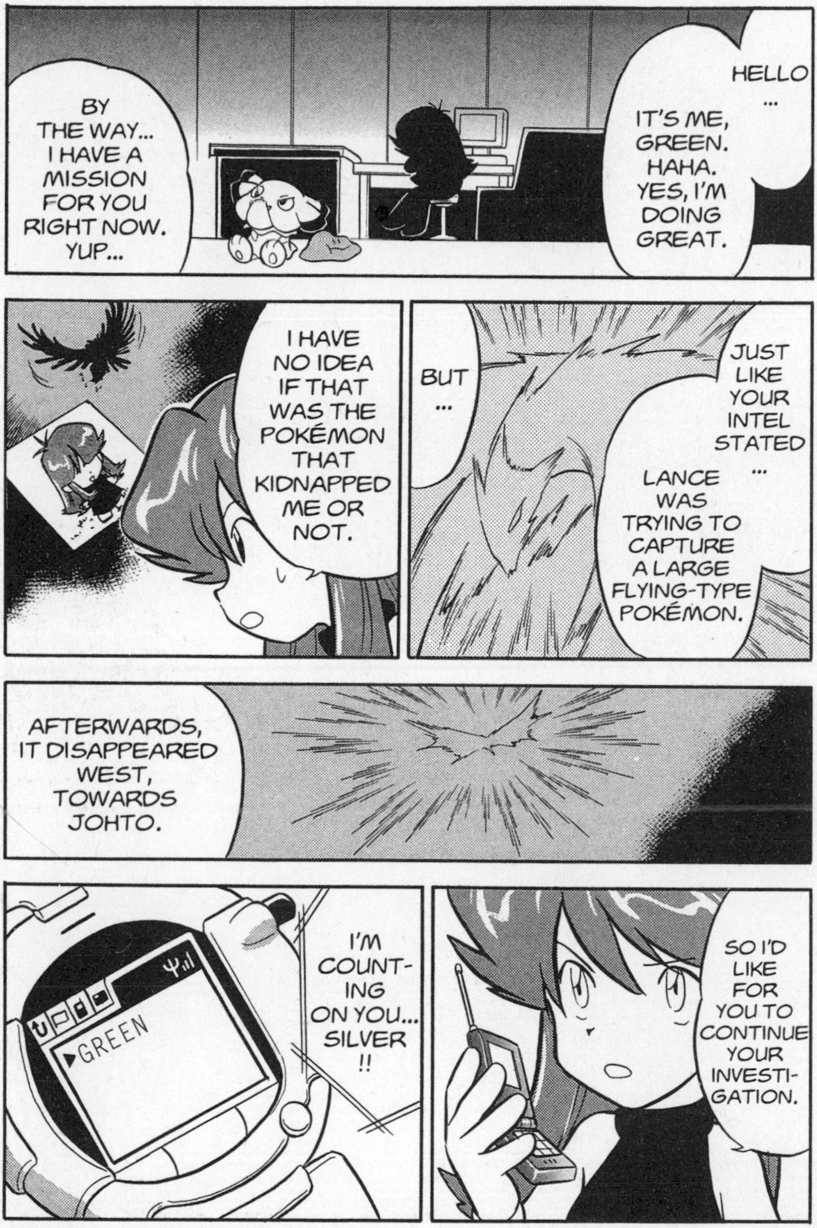
HELLO ... IT'S ME, GREEN. HAHA. YES, I'M DOING GREAT.
BY THE WAY... I HAVE A MISSION FOR YOU RIGHT NOW. YUP...
JUST LIKE YOUR INTEL STATED ...
LANCE WAS TRYING TO CAPTURE A LARGE FLYING-TYPE POKÉMON.
BUT ...
I HAVE NO IDEA IF THAT WAS THE POKÉMON THAT KIDNAPPED ME OR NOT.
AFTERWARDS, IT DISAPPEARED WEST, TOWARDS JOHTO.
SO I'D LIKE FOR YOU TO CONTINUE YOUR INVESTI-GATION.
GREEN
I'M COUNT-ING ON YOU... SILVER !!

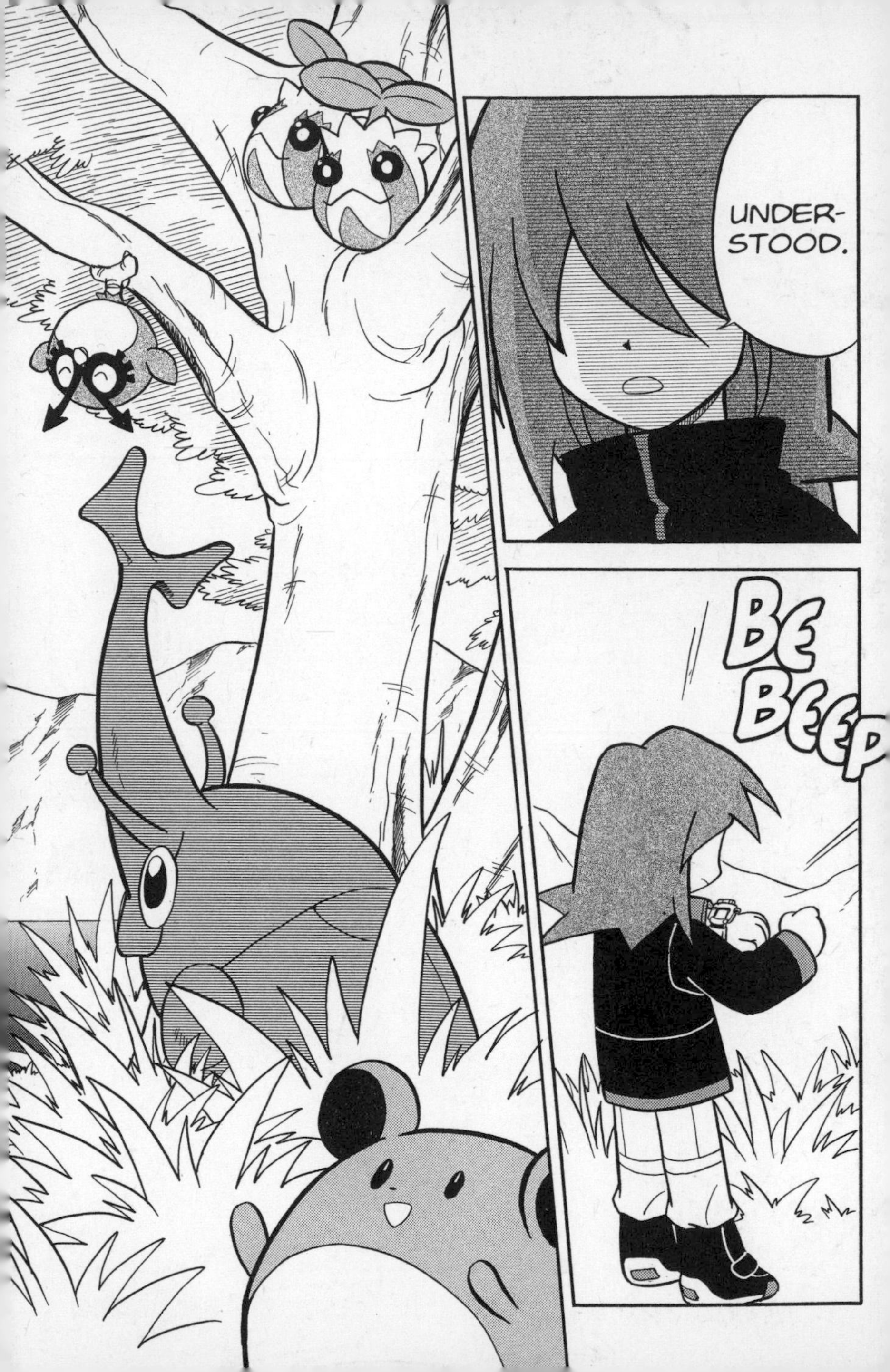
UNDER-
STOOD.
BE BEEP

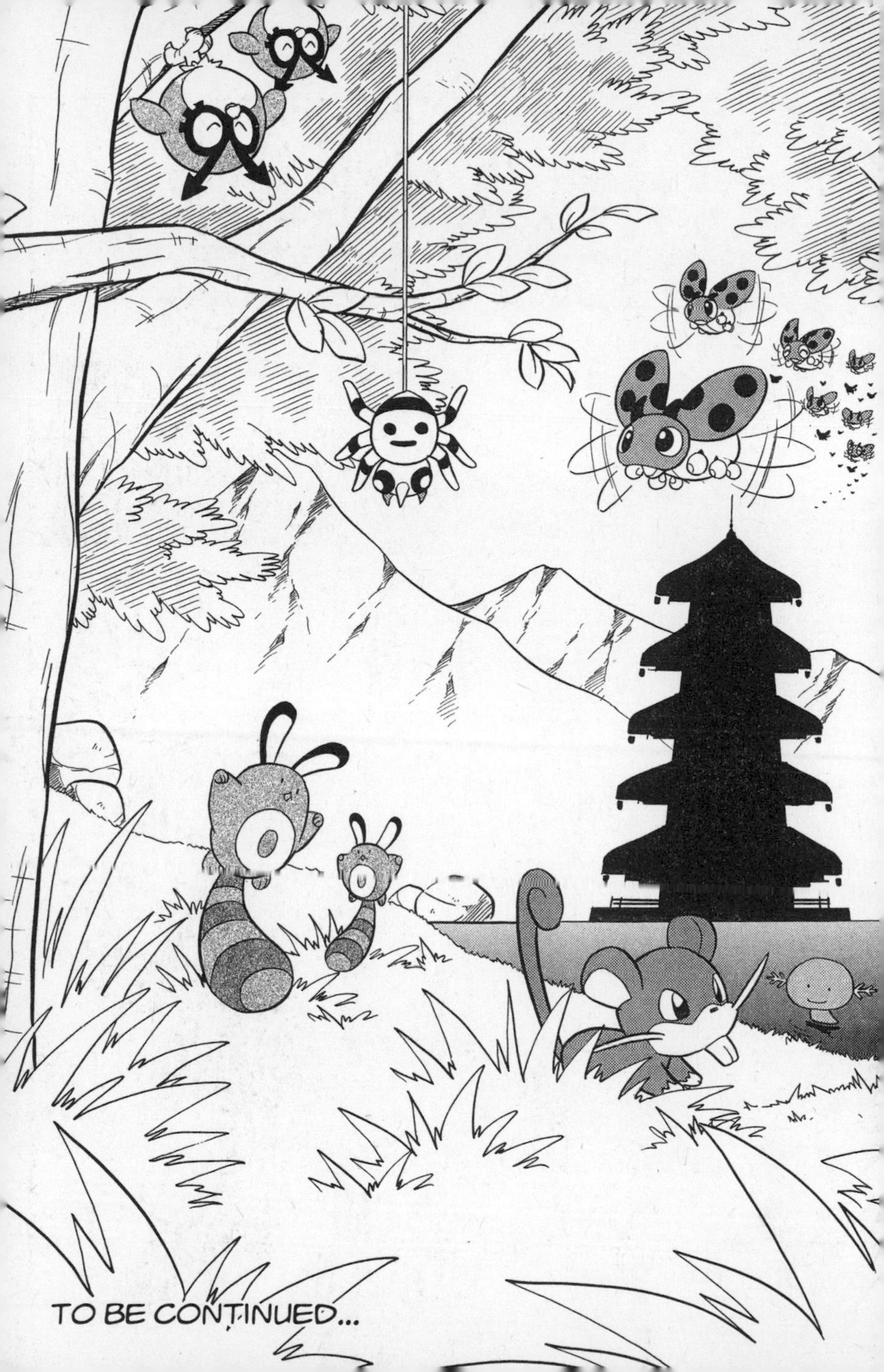
TO BE CONTINUED...

POKÉMON ADVENTURES

YELLOW

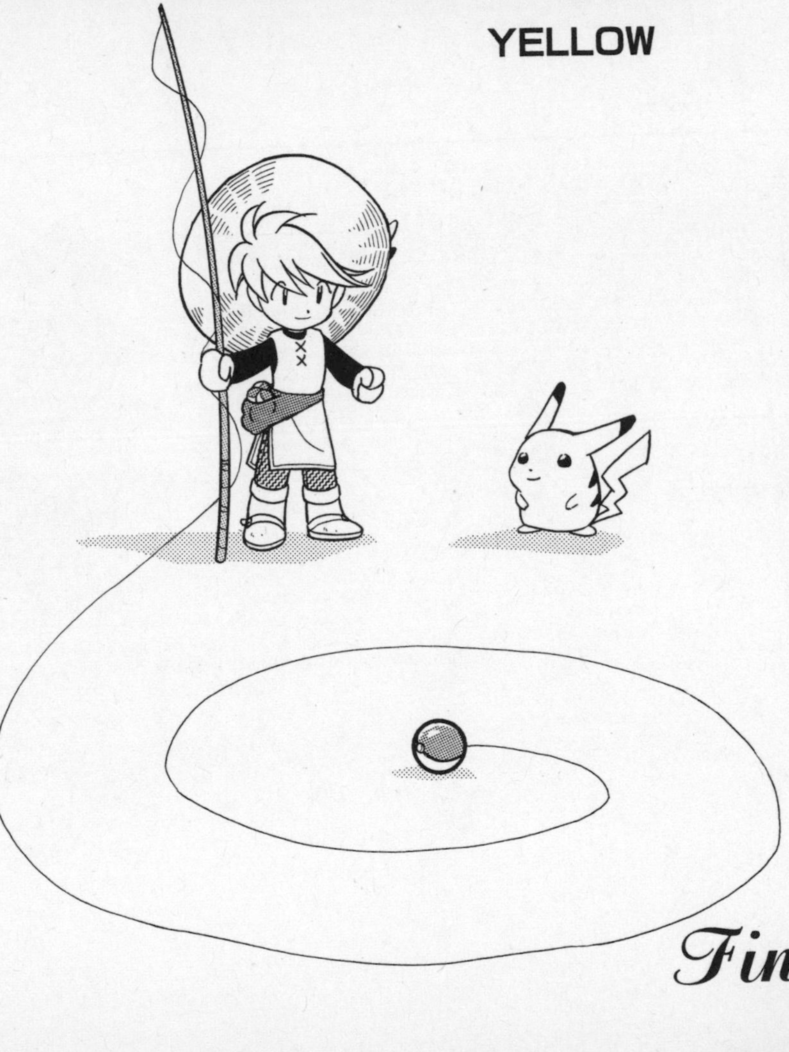

Fin

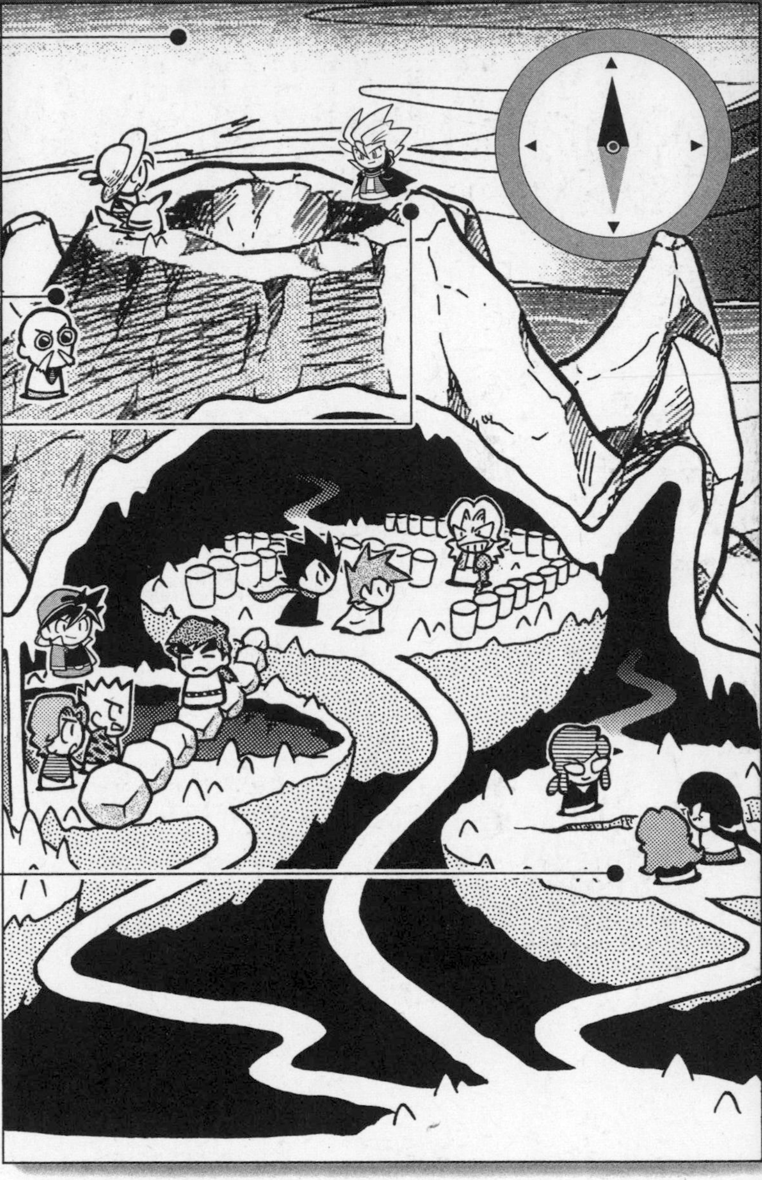

Cerise Island

Bird's-Eye View

"GOTTA CATCH 'EM ALL!!"

Adventure Route Map 7

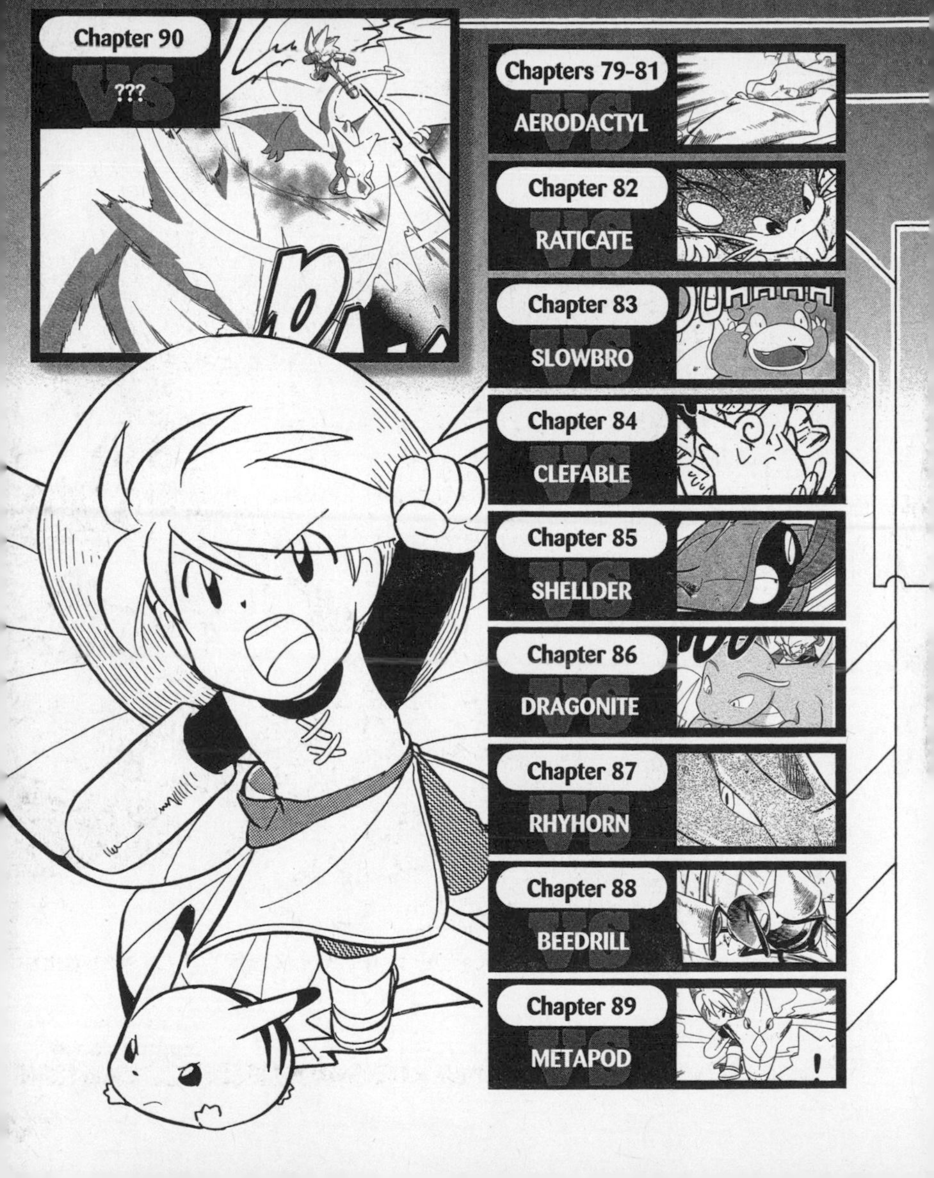

Chapters 79-81
VS
AERODACTYL
Chapter 82
VS
RATICATE
Chapter 83
VS
SLOWBRO
Chapter 84
VS
CLEFABLE
Chapter 85
VS
SHELLDER
Chapter 86
VS
DRAGONITE
Chapter 87
VS
RHYHORN
Chapter 88
VS
BEEDRILL
Chapter 89
VS
METAPOD
Chapter 90
VS
???

POKÉMON -YELLOW-

YELLOW'S POKÉDEX

POKÉDEX

008	------------
009	------------
010	CATERPIE
011	METAPOD
▶012	BUTTERFREE
013	------------
014	------------
015	BEEDRILL
016	------------
017	------------
018	PIDGEOT
019	RATTATA

TRAINER: YELLOW
BADGES: 0
POKÉDEX: 14 POKÉMON

NUMBER SEEN
81
NUMBER CAUGHT
14

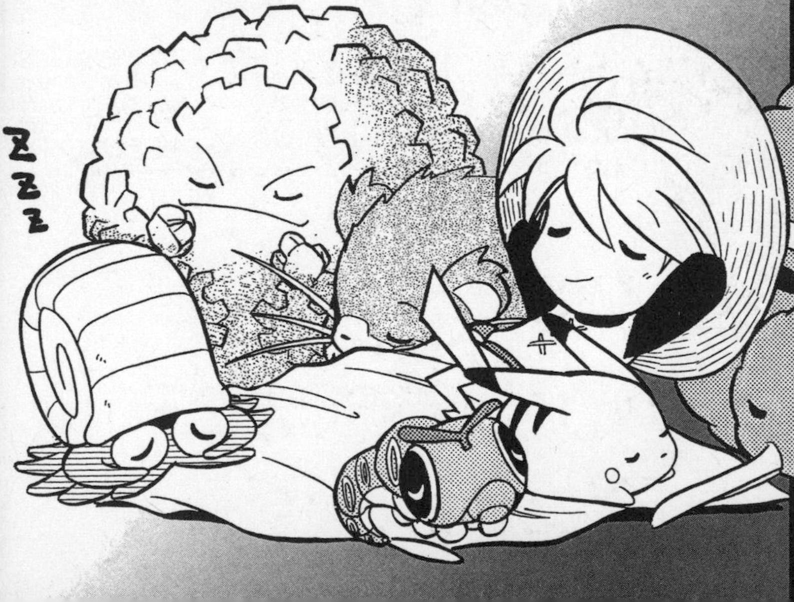
ZZZ

YELLOW'S TEAM AS OF CHAPTER 90

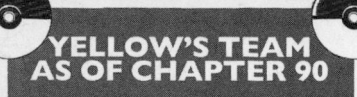

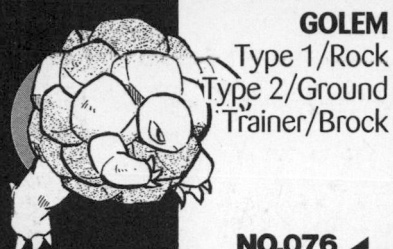

GOLEM
Type 1/Rock
Type 2/Ground
Trainer/Brock

NO.076

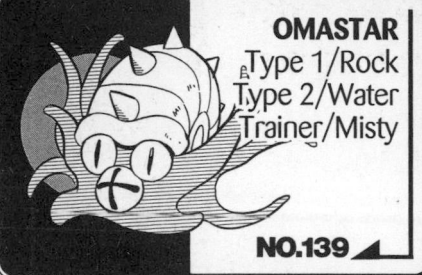

OMASTAR
Type 1/Rock
Type 2/Water
Trainer/Misty

NO.139

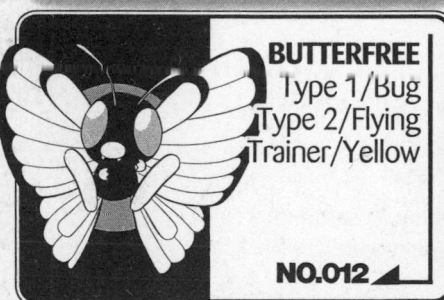

BUTTERFREE
Type 1/Bug
Type 2/Flying
Trainer/Yellow

NO.012

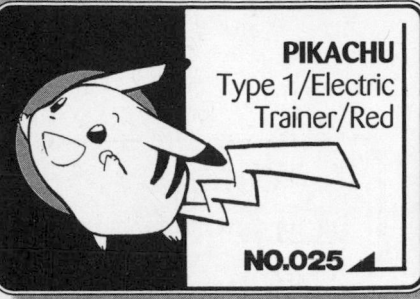

PIKACHU
Type 1/Electric
Trainer/Red

NO.025

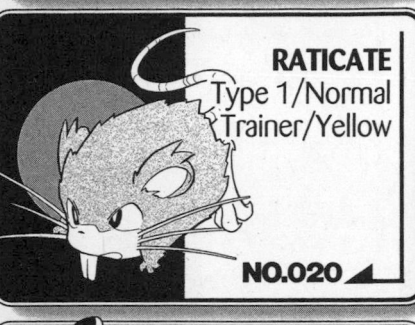

RATICATE
Type 1/Normal
Trainer/Yellow

NO.020

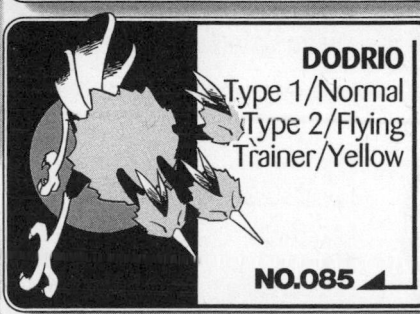

DODRIO
Type 1/Normal
Type 2/Flying
Trainer/Yellow

NO.085

▶ SEE DATA
VOCALIZATION
SEE ASSIGNMENT
QUIT

POKEMON
-YELLOW-

Message from
Hidenori Kusaka

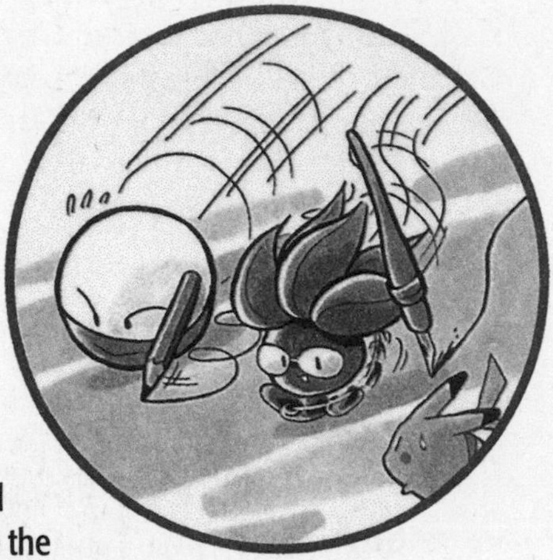

Just like that, this manga is at volume 7, which will take us to the climax of the second chapter of this adventure! How will the final battle against the Elite Four end...?! For the Pokémon and their trainers alike, this will be the final battle to test their grit! Keep a close eye on Yellow Team's battles!!

Message from
MATO

As I play the new *Pokémon Gold* and *Silver*, I'm continually surprised at how rich the gameplay is! Daily and nightly events, mysterious packages and interconnectivity with printers–there are so many things I want to try out every time I play it. But thanks to the many side-quests, my Pokédex is far from complete... or is it? How is everyone's capture rate??

More Adventures Coming Soon...

A whole new Pokémon adventure begins, starring Gold and his rival Silver! First someone steals Gold's backpack full of Poké Balls (and Pokémon!). Then someone steals Professor Elm's Totodile. Can Gold catch the thief—or thieves?!

Keep an eye on Team Rocket, Gold... Could they be behind this crime wave?

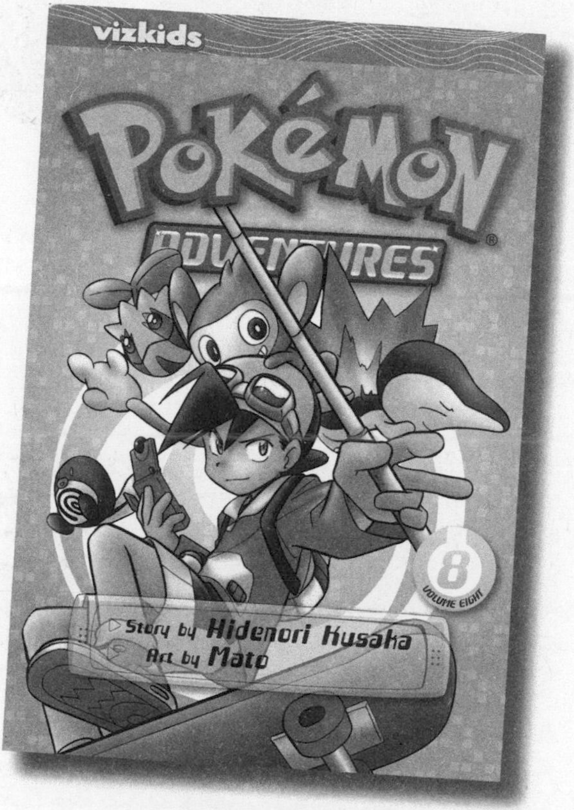
vizkids
POKÉMON
ADVENTURES
8
VOLUME EIGHT
Story by Hidenori Kusaka
Art by Mato

AVAILABLE NOW!

The adventure continues in the Johto region!

ADVENTURES
GOLD & SILVER BOX SET

Includes **POKÉMON ADVENTURES** Vols. 8-14 and a collectible poster!

Story by
HIDENORI KUSAKA

Art by
MATO,

SATOSHI YAMAMOTO

More exciting Pokémon adventures starring Gold and his rival Silver! First someone steals Gold's backpack full of Poké Balls (and Pokémon!). Then someone steals Prof. Elm's Totodile. Can Gold catch the thief—or thieves?!

Keep an eye on Team Rocket, Gold... Could they be behind this crime wave?

www.viz.com

PERFECT SQUARE

RATED A ALL AGES
ratings.viz.com